ALSO BY ALISON COCHRUN

The Charm Offensive

Kiss Her Once for Me

A NOVEL

Alison Cochrun

ATRIA PAPERBACK

New York London Toronto Sydney New Delhi

ATRIA
PAPERBACK

An Imprint of Simon & Schuster, Inc.
1230 Avenue of the Americas
New York, NY 10020

ATRIA PAPERBACK and colophon are trademarks of Simon & Schuster, Inc.

Interior design by Lexy Alemao

Manufactured in the United States of America
ISBN 978-1-63910-557-1

This book is for my parents,
who love me when I fall as much as they love me when I fly.
And for the grandmas, obviously.

Kiss Her Once for Me

Last Christmas

A Webcomic
By *Oliverartssometimes*
Episode 7: *The Girl on the Bridge*
(Christmas Eve, 11:22 p.m.)
Uploaded: February 4, 2022

Snow days are a special kind of magic.

When I was a kid, snow days meant freedom from the stress of school and from the debilitating social anxiety I felt there. On a snow day, I could wander outside and make friends as easily as packing a snowball between my gloved palms.

In college at Ohio State, snow days meant freedom from my rigorous study schedule, when my best friend, Meredith, would burst into my dorm at one in the morning so we could go sledding in South Oval on trays stolen from the dining hall.

And in Portland, a snow day seemed to mean freedom from *everything*.

My boots sink into nearly a foot of snow as I step onto the Burnside Bridge. The boundaries of the city had blurred over the course of the day, and now nothing is contained to its usual place. Grass, sidewalk, and street have all become one smooth, fluid thing—a world that looks sugar-spun and impossibly sweet. Up ahead, a couple cross-country-skis across the bridge while their portable speaker blares "White Christmas," and behind me a group of twentysomethings is having a snowball fight in the middle of the road, and beside me, a woman slips, grumbles, and curses, "Fuck the snow!" at a rather loud volume.

"Is it the snow we should be blaming?" I ask calmly. "Or your shoes?"

"The snow," she answers, clomping her boots deliberately with each step. "These boots are magnificent."

I gesture to the boots in question. "They do seem like they were selected more for aesthetics than utility, though. Like your coat."

She stops stomping through the snow and looks up. "Wait. What's wrong with my coat?"

She's wearing one of those brown Carhartt jackets so popular among a certain demographic back in Ohio and an entirely different demographic here in Portland. Hers isn't even zipped, so her flannel is exposed beneath, tucked into her light-wash jeans.

It's an aesthetic, all right.

"It's a very nice coat," I reassure her. "Not exactly practical for snow, though, is it?"

"In my defense, it hardly ever snows here."

"Yet when you left your house this morning, you knew snow was in the forecast."

She harrumphs and shakes snowflakes out of her exposed hair like a golden retriever in the rain. Her black hair is cut short, shaved along one side and long on the other, so it falls across her forehead in a damp clump. All day, I've fought against the urge to push that hair back out of her eyes.

On a snow day in Portland, you could meet a stranger in a bookstore, spend the entire day with her, and find yourself on a bridge overlooking the Willamette River at 11:23 p.m. on Christmas Eve. On a snow day, you could be the kind of person who followed a stranger anywhere, even if she did complain about the snow.

The stranger in question moves to the edge of the bridge, her eyes staring out at the black water. "Okay, explain it to me, Ohio: what's so great about snow?"

"Well, first of all, it's gorgeous." I exhale, and she turns to shoot me a sideways glance. The freckles beneath her eyes almost look like snowflakes on her light brown skin. It's only been fourteen hours since I met her, but I've already memorized the pattern on her cheeks, charted those freckles so I can draw them later.

I wrap my blue scarf tighter around my neck to hide my blush. "And it's . . . *real* snow, like this . . . big snowstorms . . . they have the power to stop the world for a minute. Snow freezes time, so the constant pressure of life is briefly suspended in a blanket of snow, and for one day, it's like you can catch your breath."

She leans against the railing, her arms lazily draped over the edge. "You know you're allowed to relax even when it doesn't snow, right?"

"When it snows," I say, more emphatically, "the world transforms. Snow is *magic*."

I gesture around us, to the night sky that shimmers light purple, almost glowing to match all the white. To the trees that sparkle an iridescent silver. To the snowflakes floating through the air, giving off the illusion that they're traveling in all directions, defying gravity. I stick out my tongue and manage to capture one, and I notice too late that she has her phone in front of her, and she is taking a photo of me with my tongue out.

"What are you doing?"

"Attempting to document the supposed snow magic. For scientific purposes."

"And from such a cute angle."

"Oh, please. You're adorable, and I'm sure—" She pauses, tilts her head to the side to study her phone screen, and winces. "Actually, maybe we might want to take that again. . . ."

I shove her arm. "I will not subject myself to further mockery."

She holds her phone in front of my face. "Come on, Ellie. Something to remember you by before the night is over."

"I don't turn back into a pumpkin when the clock strikes midnight."

"Yes." She smirks. "But maybe I do. Besides, I'll want to have a photo of you when you're a famous filmmaker. Academy Award for Best Animated Feature is part of the ten-year plan."

"Twenty-year plan," I correct. "I don't want to be unrealistic."

"Ellie," she says, her tone surprisingly serious. "I have full faith that you will accomplish whatever you set your mind to. Now." She holds up her phone again. "Look like you don't want to murder me, please."

I drop my arms limply to my sides and shrug, as if to say, *Like this*?

She shakes her head. "No, show me *you*. This does not capture your essence."

"I'm not sure you've known me long enough to comment on my *essence*."

She eyes me through her phone screen. "I know your essence is not an awkward shrug."

"Are you sure? An awkward shrug could *definitely* be my essence."

She makes a restless, impatient sound with her tongue, and, not knowing what else to do, I lift my arms in the air, like a standing snow angel, and I twirl on one foot in a slow, sweeping arc in the middle of the bridge. Eyes closed, tongue out.

"How was that?" I ask, slightly dizzy and struggling to reorient myself.

She studies her phone with an unreadable expression, then takes a step closer to me. "Here." She shows me. The photo is blurry, a few snowflakes sharply in focus in the foreground, and me in the background, a contrasting swirl of color: the muted dark brown of my braid and the pale white of my skin against the purple of my jacket, the blue of my hand-knitted scarf, the little slice of red that is smile and tongue.

"I think it's perfect," she says.

"My turn." I snatch her phone and wheel it around on her. There she is, in portrait mode, nearly six feet tall, steady with her feet in the snow. "Show me your essence."

She shoves her fists into the pockets of her khaki coat, flashes me a sideways smile, and leans back against the guardrail separating the bridge from the river below. Her essence: perfectly distilled into a single pose, as if she knows, so unequivocally, who she is.

I take the picture.

She reaches out for me. "One more," she murmurs before she wraps an arm around my waist. I know I can't really feel her body between all our layers, but I imagine I can, imagine what it would be like to have her skin against my skin. I can smell the eggnog, the maple-bacon donuts from Voodoo, and the freshly baked bread scent that lingers on her clothes. She looks like she should smell like pine trees and campfire, like the wild and untamed parts of the Pacific Northwest. Rainwater and damp soil and moss.

But actually, she smells like bread. Like warmth. Like something that would fill you up.

"On the count of three," she starts, and on the screen of her iPhone, I can see our faces cheek to cheek. Me and the beautiful girl with the impractical jacket and the half-moon smile. Snowflakes in her black hair and city lights sparkling behind us.

We both smile.

"One . . . two . . . *three*."

Her thumb swipes at the screen to pull up the photo, and I stare at the girl captured on her phone.

"On a snow day," I tell her, "you can be a different person."

With her arm still around my waist, she asks, "What kind of person do you want to be?"

Not an awkward shrug. I want to be the kind of person who pulls a stranger close in the snow, so I do it. I wrap my arms around her, pull her in, until our bodies are flush, entangled, moving slightly to stay warm.

And then we're slow-dancing in the snow. She's humming the tune to "White Christmas" in my ear, and the rest of the world falls away as we dance on a bridge while the minutes tick down until Christmas. All that exists is her breath, her voice, her arms, and all the places our bodies meet. We're suspended in a perfect snow globe built for two.

On a snow day in Portland, you could fall in love.

Chapter One

There is almost an inch of snow on the ground, so naturally, the entire city is on the verge of collapse.

Since buses are delayed, I tighten the red, hand-knitted scarf around my neck and plow angrily down Belmont Street. Cars are Tetrised bumper to bumper from the arcade all the way to the dispensary because no one here knows how to drive in the snow. Schools have prematurely closed for the day, and children appear in every doorway and walkway, dancing joyfully, catching snowflakes on their tongues. Up ahead, I watch two kids attempt to make snowballs that are at least 90 percent dirt.

Leave it to Portland, Oregon, to be simultaneously so delighted and so horrified by such a modest amount of snow.

And, quite frankly: *fuck the snow.*

By most meteorological definitions, this doesn't even constitute snow. It's small and wet, falls too quickly, and halfway melts into the concrete as soon as it lands. Still, it's enough to delay the buses and completely derail my day.

I reach into the pocket of my puffy jacket and pull out my phone to check the time again.

Three minutes. I have three minutes and ten blocks to go, which means I'm going to be late for work. And if I'm late for work, I definitely won't get the promotion and pay raise I so desperately need. And I'll probably get fired. *Again.* And if I get fired again, I'll probably lose my apartment.

Two days ago, the neon-yellow flyer appeared in the slit of my front door, informing me of the raise in rent January first. Fourteen hundred dollars a month for four hundred square feet of subterranean hellscape in Southeast Portland.

If I lose my apartment, I will have to find housing in a city with a horrible housing crisis. And if I can't find a new place to live . . .

The anxiety extrapolates and catastrophizes all the way to its natural conclusion: if I'm late for work again, my trash heap of a life will finally be put in the compactor and crushed into a cube of steaming hot garbage once and for all.

Why does Portland snow always insist on ruining my life?

The image creeps in. The girl with fire in her eyes and snow in her hair. Dancing on a bridge at midnight. The sound of her laugh in my ear and her breath on my throat and her hands—

But no. There's no point in torturing myself with the memory of last Christmas.

I look down to check the time again just as my phone buzzes with an incoming call. The cracked screen on my iPhone 8 flashes with the name *Linds* along with a photo of a woman holding a two-gallon alcoholic beverage outside the Bellagio.

I briefly consider ignoring the call, but Catholic guilt, solidified in infancy, wins out. "Hey, Linds—"

"Did you Venmo me that money?" my mother starts as soon as the call connects. It's abundantly clear that *no*, I did not Venmo her the money, or else Lindsey Oliver would have no reason to call me.

"Not yet."

"Elena. Lovey. Baby girl." Linds adopts her best mom voice—the one she probably learned from watching Nick at Nite reruns while stoned through the better part of the late nineties. Lindsey Oliver insists everyone, including her only child, calls her Linds, while she exclusively calls me *Elena* despite the fact that I'm Ellie, that I've always been an Ellie, that Elena fits me like a too-tight pair of jeans.

"I really need that money, sweetheart. It's just two hundred dollars." I can perfectly picture my mother's pouting face on the other end of the line. Her dark brown hair, which she dyes a stark blond; the natural waves she straightens every morning; the pale skin she's eradicated through numerous tanning salon punch cards; the high cheekbones she highlights through contouring.

I can picture her face because it's *my* face, except I still have the curly brown hair Linds calls "frizzy" and the pale skin that makes me look "washed out." If my mother isn't asking me for money, she's probably criticizing my appearance.

"I promise, this will be the last time I ask," she insists.

"I'm sure it will be," I huff as I jog to catch the tail end of a "Walk" sign. Not for the first time in my life, I regret that my only means of physical exercise is the occasional kitchen dance party while I wait for my frozen burrito to heat up in the microwave. "I'm just a little strapped for cash at the moment with my student loans and my rent, but hopefully I'll get this promotion to assistant manager, and—"

"It's not my fault you insisted on going to college forever and got fired from Lycra Studios," she snaps.

"Laika Studios," I correct her for the dozenth time. My mother may switch her career goals as frequently and thoughtlessly as she shuffles through husbands, but she never misses the chance to remind me of *my* greatest failure. I don't let her see how these words affect me, though—don't let her know about the hot kernel of shame that blossoms in my stomach. "And I didn't go to college forever," I manage casually. "I got a master's of fine arts in animation."

"And what's the point of having that fancy degree if you can't financially provide for your elderly parents?"

Linds is forty-six.

Her rant is really starting to build now. "For eighteen years," she laments, "I clothed you! I fed you! I kept a roof over your head!"

Her claims of providing for my basic needs are greatly exaggerated. When I was twelve, I'd asked my mother for money for new art supplies. Linds hadn't taken it well.

"Do you know how much it costs to raise a child? And you want more?"

"Add it to my tab!" I'd screamed in a fit of preteen surliness.

And Linds had screamed back, *"Maybe I will!"*

And she had. Lindsey had calculated the cost of my existence down to the nickel, and she expects full reimbursement. Unfortunately, saying no to my mother is not a skill I developed in the first twenty-five years of my life. I exhale a lifetime of parental disappointment into the wet, snowy air. "Okay. I'll see what I can do to get you the money."

Her voice goes soft on the line as she coos, "Thank you, Elena, my darling."

And this is it. This is my moment. I need to strike while she's briefly filled with maternal pride and affection.

"So, Christmas is less than two weeks away," I hedge. "Any chance you'll make it up to Portland for the holidays this year?"

There is a desperate hopefulness in my voice, even though I already know the answer. She didn't come last Christmas, and she won't come this Christmas, and I'm only setting myself up for heartbreak.

And is that even what I really want? To spend Christmas morning scraping a hungover Linds off the floor between suffering her rants about everything from my lackluster physical appearance to my even lacklustier love life? The last time we spent Christmas together back in Cleveland—before Linds followed husband number three to Arizona—she dragged me to a nightclub, tried to set me up with a handsy forty-year-old Realtor named Rick, and then promptly ditched me so she could go home with Rick's friend. I didn't see her for three days after that.

I was nineteen. My mother had provided the fake ID. *Happy fucking holidays.*

Is that *really* my Christmas wish?

The answer is, apparently, *yes.* I don't have anyone else. If last

Christmas is any indication, it's best I'm not alone for the holidays. I tend to make misguided life choices in the name of loneliness.

"Why would I leave Phoenix for somewhere wet and cold?" Linds asks, reminding me that my Christmas wishes are always irrelevant.

"Because *I'm* here?"

She smacks her lips into the phone. "Elena Oliver, don't do that."

"Don't do what?"

"You're so dramatic. You've always been like this. Don't get all sensitive and try to make me feel guilty for not wanting to spend Christmas in the rain."

"I wasn't—"

A deep voice growls in the background of the call, and Linds mutters something under her breath in reply. "I gotta go."

"I could always fly down to Phoenix," I offer pathetically. So very *pathetically*. Just a twenty-five-year-old woman, begging her mother to spend Christmas with her.

"Now's not a good time for that. Just Venmo me the money by tonight, okay?"

That's it. No *happy holidays*. No *I love you*. The call disconnects before I can even say goodbye. The earlier shame in my stomach is eclipsed by the aching hole of loneliness in my chest. I'm going to spend Christmas by myself in my squalid studio apartment, eating a five-dollar rotisserie chicken over my kitchen sink for dinner.

Homesickness sluices through me, but there is no home to be sick for, nothing waiting for me here or anywhere.

I don't let myself think about the brief moment last Christmas when I thought I'd found someone to ease the ache, a person to call home.

But I'm always alone, have always been alone, and just because it's Christmas doesn't mean there's any reason for that to change. You can feel just as lost and aimless at Christmas as any other time of the year.

I pause as I wait for a walk sign, and around me, the snow is already turning to rain.

The thing about snow is, it never lasts, and you're always left a slightly dingier version of the world when it starts to melt.

I stare down at my cracked phone screen. I'm already four minutes late for work.

Snow magic, my ass.

Chapter Two

"You're late."

These are the words that greet me when I come huffing into Roastlandia at 10:06 a.m. Through glasses obscured by the snow-rain, I catch sight of my reflection in the coffee shop front window. My brunette braid is waterlogged, my bangs are plastered to my forehead, and my pale skin is flushed from anxiety and exertion. In short, I look like someone who's about to get fired.

My boss, Greg, stands by the front door awaiting my arrival, his ginger-bearded face scrunched up and condescending.

All I can do at this point is grovel. "I know. I'm so, *so* sorry. The buses were delayed because of the snow, and I had to walk here, and—"

Greg simply *tsks*. "I don't need to hear excuses, Ellie. Just clock in."

I don't argue with the man who holds my fate in his grubby, mustache-sculpting-wax-stained fingers, but I *will* draw him vindictively later—exaggerate his neck beard and his skim-milk complexion and those beady little eyes. He's wearing his threadbare "This Is What a Feminist Looks Like" T-shirt, which means he's the only person in Portland under forty being ironic unintentionally.

As if to underscore the irony, he looks me up and down and scoffs. "You look like a basset hound who got stuck in a washing machine. What are the customers going to think when they see you?"

"Sorry, Greg," I say again as I follow him into the back. "It won't happen again."

He looks skeptical at best.

I want to point out that I've never been late before, not once in the nine months I've worked at Roastlandia. That I do dishes while my coworkers take their vape breaks, that I've worked through numerous lunches at his behest (*without pay*) and never once complained. But there's no point with Greg.

When I got fired from my last job, and my ten-year plan fell apart, I was just desperate to put some of the pieces back together. So I got a job at a coffee shop in a city full of incredible coffee, and I figured it would be a great place to work while I got back on my feet.

But it turns out I'm a failure at serving coffee, just like I was a failure of an animator.

Roastlandia is in the late-morning rush, and I quickly join my coworker Ari behind the counter. She's at the register, humming along to a Christmas song that sounds tinny through the speaker. The same speaker I've already threatened to rip off the wall a half-dozen times already this holiday season if it plays Michael Bublé one more time.

"You're like the cynical, city-dwelling, career gal at the beginning of a Hallmark movie who hates the holidays and has her heart melted by the strapping, small-town Christmas tree farm owner," Ari said the other day as I complained under my breath about Greg's obsession with garlands.

"Yes, except the part about being a 'career gal,'" I replied, gesturing around us.

The second he'd digested his Thanksgiving tofurkey, Greg decked out Roastlandia in twinkle lights and holly and started his Spotify Christmas playlist on repeat, convinced customers love the cheer as much as they love the overpriced holiday-themed lattes. As if everyone celebrates Christmas. As if it's not the most triggering time of the year. With its steampunk-looking espresso machine and handcrafted artisan chairs and the artwork featuring overweight cats made out of recycled soda bottles for sale on the walls, Roastlandia's usual vibe is *hipster coffee shop trying too hard to seem like it's not trying at all.*

Its current vibe is all that, plus *Christmas*.

And no, I'm not particularly fond of Christmas. For very transparent, gaping-hole-of-loneliness-in-my-chest-related reasons.

I begin steaming a milk substitute for a customer's flat white as the opening notes of "Last Christmas" by Wham! float overheard, and honestly, this song feels like a personal attack.

Last Christmas, I moved across the country to work at one of the most acclaimed animation studios in the world.

This year—

"Almond milk, Ellie! I said *almond milk!* Not oat milk. Were you even *listening?*"

I flinch and almost send the stainless-steel milk jug clanging to the floor. When I look up, I see Tuesday Jeff encroaching on my personal space. The man so named for his regular Tuesday visit of terror has two hands braced boldly against the back of the espresso machine, and he leans forward with a collection of spittle gathering in the left corner of his mouth. I will definitely draw him like this for my webcomic when I get home: currently apoplectic about milk substitutes and always looking like the food critic from *Ratatouille*. This entire day will make a good story for my most recent episode.

"Sorry, Jeff—" I give him my most ingratiating smile as I make a quick switch in faux-milk containers. "I thought I heard you order oat milk."

He absolutely 100 percent *had* ordered oat milk.

"Why would I want milk made from oats? You can't *milk an oat!*" he shouts at me.

"Can you milk an almond?" I mutter quietly, before covering with a very loud, "I'm extremely sorry."

Somehow, "Last Christmas" is still playing. Or maybe playing again?

Last Christmas, my life had direction and purpose.

This year, the highlight of my day is crafting shitty latte art for a cranky septuagenarian. Tuesday Jeff doesn't even crack a smile at the impressive foam snowman I've designed on his flat white. I snap a photo for Greg to post on our Instagram, but Jeff simply troops out the door to brave the slush without so much as a thank-you.

"He's such a twat," Ari says from behind the cash register as soon as Jeff is gone. For some reason, Ari can get away with saying stuff like this about customers without ever attracting Greg's outrage. Ari Ocampo is a thirty-one-year-old woman pulling off wearing a fedora indoors, so I guess she can get away with just about anything.

"Today's a big day," Ari trills.

"Taylor Swift's birthday?"

Ari is unamused. "The day you talk to Greg about the promotion to assistant manager."

Everything inside me slides downward, like the anxiety is shifting my center of gravity to somewhere around my knees. Ari gives me a look almost as condescending as Greg's. Yet, with her thick black hair, currently punctuated with an undercut and dyed with streaks of purple, I will draw Ari as I always do in my webcomic panels: like a trans, dark-skinned, badass Rapunzel. "You've put it off as long as you can, Ellie."

"I don't know. . . . I can put things off for a shockingly long time if potential rejection is involved," I inform her.

"It's been two weeks since the interview, and Greg owes you an answer. You deserve to know if he's going to give you the job."

I make a vague sound of agreement. Of course, I *want* to know if I'm going to get the promotion. I also *don't* want to know, because if the answer is *no*—if I don't get this raise and I fail yet again—I have no idea what I'm going to do about my mom and my student loans and my rising rent. The fractured pieces of my dreams might be beyond repair.

Ari must smell the anxiety wafting off me because she backs down. "Fine. You'll talk to Greg when you're ready."

For the next few hours, we fall into our usual rhythm. Me, silent behind the espresso machine, crafting foam art like it's 2012. Ari, happily chatting with every customer. Ari loves working as a barista. She says it allows her the opportunity to nurture her extroverted soul while still pursuing her secondary calling as an apiarist. Apparently, her entire backyard is beehive boxes, and she makes home remedies using her honey that she sells at the Saturday Market.

"In other news," she says near our six o'clock closing, her perkiness not even slightly dulled by the long day of serving the over-caffeinated and pretentious, "I'm meeting up with some friends at those new food carts off Alberta after work. You interested?"

I bristle at the dilemma she's placed before me. Ari means this invitation as a kindness, but my social anxiety is of the crippling variety.

I could say yes, could agree to hang out with Ari and her Portland hipster friends later. But then *later* will invariably arrive, and I will invariably have a terrible stomachache at the thought of leaving my apartment to go somewhere new. I will agonize over how to get out of the plans until I finally send a text with some half-assed excuse Ari will see right through.

And then I'll sit on my couch watching *Avatar: The Last Airbender* for the tenth time and working on my webcomic, consumed by guilt over both my deception and my cowardice.

Regardless of whether I tell Ari yes or no, I'm going to spend my Tuesday night watching *Avatar*, so I might as well skip all the painful, anxiety-inducing in-between bits.

Besides, this is just a pity invite. "Sorry. I can't. I have plans."

Ari looks at me like she knows my plans involve dipping stale graham crackers into a container of cream cheese frosting before falling asleep with my heating pad at nine. "My friends are nice. You'll like them."

My social anxiety isn't about a fear that people will be mean to me. It's a far more nuanced kind of mindfuckery, a deep-seated conviction that every social interaction is a test I'm predetermined to fail. "Maybe next time," I murmur.

Ari cocks her hip and stares me down. "Is this serving you?"

I roll my eyes. "We get it, Ari. You follow Brené Brown on Instagram."

"Don't attempt to deflect with humor. As your best friend, I have to ask—"

"My *best friend*? We're casual workplace acquaintances at best. . . ."

Ari ignores that and barrels onward. "Is this whole sad-hermit thing you've got going on serving you?" Ari makes a circling gesture in my direction, indicating *my whole thing* just as the bell dings above the door to signal a new customer. "Like, is this making you happy?"

I laugh uncomfortably. "Of course I'm not happy! I'm a twenty-five-year-old with massive debt from two degrees I'm not using who got fired from her dream job and now works for a dickweed serving coffee to snobs in this shithole."

"Shithole, is it?" asks a lush male voice. I turn away from Ari to discover that the customer who just entered Roastlandia isn't a customer at all. It's *him*.

Andrew Kim-Prescott. Roastlandia's landlord. And he heard me call this place a shithole. Which is just *fuck*.

If I'm really lucky, maybe he heard me call my boss a dickweed, too.

A visit from Andrew Kim-Prescott is usually a highlight in my sad-hermit life, but this is just the flammable tinsel on the dried-out Charlie Brown Christmas tree of my day.

"Mr. Kim-Prescott," I say, adjusting my glasses on the bridge of my nose. "Would you like your regular?"

He nods. "Please. And Ellie?" He flashes me his most winning smile. "You can call me Andrew."

If a Burberry coat were a person, it would be Andrew Kim-Prescott. This evening, he's wearing a navy pin-striped suit under a herringbone trench, his black hair arranged in its signature wave over dark brown eyes and a luxurious pair of cheekbones. He checks the gold Bulova watch on his wrist, and I swoon.

I like my men like I like my life goals: unattainable.

It's not even that he's wealthy (though he is). And it's not even that he's laughably handsome (though he *really* is). I look forward to Andrew's visits because for the length of time it takes for me to prepare his sixteen-ounce green matcha latte with cashew milk, I'm distracted from thoughts of selfish mothers and mean bosses, of social anxiety and failure, of being lonely and lost. Because it's impossible to look at Andrew's face and experience negative thoughts.

"Hey, Andrew," Ari says casually to the man who owns this building, and the building next to it, and the building next to that, like a young, surprisingly hot Dickensian landlord. (That's how I usually draw him, anyway.)

He's technically not our boss, but without him and the real estate investment firm his family owns, Greg never would have fulfilled his dream of selling overpriced, over-roasted coffee. Andrew comes by at least once a month to get updates on the business and drink his hipster hot beverage.

"Ari. Good to see you," Andrew purrs. Even his *voice* is expensive, like cashmere, or ordering an appetizer before your entrée instead of ordering an appetizer *as* your entrée.

He finishes paying and comes around the counter to stand across from me like Tuesday Jeff did. "So, Ellie. Do you have any plans for this evening?"

This feels like a trap, like he and Ari are setting me up to uncover my lies. I don't have plans. I *never* have plans. "I—"

"Andrew! You're here!" Greg comes flying out from the kitchen, because he has a preternatural ability to smell Andrew's presence. Which, incidentally, smells of bergamot and lots of money. "I read about your grandfather's passing in *The Oregonian*," Greg says with his usual amount of tact. Which is to say, none. "Our condolences."

Andrew conjures a charming smile. "Thanks."

Roastlandia's landlord is the heir apparent to Prescott Investments, a major firm that owns a healthy chunk of Portland's real estate. For a city that prides itself on being distinctly anti-capitalism, Portland *loves* the Prescotts. Maybe because they're good at appearing philanthropic even as they erect the same generic apartment buildings all over town, gentrifying everything from the Columbia River down to Sellwood.

Richard Prescott, the firm's founder and Andrew's grandfather, died from pancreatic cancer last week. It was on the front page of *The Oregonian*.

I set his green matcha latte on the counter, and Andrew reaches for it, giving me a playful wink. "Greg, you wanted me to check on the electrical issue in the kitchen?"

Greg nods obsequiously, and Andrew follows him through a swinging door into the back office. As soon as they're gone, Ari releases a knowing *tut*. I turn. "What?"

"As your best friend, I think you should date Andrew Kim-Prescott," she announces.

"Why do you keep calling yourself my best friend?"

"Do you have other friends in Portland?"

"That's—" *a fair point.*

Ari squints as if contemplating it further. "Yes, absolutely. I've decided. You should *definitely* date Andrew. Andrew would help you shake up your life. He's charming and well-connected and fun, and you're . . . well, you know." *The opposite of that.*

I find myself thinking about last Christmas again—about the bridge and the snow, about thinking I could become a different version of myself, even if only for one day. "Andrew Kim-Prescott does not date people like me."

"He winked at you."

"He probably had something in his eye. Dust keeps gathering in these sprigs of holly, and I'm the only one who cleans them."

"Come on. You know you're adorable. You're tall. You've got this thick, luscious hair going for you, and *huge*"—I self-consciously cross my arms over my ample chest—"blue eyes," Ari finishes. I drop my arms. "You're like if Zooey Deschanel stopped taking her Lexapro."

I hold my hands in a prayer pose beneath my chin. "My kingdom for off-brand escitalopram."

"See? That whole quirky vibe. Men love that shit."

"I'm not *quirky*. I have generalized anxiety disorder, and trust me, there is nothing cute about it." Unless you find chronic gastrointestinal distress, anxious vomiting, and shutting down at the first sign of conflict *cute*.

"Dude, this is Portland. We all have GAD. Get yourself a therapist already."

"I have a therapist," I mumble. Her name is Anna, I see her twice a month through an online service. Based on the fact that she told me I'm "thriving" at our last session, she's obviously awful at her job.

"I think you should ask Andrew out," Ari reiterates.

There is nothing worse than happily coupled people meddling in the romantic lives of the perpetually single. Though, I guess in Ari's case, it's happily *throupled* since she's been dating a married lesbian couple for the past two years. They both come into Roastlandia sometimes, and the three of them are sickeningly cute together. "Ari. You've known me for nine months now. Do you really think I've ever *asked someone out*? Besides, Andrew isn't really my type."

I can feel Ari's eyes on the side of my face. "Because he's Asian?"

I wheel around. Ari is Filipino and five seconds away from garroting me with Christmas garlands. "What? No! Of course not!"

She looks slightly less murderous. "Because he's a dude? I thought you were into dudes."

I shift anxiously on my feet. I came out to Ari my first week at Roastlandia, when we caught each other checking out Hot Yoga Janine in her Fabletics. It wasn't a particularly profound moment.

"You into women?" Ari had asked me point-blank.

To which I'd eloquently said, "Uh, yeah, I'm generally into everything," like I was commenting on which pizza toppings I prefer.

This was followed by Ari punching me in the shoulder and saying, "I *thought* you were one of us."

And sure, I fell a little bit in love with Ari in that moment, but we didn't exactly dive into the nuances of my sexuality. "I mean, I'm bi," I stammer now, "so *technically*, yes, I'm into dudes, but I'm also demisexual, which means I don't experience sexual attraction at all without a strong emotional bond."

"I know what demisexuality is," Ari cuts in.

Right. Of course. This is Portland. It's not like all the times I tried to explain myself on third dates back in Ohio and was met with blank, uncomprehending stares. "Okay, well, for me personally, I can look at people and find them physically attractive in, like, an objective way. And I can develop crushes. But unless there is deep trust there, that crush is always going to feel kind of distant and abstract."

Ari—who proudly wears a trans flag pin beside a lesbian pride pin on her Roastlandia apron—gives me a look that says *my question did not require a dissertation.* "But if you do form that emotional bond, you are capable of being sexually and romantically attracted to men?" she asks slowly.

I nod. "In theory." In practice, it hasn't happened before. Needing emotional intimacy in relationships while also having an anxiety disorder that makes emotional intimacy nearly impossible is just rude as hell on the part of my brain.

"Well, if I were into dudes," Ari declares, "I would be all over Andrew, so you should definitely form an emotional bond with him."

"It's not really that simple. And besides, Andrew is almost *too attractive.* The money and the suits and the hair . . . Andrew's life is perfect and being around him would only remind me of how *imperfect* my life is."

I'm content with my distant and abstract crush on Andrew Kim-Prescott.

Ari adjusts her fedora so it sits jauntily over one eye. "No one is perfect, Ellie."

Before I can respond, the swinging door opens again, and Greg and Andrew emerge. As Andrew asks Ari to transfer his latte into a to-go cup, Greg turns to me. "Ari mentioned earlier that there was something you wanted to discuss with me?"

Andrew and his hair are suddenly the furthest thing from my mind. It's this conversation or eviction. I take a deep breath. "Yes, uh . . . did you . . . um, did you have the chance to, uh . . . Did you make a choice? About the new assistant manager?"

Greg sighs. "I'm not sure what you want me to do here, Ellie. I need an assistant manager I can depend on, and you were six minutes late today."

"I'm sorry," I say instinctively. "I'll never be late again. It's just—I *really* need this promotion. I just found out my building is raising my rent January first, and with my student loans, I can't afford to pay fourteen hundred a month making fifteen dollars an hour—" I don't tell him where most of my money actually goes. Greg Radzinski doesn't deserve to know about my fucked-up family dynamics. "And I know you want me to have schedule flexibility, so I can't get a second job unless—"

"I can't make you the assistant manager because I feel *sorry* for you," Greg interrupts. "This is a business."

The conversation is going about as well as I could've predicted, really. "If maybe I could just get an advance on my next paycheck, then."

"I don't think anyone has given pay advances since nineteen eighty-seven."

"I'm going to get evicted," I mutter, on the verge of tears now. I imagine drawing *myself*, standing before my boss, sniveling. Portrait of a Sad Woman Shaded in Blue. One panel in a sequence of a thousand similar panels in the slightly fictionalized webcomic about my life. Title: *The Perpetual Suck.*

I wish I could conjure a different version of myself—a version of Ellie Oliver who didn't snivel and beg for people to treat her with even a modicum of respect.

"Don't cry." Greg's face goes momentarily sympathetic, and he reaches over to massage my arm. I honestly can't remember the last time anyone touched me so intimately.

Except I suddenly *can* and remembering is so much worse. Because remembering the way she held me opens the hole in my heart wide enough to consume me from the inside out.

Last Christmas, I—

"Ellie," Greg starts, his voice laced with compassion. For a second, I think maybe my impending tears have softened his hardened heart, that maybe Greg will keep me from completely falling apart. "You're a resourceful girl," he tells me, squeezing my flesh through my cardigan. "I'm sure you'll figure out a side hustle."

And there it is. That's the extent of Greg's advice. Then he's pushing his way through the swinging door into the kitchen again, and I'm still standing there, only now I'm outright sobbing. I turn and see the pitying faces of Ari Ocampo and Andrew Kim-Prescott. And I promptly dart toward the bathroom.

Last Christmas, it felt like the pieces of my life were finally clicking into place.

This year, I'm watching them shatter.

Chapter Three

Crying in a bathroom is nothing new for me. I've cried in a lot of bathrooms. Hell, I've cried in *this* bathroom more than once. It's just—I don't usually let anyone see me cry. Usually, I wait until I'm safely ensconced in a stall, hunched over on a toilet seat, before I let the anxious tears fall.

I drop my head into my hands.

This isn't terrible, I attempt to reason through the all-consuming dread in my stomach. This is exactly what I thought would happen. This is all *very Greg* of Greg. He hadn't been willing to work with my schedule when I got offered a second job in a restaurant kitchen, and since they could only offer twenty hours a week, I hadn't been able to take advantage of that particular "side hustle." I shouldn't be surprised he's passing me over for this promotion while still expecting me to produce cute latte art for Roastlandia's Instagram.

I take a deep breath and try to think about this logically instead of emotionally. I'm sure there is a way to pay my rent and my mother's expenses and my exorbitant student loan debt. I just haven't thought of it yet.

Without a car, my options are fairly limited in the gig economy. I tried walking dogs for Rover a while back but quit when a woman's Tibetan mastiff dragged me through Laurelhurst Park. Greg threatened to fire me when he saw the gravel burn on my face. I tried cleaning houses through Handy but quit when a creepy old man tried to coerce me into giving him a bath. I delivered groceries through Instacart for people in walking distance of the Fred Meyer, and when that fell apart, I got a job at Fred Meyer unloading pallets from trucks at night. Except it turned out my mental health couldn't endure the lack of sleep, and during a particularly rough bout of depression, I got fired from that job, too.

Perhaps I should admit total failure and move back to Ohio, but it's not like there's anyone back in Ohio waiting for me anymore.

My phone buzzes in my butt pocket, and I try to pull it out without dropping it into the toilet. Thankfully, it's not my mother demanding more money. It's a text from Meredith, who only sends me two things: TikTok videos of animals and screenshots of online dating profiles. Today, I'm facing the latter.

I stare down at what I can only assume is a swimsuit model, artfully standing on her paddleboard alongside her border collie. She looks like the lesbian character on a CW show.

My best friend lives in Chicago, where she moved six months ago to get a job working for a legal aid organization while she studies for the bar exam, but she pays extra for Tinder Passport to say she's a bisexual woman living in Southeast Portland. It's how she stays abreast of my dating options. Like catfishing, but altruistically.

Despite the current toilet-sobbing situation, I immediately text Meredith back: *I'm not outdoorsy enough to date the women in Portland.*

I don't mention that a third of the women on the dating apps here are married ladies with a "hall pass" or couples looking for a bisexual to be their third, neither of which particularly appeal to my demi-ass self.

Within ten seconds, I'm staring at a different profile picture on my phone. This one is of a man deadlifting in front of a gym mirror.

You know I hate public displays of physical exercise, I text in response. *Plus, I can see the entire shape and size of his penis through his gym shorts.*

Meredith's immediate response: *I thought that was the basis of his appeal. No surprises. You hate surprises.*

I hate dating, I correct her.

"Suck it up, buttercup," Meredith says as soon as I accept her FaceTime. "Dating is a necessary evil for people who want a relationship."

"Who said anything about wanting a relationship?"

On my cracked screen, Meredith simply glares. Her pale cheeks are flushed, her red ponytail bobbing and swishing over her yellow legal pad. The bar exam is in two months, so she's studying and chastising me at the same time. I shouldn't be surprised. Meredith O'Reilly could study for the bar while simultaneously answering every question correctly on *Jeopardy!*, knitting me another scarf, and Instagramming photos of her tabby, Kagan. That is Meredith in a nutshell: a smart-as-hell, attractive version of a cat lady. I miss her terribly, but I also can't handle a lecture from her right now.

"I'm having a really bad day, Mere."

"So it would seem. Are you crying on a toilet again?"

"Crying on toilets is not a thing I do."

"You know what would cheer you up?"

"Pie?"

"Leaving your apartment," Meredith says bluntly.

"I've never heard of that kind of pie. Do they sell it at Fred Meyer?"

"When was the last time you went on a date?"

"You sound like my mom whenever she remembers to actually pay attention to my life."

"Linds is an anti-feminist succubus with your nose," Meredith counters. "*I* am your loyal, loving best friend of seven years who thinks it might be time for you to put on your good bra and try making connections with some new people."

"You never date either," I say very maturely from my toilet seat.

"Yes, but the difference is I don't date by choice, because I'm prioritizing different facets of my life right now. You, on the other hand, don't date because of past heartbreak and a fear of failure."

"Did you and Ari coordinate these interventions? Are you in cahoots with Greg and the half-assed snow and the TriMet public transit system to make this day as humiliating as possible?"

Meredith grunts unsympathetically. "Is this still about that woman from last year?"

I play it cool. "What woman?"

"You know what woman I'm talking about," she snaps, because I've never played anything cool in my entire life. "The woman you met at Powell's on Christmas Eve and fell madly in love with, only to have your heart smashed into a million pieces."

I don't let myself think about fiery eyes and freckles. "I did not *love* her. I barely knew her. We spent *one day* together. And that's all it was ever meant to be. One perfect day. How pathetic would it be if I were still hung up on a random woman from a year ago?"

Meredith sees right through me, all the way to the core of my pathetic heart. "Girl, you completely U-Hauled."

"First of all, as a straight, I don't think you're allowed to say that," I deflect nimbly, "and second, sure, I fell hard, but we were never going to last beyond that one day. I haven't even thought about her since."

Much.

"Did you or did you not write an entire webcomic series based on your relationship with her?" Lawyer-Meredith asks me.

"That was . . . catharsis. That was turning pain into art."

"A-*ha*! So you admit that she caused you pain?"

"Very briefly," I concede. That is the downside to needing emotional connection to feel sexual attraction: there is no physical intimacy without the risk of having my heart broken. "But then I poured my pain into the fictionalized *Snow Day* webcomic and promptly forgot the entire thing."

"You're so full of shit. You haven't dated anyone in the past year. You've barely *left your apartment*. At some point, you've got to confront the fact that the whole thing messed you up more than you're willing to admit."

Last Christmas, I gave someone my heart.

And the very next day, she gave it away.

I would be happy to never *ever* hear that song again.

"What fucked me up was moving across the country for a job and getting fired three months later."

Meredith sighs, as if our friendship is the most emotionally exhausting part of her day. "Do yourself a favor, Ellie. Go out to a bar or swipe right on some Tinder himbo. Meet someone new. Strike up a conversation. You need emotional intimacy, and you're not going to find it on your futon."

"I don't know . . . I really feel like me and my left hand have reached a new level of connection." On that note, I hang up on Meredith and step out of the bathroom. And step directly into Andrew Kim-Prescott's chest.

"I was coming to check on you," he explains, staring down from about three inches above me. Then he adds: "And I did not hear that last part of your phone call through the door."

It's almost poetic that this day would end with Andrew Kim-Prescott overhearing me discuss my masturbation habits.

"Everything all right?" Andrew asks slowly, still staring down at me with concern twisted into his inky eyebrows. He has an embarrassment of eyelashes, and he's putting those to good use at the moment, too. The whole tableau is one of smoldering concern.

Usually, I would be into it, but I don't need pity about my financial woes from a man wearing a Gucci belt. "I'm fine. Thanks."

It's six o'clock, which means my shift is over, and I can *finally* go cry in the privacy of my own shithole. Before I can make my escape, though, Ari comes around the counter. "Ellie, I'm so sorry about Greg. I didn't know your financial situation was that bad. You can totally move in with me if you get evicted. We have an extra bedroom in my house. Well, an extra closet, really, but you could definitely fit a twin bed in there!"

"Thanks, Ari," I say. "I appreciate the attempt to help, but if it's okay with you, I'm just going to clock out, go home, and cry into whatever freezer-burned dessert I can find."

Ari raises a single eyebrow. "I thought you said you had plans tonight."

"Yes," I say. "Plans to cry."

I go into the back to grab my coat, and when I return, Andrew is still there, studying me like I'm a fascinating new exhibit at the Oregon Zoo. *A poor person in her natural habitat.*

"It's raining," Andrew says, pointing out the obvious. The half-assed snow has long since turned to full-assed rain. "Do you want a ride home?"

"Oh." I zip up my coat and shoot Ari a look. Three guesses who told Andrew I don't have a car. "That's not necessary. I only live about twenty blocks from here, and I can take the bus."

"She'd love a ride!" Ari bulldozes, using the power of her positivity to nudge me toward Andrew. Then she *literally* nudges me, with her elbow. I'm stronger than her, though, and firmly rooted in place. "In fact, you know what I think Ellie really needs after today? *A drink.*"

Andrew smiles and smolders. "I would love to buy you a drink."

I sigh. I would not love that. I just want to curl up in bed and cry for an indeterminate length of time. I want to take off my hard pants and my bra, and I want to eat all the things. I want to sketch today out in panels until it all seems more comic than tragic, upload the fictionalized version of my life to Drawn2 so the reality feels less painfully real.

But I think about Ari's elbow in my lower back and her voice asking *is this serving you?* I think about proving to Meredith that I am not still hung up on a girl who once twirled me in circles in the snow on Christmas Eve. I think about destroyed life plans and broken pieces and being paralyzed by my inability to put it all back together.

When Ari nudges me again, I let my feet move toward Andrew. "Actually, a drink sounds great."

Andrew gives me a look I can't quite parse before he breaks into a grin. "Perfect. Drinks it is."

See, Meredith? I think as Andrew flashes me that charming smile. *I'm totally over her.*

Chapter Four

Andrew drives a Tesla, which seems unnecessary.

When we get to his car, he opens the passenger-side door for me, which *also* seems unnecessary, but kind of nice.

Once I'm nestled into the leather seat, the absurdity of the situation begins to dawn on me. I've agreed to a date (*is this a date?*) with Roastlandia's landlord—Portland's "Thirty Under Thirty" local celebrity, a man who is a total stranger to me outside of his coffee order. He navigates the Tesla away from the curb, and I can't seem to figure out what to do with my hands, or where to put my shoulder bag, or what the hell I'm supposed to *say*.

Blessedly, Andrew breaks the silence first. "I'm sorry about the promotion. That sucks."

That sucks is not the expression of condolence I expect from a Burberry coat. "Thanks. It'll be okay. Probably. Somehow."

"You know, I haven't had the best day, either. . . ."

My shoulder bag is still on my lap, and I give it a tight hug. "Yeah. I'm so sorry about your grandpa." As soon as I get the words out, they feel empty and generic, a useless platitude.

"Nah, it's fine," Andrew says with a one-shoulder shrug. "He was actually a total bastard."

Oh. Huh. I side-eye him across the center console. The Burberry coat is starting to look an awful lot like a snapback and a pair of Adidas sliders with socks.

"Like, he has floor seats to the Blazers," Andrew starts, "but did he ever let anyone use his tickets when he was in Europe? Never. The seats would just sit there, *empty*. And he banned me from the vacation home in France because of *one* incident involving absinthe, even though what happened to the head on that fountain sculpture wasn't even my fault. And nothing I did could ever live up to his impossible expectations."

I try to recalibrate for this new frat-bro version of Andrew that has materialized in the seat next to me. "I know a thing or two about bastard family members," I say.

I suppose if your primary method of communication is seductive arches of the eyebrow, this passes as emotional vulnerability, because Andrew's face softens as he reaches over and puts a hand on my knee next to my backpack. "Thanks."

I stare at his hand, hanging out on my knee uninvited. I'm not sure if this is an old-man-in-a-bathtub situation or simply how allo-sexual people express gratitude, but I cross my legs so his hand has to fall away. Out the window, I see the Burnside Bridge in the distance as we cross the Willamette. "So. Where are we going, exactly?"

It turns out our destination is a laughably upscale bar in the Pearl District packed with working professionals, blue mood lighting, and kitschy Christmas decorations. My Moscow mule costs *fifteen dollars*, but Andrew whips out his black AmEx like a knight in shining Tom Ford. While he charms the surly Portland bartender, I snap a discreet picture and send it to both Ari and Meredith.

Caption: *My evening plans.*

Their responses range from romantically hopeful (Ari) to mildly perverted (Meredith). Andrew grabs our drinks and cuts through the crowd of people around the bar. He confidently seizes a cramped table in a corner from a couple who is getting ready to leave, and I can't imagine moving through the world like that. He's so fucking *sure* of where he belongs.

I wish I could be like that, but I'm overwhelmed by the *newness* of everything. The newness of this bar, where I don't know the protocol for finding a table. The newness of this man, who put his hand on my knee and keeps smiling at me. The newness of leaving my apartment for anywhere other than work for the first time in weeks. New sounds, new smells, new social rules. Before we even reach the table, I take three giant sips of my Moscow mule to calm my nerves.

"Is this a date?" I blurt before he's finished stripping off his jacket.

He raises one black eyebrow at me and smirks. "Is that . . . relevant to the enjoyment of your mule?"

"Um, yeah. Actually. I tend to do better if I have clear parameters for the social situation."

He slides elegantly into the booth across from me and studies my nervous sweating over the rim of his old-fashioned. "Do you *want* this to be a date?"

"Honestly?" I exhale. "I almost always want to be home under a weighted blanket, not at a bar with an attractive man who's looking at me like I'll make an amusing anecdote when he recounts this story to his gym buddies."

Andrew's smile widens. "Okay, well. What if *I* want this to be a date?"

"I'd be inclined to accuse you of lying. I've seen the people you date on Instagram. I'm not it."

He takes a self-congratulatory sip of his drink. "You've been stalking my Instagram?"

I take an evasive sip of ginger beer and vodka and admit to nothing.

"Oliver," he starts, "that's your last name, right? Can I call you Oliver?"

"No," I answer.

"Oliver," he continues, "ever since you started at Roastlandia, I've been wondering why you choose to work in a—what did you call it? A shithole? With a dickweed? When you so obviously hate it."

So he did hear that. *Damn.* I glug down my mule. "That was a . . . a joke. I don't think your investment property is a shithole."

"But you do think Greg is a dickweed?"

More glugging.

"It's okay." Andrew shrugs. "You're allowed to hate your job. Plenty of people do."

"It's not that I think there's anything wrong with working as a barista," I rush to explain. "It's just . . . I moved to Portland a year ago to work at Laika Studios as a character animator. That's the animation studio that made *Coraline* and *The Box Trolls* and—"

"Yeah. I know what Laika Studios is. Phil Knight—the founder—he's a family friend."

Half a mule in, and I can't suppress a massive eye roll. "Of course he is. And Phil Knight didn't actually found Laika, you know."

"What happened? At Laika, I mean?"

I'm not ready to open up to this man about any of that. "It, uh . . . it didn't work out."

With that, I slurp down the end of my first drink and a waiter instantly appears at the edge of the booth with a second round. I've never seen such customer service in Portland, but for all I know, Andrew's daddy owns this bar, too.

"What about you?" I ask as Andrew tucks into his second drink. "Did you dream of working in real estate investments as a kid?"

"Let's see, I wanted to be, in this order . . . a firefighter," he counts his dream jobs off on his fingers, "a fashion designer, Cristiano Ronaldo, a member of a Korean boy band, a model. . . ."

"So practical. Where did it all go wrong?"

He gives another shrug. "Stanford was always the plan. Business school was the plan. Prescott Investments was the plan." With that, Andrew launches into several long-winded and involved stories about the local properties he's acquired in the past five years. Since I'm still unclear as to whether this is a real date or an elaborate prank, I put on a first-date performance, listening and nodding at the appropriate moments as I suck down a second drink. Suddenly, the third round is arriving at the table, and we still haven't ordered food to go with all this booze. Apparently, Andrew can sustain himself on stories about investment revenues and top-shelf whisky alone.

"I'm very privileged to be able to work for my family's company," he eventually says, "even if that has meant, you know, working with my family." Andrew shifts his weight in the booth. "Do you—do you want to hear the *real* reason I wanted to get drinks with you tonight, Oliver?"

"It's not because I'm such a witty conversationalist?"

Andrew scrubs one hand across his face, looking serious. I sit up straight. "Okay, sorry. What is it?"

"I got some real shitty news, and I needed a distraction. The executor of my grandfather's will called this morning," Andrew explains. "You see, there's this trust—two million dollars set aside to become mine on his death, but I found out my grandfather added a stipulation to my trust fund before he died." He stares darkly into his drink. "I can only inherit once I'm married."

"What kind of fucked up, patriarchal, Regency-era romance bullshit is that?" I explode. Because I'm clearly drunk. Sober, it would be harder to feel pity for a man who's been denied two million dollars in generational wealth when you're sustaining yourself on Top Ramen and El Monterey frozen burritos.

Andrew sighs and takes a solemn drink. "I probably shouldn't have told you that. I—I haven't told anyone since the executor called to give me the heads-up. The thing is, my dad's side of the family is *obsessed* with legacy. My grandfather believed I was his only shot at continuing the Prescott name with biological children, and now he's blackmailing me into matrimony from beyond the grave. Like one giant *fuck you* for all the ways I never lived up to his impossible expectations."

I do feel the smallest ounce of pity for Andrew now. "Is that even . . . allowed?"

"It's his money. He can add whatever strings and stipulations he wants."

"It's too bad you're hideous." I take my straw to the dregs at the bottom of my glass. "And rich. I don't know how you'll ever find someone to marry you."

"The problem is I don't want to get married! I'm only twenty-nine!" He slams down his now-empty third—*or is it fourth?*—drink. "And I definitely don't want to dupe some unsuspecting person into marrying me so I can inherit two million dollars."

"*Dupe?* Dude, just ask politely. You drive a Tesla, and you have the hair and jawline of a young Matthew McConaughey. Any woman in this bar would happily marriage-of-convenience you."

"I'm not sure that's true. . . ."

I drunkenly continue, "You don't need to *stay* married. You just need someone to marry you until the inheritance hits your bank account, right? Then you can divorce them? It's not like your dead grandpa is going to take back the money if your marriage falls apart."

Andrew sits up straighter in the booth, and I briefly worry I've offended him. But his eyes go wide beneath his eyelashes. "Wait, you mean, kind of like a green-card marriage?"

Not offended, then. "Exactly. Happy to help." If only solving my own problems was this easy.

He pinches the bridge of his nose for a second, and the gesture cuts through the Moscow mule fog like a dart to my memory. I see her standing in the snow, pinching the bridge of her nose almost exactly like that.

"You really think I could find someone who would do that for me? Fake-marry me?"

"Sure. It happens in romantic comedies all the time."

He puts both hands flat on the table and leans in even closer, all eyebrows and that fucking smile. "Would *you* do it?"

I laugh-belch in his face. "I think you can aim higher in your aspirations for a fake wife."

"I'm serious. What if we split the inheritance? Well, not split. I could give you . . . ten percent?"

I attempt drunk math. "You'd pay me twenty thousand dollars to marry you?"

"Two *hundred* thousand dollars," he corrects.

"Fucking Christ." I can barely fathom that kind of money when sober, but *drunk*—it's like Andrew's eyes have turned to slot machine readouts with money bags on them. *Two hundred thousand dollars.* I could get an apartment that's *aboveground.* I could buy a car. I could afford to eat *fresh vegetables.*

I could afford a therapist who actually listens to me.

Still, I'm not drunk enough to think *that* is a good idea. "Sorry, but no. Not me."

"But you said anyone would happily marry me."

"Anyone but me."

"Are you sure? This really seems like a win-win. I can help you with your financial problems. You can help me with my inheritance." His eyes are lit up and hopeful, and every people-pleasing cell in my body screams at me to agree to this ridiculous plan. But I can barely handle a maybe-date without getting completely shit-faced to numb my anxiety. I can't imagine how I'd survive . . . whatever he's suggesting. Even if that's a life-altering amount of money.

"Andrew, I just . . . can't."

He chuckles. "Oliver, have you ever done anything spontaneous in your entire life?"

It's the Moscow mule that answers him before my sober self can stop it. "I once fell in love with a woman over the course of a single snow day."

That revelation renders him speechless, his mouth hanging open in shock like that of a very attractive idiot.

Actually, Andrew's mouth is always open about a half an inch. I can't tell if it's because he thinks he looks hot that way, or if he's just a mouth breather.

Either way, I do find it kind of hot.

"Well, not *love*," I backpedal, "just very intense *like*."

"Talking about someone else on a first date." He releases a low whistle. "Bold move."

"Did we officially decide this is a date? I was getting more unload-emotional-baggage-at-each-other vibes."

Andrew leans back in the booth. "I'm okay with those vibes. Tell me more about your snow girl."

Snow Girl. That was what I called her when I poured my heartbreak and grief into the panels. I hadn't planned to draw a ten-episode web series about that day—hadn't wanted to immortalize those twenty-four hours—but after everything that happened, I needed some way to cope. So I turned to art, as I always had.

I changed names and identifying details, told the story to myself to try to figure out where it all went wrong. Then I posted that art anonymously on Drawn2 because isn't the purpose of art to make yourself and others feel less alone?

"Do you remember last Christmas Eve?" I say to Andrew. "When we got that freak snowstorm?"

"I was at my parents' cabin for Christmas, but yeah."

"I met her that morning. At Powell's. We sort of . . . ended up spending the entire day together." Some combination of the alcohol and the constant reminders of her all day make it impossible for me to stop talking once I've started. "I was upset that morning because my mom was supposed to come to Portland and see my new place for Christmas, but then she canceled her plans at the last minute. I didn't know anyone in town, so I was completely alone for the holidays, and there she was, like the universe had handed her to me when I needed her most. And damn—she was really beautiful. She had this hair," I say. Or maybe I slur it. "And this mouth and these big, brown eyes and these . . . these *hands*!"

"You're painting a very clear picture here."

"She had this presence—this way of taking up space. She always talked at full volume, and she stomped around in these giant boots, and she just—didn't give a shit what other people thought about her. That's always been my problem. I give way too many shits."

Andrew's eyes flutter down to the table. I'm not sure when I pulled the pencil out of my bag, or when I started absentmindedly drawing on a napkin, but a shape is starting to take form beneath my fingers. The shape of a woman. Tall, with wide shoulders, narrow hips, strong thighs. She's faceless, silhouetted, but her hair is there, falling into unseen eyes.

"So . . . what happened with her?"

I close my eyes and wish I could forget it all. The way she led me back to the Airstream trailer where she lived. The smell of her skin and the taste of her body. It had only been sixteen hours, but I'd never felt more emotionally bonded to another person. I'd never felt so *safe*. Safe enough to want. Safe enough to feel desire.

I'd convinced myself that it all *meant something*. But it hadn't.

"It was just a one-day thing. Two people, meeting by chance, crossing paths. The next morning, I learned it hadn't meant anything to her."

He nods slowly, and I struggle to remember how I got here, how in the course of two hours and four drinks, I somehow unloaded my romantic history on a hot investment bro sitting there with his mouth half-open. "I get it now," Andrew Kim-Prescott says knowingly. "You won't fake-marry me because you're a hopeless romantic."

I snort. "There are a lot of reasons I won't fake-marry you."

A tray of shots materializes on the table. I have no memory of Andrew ordering shots, but he picks one up and raises it in my direction. "To living spontaneously."

I stare down at the napkin, at the brutal evidence that my fingers know what the rest of me refuses to admit. That I'm stuck on a memory, on a moment, on a person. That I'd been so terribly wrong about what we had.

"To forgetting," I mutter as I throw back the whisky, but there isn't enough alcohol in the world to make me forget her.

A Webcomic
By *Oliverartssometimes*
Episode 1: *The Meet-Awkward*
(Christmas Eve, 10:18 a.m.)
Uploaded: December 26, 2021

Creator note: Hi everyone! I'm excited so many of you have found your way to this first episode of my new webcomic! Just a friendly reminder that this is not a romance. Readers expecting a happy ending should proceed with caution. For more original characters, fan art, and commissions, follow me on Instagram @Oliverartssometimes.

There is almost an inch of snow on the ground, and I'm crying in a bookstore.

The tears and the snow are mostly unrelated.

Crying on a snow day feels particularly unjust. Snow days are for freedom and magic and joy, not publicly wiping snot onto your sleeve while you sob in the Gold Room at Powell's City of Books.

This is supposed to help, I think as I look up at the floor-to-ceiling shelves in the graphic novel section. *Why isn't this helping?*

I've only been in Portland for a month, but I've already come to this city-block-size bookstore a dozen times, sought solace in the color-coded rooms housing approximately one million books. After my onboarding meeting at Laika, where one of the animation bros called my grad school thesis short film—which had earned me praise and accolades from all my professors—trite and immature, I went straight to the Rose Room and sat among the children's books with their beautiful illustrations. After my first seventy-hour workweek, I retreated to the Blue Room, grabbed an armful of romance novels, and sat on the floor reading for an entire Sunday until I forgot the real world completely. And after my direct supervisor ridiculed my work publicly and told me he "didn't want to regret hiring a young girl," I cried in the bathroom, yes. But then I took the MAX to Powell's, went to the café with my bullet journal, ordered a large iced coffee, and hashed out a new plan for how I'd work harder, be better, and prove them all wrong.

And, of course, when my mom called me on Christmas Eve morning to tell me she wasn't coming to visit, I came here, to the graphic novels of the Gold Room. Yet even the graphic novels aren't helping.

I am still crying in an empty aisle at nine in the morning.

"I guess you're my only friend now," I tell the footstool next to me. "You won't abandon me at Christmas like my mother, will you?"

Incidentally, the two-foot-tall stool does not respond to my pathetic question. A well-adjusted individual wouldn't be talking to inanimate objects in public, but I am medium adjusted at best, so I continue. "If Linds was your mom," I tell the footstool, "you would be crying in a bookstore, too."

I turn back to the shelves, searching for *Fun Home*. Because nothing says "wallow in your feelings of family dysfunction" quite like Alison Bechdel's graphic memoir. I spot the bright green spine and reach for it, and . . . someone else reaches for it at the same time.

There was no one in the aisle, and then suddenly, a person. My arm brushes someone else's arm, my hand brushes someone else's hand. A hand with long fingers, dark knuckles, squared-off nails. It's the kind of rugged hand I instantly itch to draw.

I freeze. The owner of the other hand freezes. Two hands suspended in front of the spine of *Fun Home*. My eyes follow the hand to its surprisingly delicate wristbone, to the peekaboo of tattoos beneath a khaki sleeve, then all the way up to the face of this stranger.

The face that is *way too close*. I register an intense pair of brown eyes behind hip Warby Parker frames, prominent cheekbones, a smattering of freckles on light brown skin, a full mouth with a little white scar like an apostrophe through their upper lip. And then I'm taking a massive step backward to put socially acceptable space between us, but the fucking footstool catches my heel, and I begin to topple over. The stranger moves quickly and grabs the wrist of my coat to keep me upright.

I'm briefly grateful for the help, until I remember the crying and the talking-to-a-footstool and the statistical likelihood that this stranger witnessed both of these things. Then, my anxiety feels like a knot of tangled Christmas lights inside my chest.

I flinch away. "Uh . . . sorry."

The stranger seems, for the moment, entirely unfazed by my socially awkward behavior. They reach for the copy of *Fun Home*, then slowly turn to face me. "Are you okay?" they ask in a surprisingly loud voice for such a sensitive question. Their voice booms like a drum in the empty aisle, but it's also coarse and low, like sandpaper on untreated wood.

"Completely fine," I croak.

They arch a black eyebrow at me. "Are you sure? Because you're crying in a bookstore on Christmas Eve."

"I—I wasn't crying."

They arch a second eyebrow, creating a look of surprise on what I'm beginning to notice is a rather attractive face. "You know I can see you, right? There are still tears in your eyes."

They gesture to my friend. "And you told this footstool you're crying."

"What footstool?" I ask in a ridiculous attempt at self-preservation. I even sort of shift my body, as if blocking the footstool will somehow erase my humiliation from this stranger's memory.

"That footstool." They point around me. "The one you just tripped over."

"I wasn't talking to a footstool." The anxiety is causing unprecedented amounts of verbal idiocy, and I wait for this person to slowly back away from me. Instead, they bite the corner of their mouth, pinning a smile in place.

"Huh. I guess I must've misheard," they say with a shrug. "Someone the next aisle over must have been talking to a footstool about their shitty mom."

I nod. "I've heard it's a common situation at this particular bookstore."

At that, they burst out laughing. They're *laughing at me*, and it's not a particularly flattering laugh. It contains some combination of honking and snorting, and it's so loud, I'm pretty sure it can be heard all the way on the fourth floor. But the sound of this atrocious laugh is enough to loosen the tangled anxiety in my chest by a smidge, enough so that I'm able to take full stock of this other person.

They look like nineties Keanu Reeves mixed with nineties Leonardo DiCaprio, but with the subtlest hint of curves beneath their clothes. Their hair is black, shaved on one side and long on the other, so it flops over their forehead. They're wearing heavy work boots, loose-fitting jeans, and a flannel beneath a khaki jacket—none of which is appropriate attire for the snow in the forecast. They have wide shoulders, muscular thighs, and an easy-limbed indifference I could never channel no matter how hard I tried. There's something solid about them. Grounded.

Fixed. They are also *tall*—at five foot ten, I don't have to look up to meet people's eyes often, and I find it disorienting now.

"Do you work here?" I ask, because they have the look of someone who could lift a forty-pound box of books while simultaneously scolding you for mispronouncing *Sartre*, some kind of hot bookstore fantasy.

"Nope," they say, flashing me the cover of *Fun Home* tucked under their arm. "I just had the typical Christmas urge to read a depressing graphic novel about a lesbian."

"Did you . . . um . . . ?" I swallow. "I mean, did you just come down this aisle because you saw me crying?"

The stranger smiles then, a quarter-moon curling only one edge of their mouth. "I thought you said you weren't crying?"

The heat creeps up my cheeks because pretty people with freckles make me oh-so-stupid.

I wonder, vaguely, if this person would protest to being called pretty.

They're fucking *beautiful*. My fingers are desperate for the pencil in my shoulder bag so I can sketch the straight line of their nose and the slope of their jaw before I forget what they look like.

"I promise I didn't come over here to bother you," they say, leaning their long torso sideways against the shelf of books. "I've been telling my friend I'd read *Fun Home* for years, and I figured I could finally get to it during my time off for the holidays. It looks like I stole the last copy, though."

"Oh, that's okay," I mumble. "You can have it."

"That hardly seems fair." They bite down on the corner of their mouth again. I have no idea what's funny, but I'm sure it's me. And possibly the way I'm nervous-sweating. "You were here first."

"It's okay. I've already read it. Like, ten times, actually. It's amazing. And sad. And amazing."

They glance down at the cover, at the abstract green leaves, at the illustration of an unhappy family trapped inside a picture frame, at the words *A Family Tragicomic* scrawled beneath the title. They slowly shake their head and sweep aside their hair. "I'm not much of a reader, but I heard this book has pictures."

"Uh, yeah. It's a graphic novel."

They flip through the glossy pages. "Oh. Huh. Look at that."

"You don't read . . . like . . . *at all*?"

They shake their head, and their hair sways a bit across their forehead. "Not really. There's too much . . . sitting involved."

So much for my bookstore fantasy. It's only now that I realize, along with leaning against the shelf behind them, they have one leg hooked in front of the other, and they're shaking their right foot, as if to the beat of an unheard song. "There are audiobooks," I suggest. "You can listen to those while doing . . . whatever you do."

"I bake," they answer. "For my job. I work in a bakery kitchen. I bake cookies, cakes, pastries—that's what I do."

"Oh." I try to imagine this tall, loud, restless, person piping intricate frosting details on a cupcake, designing shapes in fondant. I picture those long fingers kneading dough. . . . "You can do that while listening to audiobooks."

They cock their head to the side. "You're very concerned about my literacy."

"Well." I start windmilling my arms at my sides nervously. "It's just . . . books are great. And based on the last five minutes of conversation, you seem also . . . great. You know, with the general concern about women crying in bookstores. That's the trait of a great person. And I love uniting two great things whenever possible. So."

I flail my arms more for good measure. The stranger's smile breaks free of their teeth, their mouth twisting into a half-moon, pulling the white scar through their lip into a fishhook shape. I feel that fishhook snag on my stomach as if it's pulling me closer to them.

I do not like that feeling.

"I should go!" I shout abruptly, stepping around them to make my escape. Their hand comes up again and reaches for my sleeve.

"Wait. What about the book?" They flash me *Fun Home* again.

"I said you can have it."

Two fingers are hooked on my sleeve, and they stare at me intensely. In this lighting, their dark eyes are almost incendiary, like they could burn right through me. They're *still* staring, and I squirm under their gaze. I want to look away. I unexpectedly want to ask this stranger what they see when they look at me.

"I was thinking a shared custody arrangement might be in order. You know." Their smile widens. "An every-other-weekend kind of deal. You could have the book for Christmas, then we'd meet up for an exchange so I could have her for New Year's."

"I'm not sure it would be healthy for the book to be carted back and forth like that."

"Hmmm . . ." they murmur. Even their murmur doesn't have an inside-volume. "You're probably right. Maybe we should stick together. For the book's sake."

"If we're going to be co-parenting," I say slowly and cautiously, still worried this person is going to flee, "I should at least know your name."

They release my sleeve and reach for my hand. "I'm Jack."

"Jack?" I repeat as their cool hand slides into mine. Something flips in my lower stomach, and I'm not sure if it's the way Jack's calluses slid against my palm, or if it's my nerves at screwing this whole thing up. This is Portland, not Ohio, and I'm probably going to do this wrong, but—"I'm Ellie," I mutter clumsily, "and my pronouns are she/her. What . . . um . . . what are your pronouns?"

Jack's entire face breaks into a genuine grin. "She/her," she confirms, and I think maybe I didn't fuck that up, after all. "Ellie." She repeats my name, saying it like it means something. "Shall we?"

I hesitate. "Shall we . . . what?"

Jack straightens, steady as an oak tree, and takes a confident step up the aisle. "I figured I could start by buying my co-parent a coffee."

I turn to the window behind us, to the snow piling up on the sidewalks, turning the grimy Portland streets pristine white. And I think about freedom and joy and magic. "I—I shouldn't get coffee," I hear myself say. "I have a lot of work to do this weekend, and—"

"Do you celebrate Christmas?"

"I do, but—"

"So, you can't work on Christmas Eve." When I look back at her, she has her arms folded tightly across her chest, a playful smile lighting up her face. "I cannot allow it."

"Do you celebrate Christmas?"

She nods.

"Then don't *you* have somewhere better to be on Christmas Eve?"

The woman named Jack shakes her head. "Absolutely not. Besides, it's Christmastime." She shrugs again, and I get distracted by the tug of fabric over the expanse of her wide shoulders. "And it seems like you could use a friend."

I glance at the snow one more time. Maybe, on a snow day, you could befriend random strangers in bookstores.

"You know," Jack says, "a friend who isn't a footstool."

This Christmas

Chapter Five

When I wake up, everything is spinning. I try to puzzle out if it's because I'm hungover or still very, very drunk.

The blankets are heavy and hot against my skin, and I kick my legs out to stand, but I can't seem to find the edge of the futon. Silky sheets slide across my naked limbs.

But I don't have silk sheets, and I *never* sleep naked. The bed also feels softer than my futon, and my head is buried in feathery pillows that *definitely* aren't mine, next to . . .

Someone else's head.

"Fucking fuck!" I snap sideways, away from the other naked human in the bed beside me.

Andrew Kim-Prescott makes a half-asleep sound of confusion.

"Oh my God! *Oh my God!*"

I fumble for my glasses and frantically assess the situation while he takes his sweet time rolling onto his back and stretching. I'm not entirely naked, in fact. I still have my underwear and a camisole on, but that is somehow *more humiliating*. My underwear is nude and high-waisted, and I bought it in a Target eight-pack two years ago. There is a small hole in the elastic waistband above my right hip bone.

My cheap underwear should be the least of my concerns, though, because there appears to be a ring on my finger. A huge fucking ring on one very specific finger. "Shit!"

"What's wrong?" Andrew asks with a lazy yawn.

"What's wrong! I think we got married!" I shove the ring in his face across the California king.

"I might not remember much of what happened after we left that club," he starts calmly, "but I definitely don't think we got married."

I don't have any memory of a club, so he's got one up on me. "We drunkenly *eloped*!"

"You can't drunkenly elope in the state of Oregon."

"And we had *sex*!" My anxiety has completely overpowered my hangover, so I'm running on pure panic fumes, impervious to any attempts at logic from the male participant in this clusterfuck.

"We did not have sex."

I start pacing the foot of the bed because it seems like moving might help the slithering feeling in my stomach.

It does not.

"I can't believe I got drunk and came home with you! I'm not even sexually attracted to you!"

Andrew cocks his head at me. "Wait, you're not?" He sounds confused by the statistical anomaly.

"Fuck. *Fuck.*"

"Calm down, Oliver." He climbs out of bed, and I see he's in a pair of snug red briefs that probably cost more than my entire wardrobe. Otherwise, it's all muscular thighs and broad shoulders and the kind of V-shaped muscle configuration I didn't know truly existed in the wild. And damn—he is *really* attractive.

"We did not have sex," he says reasonably. "As tempting as you are in those old-lady underpants"—I fumble to cover myself with my jeans—"you were blackout drunk, and I absolutely did not try to have sex with you. I may not remember much, but I know that for a fact. And to be honest, I think I was too drunk to—you know." He points demonstratively to his crotch bulge. "Perform. There is no way we had sex."

I consider this amidst the rollicking nausea and the migraine blooming behind my eyes. "Why would I have come back to your apartment, then? Why am I wearing *a ring*?"

Andrew pinches the bridge of his nose. "I . . . I don't know." He grabs his pants off the floor to fish his phone out of the pocket and a folded napkin comes along with it. "Ah. Well. This might clarify some things."

He hands me the napkin. On one side is my drawing of Jack. On the other, scrawled across the top are the words *ANDREW AND ELLIE'S CONTRACT OF MARRIAGE* in my handwriting. "*Fuck.*"

Below that are four enumerated agreements:

1. Elena Jane Oliver agrees to marry Andrew Richard Kim-Prescott as soon as a marriage license can be obtained;

2. Until the license can be obtained, Elena Jane Oliver will perform the role of Andrew Richard Kim-Prescott's fiancée, including, but not limited to, attending Christmas at his parents' cabin;

3. Upon marrying, Andrew Richard Kim-Prescott agrees to give Elena Jane Oliver 10 percent of his subsequent inheritance;

4. Elena Jane Oliver and Andrew Richard Kim-Prescott will remain married for twelve (12) months before dissolving their union, at which time Andrew Richard Kim-Prescott will cover the expense of the divorce.

Below that, there are little *x*es next to lines on which we signed our full names. Because apparently our drunken selves were formal as hell. I'm about 90 percent sure a drunk napkin contract is not a legally binding document, but that remaining 10 percent is wreaking havoc on my anxiety. My stomach heaves, and I think I might be sick right here in Andrew's monochromatic bedroom.

"This is not good."

"*This* is worse." Andrew is staring down at his phone. "I think I've managed to reconstruct a partial timeline of our evening."

His phone contains the horrifying photographic proof: a selfie of the two of us doing shots at the upscale bar; dancing in a circle of half-naked clubgoers; purchasing a ring at what appears to be the City Target; me, posing with the ring while Andrew kisses my cheek. I'm so drunk, I don't even look like myself. That isn't even my face.

Also, this ring is clearly cubic zirconia.

"Oliver," Andrew says, sounding worried for the first time all morning, "I posted all of these to Instagram. I have hundreds of comments. Thank God my parents are spreading my grandfather's ashes in Bordeaux and my sister doesn't have social media, but *shit.* I have thousands of followers!"

"Um, good for you?"

"I mean, thousands of people have seen these photos and liked them and commented on them." Andrew joins me in pacing the carpet. "Okay, okay," he says, mussing his hair with one hand. "Hot take: maybe this is actually a great thing."

"It's not."

"No, listen." He does a quick search on his phone. "To get a marriage license in Multnomah County, you just have to apply at the courthouse and wait three days before getting married. We can go this Thursday on my lunch break and then get married the week after Christmas."

My head is spinning, and I drop it into my hands.

"Seriously, we could do what the napkin says. We could pretend to be happily married for a while, separate after a few months, and have the divorce paperwork fully signed by next Christmas."

"I can't be married to you for the next twelve months, Andrew."

"Why not?" He looks me up and down. "It doesn't seem like you have much going on."

I snatch up the rest of my clothes and begin frantically shoving my arms into my cardigan sleeves. "I have some stuff going on. And we're *strangers*! How the hell would we fake being engaged? I don't know the first thing about you!"

"We'd get to know each other!" he insists as I grab my shoes and trip my way into the hall. He follows. "And you'd come to Christmas at my parents' cabin, and I don't know. . . . I haven't thought it all the way through, and I'm a bit hungover."

"What about your parents? They'll be fine with your getting married just to claim your inheritance?"

"My parents don't know about the addendum to my grandfather's will! He only added it a few weeks ago, and the executor gave me the heads-up because we went to Stanford together. That's why this is such a brilliant plan!"

I scoff.

"Think about it, Oliver. No one would know the truth but us. We would tell everyone we're in love, and then—"

The anxiety in my stomach turns to acid burning its way up my throat. I need to get out of here before it also turns to a fresh wave of hot tears. I shake my head. "Goodbye, Andrew."

• • •

It isn't until I'm outside Andrew's apartment building that I realize I have no idea where I am or how to get home. I end up paying twenty bucks for a rideshare, and the fact that I don't vomit on the floor of this Ford Fiesta is quite a life accomplishment.

By the time I'm home and have purged last night's mistakes respectably into the toilet, it's just before eight. My shift at Roastlandia starts at ten, so somehow in the next two hours I'll have to figure out how to be a person again and not a wrung-out sponge of whisky shots and puke and shame. God, Greg is going to be cruel when he sees me.

On the tile floor beside the toilet, my phone starts to buzz. I groan.

"Put me on FaceTime, you little minx!"

"Meredith, what's wrong? I'm sick, and I need to shower before work."

"What's wrong? *What's wrong?*" I hear her slam down a pencil. "My best friend apparently got engaged last night, and I had to learn about it from Instagram. *That* is what's wrong."

"Oh. Fuck."

I go ahead and take a little lie-down on the bathroom floor. "It's not real. I was blackout drunk."

"No shit. That barely looked like your face."

"How did you even see the photos? I thought they were posted on his Instagram."

"He tagged you, and then you shared them on your story."

"Have I already said *fuck?*"

"I can't believe I told you to find a himbo and you actually did it. And in a classic Ellie overachiever move, you took it a step further and got engaged. We should talk about your perfectionist tendencies at some point, but I'm honestly proud of you."

"The engagement isn't real," I mumble. Everything starts spinning again as I tell Meredith about the two million dollars and the napkin contract and Christmas at his parents' cabin.

"Let me get this straight," Meredith says in her lawyer voice. "A man wants to pay you two hundred thousand dollars to be engaged to him for two weeks, marry him, and then divorce him a few months later, and you're going to say *no?* What the hell is wrong with you?"

"As my unofficial lawyer, I don't think you should be advising me to commit fraud."

"As your official best friend, I am advising you to not be a fool. You desperately need this money, especially since you refuse to tell Linds where she can shove her credit card debt."

I make a sound oddly reminiscent of a dying raccoon.

"Plus, this will get you out of your apartment for a change.

Wouldn't it be nice not to spend your Christmas eating a rotisserie chicken alone over your kitchen sink?"

"That . . . wasn't my plan."

"Yes, it was."

I groan again.

"I love you, Ellie, but this past year has been rough. You experienced a few setbacks, and you just *froze*. You are frozen, like a microwavable burrito pre-microwave. You need a little shock to your system. And *two hundred thousand dollars*? You can't walk away from that kind of money."

"I can admit that I've . . . stagnated a bit." I can also admit this is a total understatement. "But does that shock to my system really need to be a fake engagement to a handsome millionaire?"

"Honestly? Maybe it does. Nothing else has managed to shake you from this hibernation. You'll be like Sandy B, and he'll be your Colin Firth. You'll pretend to be in love, and then you'll fall in love *for real*."

"What movie is that?"

"I don't know . . . all of them?"

"But I don't want to real-date Andrew. I'm not looking for a relationship right now?" I can't even stop myself from inserting a question mark at the end of that pathetically declarative sentence.

"Fine. Then don't do it for a chance at romance with Andrew. Do it for the money." When Meredith makes declarative statements, there is never a misplaced question mark. You can almost feel the universe bending to her will.

Two hundred thousand dollars. I grew up in a world of Goodwill bargain bins and living paycheck to paycheck, and I've never even let myself imagine the life that kind of money could buy.

"I—I need to shower."

"Classic Ellie avoidance pivot."

"Yes, but Ellie has vomit in her hair, so you should allow it."

"Okay, but what are you going to do about these engagement photos? They're out in the world now."

As always, Meredith is right. The photos are out there, and when I walk into Roastlandia (five minutes early), Ari squeals a congratulations at me. "Holy shit! You took my advice and *got engaged* to Andrew! Kind of extra, but I love it!"

"Last Christmas" is playing again, the Taylor Swift version this time, and Ari is wearing a feathered headband and star stickers beneath her eyes, like a human Snapchat filter. She grills me about my supposed engagement, and since it feels wrong to tell her about Andrew's inheritance, my silence seems to confirm what she already believes. Greg appears from the back to lecture me on "professional conduct in online spaces" as overhead, Taylor laments—*once bitten, twice shy.*

After my eight-hour shift, I return to my tiny, subterranean studio apartment, like always.

I heat up a frozen burrito for dinner, like always.

I sit on my futon, reach for my iPad, and open up the Clip Studio program, like always.

Frozen like a microwave burrito.

Gripping my Apple pen, I begin to draw rough panel sketches of yesterday for the newest episode of *The Perpetual Suck.*

Art is the only thing I've ever been good at, until I guess I sort of stopped being good at it. *This*—creating webcomics—started as a way to process what happened with Jack. I'd always done my own passion projects alongside my animation classes, drawing fanart of my favorite ships and posting it to my anonymous art Instagram. I built a small but loyal fan following who showed up in the comments whenever I posted original character art. I'd toyed with the idea of a webcomic or a graphic novel, but it was too time-consuming when I was in school, and focusing on it fully was too much of a risk.

A master's in animation would allow me the opportunity to do art with a steady paycheck. Webcomics would not.

But then Jack happened. She stomped into my life in thick-soled work boots and a Carhartt jacket and she shook up all my carefully crafted plans and ideas about what my life should be, and then she left me alone to figure it all out in her wake.

So I drew our story, or something that vaguely resembled it. Instead of posting it to Instagram, I uploaded the comic to Drawn2, the online community for web-published comics. Within a week, the first episode had twenty thousand reads. My small fan base exploded into a hungry mass of readers who wanted to know what would happen between the two girls at the center of *Snow Day*.

And then fans did find out what happened, and they were disappointed.

And then I lost my job.

And then I started a new series loosely based on my life in Portland, and I called it *The Perpetual Suck*. Some readers followed me to that story. Most didn't. It doesn't really matter to me either way. I don't post my webcomics for the likes or the followers or the praise. I post it because even if I'm not good enough to do art professionally, I don't quite know how to stop processing the world this way. Drawn2 is the one place my art doesn't have to be perfect, because no one knows it's mine. It's the one place my work is allowed to be a draft instead of a finished product.

So I start outlining the past twenty-four hours in a fictional form: the promotion, the maybe-date, the arrangement with Andrew, the Target ring. I fictionalize it, but I barely have to dramatize it—the whole thing is absolutely absurd. By the time I've distilled it down to a short, succinct narrative that can be consumed in a series of images, it's almost four in the morning. I usually sleep on an episode for a night before posting it, so I can come back to it with fresh eyes the next day. But I'm beyond my capacity to care about a few technical imperfections, and I prepare to post it to *The Perpetual Suck*.

Except . . . I study the panels in front of me. They don't quite fit with the other episodes of *The Perpetual Suck*: anecdotes about the time someone brought a chicken onto the MAX and it pecked a hole through my favorite leggings; the time a customer at Roast-landia insisted I call our harvesters in Ethiopia to verify the beans were never stored in plastic; the time I saw Fred Armisen outside of ¿Por Qué No? (That one didn't suck, though the line for tacos did take an hour.)

This—the panels about Andrew—feels different. It feels like something *new*.

I haven't wanted to create something new in a long time.

I make a snap decision. Instead of uploading the new episode to *The Perpetual Suck*, I create a new series and title it *The Arrangement*.

"Episode One: When a Man Asks You to Fake-Marry Him."

I post it before I can think twice. Then I make another perhaps-unwise 4 a.m. decision. I open Instagram, and for a minute, I stare at Andrew's perfectly curated grid, a mixture of hiking selfies, gym selfies, and shirtless mirror selfies.

Two hundred thousand dollars. I could create an entirely new life.

I take a deep breath. Then I click on the message button on his profile and begin to type.

Chapter Six

"I thought only racoons lived in this building," Andrew says on my doorstep Saturday afternoon. Then, peering around me into the caverns of my apartment: "Oh. I see only racoons *do* live here."

"We can't all be heirs to Fortune 500 companies. And, you know, there is a serious affordable housing crisis in Portland."

"But *the smell*."

"Let's just go." I attempt to shield his view of my pitiful abode, but he steps around me.

"I should probably know where my fiancée lives."

I flinch at that word, even though it's accurate. *Fiancée.*

Three days ago, I agreed to be Andrew's fiancée in exchange for two hundred thousand dollars. Andrew had only two conditions. First, that no one can know the relationship is fake. And second, that I have to spend Christmas with his family at their cabin on Mount Hood. Of course, Greg had scheduled me to work the holidays.

So, on Thursday, I went into Roastlandia, threw my apron down on the counter and quit. Ari cried as she hugged me goodbye.

Yesterday, Andrew and I spent five hours in line at the courthouse to apply for a marriage license, and I had a panic attack in a dimly lit hallway thinking about spending an entire week at a cabin with strangers. By last night, over fifty thousand people had liked the first episode of my new webcomic. I'd feel awful for vaguely exploiting Andrew's life story if it weren't for the fact that he says,

"You're not a serial killer, are you?" as he does a slow pivot around my studio apartment. He takes in the sight of the futon (which doubles as my bed), the desk (which doubles as my kitchen table), the shower rod in the corner of the room where I hang my clothes. "Because I'm getting distinct serial-killer vibes."

"I'm just poor, you asshole," I say as I sling my shoulder bag across my body and reach for my duffle. "Don't criminalize poor people."

He looks positively aghast. "I'm not! But Oliver, this is horrible. Quite possibly the worst thing I've ever seen. And I once spent two weeks on a party boat sailing around the South Pacific with twenty guys from my frat, and the plumbing stopped working on day three."

"Thanks for that comparison."

Andrew looks truly stricken. "This is the apartment you never leave? This cannot be good for your mental health."

"It's not." As much as I'm dreading the next week, I don't want to spend another minute with Andrew in my apartment. "Can we go?"

"Wait, is that what you're wearing?" he asks, one prim eyebrow arched in judgment.

I look down at my winter boots, my Old Navy jeans, my She-Ra T-shirt, and the gray cardigan I threw over the top. "Yep. This is what I'm wearing, and if this arrangement is going to work, you can't micromanage my wardrobe, and you *definitely* don't get to dress me up to make me look more respectable for your family. I'm not Julia Roberts in *Pretty Woman*."

Andrew fights off a smile as he reaches out to take my duffle. "We'll add it to the napkin. No *Pretty Woman*–ing you."

Add it to the napkin was his response every time I texted him with a new stipulation to our agreement over the past couple of days. Well, and one time he responded, *I don't know any notary publics who work at one in the morning, but I promise to have my lawyer draw something up.*

I wasn't going to marry a man—wasn't going to spend *Christmas at his parents' cabin*—without a guarantee that I'd get my two hundred thousand dollars when this was over.

•   •   •

"Should we work on our flash cards?"

As soon as we're situated in the Tesla, I bend down to pull out a binder-clipped stack of multicolored flash cards from my shoulder bag. To counterbalance my anxiety about spending over a week with his family, I created flash cards to help us get to know each other better. It takes about an hour and a half to drive to his parents' cabin, and that's a little too much prolonged silence between us for my taste. I pull out the first card, green for Andrew. Across the front it says the words *My parents*. I answer as prompted.

"Katherine Kim and Alan Prescott," I recite. "Your dad comes from a long line of wealthy WASPs and grew up here in Portland. Your mom's family is from Korea, but she was born in Los Angeles. They met in Harvard Business School in the early eighties."

Andrew hits me with an impromptu follow-up question: "Careers?"

"Alan is the current CEO of Prescott Investments, which he took over from your grandfather two years ago when he got the pancreatic cancer diagnosis. Katherine used to work as a professor at Portland State University, but she took a break when you and your sister were born, and eventually resigned to become a full-time mom. She now serves on the boards of four different nonprofits." I list those nonprofits in alphabetical order.

"Impressive. You're good at this." Andrew gives me an approving nod. "Your turn."

I don't bother reaching for a new card. "Same question to you. My parents."

He squeezes the steering wheel in concentration. "Um. Uh. Jed and . . . Lauren?"

"Lindsey," I correct. Andrew is *not* good at this. "And what's noteworthy about my parents?"

This, at least, he can recall. "Your parents were sophomores at Ohio State when they got pregnant with you. Like good, guilt-ridden Ohio Catholics—your words—they got married, dropped out of school, and got jobs at the local Dairy Queen to take care of you."

"And how old was I when that genius life plan failed, and they got divorced?"

"Three? Sixteen?"

"Definitely in between there somewhere."

Andrew throws his head back against his seat. "This is *hard*."

"You went to Stanford. I think you can remember I was nine when my parents divorced."

"Yeah, well, I mean . . . I had *help* at Stanford," Andrew grumbles sheepishly.

"I'm sure there was no shortage of cute girls who were willing to do your homework while you were judging wet-T-shirt contests."

"Excuse you. I would never objectify women in that manner." He smirks. "I was *competing* in wet-*boxers* contests."

I circle back to my parents, determined to make Andrew memorize these details. He's the one who insists his family has to believe we're a real couple. "After the divorce, Jed and Linds both went through huge party phases to—as my mom told me on my tenth birthday—'reclaim the youth I robbed from them.' That is how she justified the keg she bought for the party."

"How did you end up so straitlaced?" he asks, and I don't know how to explain it to him. How important it was for me to feel in control, all the time, amidst the twin tornadoes of my parents.

I think of Linds in her Daisy Dukes, handing thirteen-year-old me the car keys and telling me to drive home from my art show because she'd consumed a wine bra's worth of Merlot. Jed gifting me a roll of quarters for my eleventh birthday, two months late, and then vanishing for another six months without so much as a phone call.

The truth is: the world is full of selfish people who become selfish parents. It's hard to explain to anyone who grew up with stability and safety and guaranteed love what it's like to both hate your parents and desperately want their love at the same time. To still, at twenty-five, get sucked into little fantasies where they show up one day, sober and sorry, and finally acknowledge all the times you had to tuck yourself into bed.

All I've ever wanted is to make sure I don't become them. A fuck-up. A failure. A mess.

But I guess genetics are winning out.

Andrew Kim-Prescott could never understand any of this, so I merely pull another card from the stack. This one is labeled *Other cabin guests*.

"Okay, both of your grandmothers will be there," I respond.

"Well, technically, two of my three grandmas will be there," he jumps in. "Halmoni, my mom's mom, died when I was a kid, so this is my dad's mom and stepmom. We call Grandpa's first wife Meemaw and his second wife Lovey, because her name is Laverne."

"As a grown-ass adult, you call your grandma *Meemaw*?" I ask incredulously. Andrew just shrugs. "And your late grandpa's two wives are cool spending the holidays together?"

"Oh yeah, Meemaw and Lovey are best friends."

"Okay, so your meemaw and your grandpa got divorced before you were born, right? She's been married three times since then but is currently single. And you describe her as—"

"Boozy," he supplies. "I know it seems wrong to say that about an eighty-two-year-old, but it's accurate. I got my love of sangria and questionable romantic choices from her. She's an artist, and she's going to love you."

I try to suppress the cloying warmth that rises at the idea of someone's grandmother loving me. "And Lovey is—"

"Also likely to be drunk. And possibly high because she got really into edibles after her hip surgery."

I glance down at the flash card again. "And then there's your sister and your sister's childhood best friend, who always spends the holidays with your family."

The mood in the car immediately changes as Andrew shifts uncomfortably in his seat. He clears this throat. "Yeah, my sister's friend Dylan." I watch his jaw tighten as his steely gaze stays focused on the road. "Dylan's dad used to work for Prescott Investments, which is how we met. In college, Dylan came out as nonbinary, and things got unpleasant with their parents, so now they spend the holidays with us every year."

"And Dylan lives in Gresham and works as a kindergarten teacher?" I say, remembering their flash card.

Andrew nods.

"And your sister?"

"Jacqueline."

His voice sounds tight when he says her name, and I shoot him a look. Andrew is all strong jaw and Roman nose, sleek eyebrows and a four-hundred-dollar herringbone peacoat. Frat boy turned real-estate investor. But when he talks about Dylan and his sister, tenderness creeps in. Tenderness and . . . protectiveness?

And secrecy, like he's holding me at arm's length from fully knowing them. His sister, especially, has been a mystery. He barely mentioned her in our flash-card sessions, and he usually finds some way to change the subject when I bring her up. "Are you and your sister . . . not close?" I broach.

"We're extremely close," he says, but his hands are still tightly clenching the wheel. "We're only eighteen months apart, so we did everything together growing up. It's just . . . she has a contentious relationship with my parents, my dad especially. And she absolutely can never find out we're faking this for my inheritance. It's just—" He rolls his shoulders, and his tone turns defensive. "My sister can be stubborn in her quest for independence. She refused to take the Prescott Investments route and dropped out of college. My parents stopped helping her financially after that, and she basically had to become a full-blown adult while I was still at Stanford partying on my monthly allowance. I . . . she . . . she can't ever find out about the addendum, okay?"

There's something he's not saying, and unfortunately for both of us, Andrew isn't good at hiding things. Still, I don't push it, because I'm his *fake* fiancée, not his real friend.

"You'll like her, though," Andrew adds. "My sister, I mean. Everyone loves her."

I bite my tongue. Jacqueline is the name of someone who has a country club membership and a Pomeranian. I do not foresee us bonding.

I take a long, deep breath through my nostrils. *Two hundred thousand dollars.* I'm doing this for two hundred thousand dollars.

Our flash cards are forgotten as the car climbs in elevation and the road conditions become more treacherous. At first the snow is just sprinkled on the side of the road, then it's banked on the side of the road, then it's covering the roads. We pull over so Andrew can put chains on the Tesla—a truly ridiculous choice of vehicle for snowy terrain—and I white-knuckle the dashboard the rest of the way on Highway 26.

Eventually, Andrew turns the Tesla onto a steep country road, and the chains grind against the fresh snow. He calmly maneuvers the car going ten miles per hour, past silvery evergreens and the dense forest in the distance. We turn a final corner, crest a hill, and the trees thin to reveal a house.

"Andrew!" I shout.

"What?"

"*Andrew!*"

"*Oliver!*"

"Andrew! I thought you said your parents had a cabin?"

"They do." He gestures ahead of us. "It's right there."

"This is not a cabin! It's a fucking ski chalet!"

He looks confused. "You can't ski here. We drive up to Timberline to do that."

"You're missing the point. That—" I jab my finger against the windshield. "That is a Swiss mansion, not a cabin."

"It's a log cabin."

It *is* seemingly made of logs—or at the very least, meant to look like it's made of logs—but the four-story monstrosity sprawled out on the snowy hill in front of us looks like a hotel. As dusk settles on the mountain, a hundred porch lights bathe the giant home in a golden glow. The ground floor is a whopping five-car garage and there are stone freaking columns.

"I'm confused as to why you're so hung up on the semantics of the word *cabin*."

"Because there are balconies!" I count them. "Six. Visible. Balconies!"

Andrew pulls the Tesla into the driveway but doesn't turn off the engine. "Well, if I'd known about your balcony-phobia . . ."

I slink down in my seat, hoping it will absorb me, make me part of its leather so I never have to get out of this car. While I knew the Kim-Prescotts were wealthy, it's another thing entirely to be confronted with a multimillion-dollar vacation home. I could fit every place I've ever lived *combined* inside this alleged cabin, and there is no way I can walk in there in my Old Navy jeans and cardigan with a hole in the armpit and introduce myself as Andrew's fiancée. I should have let the bastard *Pretty Woman* me.

And more to the point, I never should have left the safety of my apartment. I won't know how to talk to these people. They're wealthy and normal, and they'll know right away that my childhood was marked by dysfunction, not decorating Christmas cookies.

Andrew notices the whole-body anxiety melt taking place in the passenger seat. "What is this? What's happening?"

"I can't go in there."

"Well, we're not going to spend the entire week outside."

"Seriously." I'm clutching the door handle. "I can't do this, Andrew."

"Hey there." He pats the crown of my head in an attempt to be comforting. "Don't worry. Everyone will be really nice to you. Even my dad. At least to your face."

Sweat pools beneath the thick layer of my cardigan. So, naturally, I flail my hands under my armpits like little fans. Because the best thing to do with pit stains is draw needless attention to them in front of the handsome man who wants to fake-marry you.

"This—this was a mistake. We can't get married. I can't spend a week with your family."

"Yes, you can." He shuts off the engine. His voice is cutting and impatient, almost as if two million dollars were on the line. "Because you have no other choice. We're already here."

Chapter Seven

"You must be Ellie!"

Someone screeches these words the second Andrew opens the front door. I barely have time to consider how I would draw the entryway—high ceilings, oak paneling, large windows lining the backside of the house—before I'm accosted by a pair of soft arms that encircle me in a surprisingly tight hug. The anxiety I felt in the car moments before begins to seep out of me and into the arms of this woman who smells like red wine and ginger cookies. *God*, when was the last time someone hugged me?

"Sugar, it's so good to meet you!" the woman coos into my hair. "And such a pretty little thing! Let me get a good look at you."

The woman seizes both my shoulders and holds me at arm's length, and I finally get a good look at her, too. She is an elderly white woman who can literally only be described as *boozy*. There's a poof of gray hair circling her head like a chaotic halo, orange lipstick not quite colored in the lines of her mouth, a ruched top cut low enough to reveal a spectacular (if somewhat wrinkled) pair of breasts.

In describing his meemaw, Andrew neglected to mention that she is incredibly Southern, six feet tall, and the human antidote to an anxiety attack.

"Bless you." She gives me another hug, and I never want to let go. "Aren't you a doll?"

Then Meemaw plants a wet kiss on my cheek, and even though I can feel the imprint of her orange lipstick, I really don't mind. "Welcome to the family, sugar." She eats the *r* at the end, so it's a musical *suga* rolling off her tongue.

"It's nice to meet you, Mrs. Prescott."

She swats my arm. "None of that formalness. You can call me Meemaw, and this here is Lovey."

She gestures to the equally boozy-looking white woman on her right, who is sucking on what appears to be a vape pen. Likely to be high, indeed. To each octogenarian her own, I guess.

Laverne Prescott is wearing a Patagonia vest over a moisture-wicking button-down, a pair of patterned yoga pants, and Crocs with socks. She barely comes up to my shoulders, but her hug is just as soft and just as comforting as she wraps her arms around my middle. "Um, I was very sorry to hear about your recent loss," I say, stupidly and uselessly to a woman who just lost her husband of almost thirty years.

But Lovey's only response is, "You're so tall! Pah! That's the last thing I need! Another granddaughter to tower over me."

My heart flutters at the base of my throat. *Granddaughter.*

And really, did Richard Prescott's *entire* family despise him?

"Oh, well. I guess I'll just have to get used to it. I'm doomed to a family of giants. Can I get you something to drink?" Lovey offers with her head still pressed against my shoulder. "Barbara made sangria."

"You absolutely need sangria!" Meemaw announces, and she's somehow conjured a glass of sangria to thrust into my hand. "Now! Andrew tells us you're an artist. I've just recently gotten into glass-blowing, and I found this instructor in Lake Oswego. He's got an ass like a peach and hands like Michelangelo. Have you ever worked with glass? Or Italian men?"

I shake my head.

"Barbara, let the girl catch her breath," Lovey scolds as she takes another hit off her vape.

Meemaw ignores her. "Ellie. That's a pretty name. Short for Elizabeth?"

"Elena."

Meemaw studies me for a moment, one eyebrow quirked. "Ah. Well, I can't believe this one is finally settling down." She thrusts a thumb at Andrew, who is casually standing back by the front door with an expression of gentle amusement. "Never thought he'd stop ho'ing around."

"Hello, Meemaw." Andrew smiles. "It's always a pleasure to be harassed by you. And Lovey." Andrew accepts two kisses from Meemaw before he stoops to embrace Lovey. The latter presses a papery hand to Andrew's cheek, and the gesture is so tender, I have to look away.

The house smells like pine cones and winter spices, and John Lennon is crooning, "So this is Christmas," over a speaker system, and he's right. This *is* Christmas, the way I've always seen it in movies but never experienced firsthand. Grandmas who greet you with warm hugs. Holly up the banister and mistletoe in all the doorways, a collection of illuminated porcelain houses along a buffet table. Later, I will draw this place like a fucking Norman Rockwell painting. It makes me oddly nostalgic for something I've never had.

"Come along, now." Meemaw loops her arm through mine. "Katherine is dying to meet you."

Meemaw drags me through the house, past the giant living room where the stockings are already hung along the fireplace mantel. Someone has added a plain red one to the end of the lineup, with the name *Ellie* written in glitter glue. My heart is in my throat as we turn the corner and see a woman in a dark green dress arranging a floral centerpiece on a formal dining room table. Behind me, Andrew clears his throat. "Mom?"

Katherine Kim looks up. She's a gorgeous, flawlessly tailored Korean American woman in her early sixties, and I lament my Old Navy jeans once again. But Katherine only has eyes for her son, not my haggard appearance, and her face breaks into a smile. "Andrew!"

She throws herself at him. "Oh, Merry Christmas! I'm so happy you're here! It's so good to have the family together!"

She plants kisses on both of his cheeks, and Andrew relaxes into his mother's hug. "Mom," he says when they break apart, "I want to introduce you to Ellie, my fiancée. Ellie, this is my mother, Katherine."

Katherine is pulling me into a choke hold before I realize what's happening. "Hello, Mrs. Kim!" I cough as she crushes me against her bony chest. "You have a lovely home!"

She releases me and waves her slender arms around. "No, no, it's an absolute mess. Please, don't even look at it! I came up yesterday to try to get things sorted, but there's always so much to do around the holidays! But my goodness, dear, look at *you*!" She absently touches the tip of my braid. "It's so nice to finally meet you!"

Finally? They've known about my existence for three days, at most. I try to think of an appropriate response, but a loving mother is touching my braid, and I'm feeling too much in this giant house, surrounding by these loud people, consumed by the unequivocal *family Christmas* of it all. I hadn't expected this. In all the dread and panic leading up to this trip, it didn't occur to me that I would be spending *Christmas* with a *family*.

Before I can respond, Katherine Kim bursts into tears.

"Mom!" Andrew moves closer to her with concern. "What's wrong? What is it?"

Katherine waves her arms around again. "I'm sorry. I'm so sorry—but I just can't believe you've had a girlfriend for three months and we haven't met her. And now you're engaged, and she's a stranger to us, and I feel like I've failed as your mother, like I haven't—"

Katherine chokes on a mom-guilt sob, and Andrew sweeps in with another hug. "No, *I'm* sorry," he says as he holds her against his chest. "With Dad out of the office dealing with Grandpa's passing, I've been working too much. But Ellie and I are here now, Umma."

With that, Andrew reaches out to thread our hands together.

Mine is definitely sweaty from all the excitement, but Andrew doesn't seem to mind. This person, *this* Andrew—he isn't a Burberry coat or a snapback. He's a well-worn sweater, comforting and familiar. An investment banker dude bro who genuinely loves his family.

And maybe, I think, full of sangria and drunk on secondhand familial affection, I *could* love him. Especially if loving Andrew means having the love of his family. Maybe Meredith was right, and maybe fake feelings will turn real. Maybe Andrew is someone I could build an emotional connection with.

"We'll have over a week of family time!" Andrew tells his mother, and my heart turns to putty in my chest. "I didn't even bring my work computer."

Katherine blinks up at her son. "You didn't?"

"Well, no, I mean I brought it. But I promise I won't use it unless it's an emergency."

"No work," Katherine echoes, demurely brushing away the evidence of her tears.

"Speaking of . . ." Andrew glances behind his mother into the large, modern kitchen. "Where's Dad?"

Katherine drops her gaze and begins smoothing out an invisible wrinkle on her dress. "Your father couldn't make it today. Something came up at work."

"At . . . work?" Andrew repeats.

"Yes, he said he has that big land deal in the works with the South Waterfront property, and he missed so much time with the trip to France for your grandfather, so he needed to work through the weekend. But he said he'll be here Monday morning."

"Right. The land deal," Andrew says, and his words are clipped, his loving expression now stern and unforgiving, with the same sense of secrecy he had in the car about his sister.

In the background, Burl Ives starts chanting, "Have a holly, jolly Christmas."

It's the best time of the year.

"Who needs more sangria?" Meemaw blurts, and she's refilling my glass before I can protest.

Andrew is still glancing around the house. "And what about . . ." He coughs. "Is, uh . . . is Dylan coming this year?"

Katherine has returned to fluffing the flowers in the centerpiece. "Yes, of course. They're driving up with your sister, who should be here any minute. In fact, she should have been here an hour ago, but you know how it is with her. She *insists* on towing that damn thing up the mountain." Katherine turns to me with an apologetic expression. "My daughter lives like a nomad."

"Jacqueline lives in an Airstream," Meemaw explains for my benefit as she slurps down her own large glass of sangria. "She parks it in a friend's backyard for most of the year, but she brings it with her when she comes to the cabin because *someone* doesn't like having the dog sleep in the house."

"I told her the dog is welcome to sleep in the garage." Katherine bristles, and Meemaw comes back with another retort about millennials and their dogs.

"If Jacqueline had a child, you wouldn't ask *them* to sleep in the garage!"

They continue back and forth, but my brain has lost the ability to track this conversation. It's stuck on one word.

"An *Airstream*?" I ask when I finally find my voice.

"It's actually really nice," Andrew reassures me. "Kind of like a tiny home, but on wheels."

I see her in the low light of memory, standing beside the shiny trailer in the snow.

"Your sister named *Jacqueline* lives in an Airstream?"

It's—it's a coincidence. It has to be. There is no other explanation. Except—

"Yes . . ."

"An Airstream?"

Andrew shakes his head. "Is this a cabin thing again?"

"Is she having a stroke?" Meemaw wonders.

"I've had a stroke," Lovey throws in. "This ain't it."

It *feels* like a stroke. This feeling of numbness creeping down my arms, this tightness in my chest, this tingle around my skull as realization competes with reason. He has a sister named *Jacqueline* who lives in an *Airstream*—

"She's here," Katherine announces, though I can barely hear anything over the blood roaring in my ears. A second later, an Australian cattle dog bursts into the room, nails skittering across the hardwood floor as he makes a beeline for my crotch.

"Paul Hollywood, no!" Andrew scolds. "Down."

The dog looks up at me with his tongue lolling sideways out of his mouth, piercing blue eyes amidst tufts of gray fur. He stands on his back legs to try to make a play for my face, his tongue licking my throat instead.

And *fuck*. It's not a coincidence.

I know this dog, just like I know the woman who bounds through the back door into the house with equal doglike energy. She's wearing rubber-soled work boots, loose jeans, a red-and-brown flannel, and that coat. That same impractical-for-winter-snow khaki coat. The one that smelled like freshly baked bread.

I don't have to speculate about how I would draw her. I've drawn her a hundred times in the past year, and now she's here. Not on a napkin sketch, but in 3-D and flesh. At the Kim-Prescott family cabin.

My brain trips and falls over the *how* and *why* and *for the love of God* of it all.

"Jack!" Meemaw cries as her granddaughter pounces, landing a kiss on her cheek. "So happy you could make it this year, sweetheart."

It's Jack.

Jacqueline.

Jacqueline *Kim-Prescott*, apparently.

I've agreed to marry the brother of my one-night stand from last Christmas.

A Webcomic
By *Oliverartssometimes*
Episode 8: *The Airstream*
  (Christmas Day, 1:12 a.m.)
Uploaded: February 11, 2022

"An Airstream?"

Jack grins at me over her shoulder. "Shut up."

She tugs me by the hand, and we trip our way down a stone path, through a gate into the backyard of her friend's house where she parks it. The trailer shines in the dark, silver in the glow of the snow, lit up with the Christmas lights she strung along the top. "No, it's *perfect*. A pastry chef who lives in an Airstream? I think I've seen that episode of *The L Word*."

"You know, I think I liked you better when you were too nervous to tease me."

"You liked me *better* when I had crippling social anxiety?"

She seesaws her hands in the air. "I mean . . ."

I hoist myself onto the single metal step leading to the door so I can be taller than her, just for a minute—tall enough to push both of my hands through her hair, fisting the ends, kissing a mouth that tastes like spiced eggnog. My body thrums as I think about two hands reaching for the same book that morning—how I didn't feel any of this then, how strongly I feel it all now. "Is this the real reason you came into the graphic novel aisle?" I ask as I tilt my head out of the kiss.

"Because I wanted to lure you back to my Airstream and kiss

you in the snow?" she asks, sounding affronted. "Absolutely not! I was doing my civic duty by aiding a sad woman crying in a bookstore!"

I narrow one eye at her, but she just wraps her arms around my waist, pulls me close. "Kissing you in the snow? Minor perk to being a good Samaritan. Now. Inside?"

I detach myself from her long enough for her to unlock the door. A fifty-pound ball of fluff charges at Jack as soon as she steps inside. "Yes, my little baby boy." She crouches down to vigorously rub the dog's ears. "I know. I left you all day like a bad mom. Who's a good boy for not pooping in the Airstream?"

She leaves the door open, and the dog rushes into the backyard, unleashing a terrific stream of pee before he flops down in the snow and rolls back and forth, making the dog equivalent of a snow angel. "So, that's Paul Hollywood."

"He's less dignified than he seems on *Bake Off*."

"They say you should never meet your heroes."

She begins stripping off her layers, and as much as I want to watch her, the desire to survey her house takes precedence over my unexpected lust. I do a slow circle in spot, taking in the details of her messy, cramped living quarters. It feels like a study in contradiction: she lives with wheels beneath her, always restless, always ready to be on the move, yet this trailer is a *home*. She's nested here, accumulated a life. There is an unmade bed on one end of the trailer, a stack of what looks like unfolded clean laundry in the corner. Shelves overhead house dog toys and boxes of treats, half-finished macrame projects, mason jars with rings of cold brew crusted to their bottoms.

On the other end of the trailer is a kitchenette with cookbooks stacked on every shelf, bulk ingredients in glass jars, a stand mixer and a food scale, a small trail of spilled flour. There are prints on the walls, succulents behind the sink, the smell of dog and body sweat, of peppermint tea and freshly baked bread, always bread.

It is both fixed and transient, restless and grounded, subtle control amidst unbridled chaos. In short, it's Jack.

"I can't believe you live in an Airstream. It's so . . ." *Romantic*, I don't say.

Paul Hollywood comes bouncing back inside, and Jack closes the door. The dog circles three times and flops down in a fluffy bed on the floor packed with half-chewed stuffed animals. "How are your feet?" Jack asks me.

I groan. "Still frozen and sore. And I think there's a good chance several of my toes have detached and are just rattling around inside my boots at this point." We'd walked three miles to get here, across the Burnside Bridge, where she'd held me in her arms and whispered the words to "White Christmas," then on through the neighborhoods of Southeast Portland. "How are yours?"

She shrugs. "I'm not worried about my feet."

"Oh, really? Miss 'Fuck the Snow'?"

"Sit down," she orders, pointing to the bed behind me.

I sit down. On the bed. On *her* bed.

I wait for the alarm bells to go off in my brain. The signal that usually tells me it's too much, too fast. The alert system that tells me to flee when people get too close before I'm ready. This isn't me. I don't follow a woman home after a single day together, but for some reason, over the course of a few hours, I feel like I know this woman better than I've ever known anyone.

She crouches down before me, kneeling so her face is level with my torso. Her quarter-moon smile and her white scar and her sweet freckles so close. My pulse throbs against every inch of my skin as she bends forward, her hair falling over her eyes. She begins to untie the laces on my boots. "Do you want to know why I live in an Airstream?" she asks quietly. Well, quietly for her, which is still sort of yelling.

And I want to know every fucking thing about her, and she has to realize that by now. We've spent the day bartering for facts about each other, collecting them like seashells on the Oregon coast. My pockets are full of pieces of Jack, and I want to spend the rest of this snowstorm begging for the rest of her story, putting it all together until I can draw her accurately on a sketchbook page, figure out all the lines of her.

"My parents had a rule for me and my brother. As long as we were in school, they would continue to financially support us," she explains, her fingers still working my laces. I don't speak. I can barely breathe. She slips off my boots to reveal the soaking wet wool socks underneath. "But I dropped out of college at nineteen, so my parents cut me off. I spent a few months couch surfing with friends until I got the job at Patty's Cakes. Patty took care of me in a way my parents couldn't at that time in my life. She taught me how to stand on my own two feet, without my family's money, and she made me feel like I could be happy, even if I didn't follow the prescribed plan for my life. Patty's brother was going to sell this Airstream, but she convinced him to let me pay for it in monthly installments so I could have my own place. It's the first thing I ever bought on my own, with money I earned. The first thing that's ever truly been *mine*."

Carefully, tenderly, she peels off my socks one at a time, her warm fingers grazing the cold skin on my ankles. I shiver.

"So, yeah," she says with another shrug. "I live in an Airstream, because it reminds me every day of what I value most. Now, would you look at that?" Jack asks in her too-loud gravelly voice as she bends low over my bare feet. "All your toes are still attached."

She takes my sweaty, damp right foot between her hands and

rubs, trying to warm my skin. Then she presses my foot against the soft flannel of her clearly beloved shirt, pressing my foot to her heart. It is the grossest thing anyone has ever done for me.

It is the most romantic thing anyone has ever done for me.

"How does that feel?" she asks, kneading my skin like her fingers knead dough.

I swallow. "Better."

Chapter Eight

I can't believe she's here.

Or maybe I can't believe *I* am here.

I can't believe that of all the people living in the Portland metro area, Jack and Andrew are related.

Not just related. *Siblings.*

The woman I met last Christmas Eve is standing ten feet away across an ornate dining room table in a goddamn ski chalet. For almost a year, she's lived exclusively in my memories and in my webcomic panels, but now she's *here*. Ten feet away. And I have her grandmother's orange lipstick on my cheek.

"Meemaw! Lovey!" She pulls her grandmothers into one joint, enthusiastic hug. "Merry Christmas!" she says in that voice. *That voice.* Low and rough, like the feeling of her callused fingers on the back of my neck. Loud, like she's never afraid to take up space. "I brought rice cakes!" She holds out a cookie tin, and both grandmas absolutely lose their shit.

She hasn't seen me yet, vibrating with nerves and sweating profusely beside her brother, our hands still intertwined. Five minutes ago, I was surrounded by the loving embrace of three older women, pleasantly contemplating the possibility of falling in love with a man who might let me be part of his family traditions. And then, Jack.

Jack's outside voice. Jack's heavy-footed stomp. Jack once again barreling into my life without warning. She's not wearing her glasses, and her eyes burn so bright in her face, I feel myself heat up beneath my clothes.

Paul Hollywood barks three times, and as I turn to face him, he leaps up onto his hind legs, pressing his front paws to my thighs and bodychecking me backward into the table. I release Andrew's hand and stumble directly into Katherine's floral centerpiece.

"Jacqueline, darling. Please control your dog."

"Hi, Mom." Jack plants a kiss on her mother's cheek. Then: "Paul Hollywood, sit."

The dog promptly drops his butt onto my feet. Jack glances up, and I watch as her dark brown eyes pass over my face. They narrow, barely, her mouth ticking in the corner. "What—?"

Andrew steps between us. "Jacqueline, this is my fiancée. And this is my sister."

The fire keeps crackling and Bing Crosby keeps singing and Paul Hollywood's tongue keeps wagging, but I feel like the entire world grinds to a halt in my bones. Jack is looking at me, and I'm looking at her, and I'm waiting for her to say something, *anything*, to give us away.

Confusion flickers across her beautiful face. I would give anything for her to be less beautiful than I remember.

"Hi," Jack says, outstretching a hand toward me. "Sorry, I think I missed your name."

The world starts spinning again, tilting, knocking me sideways with its centripetal force. Does she not remember me?

What if she doesn't remember me?

What if, to Jack, I was one of many nameless, faceless women she brought back to her Airstream? What if to her, what happened between us was ordinary and entirely unremarkable, and she forgot about it instantly, while I've been carrying it around in my heart for a year?

That would be . . . even more humiliating than what happened the morning after.

"It's—it's Ellie," I stammer, and I wait for recognition to jar across her features.

"Ellie," she repeats, as if the name means nothing to her. Then her skin envelops mine in a handshake. Her hand is cold and callused, and I don't look down at the familiar shape of it. I tell myself to feel nothing, standing in this cabin, shaking the hand of this woman who doesn't remember me.

"And this is . . . Dylan," Andrew says, and I quickly drop Jack's hand. Andrew is gesturing to someone who must've come in with Jack, but I was too distracted to notice. They wear steel-toed boots and what appears to be a homemade anti-fascist T-shirt with an illustration of a beheaded Alexander Hamilton. I take in the rest of them: giant gauges, the faintest stubble along a fine jaw, at least three facial piercings, and a neck tattoo of a knife against brown skin.

"Oh, hi!" I say to Dylan Montez, Jack's childhood best friend.

Dylan eyes me skeptically. "Are you okay?" they ask in a scratchy voice, and I wonder what's worse: the way I'm blushing or the way I'm sweating.

I press the back of my hand to my forehead. "Low blood sugar, I think."

Low blood sugar and seeing the ghost of one-night stands past.

"Don't worry. Dinner is almost ready," Katherine announces, darting into the kitchen with Lovey on her heels. Meemaw quickly follows, muttering something about another batch of sangria in the fridge.

"It's nice to meet you." I outstretch my hand again, this time toward Dylan. "I'm Ellie."

Dylan stares down at my hand like it's something grotesque they wouldn't touch in full PPE. Then, slowly, their eyes flit up my body. They seem thoroughly unimpressed by what they see. Still, they refuse to take my hand, so it dangles there like a dead fish between us.

"Dylan." Jack releases a warning puff of air. "Tone down the open hostility just a bit."

"What?" Dylan holds up two hands apologetically without actually looking remotely apologetic. "Come on. Andrew brings home some woman we've never heard of and we're just supposed to act like that's normal?"

Andrew pinches the bridge of his nose. "I knew you were going to be like this," he mutters under his breath.

"You knew I was going to be weird about you bringing home a *fiancée* out of the blue? Wow. Very astute, Andrew."

"When would I have introduced the two of you!" Andrew raises his voice. "We haven't even seen each other in six months!"

Dylan clenches their fists at their sides. "And whose fault is that?"

Jack holds up both hands like she's ready to physically restrain them if it comes to that. "Come on. What's going on with the two of you?"

"Nothing!" they shout in unison. Quite convincingly.

In the awkwardness of the moment, Jack swings around to face me, to look at me directly for the first time since we shook hands. "I—I like your T-shirt," she says loudly, redirecting the tense conversation by sheer force of will.

I have to look down to remember what shirt I'm wearing. Jack is looking at me for the first time in a year, and I might as well be naked in this dining room.

Oh. Right. My She-Ra shirt. "Yeah. Thanks."

She's still staring at me. "It's a good show," she says, and she holds my gaze. My brain proceeds to jump to outlandish conclusions. Does she remember that it was me who told her to watch *She-Ra*? Did she watch it *because* of me? And if she did, what the hell does that *mean*?

"Ellie is an animator," Andrew says.

"Um, yeah. Yes."

"Well, I guess she's an . . . *aspiring* animator," Andrew corrects. "Or a former and future animator? I don't know, babe, how would you describe it?"

I have no desire to describe it at all, not in front of Jack, who is looking at me with an intensity I don't understand. Not in front of Dylan, who is looking at me with a hatred I understand even less. My social battery is running on fumes, yet I turn to Dylan because they seem to be the lesser of two evils at the moment. "So, you're a . . . *kindergarten* teacher?"

"You sound surprised," Dylan monotones. "I'm nurturing as fuck."

"Yes, that's the impression I got from the knife tattoo."

Dylan stares at me like they're contemplating disembowelment. "Sometimes, when you're eighteen and pissed as hell at the world," they say dryly, "the only thing that makes sense is getting a knife tattoo on your neck."

I nod. "I totally get that. After I came out as bi to my mom, I got an asymmetrical lob."

Their expression clearly states that these two life choices are not comparable.

Jack comes in with another clumsy conversation change. "So, how did the two of you meet?"

And *sure*, why don't I just tell the woman I hooked up with a year ago the fabricated story of how I met her brother, my fake fiancé. This is all very normal. Very fucking Norman Rockwell.

"Work," is all I manage to say.

Andrew, remembering our flash cards, fills in the rest. "Ellie works as a barista at one of my properties. Three months ago, I came in at the end of her shift, and it was raining, so I offered to give her a ride home. We ended up getting drinks, and the rest is history."

Dylan snorts. "Sounds like the perfect meet-cute."

I don't think about two hands reaching for the same book.

And then I can't think about anything, because Andrew is suddenly reaching for my chin. I'm not sure why Dylan's clearly sarcastic comment has prompted this moment of intimacy, but before I can sort it out, he tilts my face toward his and kisses me. In the middle of the dining room. In front of Jack. While Michael fucking Bublé is playing, Andrew kisses me *on my mouth*.

On-the-mouth kissing was not negotiated on the napkin contract. The surprise prompts my mouth to drop open in shock, and Andrew seems to interpret this as an invitation for his tongue to occupy that space, and now we're kissing *with tongue*.

I realize some part of me wants it to be a good kiss. I'm being kissed by a beautiful man, who is funny and charming and sweet to his mother, and I wish that was enough to make me feel something toward him.

Unfortunately, this is a terrible kiss, and I feel nothing, though I am not sure if the problem is with Andrew's skills, my mild horror, or the fact that he tastes like sangria.

Even more unfortunate is my knowledge that Jack is an exceptional kisser. That she once kissed me like this in the snow, and it had actually meant something.

At least, it had meant something to me.

Andrew finally detaches himself from my face, having proved with a few aggressive strokes of his tongue that we're madly in love, I guess. I wait a few seconds before wiping his saliva off on the back of my hand. Dylan doesn't look appeased. Jack looks, well . . .

I can't actually stand the thought of looking at Jack, so I blurt, "Bathroom!" and I don't even wait for Andrew to point in the right direction before I take off at a brisk pace.

And I can't . . . I can't *do this*.

I can't stay here in this cabin, pretending to be Andrew's fiancée, when it turns out he's Jack's *brother*.

This cabin is so comically large, I get turned around, and since I don't actually need a bathroom, I dart through a back door onto one of the many balconies. This one is a large, covered patio with a table and covered grill. It's freezing, but the fresh air feels good as it burns my lungs. Below the deck, on the other side of a giant hot tub, is the Airstream, still hitched to Jack's truck and parked in the snow.

It had seemed so romantic that night, the idea of living in an Airstream. Jack was adventurous and unpredictable, independent and fearless, so of course she lived with wheels under her. It felt like being with Jack meant I could end up anywhere.

But the next morning, when I stumbled out of the trailer in tears, the Airstream felt more like a metaphor for her impermanence. We were never meant to last. And I was naïve for thinking otherwise.

I grab the porch railing and try to breathe through the waves of anxiety rolling through me.

"Fuck, Dylan!" I hear Andrew's voice before I see the source. A few dozen feet away, on a different balcony off the dining room, I spot Andrew stepping outside, quickly followed by Dylan, then Jack, then Paul Hollywood at Jack's heels. The lights on my balcony are off, and in the dark, they seem collectively unaware of my presence.

"I just asked where you found her!" Dylan is yelling. "Did you hold a casting call for generic white girls who will ingratiate themselves with your parents?"

"She's my fiancée!" Andrew shouts into the night. "We're in love!"

I wince. I'm not sure *we're in love* is something you declare quite so matter-of-factly if it's actually true, but Andrew looks confident and stubborn in the glow of the porch lights. In front of him, Dylan looks positively feral.

"Is she pregnant?"

Jack breaks her silence with a guffaw. "Of course she's not pregnant! Wait, shit, Andrew, is she pregnant?"

"No!"

"Is this a *Walk to Remember* thing? Is she terminally ill?"

"No, Ellie isn't dying!"

"Does she need a visa? Is she Canadian?"

"No!"

"Are *you* secretly Canadian, Andrew?"

"No one is Canadian!"

"Then I just don't get it!" Dylan throws their arms up. "What the hell? Years of running from commitment, and then suddenly you're engaged after *three months*?"

"When you know, you know!" Andrew argues. "And with Ellie, I just know!"

The night goes quiet save for the sound of my own heartbeat thudding in my ears.

"What's so special about *her*?" Dylan finally asks.

"Dylan has a point." Jack exhales, and, concealed by darkness, I watch the wisps of her breath float around her face. "I mean, why *her*?"

The incredulity in her voice feels like a knife between my ribs. I gasp, like a wounded creature dying out in the wildness, and then I clamp my jaw shut and hope none of them heard me.

Of course, I'm not quite that lucky.

Paul Hollywood launches himself into a patio chair and begins barking frantically in my direction. I duck behind a covered grill, hold my breath, and wait until the barking stops.

Then I wait even longer, until the silence stretches for several minutes, and I'm certain they've all gone back inside for dinner. I wonder what would happen if I never went back inside, if I climbed down this balcony and disappeared into the night. Would Andrew come after me? Or would he just find someone else to help him get his inheritance?

It doesn't matter, because I have no way back to the city. We're up on a mountain, and as far as I can tell, there's not another house for miles. I'm completely and utterly *stuck*. I carefully climb out from behind the grill and brace myself to face the family.

"Hey, there," says a loud, husky voice in the night.

Jack is still outside, Paul Hollywood obediently sitting at her feet. She's moved to the end of her balcony, and I'm at the end of mine, so we're only fifteen feet apart now, separated by a gap of air and snow. "Are you okay?" she asks, just like she did that day in Powell's.

"Oh, fine," I say, dusting the snow off the back of my jeans. "I, um . . . couldn't find the bathroom?"

"Incidentally, it's not outside," she says with a half-moon smile I can barely make out in the dark. "What are you doing here?"

"Well," I try, "I was looking for the bathroom, as you know, and then I ended up outside, and then I heard Dylan asking if I was a dying pregnant Canadian, and I thought it might be best to pretend like I couldn't overhear it, so I hid behind this grill, and—"

"No, Ellie," Jack says. "What are you doing *here*? At my family's cabin? With my brother?"

I take a sharp breath. "He's my . . . fiancé."

"Elle," she says, and that one syllable rips through me like shrapnel. That name. My name. The name she called me that entire day. The name she called me when we were tangled in each other's arms. "I haven't seen or heard from you in a year, and then you show up for Christmas *engaged to my brother?*"

I turn away from her and stare at the Airstream nestled in the field of snow. "I thought you didn't recognize me."

"What?"

"In there. You acted like you didn't know me. I thought maybe you forgot."

"You thought . . . I forgot you . . . ?" I glance back across the separated balconies. She's staring off into the distance, too, her profile highlighted in gold from the lights. "I didn't forget you," she says. "I just . . . panicked. You were standing in my dining room, and I didn't know what to do."

She admits this so easily, always handing over the truth like she has nothing in the world to hide. Except she does. Or she did back then. I just found out about it too late.

"I panicked, too," I confess, knowing she can't see the heat of my face.

"So, you didn't know?" she asks. "You didn't know you were engaged to my older brother?"

"What? No! Of course not!" I sputter. "You and I weren't exactly on a last-name basis. And Andrew calls you *Jacqueline*, and there are no pictures of you on his Instagram"—I *definitely* would've noticed—"and he said your family spends every Christmas here, when I happen to know this is not where you spent last Christmas."

All of this is true. On paper, there was nothing to connect Andrew and Jack before she showed up here. Of course, now that I'm confronted with the truth, the signs are more obvious. The shared casual lean. The shared eyebrow pinch. The shared pouty mouth, the shared staggering bone structure, the shared gorgeous brown eyes and soft black hair. They're both built like Olympic swimmers. They both have the same tendency to flash a charming smile and completely upend my life.

She props her arms against the railing between us and leans forward. "What are the odds, huh? Of all the people in Portland . . ." She laughs her too-big belly laugh, like it's the funniest thing she can imagine. I grab the railing on my balcony, too, so our bodies are mirror images of each other. But I'm distinctly not laughing.

"It's . . . it's good to see you again, Elle." Jack exhales with that same easy honesty. "I didn't think I ever would, but . . ." She reaches up to push aside the flop of hair falling into her eyes. "You look good. Are you good?"

"I—" *No*, I almost say. *No, I'm not good*. I'm a frozen burrito. My ten-year plan crumbled, and I crumbled along with it. I'm so lonely and desperate, I agreed to a marriage for money. "Yeah. Yeah, I'm good."

"Good." Jack smiles fully, and I look away again. "What are we going to do?" she asks, and for a moment, it feels like we're on the same team again. I almost reach out for her before I remember there's a fifteen-foot drop into snow between us.

"I don't know," I say.

She pushes back from the railing. "I don't think we should tell Andrew the truth. About us."

I'm not sure what I expected her to say, but it isn't this.

"It . . . it will only hurt him, I think," Jack announces casually. "So we should just keep what happened last year between us, okay?"

"Oh, okay," I stammer in agreement.

She flicks her hair out of her face again. "It was only one day, right?" she says, her quarter-moon smile pale in the dark. "It's not like it meant anything."

"Right," I say. "Of course. It didn't mean anything."

Jack nods once, then turns on the heel of her work boot and stomps back inside the house, Paul Hollywood following closely. The door closes between us with a snick.

I stare at the empty balcony across from me long after she's gone. I already knew what happened between us a year ago meant nothing to her. So why does it feel like my heart is breaking all over again?

Chapter Nine

"Well, that went off without a hitch," I snap when Andrew and I are finally alone in our shared bedroom for the night, our stomachs full of Katherine's short rib and Meemaw's sangria, our fake smiles distorting our facial muscles.

Andrew leans back against the closed door and sighs. "It could have gone better, I suppose." He smiles at me, like he believes his smile will solve all of our problems.

"Could have gone better? We are lying to your sweet old grandmas, and your sister's best friend is like the Sherlock Holmes of fake-dating!"

"But tomorrow is a new day," he says cheerfully. "The good news is, my grandmas and mom ate it right up. They're all so desperate for me to settle down and make them grandbabies, they saw what they wanted to see: me, helplessly in love. As for Dylan, we'll just have to be more convincing."

"How do you propose we do that, exactly?"

Andrew scrunches up his nose. This is clearly his *thinking very hard* face. "I could kiss you more?" he suggests.

"Please don't."

"If you insist." He crosses the room and flops down on the queen-size bed.

"There's only one bed," I point out to him. "Aren't you going to valiantly offer to sleep on the floor?"

Andrew gets up, reaches for his rolling suitcase, and pulls a black leather toiletries bag from the front pouch. "No, I'm not."

"In romantic comedies, the gentleman always offers to sleep on the floor in these situations."

"I'm not a gentleman, and this is not a romantic comedy. Besides, we are two mature adults who've shared a bed before." He pulls off his sweater and tosses it inside a giant armoire in the corner of the room before he sits down at a little vanity table and begins performing a multistep nighttime skin care routine.

For a moment, I stand there, awkwardly watching him dab cream beneath his eyes, thinking about grandma hugs and home-cooked dinners, and Jack on a balcony saying, *Why her*? "Andrew," I eventually croak. "We can't do this."

He eyes me over his shoulder in the mirror. "We can't . . . share a room? I think it might give us away if we sleep in separate beds."

"We can't *lie* to your family."

And I can't lie to you about Jack. Or lie to Jack about you.

"Of course we can! We'll get better at it, I promise."

"It's not a matter of our ability to lie. It's about the morality of lying!"

"You were fine with compromising your morals for two hundred thousand dollars a few hours ago."

"That was before I met your family and realized how lovely they all are." *And before I found out I slept with your sister.* "And before Dylan expressed their utter disbelief you could ever be marrying a girl like me unless I'm terminal."

Andrew winces. "Wait . . . you overheard that?"

I don't bother trying to explain the mechanics of my balcony eavesdropping. "Yeah. I did."

He presses a jade roller across his forehead. "I guess I should've assumed they might be intense about this whole thing."

"Why would you assume that? What's going on with you and Dylan?"

"Nothing!" Andrew swivels around in his chair to face me, jade roller twisting between his fingers like a baton. "Well, I mean, we sort of, kind of . . . used to date?" Andrew is also guilty of misplaced question marks because it's obvious there is no *sort of, kind of* about this.

"Does everyone know about this? Does *Jack* know?"

"It's . . . complicated?"

"Well, that's a no. Why didn't you tell me you and Dylan used to date *before* I got here?"

"I didn't really think it was relevant information," Andrew grumbles. "They're not here as my ex. They're here as my sister's best friend."

"Well, your sister's best friend hates me, and now I'm starting to see why! Which makes it relevant, Andrew!"

Andrew slumps in his chair. "Dylan isn't jealous, if that's what you're implying."

For someone so successful, Andrew can also be so very oblivious. "They are *absolutely* jealous."

Andrew attempts to pinch his brow, but it's currently slick with rose oil. "Our thing was a million years ago," he reassures me. "Dylan and I hooked up a few summers in college. We were never going to last. We want different things."

"So, you just casually dated your sister's best friend–slash–kind of surrogate sibling?"

"It was mostly casual." Andrew chews on his bottom lip before he finally confesses: "And we maybe sort of relapsed last Christmas when Jack didn't come to the cabin and we were alone together."

I throw up my arms. "This is the real reason you brought me, isn't it? I'm here as your beard!"

Andrew slams the jade roller onto the vanity table. "You're not my beard. Everyone knows my sexuality is like a Rorschach test."

"What does that even mean?"

"What you see when you look at me says a lot more about you than it does about me."

I don't have the time or the energy to parse out that metaphor. "Whatever, you brought me here to be your sex shield!"

"*No.*" Andrew sits stiffly in his chair. "You're here to help me get my inheritance."

"In that case, is it cool if we come clean to Dylan about the fake engagement?" I make a feint toward the door. "I mean, since I'm only here to help you get the money, I don't see any reason to lie to Dylan."

Andrew leaps up from his chair and grabs me by both arms before I can leave the room. "Fine!" He relents. "You might also sort of be here to help block my cock from certain, potentially detrimental actions."

"*Andrew!*"

"I'm sorry!" He massages my shoulders in a feeble attempt at apology. "But I need Dylan to think I'm in a relationship so we don't . . . backslide."

Here I thought I'd stumbled into a weirdly incestuous love triangle, but it's actually some kind of dysfunctional love trapezoid.

"I'm sorry I didn't tell you the whole truth, but I did not lure you here under false pretenses. This really is just about the inheritance. I need that money."

"Why?"

Andrew drops his hands from my shoulders. "I—I can't . . . it doesn't matter why. I just need it."

I feel the need to pinch my own brow to fight off the impending tension headache. "I don't get it. If you have a weird on-again, off-again thing with Dylan, why didn't you ask them to be your fake fiancé?"

"Because it would be too confusing! Look, I know how Dylan comes across when you first meet them, but they're really just a giant marshmallow—you know, one of those marshmallows that got burned while making s'mores, so the outside is all crispy, but the inside is pure goop—" Andrew makes hand gestures to aide him in this new metaphor. "Dylan is that marshmallow. They're usually a serial monogamist, and a fake engagement might . . . I don't know . . . give them the wrong idea."

"Because you don't want a real relationship with them?"

Andrew shoves his hands into his hair. "You heard Meemaw. I'm a ho. I'm a pretty face with a trust fund and a good time at a party. I'm not what Dylan wants or needs."

I'm acutely aware that Andrew didn't answer my question about what *he* wants, but after everything that's happened in the past six hours, I'm too emotionally drained to push it.

"My parents . . . they don't have the best marriage," Andrew offers with the same level of trust his sister always showed me. "I've watched my dad hurt my mom my entire life. I don't want to hurt Dylan like that, okay?"

And *there it is*. The legacy of shitty parents, the looming specter of morally questionable genetics. I know that fear in my bones, and I didn't expect to see it so clearly etched into Andrew's handsome face.

"You're nothing like your father," I tell him.

Andrew snorts. "You don't know that. You haven't even met him."

"You're *here*," I say. "You aren't at the office. You're here for your mom, for your grandmas. You showed up, and your dad didn't."

He smiles wickedly. "I knew you wanted me, Oliver," he teases, and the funny thing is, a few hours ago, I really did want him. Or, at the very least, I *wanted* to want him.

Andrew eyes the one bed, and his smile turns downright lascivious. "Are we going to do this thing or what?"

I reach out for his hand and lace our fingers together instead. "You don't have to be that guy with me, you know."

He does another scrunched confused face. "What guy?"

"The guy who's only a fun time at parties." I pull him down on the bed so we're sitting side by side. Andrew is quiet for a moment as he fiddles with our joined hands.

"You know," Andrew says thickly. "You're kind of a great fake fiancée so far."

I give his hand a squeeze. "You're mediocre, if I'm being honest," I say, and Andrew smiles again. "But tomorrow is a new day."

Unfortunately for Andrew, I don't plan to be here tomorrow.

A Webcomic

By *Oliverartssometimes*

Episode 2: *The Honesty Game*

(Christmas Eve, 11:07 a.m.)

Uploaded: December 31, 2021

I think I'm about to have a heart attack in the coffee shop at Powell's.

This is—I press my hand against my chest—*yep*. This is definitely a heart attack.

I'm too aware of my heart thrashing against my ribs, and it feels like there's something lodged in my chest, a too-crowded, overwhelmed feeling. Every time I attempt to breathe, there's a sharp, stabbing pain. I clutch my rib cage and try to inhale slowly, but nope—it hurts too much.

This is probably it. I'm probably dying.

Except. Well. It's statistically unlikely that I'm actually going to die from a heart attack while standing in line for coffee at eleven in the morning.

I remind myself to go through my pre-scripted self-talk. *You're not having a heart attack, because first of all, you're twenty-four years old, Ellie, and despite your love of microwave dinners and your hatred of physical exercise, it's unlikely you're having an unprecedented cardiac event.*

Secondly, because you've been here before, confusing a panic attack for something else, going to the emergency room in the

middle of the night to have EKGs painfully point out that your
health problems are not in your chest.

I take my first full breath.

What I'm having, in fact, is a minor panic attack. A brief flash of intense anxiety. The kind you might experience when you agree to follow a stranger to a second location. Even if that second location is just the coffee shop inside of Powell's.

I take a few more calming, cleansing breaths. The woman named Jack orders our coffees, then leads the way to an empty table beside a wall of windows. Most of the tables are empty, actually. Outside, there's at least three inches of snow now, with gridlocked cars lining Burnside and fat flakes still falling. Jack shrugs out of her khaki jacket, and my heart clenches for some reason. A beautiful woman with long fingers wrapped around a praline mocha sits down across from me, and my cardiovascular system is going haywire trying to figure out if this is some kind of date.

"Don't worry. This is not a date," she says, leaning back in her chair like she's just read my mind.

"Oh." I'm relieved. Am I relieved? *Why am I not more relieved?* "Oh, right. Um, of course not. I didn't think—"

"This," she continues, cutting off my rambling, "is a meeting between co-parents to discuss the future upbringing of our book."

The copy of *Fun Home* she purchased sits on the table between us, and she gravely places her hand over it.

"And because this isn't a date," Jack says, "normal date rules don't apply."

That is somehow *worse*. At least I understand the rules of dating and know what's expected of me socially. This is something lawless. Under the table, Jack jostles her foot, and I feel it rattling through my bones. "Normal date rules?" I finally ask.

Jack hums. "Yes. On a normal first date, you're not allowed to unburden your childhood traumas, but because this isn't a date at all, I think you should tell me why you were crying in a book-store on Christmas Eve."

I shift in my seat. "I wasn't—"

"Don't," she interrupts, raising one stern finger. "Do not lie and say you weren't crying. It sets a bad example for our child." She pats the book. "New rule. We both have to answer every question the other person asks honestly."

"I–I don't agree to those terms."

Jack pushes her glasses up the bridge of her nose with two fingers, and there's something so unexpectedly dorky about the gesture, I almost don't know what to do with myself. "I can go first," she offers. "Ask me anything."

A million questions fling themselves through my mind, like the platonic, anxiety edition of "36 Questions to Fall in Love," starting with the most obvious. *Why me? Why did you want to buy* me *coffee on Christmas Eve?*

Why are you being so nice to me? Is it because you feel sorry for me?

Why can't you sit still?

Why do you keep looking at me like that?

And *What, exactly, do you see when you look at me?*

"Why are you alone on Christmas?"

The woman named Jack takes a sip of her mocha. "I–I . . . I needed a break from my family this year."

I mirror her caginess by taking a sip of my black coffee. "That doesn't sound entirely forthcoming or within the parameters of your honesty game."

She ruffles her hair and glares at me. "Yes, well. My family." She takes another sip and fidgets in her chair. "Okay. Honesty? I can do honesty." She takes a deep breath. "I'm the family fuck-up." Jack makes a sweeping gesture with her hand, as if she's reveal-ing herself as an item during the Showcase Showdown on *The*

Price Is Right. "I was always awful at school, which was hard on my parents, but even harder on my racist teachers, who took one look at my last name on the roster, realized I am Korean on my mom's side, and expected me to be some kind of genius. Or at the very least, a quiet, obedient student, not a loud, outspoken slacker with ADHD and a heavy tread."

"You do have a surprisingly heavy tread," I note.

She continues to jostle her foot, and I fight the sudden, explicable urge to reach under the table and put a hand on her knee. I wrap my fingers around my warm mug instead.

"So, I hated school, even after I got the ADHD diagnosis and the right meds. The desks were too small, and there was too much sitting, and you're supposed to learn stuff from reading a book? That's a terrible system. But my parents wanted me to go to college, so I scraped by with the grades I needed to get into the University of Oregon, lasted for almost a year, and dropped out. Now I'm twenty-six, working for minimum wage, and profoundly disappointing my parents with every one of my life choices. And I just didn't feel like facing their disapproving stares this Christmas."

She finally takes a breath, and I fumble with some way to honor the vulnerability she's offered me. "At least your parents care enough to be disappointed," I try. I'm aware that it's the complete wrong thing to say.

"Is that why you were crying? Because your parents don't care?"

I inhale slowly through my nostrils. She just handed me so much of herself, and I'm not sure I know how to do the same. "It's . . . something like that."

She flicks her chin to get her hair out of her eyes, and I know this isn't enough. I reach into my shoulder bag and pull out a pencil, like a security blanket. "Honesty. I just moved to Portland a month ago because I got a job at Laika Studios, and it's been *really* challenging, way more challenging than I thought it would be. I've always been naturally talented as an artist. I mean, I've worked hard at it, don't get me wrong, but I don't think I've had to work as hard as some of my peers. It's come fairly easy to me. But at Laika, I have to work *hard*, and it's been draining.

"I bought my mom a plane ticket so we could spend Christmas together, because with everything at work, I really didn't want to be alone for the holidays. This morning, she called to tell me she didn't get on the plane. She said it was because of the snow in the forecast, but she just met this new guy named Ted, so . . ."

I trace the tip of my pencil along my napkin, outlining a vague shape. "My mom has a pattern of putting her relationships with men before me, so I'm sure Ted is in line to become husband number four. Another failed marriage to add to her growing collection."

"Do you really think that?" she asks abruptly. "That a relationship is a failure if it doesn't last forever?"

My hand pauses over the napkin. "Well, I mean, isn't forever the goal of marriage?"

Jack's jaw tightens for a minute, and I study her profile as she turns to look out at the snow. It's obvious I've said something wrong, but I'm not sure what it is. "I think marriage is just promising to love someone as long as you can for as best you can. I think relationships can be exactly what they're supposed to be," she says, eyes still on the snow, "even if they only last for one year, or five years, or even just for one day. The good parts of the time you spent with a person don't go away simply because the relationship ends."

"Isn't that exactly what happens?" I think about my mother falling in and out of love a dozen times throughout my childhood, about all the heartbroken days when she lay in bed crying. I think about my one serious relationship, in undergrad, with a girl named Rachel Greenblatt. Even if there were some good

moments with Rachel, they're overshadowed now by the knowledge that I fucked things up between us, that I let things fall
apart, that I failed.

"Is that the only reason you like art, then? Because you're
good at it?" Jack startles me with another abrupt turn in the
conversation.

"What? No! I love art because—" The anxiety control-alt-
deletes everything I love about art from my brain, so I'm just sitting across the table, floundering. I fell in love with art because . . .
because it was something my teachers praised me for. Because
nothing I did at home ever got me noticed by my parents, but
drawing—being good at *something*—got me noticed at school.
So I kept doing it, kept getting better, kept getting attention.

"Okay." Jack straightens in her chair, unable to wait for my response. Her smile is suddenly mischievous. "Honesty game: What
is your favorite Taylor Swift album, and why is it *evermore*?"

I'm ill-equipped to handle her dialogic whiplash, and I sputter,
"What makes you think I love *evermore*?"

She waves a hand in my direction. "I'm getting definite *evermore* vibes."

"Okay, for one, it's the single greatest Christmas album ever
written—"

"It's not even remotely a Christmas album."

"Agree to disagree." I take another sip of my coffee.

"Not that you asked, but my favorite album is *Lover*."

I slam down my mug. "*Lover* cannot be your favorite album.
That's offensive to her overall body of work."

"It's just nonstop bops, and I'm here for it."

I eye her across the table. "You don't really look like a
Swiftie. . . ."

"What does a Swiftie look like?"

"I don't know. . . . You're just sort of . . . cool looking?" Her
eyebrows shoot up in her face. "And, you know, more . . . *butch*."

She leans forward across the table until our faces are close together and attempts to lower her voice. "*Butch* isn't a dirty word." She's still at almost-shouting volume. "You don't have to whisper it."

"You just don't strike me as someone who enjoys pop music."

She doesn't move away from me, so I can smell the praline syrup on her breath when she opens her mouth. And beneath that, coming from somewhere on her skin, freshly baked bread. "Tell me: What kind of music is someone like me allowed to enjoy?"

I cringe at myself, closing my eyes tight. "I'm so sorry. Of course, you can listen to whatever music . . . I didn't mean—"

"Honesty game: Have you ever met a queer person before?"

"Of course I have," I snap defensively. "I mean, I'm queer, actually." I resist the urge to cringe at myself again. "I'm bi. It's just . . . you know, Portland is a little different, and I'm still getting used to it."

She studies me from across the table. "Let me guess: Iowa."

"Ohio."

"Ah, yes." She nods sagely. "Everyone in Portland is originally from Ohio."

"It's why I moved here," I attempt to explain. "I flew out here to visit the city before accepting the job at Laika, and it just felt like . . . like home. I've always felt like I don't quite fit in, but within five minutes here, I just knew it was right. Like if I could be myself anywhere, it would be here."

"Are you?" she asks.

"Am I what?"

"Yourself."

I look up from my napkin sketch and find Jack staring at me again. "For the record, I *only* listen to pop music," Jack says. "And Taylor Swift is the greatest lyricist who has ever lived. I'm pretty sure Bob Dylan listened to *Folklore* and immediately threw his Nobel Prize for literature into the fire. Are you drawing my hand?"

I look down at the napkin in front of me where I've sketched out long fingers, shadowed knuckles, square fingernails, a thick callus on the index finger. I attempt to cover the drawing with my elbow. "No, I was just—"

"Honesty game!"

I move my elbow out of the way. "Yes, I guess I am drawing your hand. In my defense, you have very interesting hands. Like, from an artist's perspective."

"You drew my hand," she repeats, sounded awed instead of creeped out. Which is something.

"I'm sorry. It's bad," I say, crumpling the napkin.

"Wait! Don't." Jack reaches out and puts her hand over mine to stop me. Then she takes the napkin and carefully smooths it out with her callused fingers. "Shit. You *are* really good."

"I basically have this ten-year plan," I explain, because I need some distraction from the serious way she's studying my napkin drawing. "I was at the top of my class in undergrad, and I earned this prestigious fellowship for grad school, which is how I scored the job at Laika. My job now is working as a character animator, and I'll probably do that for a few years before I work my way up to lead animator, so that hopefully one day, I can write my own animated movies."

"Huh." Jack glances up from the napkin to frown at me. "I thought there was an intense, overachiever smell coming from that side of the table."

"What does that even *smell* like?"

She leans forward again, even closer to me, and takes a deep breath through her nose. "Stale coffee and unresolved perfectionism."

"I'm not a perfectionist," I argue. "I just like plans." I'm flailing my hands again, and Jack reaches across the table and plucks one out of the air like she's capturing a nervous bird.

"I just don't understand how you even go about drawing someone's hand," she muses, tracing the edge of my thumb, the crescent moon of my nail. I'm scrambling again, trying to keep up with her sharp-left turns. "There are so many intricacies in the human hand."

I open my mouth to explain, but my chest feels too crowded again. I have four extra ribs, three hearts, and a fullness climbing into my throat as Jack continues to chart a path down the slope of my thumb, inward across the soft flesh of my palm. If this is how she touches a woman's hand, I can't imagine how she kisses.

Except, I absolutely *can* imagine it—it would taste like pralines and chocolate and feel like this, delicate and unhurried—and the thought curls my toes inside my boots like paper as it burns.

This doesn't happen to me. I don't picture kissing total strangers, and if I do, there isn't toe-curling involved.

I rip my hand away from her.

"Sorry." She places her hands palms-down on the table. "I should've asked before I touched you."

"No, it's not . . . um . . . I watched a lot of YouTube videos," I say, "to learn how to draw hands. In high school. That's how I taught myself how to do it."

Jack smiles fully—not a quarter-moon or a half-moon, but something unguarded and infectious and a little goofy. "Come on." She pushes back from the table and grabs her coat. "The snow is getting bad, so we should probably head to our next location."

"What is our next location?"

She shrugs into her Carhartt jacket. "No idea. I don't have a 'plan.'" I look up to find her smirking at me for a moment before her expression falls. "But look," she says, holding up that same stern finger, "I'm not your manic pixie dream butch—"

"My *what*?"

"But if you wanted to, say, spend a few hours with a kind stranger who has attractive hands"—she jazz-hands aggressively at me—"we could just . . . I don't know . . . see where the day takes us?"

Out the window, nearly four inches of snow has gathered along the sidewalk on Burnside. On a snow day, you could get away with not having plans.

Chapter Ten

"Is this a joke? You're joking, right?"

"Why the hell would I joke about something like this?"

"Um. Because you're hilarious?" Meredith guesses. "Especially when you're trying not to be."

"Okay, one, that's harsh—"

"You know what's actually harsh? The fact that you never watch the TikToks I send you—"

"And two—" I raise my voice as loud as I dare over the silence of the cabin. Everyone else is still sleeping, but I've been awake for hours, hiding in the laundry room on the ground floor, working on the panels for episode two of *The Arrangement*—current working title: "Revenge of the Snow Day." As soon as I came downstairs, I sent Meredith a frantic, all-caps *CALL ME* text with twenty exclamation points at four in the morning my time, and then anxiously waited for her to call me back.

"You should not make light of my struggles," I scold her now, even though I'm just grateful to see her face.

"You're not fucking with me, then? Andrew is Jack's brother? Jack is there? With you? *Jack*?"

"No, I'm not 'fucking with you.' She's here."

"Well." Meredith shrugs on the screen. "You definitely have a type."

"I hate you."

"I mean, statistically, you don't develop crushes on dudes very often, so it would make sense that you were crushing on Andrew because he looks like a girl you already slept with."

"So much. I hate you so, *so* much."

Meredith shakes her head. "And she told you not to tell Andrew about your history?"

"Yes, she did. Because she's clearly a garbage liar person."

"A *sexy* garbage liar person."

"That detail is immaterial to this argument."

"Feels material."

I flop back on my washing machine perch. "I can't stay here! Andrew has a weird thing with his sister's best friend, and I slept with his sister, and it's a whole love trapezoid situation that's going to end disastrously for everyone involved. So, I'm going to find a way back to Portland."

"What do you mean? You can't leave. The money!"

"I can't stay, Mere! She's his sister!"

"You quit your job! You can't just go back to Portland! Where will you live?"

"Wherever it is, it has to be better than staying here!"

Meredith sets down her torts flash cards and gives me her full, undivided attention. "It's eight days until Christmas, Ellie. You're telling me you can't suffer eight days in that house for two hundred thousand dollars? That's twenty-five thousand dollars *per day*."

"I know, but—"

"You survived with your shit family for eighteen years, and you didn't get a cent for it," Meredith points out. "Think about how you grew up. Think about what money like that could *mean*."

The problem is, I know *exactly* what it would mean. Money like this . . . it wouldn't solve all of my problems, but hell if it wouldn't solve a lot of them.

Our FaceTime lapses into awkward silence, and for a moment I think she's frozen, her curly red hair framing her sleepy face, a pencil shoved into her half bun. Then she speaks: "How was it? Seeing her again?"

I swallow. "She said it didn't mean anything, Mere."

"But you already knew it didn't," she tells me gently, "and I thought you said you were over her."

"I totally am."

I totally am not. But I want to be, so badly, and isn't that kind of the same thing?

"If you're over Jack, I don't see what the big deal is with this arrangement," she says. "Who cares if you slept with your fake fiancé's sister?"

Despite the absolute ridiculousness of that sentence, she does have a point. "I suppose it doesn't really matter . . ."

Meredith pauses. "You're *really* over her, then?"

"Mmm," I say. It's either the beginning of the Campbell's Soup slogan, or the least convincing syllable in the English language.

"Okay. It's decided." Meredith delivers this verdict with finality. "You'll stay with Andrew at the cabin for eight more days and pretend to be his fiancée. For the money. And for the creative material, honestly. I can't wait to read the next episode of this new webcomic. Did you see the numbers on the first episode? People really love a fake-dating trope. Or is this more marriage of convenience?"

I ignore her. "Okay," I say, strengthened in my convictions. Jack be damned. This is about two hundred thousand dollars. I can't allow a silly crush to ruin my chance at two hundred thousand dollars.

I can totally be over her. But just to be safe, I can also totally avoid her in this giant house for the next eight days.

• • •

The "avoiding Jack" plan lasts all of five minutes, four of which I spend uploading the second episode of *The Arrangement* even though it's more of a sloppy draft than a finished product, since I did it in five hours hunched over a washing machine. I try not to think about the people on the other side of the screen, but Meredith is right: tens of thousands of people read the first episode.

I slide my iPad back into its case and hop off the washing machine in search of breakfast. It's almost nine now, and I can hear someone banging around loudly in the kitchen. When I come up the stairs, I see that it's her.

Jack is wearing an apron over a "Stop Asian Hate" T-shirt with AirPods sticking out of her ears. She's sifting flour, so her head is bent low, a lock of hair falling across her face. She hasn't noticed me yet. She's preoccupied with measuring her flour on a small kitchen scale, bobbing along to an unheard song.

I should take advantage of her ignorance and leave the kitchen before she sees me. I don't want to hear the sound of her raspy morning voice or see the soft purple bags under her eyes. I don't want to think about how she looked when she woke up next to me, when I briefly and foolishly thought she might always wake up next to me.

Two hundred thousand dollars. You're doing this for two hundred thousand dollars.

Before I can make my escape from the kitchen, Jack's head snaps up in anticipation of adding the flour to the mixing bowl, and when she sees me standing there, her dark brown eyes go wide. She pulls out one AirPod, and I hear three seconds of "Pocketful of Sunshine" playing at damaging volume before it cuts off.

"Good morning," she says. In that raspy fucking voice.

"Hi, uh. Hey," I say, in a nervous fucking voice. "Good morning."

Her eyes linger on me for another beat before she drops them down to the mixing bowl. "Sorry if I woke you," she says. "I know I can be loud."

I smile. Calling Jack loud is like calling her decent looking: she crashes into every room, takes up all the space, demands all the attention.

"You didn't wake me," I say.

The kitchen falls silent, with Jack's concentration consumed by her baking, and my concentration consumed by watching Jack bake. I catch myself a solid ten seconds into a stare fixated on her hands and try to come up with some kind of verbal diversion. I have so many questions about what happened between us a year ago. Questions about honesty and dishonesty, about trust, about *Claire*. About how seeing me again can be so fucking *easy* for her.

But I can't ask her about any of that. So I ask, "Do you always bring your Airstream all the way up to the mountain for Christmas?"

"Paul Hollywood isn't allowed to sleep inside the house because my mom doesn't trust that he won't climb up on any furniture in the night." Jack gestures to the floor, and I peer around the island countertop to see the dog curled into a ball at her feet. "And I like being able to escape to my own space at the end of the day. As much as I love spending Christmas with my grandmas and my mom, it's best for my mental health if I have a place that's completely mine."

She offers this information freely, as if we've picked up our relationship exactly where we set it down on Christmas morning a year ago, halfway through a round of the honesty game. As if there are no boundaries between us, no hurt feelings to protect. She hands over vulnerability like it's the easiest thing in the world, and maybe it is if you're Jack Kim-Prescott. If you didn't leave last year with hurt feelings.

My heart squeezes in my chest, almost like it's shrink-wrapping itself for future mishandling. "What are you making?"

"Waffles." She cracks an egg against the granite counter and slides the egg whites and yolk into the batter with one hand. It looks impossibly cool. "I always make waffles the first morning at the cabin. It's on the schedule."

"The schedule?"

Jack uses a wooden spoon to point to a laminated schedule on the counter. It's an Excel spreadsheet with the next eight days broken down into structured activities, things like *Christmas cookies: six hours* and *finding the perfect Christmas tree: three hours.*

Christmas carols: two hours.

Family ski trip: twelve hours.

The detail-oriented side of me whimpers at the sight of such organizational glory. But the emotional, sentimental side is slightly unnerved that the organization is applied to family bonding time. "Whoa," is what I ultimately say.

"Yes." Jack nods, whisking. "That's my mother for you."

"Whoa," I repeat. Yet—there's something *sweet* about the laminated schedule, too. Katherine cares about spending time with her family so much, she's carved out two hours just for a *first family walk in the snow.* Linds can't carve out ten minutes for a phone call unless she needs money.

I feel it again, that sense of longing mixed with a nostalgia for family Christmases I've never known.

"Katherine does not play when it comes to mandatory family activities," Jack explains. "Even though we all live close, we only spend quality time together as a family a few times a year, and Christmas is my mom's favorite."

"What about your dad?" I set the schedule back down. "Does he usually have to work through the holidays?"

Jack hunches her back and leans into mixing the batter. This involves some rather obscene forearm flexing.

You're over her. It never meant anything. She's a garbage liar person.

I hear Meredith's voice. *A garbage liar person with exceptional forearms.*

"Yes," Jack finally answers. "My dad *works*. And he'll tell my mom he's coming tomorrow every night when she calls, and every morning, he will break my mom's heart all over again by not showing up. He'll probably be here for Christmas Day, but that's it. It's the same every year."

I glance back down at the laminated schedule. *Family holiday movie night: four hours.* "That's . . . sad."

Jack stops whisking for a moment and looks up at me. An immediate warmth seeps into my bones from the heat of her gaze. It's not fair. She broke my trust. She shouldn't have the power to make me blush anymore.

"It *is* sad," she agrees. "But I'm sure Andrew has told you all about our dysfunctional family."

Andrew clearly didn't tell me shit.

"I know what it's like to have a dad who can't bother to show up for the holidays," I say, setting the schedule back on the counter. "Or ever."

Jack's face and eyes go soft. In the morning light of the kitchen, her eyes shine a dozen shades of brown, each one warm and comforting. Like molasses cookies. Like medium-roast coffee. Like the worn leather spine of an old, beloved book.

No, Ellie. You're over her.

And it never meant anything to her.

And two hundred thousand dollars.

Jack's eyes travel down to the iPad tucked under my arm. "So . . . you work as a barista now?"

I nod and hope against reason that she won't ask any follow-up questions.

But of course, she does. "Does that mean you left Laika?"

I hold my computer against the front of my body like a shield. Jack knew me as the Ellie with dreams and goals, the Ellie who'd worked toward something her whole life and then achieved it. The Ellie who'd believed that most things worked out, most of the time.

Standing in front of her now as *this* Ellie—the Ellie who lost everything, the Ellie who failed, the Ellie who stopped believing in most things—I'm not sure what I regret more: my past naivete or my present cynicism.

"Yes," I say. "I left Laika."

"Why? What happened?" Jack asks bluntly. She's always blunt, always direct, never wraps my fragile feelings in bubble wrap. I love that about her, and I hate that about her, and right now, I just want to evade her questioning.

"It didn't work out."

"What do you mean, it didn't work out?" she pushes. "You moved across the country for that job. It was all part of your ten-year plan. You—"

"It just didn't work out. I failed, and there's nothing else to say about it."

"Honesty game," Jack says, reflexively, flippantly. It's only after the words are hovering awkwardly in the kitchen between us that Jack seems to realize perhaps she shouldn't have said them. She clenches her jaw.

There's a burn behind my eyes, in my chest. Part of me wants to slip back into the dynamics from a year ago, to be the girl who trusted Jack with all the secret compartments of her heart. When I got fired from Laika, she was the first person I wanted to tell, because I knew if anyone could make me feel better about my entire life falling apart, it would be her.

But it's not that simple. "There's nothing else to say," I repeat.

Jack stares at me over the carnage of her breakfast preparations. "You've changed," she finally decides, dropping her eyes to the waffle maker.

"You haven't."

She jerks her head up again, and I'm startled by the sadness in her eyes, the downward tilt of her mouth. "Ellie, I—"

"Morning!" Andrew singsongs behind me. Jack freezes as her brother strolls into the kitchen in a matching set of flannel Christmas pajamas clearly picked out by his mother. Whatever Jack was about to say is lost to this intrusion. "How are my two favorite girls?"

"We're grown-ass women," Jack grunts.

"Sorry. How are my two favorite *women*?"

Jack shakes her head. "No, never mind. It's still gross."

Andrew shimmies up to the counter next to me. "Fine. How is my favorite woman?"

"Um," I croak.

That's it. That's all I say. All other syllables die in the back of my throat, just like whatever Jack was about to say. *What was Jack about to say?*

Andrew tilts his head in a flawless performance of a doting fiancé and kisses my cheek. "Good morning, Oliver."

There's a question on Jack's face, and, never one to censor herself, she says, "Oliver is a weird pet name."

What was Jack about to say?

"It's her last name," Andrew explains.

Jack flinches at this news before quickly returning to her whisking. "Waffles almost ready?"

Jack eyes her brother. "I thought you only consumed whey protein shakes for breakfast these days."

Andrew lifts the bottom of his shirt to flash his shredded abs at his sister. "I think I can afford a single waffle." He reaches his other arm across the counter to swipe his finger into the whipped cream.

She swipes back with the whisk. "That's disgusting! I don't know where you've been sticking your fingers."

"Aw. Come on, JayJay," he croons. "You know you love me."

Jack scowls as Andrew dramatically licks the cream off his finger. "Say it, Jacqueline."

"I love you," Jack mumbles begrudgingly under her breath.

Andrew struts around the counter, cupping his ear. "Sorry. I didn't hear you."

Jack raises her voice. "I love you," and she adds, angrily, "Boo-Boo!"

Andrew grins and wraps his sister in a sideways hug. "I know you do."

"Oh God, who died?" Dylan grumbles as they strut into the kitchen wearing bunny slippers on their feet. They've got drool crusted on their chin, sagging holes for their gauges, and a gleam of murder in their eyes. I imagine this is their typical morning aesthetic.

"Uh, our grandfather died," Jack answers.

Without acknowledging my existence, Dylan slides onto a barstool next to me. "Yeah, a week ago. Why are you hugging now?"

Andrew releases his sister. "Sometimes, when two siblings love each other very much," he starts to explain in a patronizing voice.

"Don't try to make jokes, Andrew," Dylan quips. "You should stick to your strengths."

"Which are?"

"Lifting heavy things and being hot."

"Ah." Andrew winces briefly before covering it with a charming smile. "You forgot I'm also rather gifted at making fuck tons of money for people who already have fuck tons of money."

"I could never forget that, you capitalist pig."

"Children, children," Jack hisses, passing Dylan a giant cup of coffee from a French press. It's so full of nondairy creamer, it's almost yellow. "No ideological spats before breakfast."

Dylan gratefully accepts the mug and takes a bleary-eyed sip. Andrew watches them for a second before grabbing a bag of matcha powder from the cupboard. When Andrew's shirt creeps up in the back while he reaches up, Dylan distinctly notices. They're both ridiculously obvious, and this love trapezoid is *definitely* going to ruin our lives.

"Where are the grandmas?" Dylan asks after a few sips of coffee.

"Sleeping off their hangovers," Jack says, pouring another mug of coffee, black this time, and passing it to me without thinking. I hold the warm mug close to my chest.

"And Katherine?"

Jack shoots her brother a look before she answers. "Dad called last night to say he's not coming until Tuesday, so if I had to guess, she's probably crying on her Peloton."

"Sounds like a Kim-Prescott family Christmas to me," Dylan says.

"Alexa." Jack turns to the circular speaker on the island. "Shuffle Jack's playlist."

"See You Again" by Miley Cyrus fills the kitchen, and Jack does a little fist pump as she starts singing the lyrics.

Dylan shakes their head in profound disappointment. "How can I be friends with someone who has such deplorable taste in music?" they wonder.

Jack clasps her hands in mock apology. "I'm so sorry I don't listen to German death metal like all the cool kids."

"The fact that you just said 'cool kids' is a poignant reminder of how profoundly uncool you are."

"How did you two become friends?" I ask, shifting my gaze from Jack to Dylan. On the surface, they don't seem like prime candidates for best friends. Jack is open and warm and kind. Dylan is . . . a burned marshmallow, apparently.

Dylan points accusingly at Jack as she takes what appears to be homemade strawberry compote out of the fridge. "She punched me in the face."

"Interesting friendship origin story," I observe. "Why did you punch them in the face, exactly?"

"Because they were being a dick," Jack answers matter-of-factly.

Dylan slams down their mug. "Okay, first of all, I was seven—"

"Seven-year-olds can be dicks," Jack interrupts.

"And second, I was going through some heavy stuff at the time. . . ."

Andrew rolls his eyes and turns to me. "We all met because our dads worked together. And because Lake Oswego is overwhelmingly white, so the few kids of color had to stick together on the Lake Grove playground."

"That's how we *knew each other*," Dylan clarifies. "But Jack and I only became friends because she punched me in the face at recess."

Jack looks mildly apologetic about resorting to violence. "They were bullying some first graders. What was I supposed to do?"

"Oh, I definitely deserved it. Jack punched me in the face, and then she immediately took me to the nurse to get it iced and sat next to me on the cot until the bleeding stopped, and I just knew in that moment that I would love her chaotic-good ass for the rest of my days. Besides." Dylan clears their throat. "Sometimes I need a good punch in the face. I can be a bit . . . confrontational."

I take another sip of coffee. "I hadn't noticed."

"And domineering," Andrew says. "You can also be domineering."

"And antagonistic," Jack adds, peeling a waffle off the griddle. "And just plain mean."

"Okay, that's enough from both of you, thanks." Dylan scowls, but it lacks the bite of last night. They swivel toward me on their barstool, our knees creating the points on an obtuse angle. "Jack gave me a metaphorical punch in the face last night and made it clear that I, uh . . . owe you an apology. For what you overheard outside."

Dylan scratches their neck, right over the ink of their knife tattoo, and pushes out the next few words like they cause great physical and mental anguish. "So, I'm sorry." Dylan immediately cuts their gaze to Jack. "Is that a sufficient apology for you?"

"You undermined it a bit there in the end, but—"

"Extra points for the execution of humility," Andrew says. "I know that's hard for you to pull off."

Dylan glowers. "Welcome to the family, Ellie. It sucks here."

I take a sip of my delicious black coffee. It really doesn't seem so bad here.

"Oh, come on." Andrew reaches across the counter to jostle Dylan's shoulder. "You love us."

Dylan chokes on a sip of their coffee. Andrew takes several steps back from Dylan, the hand that was on Dylan's shoulder now rumpling his own hair. Alexa starts playing Avril's "Complicated."

Very subtle, Alexa.

And when I look away from Andrew and Dylan, I catch Jack staring at me from across the countertop; I quickly drop my gaze down to the laminated schedule on the counter.

Awkward interactions between Jack and Ellie: 192 hours.

Chapter Eleven

First family walk in the snow: two hours involves matching Christmas sweaters.

"Okay!" Katherine claps her hands together enthusiastically as we finish brunch. "It's Jacqueline's year to choose the Christmas sweaters." Katherine shoots her daughter a weary look. "And *hopefully*, this time, she took that duty seriously."

"*Sugar*," Jack says in a perfect imitation of Meemaw, "I take everything seriously."

Jack takes very few things seriously, as evidenced by the reusable New Seasons bags she produces, containing some of the most outlandish Christmas sweaters I've ever seen. Her own says "Don We Now Our Gay Apparel," Andrew's is somehow sexually suggestive *and* festive, Katherine's is three sizes too big, and Lovey's has a picture of a Christmas tree and the words "Get Lit" across the top. Dylan's features a tower of presents arranged to look like either a raised middle finger or an erect penis. Regardless, Dylan gives their best friend an approving chin nod. "This is dope."

I end up with the extra Christmas sweater, and it's an absolute atrocity with tinsel dangling from the waist, a weird RBG-style fringe around the neckline, and two dozen plastic presents sticking out from my breasts. Jack hides her laughter behind a well-timed cough. "That looks very nice on you, Ellie," she manages.

I glare. "Is this some kind of Kim-Prescott hazing ritual?"

Jack arches one eyebrow and shrugs. "Think of it more like a rite of passage."

"Really, Jacqueline." Katherine looks slightly horrified by her tent sweater with the words "In a World of Grinches, Be a Griswold" in loopy script across her middle. "Is this what you'll have us wearing on next year's Christmas card?"

"Absolutely," Jack says with a solemn nod. About this, she is perfectly serious. "I think Christmas 2023 is going to need some levity."

"I think these are perfect!" Meemaw does a little twirl. Her sweater has flashing lights and plays "Jingle Bells" on a loop.

Apparently, the first walk in the snow isn't about the walk at all; it's about the family photo they take together in the woods to use for the next year's Christmas card. This becomes clear when Katherine hands Andrew the tripod to carry and begins fussing with Jack's hair. The grandmas are both clutching stainless steel-thermoses, and when Katherine side-eyes them, Lovey says, "They're hot toddies. You want one?"

"It's twelve thirty."

"We're very old, dear," Meemaw explains. "We need something to keep us warm. You wouldn't want us catching our deaths out there."

Katherine ignores the grandmas. "First Christmas tradition of the year!" She beams as we bundle up over our ridiculous sweaters and set out. I wonder if Alan Prescott ever wears his heinous Christmas sweater, or if Katherine has to photoshop him into these annual pictures.

The Kim-Prescott cabin is on an expansive piece of property at the top of a steep hill, and as far as I can tell, theirs is the only place for miles. We all trudge through the snow past the Airstream and Jack's truck, toward the copse of trees that runs alongside a half-frozen stream. And for a split second, I forget about Jack, and I forget about Andrew and Dylan. I forget about my ruined ten-year-plan and the money that might save me. I forget everything but *this*. Snow. The beautiful magic of *snow*.

The woods are hushed by the thick layer of fresh powder, the silence and stillness punctured only by the sound of our boots crunching in unison. Everything is silvery and pure, and my cynicism goes out with a whimper. I've always loved this. The majestic white sweep of snow that makes the world anew, that makes the world feel slow and unhurried, like you can curl up and just be for a moment.

"What does your family usually do for Christmas?" Lovey asks, pulling me back to reality.

My gloved hand is intertwined with Andrew's, because apparently hand-holding is his solution to selling our relationship. "I don't really know. My parents aren't really . . . around?"

Lovey crinkles her brow in a question she's too polite to ask. Jack is out of earshot for the moment, clomping through the snow up ahead with Dylan and Paul Hollywood.

"They're not dead," I clarify. "They're just . . . I'm not close with my parents, and I don't have any other family," I attempt to explain. "I mean, I do have other family, but most of them disowned my parents for getting pregnant with me out of *wedlock*, and then my parents held a grudge and didn't let me see my other relatives growing up. Which would have been fine, but my own parents didn't want to see much of me, either, so I was mostly just alone a lot as a kid."

I stop blathering when Lovey reaches up to press a gloved hand to my cheek. I think she might be as lit as her sweater recommends, but the gesture is comforting all the same. Meemaw, hot toddy sloshing, declares, "Fuck 'em, sugar."

I startle. "Excuse me?"

"Fuck your parents," Meemaw says with even more force, shooting me a look I can't entirely parse. "I'm sorry if that sounds harsh, but any parent who would ignore their child at the holidays doesn't deserve the title." Meemaw takes a pull from her thermos. "Some of us are born into families that deserve us and some of us have to spend our lives searching for them. You found Andrew, and that means you're part of this family now."

Andrew squeezes my hand, and for a moment in the snow, I let myself forget this isn't real.

"All right, everyone!" Katherine announces when we arrive at the perfect spot for the family photo—a clearing with good light and a felled tree, with snow-covered branches framed perfectly in the background. "Coats off! Places! Places! You all know the drill! Dylan, you will not glare, so help me—"

Andrew sets up the tripod, and Katherine puts her iPhone on self-timer. I try to move to the edge of the photo—to Andrew's far side, where I will be easy to crop out in the future.

"Ellie, sweet," Katherine coos from behind the camera. "Get in the middle there. Yes, that's right. Between Andrew and Jack. That's perfect."

I adjust myself so Andrew is on my right, his hand still secured in mine, while Jack is on my left, in a gay Christmas sweater, beaming at her mother behind the camera. "Smile, Ellie!" Katherine taps the edges of her practiced grin, and when I smile, it comes easily, effortlessly.

Afterward, I can't stop thinking about how it will be impossible to photoshop me out of next year's Christmas card, how I'll always be there, in the middle of the Kim-Prescotts.

• • •

I should not be surprised that Meemaw throws the first snowball.

It starts innocuously enough. On the trek back to the cabin, Meemaw pauses for a moment under the guise of fixing her shoelaces, and before anyone truly sees what happens, a dense snowball collides with the side of Katherine's face.

Katherine's gloved hand wipes away the snow on her cheek. "Really, Barbara," she says primly, before she bends down, gathers up snow, and chucks it at her mother-in-law. Then Katherine— elegant, decorous Katherine Kim—*cackles*.

It's impossible to know who throws the third, fourth, or fifth snowball, because pretty soon, I'm dodging frozen missiles from all sides.

I try to hide behind Andrew, hoping he'll protect me from his maniacal family, but instead, he dumps a handful of snow down the back of my puffy jacket, and it's Dylan who grabs my hand and tugs me into the trees so we're concealed from the onslaught. I'm half convinced Dylan is about to use this whole snowball fight as a cover for impaling me on an icicle, but then Katherine and Lovey dart into the trees alongside us, and I understand: battle lines have been drawn.

"Those monsters are ruthless," Dylan grunts. "And we can't beat them unless we're willing to fight dirty, too." They turn to me with a grave expression. "Ellie, how is your aim?"

"Uh . . ."

"I assume that means bad," Dylan cuts in. "That's fine. You'll prepare our stockpile of ammo with Lovey while Katherine and I lead the assault."

A stoned Lovey gives Dylan a salute and immediately starts building snowballs for our arsenal. I shoot a glance through the trees to where Andrew, Jack, and Meemaw have all hunkered down together behind a giant stump. The hot toddy thermos is long forgotten as Meemaw seemingly draws out a plan of attack in the snow using a stick. Both Jack and Andrew have their arms folded across their chests, twin expressions of consternation on their faces.

I burst out laughing. I can't help it. They're six grown adults engaged in a snowball fight like it's a matter of life or death. It's easy to imagine, though, how this tradition might have started, if you grew up in a family like this. A seven-year-old Jack throwing snowballs at her brother like she threw punches. The grandmas egging them on, Katherine indulging them. Clinging to the tradition over the years like they cling to each other.

For all Dylan's strategizing, when it actually comes time to start throwing snowballs again, it's utter chaos. Katherine and Dylan throw a few through the trees, and some even hit their marks, but then Meemaw grabs a snowball in each hand and charges directly at us. From there, the teams dissolve, and it's every Kim-Prescott for themselves.

I hide behind the trees a few beats longer before I grab one of my premade snowballs and attempt to lob it at Andrew. I miss and hit the back of a khaki jacket instead. Jack swivels to find the source of the assault. Her face conveys the briefest flash of surprise before she unleashes an epic battle cry, gathers up a fistful of snow, and barrels toward me.

Quite maturely, I squeal and run away, deeper into the thicket of trees, holding back the bubble of laughter gathering in my throat. I feel the first blow against my back, followed quickly by another clod of snow hitting my thigh. I halt in my tracks to gather up another snowball for my own arsenal, tripping slightly from the momentum of my run, and I don't realize Jack is right at my back. She bumps into me, and since I'm already off-balance, I go tumbling down into the snow, my ankle twisting as my legs give out beneath me.

Jack reaches out to try to hold me up, but I only succeed in bringing her down with me, until we're a heap of limbs strewn across the snow.

Jack is strewn across *me*, her weight pinning me down. Even through the pain in my ankle and the wetness seeping through my clothes, I'm laughing. It's a deep laugh, the kind that catches you by surprise and doesn't let go. Above me, Jack looks stricken for a second, and then she's laughing, too, perhaps at the sound of my laugh. But Jack's laugh is ridiculous—a mix between the honk of a goose and the screech of tires on wet asphalt—and the sound of it only makes me laugh harder, until there are tears streaming down my face. Until I can't remember the last time I let myself laugh like this.

Then, all at once, the reality of the moment settles over me.

Jack is lying on top of me. We're touching in so many places: knees, thighs, arms, stomachs, chests.

I gasp, and Jack's eyes go wide. "Shit, I'm sorry—" She scrambles off me. "Sorry."

"No," I manage through the pain and embarrassment. "It's my foot. I—I think I sprained it."

I sit up, and she sits down, so we're side by side in the snow. "The hazards of all-out war," Jack muses. "Do you think you can make it back to the cabin?"

I look up. We're far from the path now, where the rest of the family is engaged in their snowball fight, and I can't see the cabin through the trees. "Maybe," I say. Now that Jack is no longer on top of me, the pain in my ankle is consuming all my attention. "Maybe not?"

"May I?" she asks, indicting my foot. I nod, and then she's slowly untying the laces on my boot. I see her that night in the Airstream, bent in front of me, doing the same thing.

I wince as she tugs the shoe off my sore ankle. She immediately takes my foot in her hands, cradling it carefully. For someone who's never heard of an inside voice, Jack has a surprising capacity for tenderness.

"Can I remove your sock?" she asks. I might be imagining it, but her voice sounds huskier, scrapes pleasantly across the exposed parts of my skin. I know she's asking to be polite—that she is establishing clear boundaries between us—but there's something about the way she waits for permission to touch me that stirs my misguided feelings back into action.

You're over her, the voice in my head screams. *You need to be over her.*

But the lust is louder than the scream when I say, "Sure," and Jack pulls down my thick sock to reveal my pale ankle. Her thumb slowly strokes the back of my heel.

"I didn't realize pâtissiers needed such intense first-aid training,"

I choke out. Maybe if I turn this into a joke, I can start laughing again instead of feeling like parts of myself are waking up for the first time in a year.

"I was a camp counselor every summer in high school," she says, still stroking my foot with her callused fingers. "And I'm going to say to you what I said to a lot of crying ten-year-olds during games of capture the flag: you just twisted your ankle. It'll probably feel fine in about twenty minutes or so."

I wait for her to let go of me, but she still has my foot in her hands. There's something so startlingly intimate about it. Her rough fingers, my cold foot, skin and skin and skin. There is something about the vulnerability of her hands on my body and the snow surrounding us that takes me back to that day, to the honesty game and the openness.

"I got fired from Laika," I blurt into the quiet of the woods. As soon as I say it, I feel like a huge weight has been lifted off my chest, the hole inside me filling a little bit. I keep going. "I couldn't hack it, and I got fired after three months. Like a total failure."

Jack doesn't look up from my foot, from the place where her fingers are still absently massaging my skin. "I know what that job meant to you, and I'm sorry. But people get fired, Elle," she says with a shrug. "Failure happens. That doesn't make *you* a failure."

I shake my head. "You don't understand."

"Okay." She sounds so casual, so unconcerned. "Then make me understand. Tell me what happened."

I close my eyes and see my supervisor pulling me into his office; he had a thick beard obscuring his expression, and he was wearing a Patagonia pullover that smelled like patchouli and burned coffee. My stomach felt like a wrung-out dish towel because my gastrointestinal distress always knows bad news is coming before my brain does.

I've avoided thinking about that day for the past year, tried to block it out and ignore it. "It was . . . it was really challenging," I say with my eyes still closed, her fingers still on my skin. "I'd always been at the top of my class, and I'd never really . . . *struggled*. Not like that."

I inhale slowly through my nose and the cold stings my sinuses. In the distance, there is a peal of laughter, followed by a shout of mock anguish. I close my eyes. "I was working all the time, putting in extra hours to try to catch up. My anxiety was terrible—I couldn't sleep, I could barely eat, and I knew I was disappointing the people who'd hired me. Then, three months in . . . there was a budget issue."

That was why my supervisor pulled me into his office. *"I'm afraid our quarterly earnings fell short of our projections, so we can only keep on two of the three new animators we hired at the end of last year."*

The shame that gathered on my skin, rolling up and down my limbs in hot waves. Shame like terror, like a sound you hear in the night, half-asleep, when you wake up in a confused panic.

"I'm sorry, but we're going to have to let you go."

My supervisor kept talking after that, but I couldn't hear the rest. There was a deep, pulsating thud in my ears, and all I could do was stare at the naked tree branches outside the window, unblinking. Because if I blinked, I would cry. I was sitting in a chair, hearing what I always suspected deep down.

I was just like my parents. Not good enough. A failure. A fuck-up.

"So, you weren't fired at all," Jack says after I've told her everything. "You were laid off."

I squeeze my eyes shut. "They'd hired three new animators, all fresh out of grad school, and I was the one who couldn't keep up. I was the one they chose to let go."

Jack doesn't say anything, doesn't argue with me about my interpretation of events. When I open my eyes, she's sitting in the snow beside me, looking at me the way Jack *looks*, like she can see through everything, to all the holes I still keep hidden on the inside. "I'd had this whole ten-year plan—this goal I'd been working toward my whole life—and it just collapsed in an instant."

I'd failed, and the worst part was, everyone *would know*. Those professors who'd praised me, and the peers who'd been impressed when I'd landed such a coveted position at Laika right out of grad school. My parents, who'd never believed in my dreams or noticed my talent. Guidance counselors who told me I would never be able to support myself as an artist. Meredith. *Everyone*.

I take another deep breath, and for the first time in months, I don't feel the sharp snag in my ribs at the inhale. It feels like someone has untangled the aching knot in my chest just a bit.

"I'm sorry," Jack says. My foot is in her lap. Her fingers are on my skin. Somewhere across these woods, her family is throwing snow at each other. "But did you even like working at Laika?"

"Of course I did," I answer automatically.

"You just . . . you didn't seem very happy there, last year." Jack absentmindedly squeezes my foot. "You seemed like you *wanted* to be happy there, because it fit with this idea you had of your life—this ten-year plan—but did it really bring you joy?"

I run my tongue along my bottom lip, considering. Was your dream job *supposed* to bring you joy?

Jack drops my foot so it sinks into the cold snow. "Sorry," she says, dropping her gaze, too. "Sorry, that was presumptuous. I–I shouldn't have forced you to open up about all of that."

I reach for my discarded sock. "You didn't force me."

Jack rises clumsily, her boots slipping before she's able to right herself. "Yeah, but I just . . ." She whips off her Carhartt beanie, ruffles her hair, then shoves it back on her head. "I just think, probably, we shouldn't—Is your foot okay?"

It hurts a bit as I shove it back in my boot, but I nod.

Jack nods, too. Emphatically, her head bobbing up and down. "Good. Cool. Good."

Someone comes crashing through the forest, and we both jerk our heads to see Andrew approaching with two snowballs. "Unhand her, you fiend!" And he launches the snow at his sister.

"I'm literally not touching her," Jack says. "And we were on the same team."

"Oliver, my pet." He drops down in front of me. "Are you okay?"

"Yeah, I just . . . twisted my ankle."

Without another word, Andrew gathers me into his arms and sweeps me away. And I have to admit: Dylan wasn't wrong. Andrew is very good at being hot and lifting heavy things.

I tell myself not to look back at his sister in the snow.

But I do.

A Webcomic

By *Oliverartssometimes*

Episode 3: *The Other Woman*

(Christmas Eve, 1:32 p.m.)

Uploaded: January 7, 2022

"I think it's time to introduce you to the most important woman in my life," Jack says. She steps onto the snowy side street, her work boots sinking up to her ankles. "Elle, this is Gillian."

She places her hand on the hood of an ancient pickup truck. "Gillian," she says to the truck, "this is Elle." She leans in close and stage-whispers. "But don't worry. You're still my number one girl."

I put my hands on my hips. "Do you always talk to your truck?"

"Don't hit me with that judgmental tone. You converse with random footstools. At least Gillian and I have an established rapport."

"I know you don't want to be stereotyped, but—" I wave my hand in a circle in front of the red truck. "This ancient red pickup truck is *very cliché.* Wait. Gillian? As in Gillian Anderson?"

"Is there another Gillian?"

"Because she's a reddish-brown color?"

"And because while some might argue she was in her prime in the nineties, I think she keeps getting better with age."

Jack wrenches open the passenger door, and the hinges release an unholy sound. "Come on."

"Where are we going now?"

After Powell's, Jack had dragged me through the snow to Voodoo to try a maple-bacon doughnut, insisting that even if it is slightly overhyped, it is still a crucial pilgrimage for every new Portlander. As we walked, we played the honesty game. She told me more about her parents and their expectations for her life, which never quite fit with who she is as a person; about visiting distant relatives in Seoul as a kid and feeling she didn't quite fit there, either; about her favorite pies to bake (marionberry and lemon meringue) and her favorite pies to eat (chocolate pecan and key lime).

And I told her more about my parents and their total lack of expectations, and how that never quite fit with who I am as a person; about my mapped-out life plans; about the loneliness of moving to a new city, even though I've been alone most of my life.

She talked about her dog and the chicken coop she was building in her friend's backyard.

I talked about Meredith and how I didn't think bacon belonged on doughnuts.

Somehow, two hours passed, and two new inches of snow accumulated around us. We were hanging out as friends, just as friends. But sometimes, I would turn and catch Jack's burning eyes on me in a way that felt nothing like friendship.

Now, Jack stands beside her truck. "We're going home."

My heart vaults into my throat. "I can't go home with you," I say with less chill than intended. "I–I don't go home with people on a first, um . . ."

Jack smiles. "I am going to drive *you* to *your* home," she says, gesturing toward me with her palms up. "And then I will go to *my* home. Because this is clearly shaping up to be a much bigger snowstorm than forecasted, and we're going to get snowed *out* if we don't get home soon."

"Oh." I stare down at my feet submerged in the snow. "Sorry."

"Why are you sorry?"

"For not wanting to . . ."

"Go home with a stranger you met three hours ago in a city you've only lived in for a month?"

I nod.

"That just seems like common sense to me," she says. "And honestly, under normal circumstances, I would not advise that you get into a car with a stranger, either, but unfortunately, the buses have probably shut down already, so I don't think you have any other option. Lucky for you, I happen to know that I'm not a murderer."

These are reasonable arguments all around, and I finally hoist myself into the passenger seat of her truck. She jogs around the cab and climbs into the driver's seat. Before she does anything, she hooks her phone up to an aux cord attached to an old cigarette lighter. The engine doesn't sound any better than the rusty doors, and it turns over a few times without catching when she cranks the keys.

"Hang on." She sticks her tongue out the side of her mouth as she leans into the wheel and tries again. When the truck finally sparks to life, her playlist clicks on, blaring "I Do Not Hook Up" by Kelly Clarkson.

"Did you time that?" I ask, gesturing to the speakers.

"I wish I had."

"I forgot this song existed, honestly. This album *defined* the fifth grade for me. What?" I glance at Jack across the cab of her truck and catch her looking at me again. Looking at me like—

"This is pretty," she says, reaching over to touch a single finger to the edge of my hand-knitted scarf. That's it. One finger. Not even touching me. Touching my *scarf.* Yet somehow, that one finger is enough to turn me inside out.

"Oh, it's, um. Meredith made it," I say.

Jack turns forward, pushing her glasses up her nose again. "It matches your eyes," she says as she yanks the gearshift into reverse and eases her foot off the brake. And—nothing happens. The tires spin beneath us, the engine whines, but Gillian does not budge.

"Uh-oh."

"What do you mean *uh-oh*?"

"I'm just gonna—" She hops out of the truck as if to diagnose the source of the problem, even though the problem is quite clear. It's the snow. There are parked cars all around us, abandoned and covered with snow, and up ahead is a snarled line of traffic on Ninth Street, cars fishtailing and peeling out.

I jump out of the truck too, and follow Jack around to the back. "I think she's stuck," Jack observes. "We'll have to dig her out. Fucking snow."

My anxiety feels like a tangle of Christmas lights again—like a horrible, inextricable knot lodged in my chest, spreading up to my throat and down into my stomach. "Won't they plow the roads soon?" I ask as Jack crouches down behind the rear tires.

"That's so cute, Ohio, but no."

"Okay, Portland, why not?"

She begins earnestly shoveling snow with her hands. "We don't have the infrastructure for snow here because we don't get it very often. Most winters, we only get about two inches or so, but every few years, there's a massive storm like this one where all the grocery stores sell out of kale and no one can go anywhere. As for plows, they'll wait until the snow stops, so maybe by midday tomorrow the main roads will be clear. You know, this would probably go faster with two people."

But it goes nowhere, even after thirty minutes of both of us attempting to dig the car out. Finally, Jack slumps back against her truck. "Gillian isn't moving today. I think we might be properly stuck."

She sounds impossibly calm, as if she hasn't just announced that we are trapped outside in a snowstorm with no way to get home. I try to take a deep breath, but it feels like all the oxygen has been siphoned out of my lungs. We're stuck. I'm stuck, with a stranger, in a city I don't know, cut off from the comfort and the safety of my new apartment.

I'm stuck in the snow, stuck, stuck, *stuck*.

"Hey." Jack's voice cuts through my mental spiral. "Are you okay?"

"No!" I gasp, clutching the sides of my ribs, struggling to breathe through this new probably-not-a-heart-attack. "We're stuck in the snow! What are we going to do?"

I wait for Jack to laugh at my overreaction, the way my parents used to. I wait for her to switch into problem-solving mode, like Meredith always does. I wait for her to tell me something horribly unhelpful, like *you're fine* or *you're going to be okay*, even though nothing feels fine and it isn't okay and I'm having a panic attack in the snow.

But Jack doesn't say anything at all, not for a long time. She simply unhooks the tailgate so it drops down into a bench, gesturing until I come and sit down beside her, my legs dangling over the edge. We sit in silence, her thigh pressed against mine, her shoulder right there, reminding me I'm not alone with my racing thoughts.

My hands are twisted in my lap, and with the same gentleness from earlier, Jack reaches over with her left hand to disentangle the anxious knot of fingers. Then she slips her warm, callused hand through mine, holding it loosely. "Is this okay?" she asks, and when I nod, she tightens her grasp. "What's the worst thing your anxiety is telling you right now?"

"Nothing," I manage. "It's fine. I'm fine."

"Elle," she says. She started doing that, started calling me *Elle* on our walk to Voodoo. One syllable, a single letter. I focus on that. "Don't make me say 'honesty game' when you're clearly having a panic attack."

"Fine," I choke out. "My anxiety is telling me that we don't have a plan, and that we're going to be stuck outside in the snow forever. That we'll never get home. That we'll catch hypothermia and our toes will fall off and we'll die."

"Yeah." Jack exhales. "That would all be less than ideal."

I study her profile, the sharp lines of her pretty face against the backdrop of so much snow. "Aren't you going to tell me that I'm being irrational?"

She turns to face me, so close, our noses almost brush. "Is that something that helps you when you're having a panic attack? Being told you're irrational?"

"God, no."

"Then, why would I say that to you?" Without letting go of my hand, Jack fishes her phone out of the pocket of her coat. "My mom has generalized anxiety disorder, and if I ever told her she was being irrational while she was having a panic attack, I'm pretty sure she'd scratch my eyes out. And I would deserve it."

"What are you doing?" I ask as I watch her jab her thumb against her phone screen awkwardly with one hand.

"I'm coming up with a plan. Okay. I live up on Stark close to Mount Tabor Park, which is . . . an hour-and-twenty-minute walk from here. Totally manageable. Where do you live?"

"Off Belmont, near Thirty-Fourth."

"Even closer. Perfect. We can leave Gillian here, and I'll come back for her when the snow clears. Does that sound like an okay plan?"

For the first time in five minutes, I'm able to catch my breath. "Yeah. Yeah, I guess . . . that works."

She hops off the tailgate, and as a natural product of our new distance, our hands fall apart. The absence of her closeness feels conspicuous on the right side of my body, in all the places the cold air can now reach now that she's not pressed there.

She shakes the snowflakes from her hair before turning back to face me. "Do you think you can trust me to get you home, Elle?" she asks with that quarter-moon smile softening the angles of her face.

And two surprising realizations hit me at the same time.

First: that I did, inexplicably, trust this woman I'd only known for a few hours.

And second: that I really, really wanted to hold her hand again.

Chapter Twelve

Jack is avoiding me.

At first, I thought I was just being sensitive—reading into things in our relationship that weren't really there, like I'd done last year.

When we all got back to the cabin after the snowball fight, everyone separated to do their own thing. The grandmas went to warm up in the hot tub, Katherine disappeared into the kitchen to prepare the beef tenderloin for the bibimbap she was making for dinner, and Andrew went off to something called "the exercise room," because apparently maintaining his hot bod required several hours of weights and cardio every day. Dylan and I decided to lounge in the living room—me working on the next episode of the comic, them working on lesson planning for after winter break. And Jack—she awkwardly hovered for a few minutes before grumbling some incomprehensible excuse as to why she needed to flee to the Airstream.

And I thought, *Sure. Who doesn't need alone time to recharge?*

But it got weirder.

For movie night, Meemaw made popcorn and cranberry mules, and in an unwavering display of our coupledom, Andrew and I snuggled under a quilt on the sectional sofa. Jack sat in an overstuffed chair on the far side of the room, but she kept restlessly fidgeting. She only made it to the narwhal scene in *Elf* before she leapt out of her seat and announced she was going for a run.

At eight o'clock at night.

In the snow.

When we woke up this morning, Katherine proclaimed that despite what the schedule said, we wouldn't be going to get the Christmas tree today, since she wanted to wait until Alan arrived tomorrow. Instead, Jack made pancakes for breakfast . . . and then didn't eat them, claiming she was still full from dinner the night before.

When Jack asked Dylan if they wanted to take Paul Hollywood for a walk together, and Andrew and I decided to tag along, Jack abruptly decided she was "gonna sit this one out."

And every time I went into a room for the past day, Jack promptly went out of it. For the past twenty-four hours straight, Jack has refused to look at me, refused to talk to me, and has barely left the Airstream.

I should be relieved. I'm not here for Jack; I'm here to convince everyone I'm in love with Andrew for two hundred thousand dollars.

Why am I not more relieved?

Unfortunately for Jack, the agenda for the afternoon is *Christmas cookies: six hours*, and as the resident expert in baking, she can't excuse her way out of it.

Personally, five minutes into the process, and I'm already confused by the mechanics. "Is there usually this much weed involved in the cookie-making process?"

Dylan looks up from where their deft fingers are rolling an impressively large joint. "Do you usually bake Christmas cookies sober?" they ask, sounding horrified by the thought.

I glance around the kitchen, at the ingredients Jack neatly laid out on the counters, at the family in their matching red aprons that say "Christmas Cookie Crew" with their names hand sewn across the top. Judy Garland is singing "Have Yourself a Merry Little Christmas."

"I have never done any of this before," I admit.

The family all turns their heads to me in shock. "You've never made Christmas cookies before?" Meemaw asks.

Katherine, who is completely unfazed by the weed on the counter next to the chocolate chips, claps her hands together. "Well, isn't this exciting!"

"You're definitely going to want to be high, then," Dylan drones. They raise the rolling paper to their mouth and lick the edge. When Dylan slides the joint between their lips, Andrew leans forward to light it without prompting. He cups a hand close to Dylan's mouth until it catches, and I watch as Dylan stares up at Andrew through their lashes, taking a sharp inhale.

Andrew steps back. Dylan rubs the back of their neck before passing Andrew the joint.

The rest of the family appears to be oblivious to this sexually charged scene. Katherine is distracted by grabbing me an apron. She's written my name in Sharpie on a piece of masking tape over what I imagine is the name Alan. Before I know it, I'm wearing an apron and the joint has made it around the entire kitchen to me. I stare at it between my fingers for a moment before deciding to lift it to my mouth. I can't remember the last time someone offered me an honest-to-God joint. Undergrad, maybe?

My inhale is shallow, only letting a little smoke into my lungs before I exhale. Still, it's been so long, I feel an immediate rush of blood to my head, followed by a slow decompression in my limbs, like I'm a piece of Ikea furniture and someone has taken a monkey wrench to all my screws and loosened them just a bit. The joint has made its way around the kitchen to everyone but Jack. I turn to face her.

For the first time in twenty-four hours, she sets her eyes on me as I stretch the joint in her direction. She holds up both hands. "No, thanks. Someone in this kitchen needs to have their wits about them. Okay, fam!" Jack declares at full volume. "Let's get started. This year, we're making cutout cookies, peanut butter fudge, and dasik."

I must involuntarily make a face of confusion because Jack adds, "Dasik is a Korean pressed cookie. We used to make them for Lunar New Year as kids, but now we usually make them at Christmas. This year, we're doing half with sesame seeds and half with green tea."

I nod as if I understand anything about baking. I'm suddenly captivated by the way Jack takes charge of the kitchen, assigning everyone in the family different jobs, sending Katherine to the stove to heat up the skillets for the dasik and Meemaw to the stand mixer to work on the homemade frosting for the cutout cookies. The sight of Jack in her red apron, the strings tied around the dip of her waist. She's wearing her glasses, which only make her *more* attractive, like a hot lesbian architect. The sleeves on her flannel are rolled up to her elbows, revealing the black swirls of tattoo ink on her arms, those glorious tendons that flex when she cooks breakfast in the morning, those fingers that move—*Shit*.

A tiny bit of weed, and my brain is already hyperfixating.

"Jack is an incredible cook," Meemaw tells me, when she catches me staring at her granddaughter.

"Mmm," I say in response, trying to focus on the dough Andrew and I are going to roll out, and not on the way Jack looks mixing the peanut butter with the sugar and melted butter.

"She works at a shop on Division, but she's opening her own bakery," Meemaw continues proudly.

All of my attention is back on Jack, watching her freckled cheeks turn the faintest hint of pink beneath her eyes. "Wait, you are?"

Jack shrugs one shoulder and pushes the hair out of her face. "Yeah, I am. Opening my own bakery, that is."

I stare down at the mound of dough on the parchment paper in front of me. Memories attempt to overtake me, but I shove them back, not wanting to think about that day or that place—about the building she showed me when she told me about her dream. When Andrew passes the joint to me a second time, I accept it.

"And Jacqueline is opening the bakery all by herself, without any financial help," Katherine notes as she meticulously roasts the sesame seeds.

"*Mom*," Jack says, in a tone that suggests Katherine's comment is something more than a casual observation. "It's perfectly fine. I took out a business loan, and I have the money—"

"But you have to pay the loan back, and if the bakery doesn't turn a profit . . . I just don't *understand* why you're willing to take this financial risk when your father's company could invest—"

"I don't want it to be a Prescott Investments business," Jack jumps in. "I want it to be *my* business."

Beside me, Andrew's body is tense, tightly coiled. "Then your grandmothers could help," Katherine continues.

Meemaw nods as she locks the stand mixer into place. "I've said I'd be happy to give you some startup money, just to get you on your feet until the bakery starts making money."

For a moment, the kitchen is quiet except for the sound of the KitchenAid whorling the frosting.

"Thank you, Meemaw," Jack finally says through a clenched jaw. "But I can do this on my own. I can open my own bakery without the family's help."

"Yes, but *why would you?*" Katherine's little outburst is met with a glare from Jack.

"Maybe I don't want to be dependent on the Prescott name to accomplish my dream," she bites out.

Lovey reaches over to put a papery hand on Jack's elbow. "Your mother is just concerned about you. She doesn't want to see you fail."

Jack shuts her eyes tight. I remember her sitting in the coffee shop at Powell's, telling me, *I'm the family fuck-up.* "Well, you can all relax," Jack says bitterly. "When I fail, I'll have Grandpa's trust to fall back on, okay?"

I flinch as Andrew's fist collides with the ball of dough in front of him. He pulls his hand away, and there's a little imprint of his knuckles.

"Andrew!" Lovey scolds in a low voice. "What's the matter with you?"

"Sorry," he grumbles, avoiding his grandmother's gaze. "Sorry, I just need some air."

He moves around the countertop, and I'm vaguely aware that, as his fiancée, I should probably follow him, but before my loose limbs can move, Dylan is abandoning the fudge. "I'll go see what's up with him."

There's a heavy tension in the air once Andrew and Dylan are gone. Michael Bublé is crooning "Holly Jolly Christmas," but there doesn't seem to be anything jolly about the cookie-baking process. Katherine presses her manicured fingers to her temples. "I have a headache." She winces to sell it. "I—I need to go lie down."

The stand mixer is still spinning away, and Jack reaches over to turn it off. "Thanks, Jacqueline, sugar." Meemaw smiles. "You know, I'm really no good at all this domestic baking business. . . ."

"Go." Jack shrugs. "It's fine. You, too, Lovey."

And just like that, the cavernous kitchen is empty except for me and Jack and a whole lot of cookie ingredients.

Jack reaches for the bud of the joint Dylan left on the ceramic spoon holder by the stove. "This happens every year," she says as she draws it to her lips.

"Your family calls you a failure and tries to get you to take money every time you bake Christmas cookies?" I ask skeptically.

The quarter-moon smile creeps onto her face, and Jack leans back against the countertop behind her. She would look so relaxed, so indifferent, if not for the way she jiggles her socked foot, one crossed over the other. "No. They ditch me in the kitchen every year and leave me to do all the baking. My family likes the *idea* of making Christmas cookies together, but they always forget it's actual work, and they end up bailing in the first hour."

Jack pushes her glasses up her nose with those two fingers, and my heart feels like powdered sugar inside my chest. I turn back to my dough and finally pick up a rolling pin.

"You don't have to do that," Jack says quickly. "Go find Andrew. Or go join the grandmas in the hot tub. I can make all the cookies."

"I don't mind helping." I press the rolling pin to the dough, but instead of flattening, the dough simply sticks to my pin.

"Here," a voice says low in my ear, and there's Jack, standing right at my back, reaching around me to take the rolling pin. "Let's use flour so it doesn't stick."

She grabs a fistful of flour from a glass container on the counter and sprinkles it over my rolling pin and the parchment paper. She's standing so close to me, I can smell that impossible scent of freshly baked bread that seems to live on her clothes. I can feel the heat of her body and the tension in her muscles from the earlier argument with her family.

"Apply pressure evenly," Jack orders, and I'm not sure why those words make my toes curl against the cool tile floor. "And don't let the pin hit the counter. Just roll to the edge and stop."

She's still standing at my back, her presence like a palpable shadow behind me. A warm, comforting shadow, one I want to lean into. I grip the handles of the rolling pin and follow orders. The dough begins to spread out before me in a nice, thin layer.

"Perfect." Jack exhales at my neck. "Just like that."

I absolutely do not think about her saying those words—*perfect, just like that*—in a very different context, her husky voice and her sweet moans of pleasure. But then, without meaning to, I arch back, and I feel the solidity of her body against mine. For one second, it's rough fabric and muscles and heat.

And then Jack is across the kitchen, as far as possible from me, stirring the fudge again.

"Keep going," she says, her eyes fixed on the saucepan. I keep going, rolling out the dough until it covers the countertop, hoping she didn't notice the part where I tried to rub up against her like a horny cat.

"So . . ." I watch the dough spread out before me. "You're opening a bakery."

Jack's only response is the sound of her stirring spoon accidentally hitting the edge of the pot. I swallow. I shouldn't have asked. It's not my place. Maybe once, when we were something else to each other, but now—

"Yeah, I am," Jack says. "I mean, I *will* be opening a bakery, if I can get everything sorted before the planned opening in two months. I've signed the lease, and I've secured the loan I need, but the renovations have been a nightmare. It hasn't been easy doing it by myself."

"You've been doing the entire thing by *yourself*?"

Jack nods. "There is so much boring business shit involved with starting a business. Which is quite unfortunate, because I get bored very easily. Plus, my finances are kind of fucked since I've cut back hours at Patty's to spend more time getting the new place off the ground."

"But you won't accept help from any of the millionaires in your family because . . . ?"

"Because!" Jack says, flicking the spoon. "Taking money from family is complicated."

I turn to face her standing by the stove top, so solid, so grounded. "Is it because if you accept help from other people, then you wouldn't be the strong, independent, self-sufficient Jack?"

"Because if I take my family's money," she corrects defensively, "it means I'm buying into their ideas about success and failure."

"And if you take their money, and your business still doesn't work out—"

"Then I'll just prove to my dad that I'm the slacker fuck-up he thinks I am," Jack finishes, mixing the peanut butter now in a rather violent fashion. Then she's scraping the frosting off the sides of the stand-mixer bowl, then she's roasting sesame seeds in a frying pan. She is somehow everywhere all at once, a blur throughout the kitchen, her brain on autopilot. She's laser focused on each task, no part of her restless or fidgety.

Jack bakes like I draw, with all of herself. It's sort of miraculous to watch. All that restless energy funneled into a beautiful purpose. "I'm going to tell you what you would tell me if our positions were reversed," I say, watching her fly through each step in the baking process like it's written in her bones. "Your bakery can't fail."

"Believe me, it can. It's a very saturated market."

"It can't fail," I say with more force, attempting to use Jack's own words against her, "because even if it never turns a profit, and even if it closes within the first year, you *tried*. You took a damn risk. People who take bold risks to go after their dreams are never failures."

"Shit." Jack looks appalled. "Do I always sound like a cheesy motivational poster hanging in the office of an out-of-touch high school guidance counselor?"

"Literally *always*."

Jack flashes me her full, goofy, infectious smile, and I feel like *that* is written on my bones. Her smile is stamped on every nerve ending in my body. *Two hundred thousand dollars*. I chant the words in my head. *I'm here for two hundred thousand dollars.*

I'm here for the chance to rebuild my life. I'm not here to stare at Jack's forearms while she mixes semisweet chocolate chips into boiling milk. And I'm definitely not here to rekindle something that only burned me the first time around.

The dough is successfully rolled out in front of me, and I open the Tupperware of cookie cutters in the shape of reindeer and Christmas trees and snowmen. There's a snowflake cutout at the bottom, and I press the sharp edges of it down into the dough. When I pull away, a perfect cookie snowflake pulls away with it.

"Look at that," Jack says. She's at my back again, with her heat and her solidness and her bread smell. She hands me a baking tray, and I lay out my one dough snowflake.

I'm not thinking about Jack with snowflakes in her hair.

Chapter Thirteen

Tuesday, December 20, 2022

Throughout most of my childhood, I responded to my parents' dysfunction and neglect by turning inward, by becoming quiet and small. My parents would drink too much and scream at each other in the kitchen until at least one of them shattered a glass, and I would hide in my bedroom for hours, disappearing inside my drawings and the fictional world of my art, building a better home inside an imaginary space where people like me triumphed, where we were celebrated, where we were loved.

My dad would take off for weeks at a time, and I would make the honor roll.

My mom would get fired from another job, and I would sign up for another Advanced Placement class.

There wasn't always food in the refrigerator or an adult at home, but I never misbehaved in class, never got in trouble, and formed unhealthy attachments to all my female English teachers. When I realized my art got me the kind of positive attention I never received at home, I built my entire identity around being Ellie the Art Girl.

For the most part, I was the perfect daughter to the world's most imperfect parents, but for a brief period of time in the seventh grade, all I wanted to do was yell at my mom. I yelled at her about her constant partying. I yelled at her about the unpaid bills. I yelled at her about the strange men she brought into our house.

And Linds, being Linds, would always yell back. I would stomp and slam doors, but Linds would say the cruelest thing in the most cutting tone. Linds would give me the silent treatment for days on end in our own house, refusing to talk to me as I ate breakfast cereal for dinner or did my own laundry. Sometimes, she just wouldn't come home for a few nights, and I would be left to wonder if she was ever coming home at all.

The fighting-with-my-mom phase was short-lived once I realized there was no guarantee that Linds wouldn't just take off like Jed had. What several therapists have deemed an insecure attachment style means I now avoid arguing with my mother at all costs. It also means that after the Christmas-cookie argument, I'm anxious that things among the Kim-Prescotts are going to be tense.

Instead, they are . . . not.

Andrew and Dylan come back inside to help me decorate the cutout cookies with frosting and sprinkles, and Katherine's headache wears off in time to press the dasik cookies using the baking molds that belonged to her halmoni. As soon as five o'clock hits, Meemaw's pulling a pitcher of sangria from the fridge and blaring some Kacey Musgraves Christmas music. The kitchen is a disaster zone, so we throw leftover short rib or beef tenderloin over bowls of rice and eat at the counter while we finish decorating. Mostly, we eat cookies for dinner because we're all a little stoned. The earlier argument about money is entirely forgotten.

I guess maybe that's how it works in families who love each other unconditionally: you can fight without fear of losing them and be honest without consequences or repercussions.

• • •

Alan promises he'll be there Tuesday morning to go pick out a Christmas tree.

He's not, and we don't.

Instead, we spend most of the day working on a giant Christmas puzzle. We go into separate rooms to wrap presents for each other to put under the hypothetical tree. I go with Andrew and watch the carnage of his attempts to wrap presents—the amount of tape he uses should be an actual crime—until he finally concedes and lets me do all the wrapping. Lovey makes vegan lasagna for dinner, and we all eat together, pretending not to notice the conspicuously empty chair at the head of the table. Everyone seems a little morose as we move into the evening's event.

Christmas carols: two hours.

At seven o'clock sharp, Katherine ushers the entire family from the kitchen into the living room. There isn't actual caroling involved in Katherine's Christmas carols, since we're isolated in a cabin in the mountains with nowhere to carol *to*. There's an upright piano tucked into the corner of the living room, and we all gather in a semicircle around it. Meemaw pours the sangria, and Dylan rushes off to fetch their guitar.

"Who's going first this year?" Katherine asks gleefully.

Meemaw whips around to face me and Andrew sitting side by side on an ottoman. "Why don't the lovebirds sing a little duet for us?" She waggles her eyebrows at us.

My singing voice is awful, but if Meemaw needs to hear Andrew and me sing a duet to believe our relationship, I'll step up to the piano.

"Oh," Andrew says, tensing. "A duet. I mean, Dylan and I usually—"

"Dylan and Andrew's duet is a *tradition*," Katherine says, and her declaration is final in this and in all things. Meemaw's request is forgotten as Andrew rises from the ottoman and slides his body onto the piano bench. He sits behind the keys like he was born there. Dylan rubs the back of their neck with the hand not gripping their guitar.

"Eh, are you sure—?" They shoot me a look. "I mean, it is a tradition, but . . . you don't mind if we—"

I wave a hand and take a gulp of my sangria. If my fake fiancé wants to serenade his secret ex in front of his family members, who am I to protest?

Dylan pulls a chair up beside Andrew on the piano bench. They both look stiff and uncomfortable with the new proximity, but then Andrew begins playing the opening notes of a song, and all the awkwardness between them dissolves.

The song in question is "Baby, It's Cold Outside," and while I have a number of issues with this choice, I forget most of them as Dylan begins to strum their guitar. Then Andrew's voice lifts over the instruments, and I fall *in love* with this stupid song. I can't help myself. Andrew's voice is rich molasses, turning the first line of the song into something luscious and sweet. When Dylan responds with a "but baby it's cold outside," it blends perfectly with Andrew's. Their voices circle and cross each other in flawless harmony.

On the couch, Meemaw films on her phone, Lovey waves a lighter, and Katherine beams with pride. My gaze finds Jack across the living room, leaning against the fireplace mantel instead of sitting with the rest of us. She smiles crookedly as she watches her brother and her best friend sing this practiced duet.

When Andrew and Dylan's voices braid together for the final "oh, but it's cold outside," Jack puts two fingers into her mouth and whistles. Andrew turns around on the piano bench, smiling almost shyly. Dylan puts their guitar aside and rubs the back of their neck again, pointedly not looking at Andrew. Andrew is very pointedly looking at Dylan.

For some reason, Meemaw is pointedly looking at me.

"Jack, take over," Andrew says as he climbs up. "I'm going to make us some real holiday cocktails."

Apparently, both siblings took twelve years of piano lessons, so Jack folds her large frame behind the piano while Andrew goes back into the kitchen. Meemaw sings next and performs a raunchy, off-key rendition of "Santa Baby," then a stoned Lovey performs "Grandma Got Run Over by a Reindeer," making me laugh so hard sangria actually shoots out of my nose. Andrew finally brings out a tray of drinks in time for Katherine to go stand beside the piano while Jack plays "I'll Be Home for Christmas," from the sheet music in front of her.

Andrew's cocktail is a variation of whisky eggnog, and as soon as the taste hits my tongue, I'm back there, sitting in a dark bar with Jack on Christmas Eve, sipping spiced eggnog while our knees brush. I'm on the metal step of the Airstream, tasting eggnog on Jack's mouth.

"If only in my dreams . . ." Katherine sings, and as the song comes to its pretty end, she turns to me. "Okay. It's Ellie's turn!"

Suddenly, there's not enough alcohol in the world to make my legs unstick from the furniture. "Oh. *No*. I don't think I—"

"Come on, sugar. We don't judge. This is just for fun."

I believe Meemaw, but the Kim-Prescotts' general decency doesn't seem like sufficient justification to humiliate myself. Andrew clearly disagrees, and he hoists me off the couch. "Come on, Oliver. You're family now. You've got to sing."

"Yeah, come on," Dylan agrees. "You've gotta," and I don't trust for one minute that Dylan isn't going to judge me.

Andrew positions me beside the piano. Jack is still on the bench, her long, square-knuckled fingers resting on white keys. She looks up at me, flicking her chin to get the hair out of her eyes. "What do you want to sing?"

"Nothing." I set my eggnog down on a coaster atop the piano. "I—I don't know very many Christmas songs."

Jack drops her head, and I stare at the lock of hair that spills forward again. My whisky eggnog brain so badly wants to sweep that hair aside.

"How about this one?" Jack's long fingers dance out the opening bars to "Holly Jolly Christmas." We've heard this song a half-dozen times just in the past two days.

"Everyone knows this song." Jack quarter-moon smiles at me, and my insides are a runny glass of eggnog. I hear the moment I'm supposed to start singing, but the words get caught in my throat, lodged behind memories of that smile and those fingers.

Jack loops the song back to the beginning to give me the cue to start again, but I'm frozen. Paralyzed by the idea of embarrassing myself.

She loops the song again. "We're okay," Jack whispers—*actually whispers*—so even Katherine close by can't overhear. "No rush. Sing whenever you're ready."

I think about Jack sitting on Gillian's tailgate. *We're going to be okay.*

And then when I don't sing again, Jack belts out the beginning of the song herself. And Jack's singing is *earsplittingly* abominable. That deep drum of a voice that always sounds half-musical to me somehow doesn't translate into actual song. It's screechy and off-pitch and not aligned to the tune she's playing on the piano.

Yet here she is, singing anyway. So when she reaches the line, I join in with "kiss her once for me." Our voices blend together not unlike the way Andrew's and Dylan's did, except where theirs were molasses, ours are peanut brittle. Inside a garbage disposal.

As we attempt to harmonize, we're both smiling through the words, half laughing at ourselves for how awful we sound. Jack looks up at me, and she's looking at me like she did that day. Like I'm a person who takes up *space* in this world.

It never meant anything.

You invented the whole thing in your head.

Two hundred thousand dollars.

But she's singing this song for me, and I'm literally goo inside a skinsuit. I feel drunker than I am—so drunk, I might do something stupid.

I might float away.

I might touch her hair.

I might kiss her, once, for me. Just once, to remember what it felt like.

The song ends, and I have to turn away from the heat of Jack's stare. I press my fingers to the hollows of my cheeks and feel the blush radiating off my skin.

"Gingerbread houses!" Meemaw shouts over the family's raucous applause. "We should make gingerbread houses!"

"Barbara." Katherine clicks her tongue. "It's nine o'clock at night."

But everyone is some combination of drunk and/or high, so Meemaw's demand that we host the gingerbread house contest *right now* is treated with a startling degree of seriousness.

"Jack. Do you have the supplies?" Dylan asks with the same intensity they brought to the snowball fight. Except, now they're lying flat on their back on a rug, swinging their glass of eggnog as they hum "Santa Claus Is Coming to Town."

"Yeah, they're out in the Airstream," she says, "but it's getting late, and I think we should maybe wind down, not increase our sugar intake."

"Don't be a party pooper, Jacqueline," Meemaw says. "Go get the goods! I'll clear the puzzle from the dining room table!"

Jack looks both annoyed and amused by her family's antics, but she throws up her hands and says, "Fine! Dylan, help me carry."

"Dylan is not able to walk that far," Dylan answers from the rug.

"Never mind." Jack backpedals. "Andrew, come help—"

"I'm not going outside," Andrew snaps. "It's cold. Make Ellie do it."

"You're going to make your fiancée go outside in the cold because you don't want to?" I ask, hoping Andrew will realize the bad optics of the situation and change his mind.

He does not, and five minutes later, I'm zipping up my puffy jacket and shoving my feet inside my boots while Jack and Paul Hollywood wait for me by the back door. We step outside onto a dark patio and take stairs down to the snow. It's not a long walk from the cabin to the Airstream, but in the silence between us, it feels as long as our hike from Powell's to Southeast Portland. A few minutes ago we were singing together, and now everything feels too serious.

We reach the Airstream and she puts one foot on the metal step. There's a slight pause before she hoists open the door, and I follow her inside the Airstream without fully realizing what it will be like to step inside this place again. It's like stepping through a wormhole into the past. Into *our* past.

There are the kitchen cabinets she pushed me up against. There are the cookbooks I knocked over when she hoisted me onto those counters. There is the bed where Jack curled herself around me. The smell of peppermint tea and sourdough bread. Me, crying with my boots under my arm, fleeing the Airstream as quickly as I could.

Jack catches me looking at her unmade bed. "It . . . it hasn't changed much since you were here last."

"No," I say quietly. "It hasn't."

Jack makes several false starts, like there's something she wants to say and can't, but when she finally gets a word out, it's "Alexa!" to the tiny Echo on her counter. "Mix Jack's playlist."

It's Fergie's "Big Girls Don't Cry" that cuts the awkward silence between us.

"You do know people have continued to make music since the aughts, right?" I ask her.

Jack smiles, and some of the tension eases. "Gingerbread house supplies," she says and grabs a tote from under the kitchen table. "Do me a favor and grab my extra piping bags. They're in the bottom drawer there."

I swivel toward the narrow drawers built into the wall between the kitchen table and the bathroom door.

"Wait, no, wrong drawer," Jack barks as I slide open the bottom drawer, just like she said. There are no piping bags. It's a drawer stuffed with winter clothes—beanies and scarves and gloves—and right on top is a hand-knitted cerulean blue scarf I recognize immediately. My drunk heart corkscrews in my chest.

"What—why? Why do you have this?"

"You . . . you left it here," Jack starts, but I'm already lifting the scarf from the drawer. It's heavier than it should be, and something falls out of the folds of the scarf Meredith knitted for me. It's a copy of *Fun Home*, and it lands on the floor with an ominous thunk.

Jack Kim-Prescott keeps the copy of *Fun Home* she bought on Christmas Eve wrapped up in my scarf. "Why do you have this?" I ask again, because I don't know what else I'm supposed to say.

Jack says nothing, and I pick the book up off the floor. I hold *Fun Home* between my hands. The spine is still crisp, and it looks unread, but there is a small bookmark sticking out from the middle. I open to the page, and there, holding a spot, is the drawing I did of Jack's hand in Powell's coffee shop.

"Elle—"

"Why do you have a drawer of my things?"

"Well, technically, only the scarf is yours," she says casually, "because I bought the book, and you gave me the drawing."

"Semantics." I shake the book in her direction, trying to understand. "Why did you *keep* these things?"

"Why wouldn't I keep them?" Jack asks.

Because it didn't mean anything. Because what we had that day hadn't meant a damn thing to her, so why does she have a drawer of mementos in the same way I have a file folder of art? I look up, and Jack has set the tote back down. She's leaning against the table with that same indifferent slouch from our first meeting in Powell's, but now, the *indifference* feels more rehearsed than genuine. She looks like someone who is trying very hard to look like she doesn't care.

"Can we not do this?" Jack asks, flicking her chin to get her hair out of her face. She needs a bobby pin. Or someone who is always next to her, pushing her hair out of her eyes.

"Not do what?"

Jack shrugs one shoulder. Had her indifference always been this poorly playacted, and I just hadn't been able to see past her carefully crafted coolness? "It's embarrassing, Elle," Jack spits out.

"I don't get it. Embarrassing *how*?"

Jack straightens. "Look, you ghosted while I was in the shower, okay? And it's fine. It's whatever. I thought our day together meant something else, but it hadn't, and that's whatever."

I shake my head. *No.* No, that's not what happened. . . .

"It was a one-night stand, and that's chill," she says, but there's nothing "chill" about her now, about the way she's pushing out her words in a frantic rush. Like it meant something then and it means something now and she's trying so hard to protect herself.

But that's not right. Because *I* was the one who thought it meant something. I was the one who had my heart broken. Not Jack.

"And now you're engaged to my brother, of all people," Jack is rambling, "and there is no point rehashing the past or what happened or why you left. So, yeah. It's embarrassing that I kept your stupid scarf."

The stupid scarf in question is draped over my right arm, and I set down *Fun Home* so I can take the scarf in both hands. I'd been in such a hurry to leave that morning, crying and grabbing my things from around the Airstream, that I'd forgotten the scarf. I'd taken it off before we slept together, set it down on the kitchen counter next to the flour. Now the scarf smells like her.

"That isn't how it happened," I finally say. I can't look up at Jack as my fingers wind deeper into the yarn. "That . . . that isn't what happened that morning. I—I didn't *ghost* you. I left because . . ."

"Because *why*?" Jack asks when I trail off. She takes a step forward, and in the crampedness of the Airstream, one step brings her so close to me, I can smell the whisky eggnog, the past slamming into the present, and it's all too much. "Why did you leave that morning? What did I do wrong?"

Jack's voice cracks over the question, and there's no shield of indifference to keep her safe. There's nothing to keep me safe, either.

Jack *cares*, but that's not what happened between us. That's not the story I've been telling myself for the past year. That isn't the version of events I immortalized in my webcomic.

"Never mind," Jack says suddenly, putting space between us again. "We shouldn't . . . you're engaged to my brother, and I can't—"

Jack grabs the tote of gingerbread house supplies, and before I can open my mouth to speak, she's back outside in the snow. I'm left behind in the Airstream, in this perfectly preserved time capsule of one of the worst days of my life, trying to put all the pieces together.

There's a scarf in my hands and a drawer of my things and Jack *cares*, and none of that aligns with the version of events from that morning. I've relived that morning a hundred times. I remember every detail—how Jack and I fell apart as quickly as we came together. And for once, the failure had nothing to do with me.

A Webcomic
By *Oliverartssometimes*
Episode 10: *The Missus*
(Christmas Day, 10:02 a.m.)
Uploaded: February 25, 2022

"Honesty game: how long have you been watching me sleep?"

She stretches her arms up over her head in a massive morning yawn.

"Not long," I say.

"Liar." Her voice is especially raspy first thing in the morning, thick with sleep and hoarse from other things, and she looks—*fuck*.

Jack first thing in the morning is just *fuck*.

Her black hair is matted in the back, with the front sticking straight up in a greasy wave over her forehead, and she is unabashedly naked. As she wakes up, she makes no effort to hide her body under blankets. I can see her tattooed arms, her dark armpit hair, her soft stomach and her strong thighs, her muscular legs stretched out beside Paul Hollywood, who climbed up onto the bed at some point in the night.

I bury my smile into my pillow. "*Long* is subjective."

"Creep. I brought home a creepy stalker." She hits me with an extra pillow. "Did you sleep at all?"

I shake my head. It felt like if I closed my eyes, I would wake up to find the snow had melted, that the magic between us had dissolved, too. "Not too much sleep," I say.

She rolls onto her side to face me in bed. "How are you feeling?"

And I know what she's really asking me. *Do you regret this? Would you take this back?* I'd only ever felt this way with one other person, and it had taken *months* for me to feel safe and comfortable with my college girlfriend. We were friends for almost two years before we even kissed, yet here I am, naked with this person I've known for a day. And I've never felt more certain of anything than I am of whatever this is.

"I'm feeling really good," I tell her.

It's her turn to hide her smile against her pillow. Under the blankets, she slides her hands toward me, her fingers hovering half an inch above my bare stomach, ghosting over my skin in some kind of tantalizing whisper. It feels almost better than when she touched me there last night—when she touched me *everywhere*, claiming every uncharted corner of me as her own.

"Are you hungry?" she asks.

"*Starving.*"

She leans over and bites softly on my shoulder before smoothing the mark with a kiss. "I'll shower, and then I'll make you biscuits and gravy."

"That's not exactly what I had in mind. . . ."

"Well, you haven't tried my homemade biscuits yet."

"I would very much like to *try your biscuits.*"

Jack laughs, groggy and throaty, shouting, "Creep!" even louder. I reach for her. She comes willingly, rolls on top of me, settling herself between my legs, kissing my throat, my earlobe, my mouth. Sweet, unhurried kisses, like we have nothing but time, like the snow outside will never melt, and we'll live in this little bubble forever.

"Okay. Okay." She exhales against my collarbone a few minutes later. "I really do need to shower."

I wrap my legs around her torso to anchor her to me. I have

no intention of ever letting her go, not even for homemade biscuits. "I'm afraid if you get up, you won't come back," I confess into her shoulder.

That's the thing about our honesty game: it made telling the truth easier, even when she wasn't demanding it.

"Well, it's my Airstream, and the bathroom is attached, so—"

"I'm afraid if you get up," I clarify, holding her tight, "that this will be over."

She pulls her head back just enough so her mouth can find my temple. "I'm not a pumpkin, Elle," she whispers. "And I would really like to make you breakfast."

"Not a pumpkin," I repeat, willing myself to believe it.

"But I have to shower first," she insists. "My hair is a disaster."

"I love your disaster hair," I say, running one hand through the grease.

Propped on her elbows above me, Jack sucks in a sharp breath, her eye contact burning through my entire body. "I love your hair, too," she says back, touching what's left of my braid from the day before.

I release her, and she climbs off the bed. She struts—truly struts—to the tiny bathroom, still unapologetically naked, and I watch her until the door closes between us. The shower turns on, followed shortly by the sound of her phone blasting a Jordin Sparks song I forgot existed. Of course Jack can't shower without music. I smile to myself and sit in her bed, pressing my open palm to the too-much feeling in my chest.

There's a pounding on the door to the Airstream, and Paul Hollywood awakes with a start, barking wildly at the intrusion. I scramble out of bed, searching for my underwear. "Jack!" I attempt to shout over the sound of the shower. "Someone's here!"

She doesn't seem to hear me over the water and the music and the barking, and I quickly slide my arms into the sleeves of her flannel and button it over myself. It looks like a dress. Like a very short dress, but an acceptable one for answering the door at nine in the morning on Christmas. I stub my toe on the edge of a cupboard as I trip over to the door, Paul Hollywood barking maniacally at my feet.

When I open the door, I'm temporarily blinded by the iridescent snow, and by the morning light reflecting off every surface. I put a hand up to shield my eyes and squint, and it's then that I notice the woman standing below me. She's short, with magenta hair cut to her shoulders, half-covered by a black beanie, the rest of her covered by a Patagonia coat. "Hi," I greet her awkwardly as Paul Hollywood leaps outside and runs circles around the woman's feet.

She eyes my bare legs, then looks up at my face. "Hi," she says back. "Who are you?"

I tug on the hem of Jack's shirt. "Um. Ellie? I'm Jack's . . . friend. Who are you?"

"I'm Claire," the woman with the magenta hair says. "I'm Jack's wife."

The crowded, too-much feeling in my chest recedes, hollows out, until I'm standing there with a black hole of absolute nothingness where my rib cage used to be. "I'm sorry." I blink at this woman. "Who?"

Claire smiles and cocks her hip. "Did she not tell you about me?"

I try to take a breath, but there's nothing but dead space where my lungs should be.

"Don't worry." Claire laughs. I'm standing there half-naked in a stranger's shirt, and Claire is *laughing at me*. "I'm not upset or anything. We have an agreement. In fact, I told Jack to go out and have a one-night stand. I just didn't think she'd actually do it."

A one-night stand.

A one-night stand.

One night.

Claire looks me up and down again. "And I definitely didn't think you were her type, but more power to her, I guess. Sorry, I'm intruding." The woman . . . Claire . . . Jack's wife . . . she takes a step backward. "I told her I wasn't coming by this morning, but I was down the street at her favorite coffee place, and I got her a praline mocha. . . ." Claire shakes the coffee cup in her hand. "You know what, actually, don't tell her I was here. I don't want to interrupt her special morning. This can be our little secret, right, Ellie?"

She half turns in the snow, ignoring Paul Hollywood at her heels. "I'll just come back later this afternoon to wish her a Merry Christmas. You'll be gone by then, right?"

I am gone before Jack is out of the shower.

Chapter Fourteen

Wednesday, December 21, 2022

One night.

It was just one night. That was what Claire said as she stood in the snow outside the Airstream. Like a naïve fool, I'd abandoned all reason and logic and *plans*. I'd let myself fall for a woman I barely knew on the basis of snow magic. And the next morning, *her wife* had shown up to remind me that there is no magic. That falling in love with a woman in a single day is irrational, because you can't possibly know a person after only twenty-four hours with them.

I hadn't known Jack was married, or that I was just an experience her wife wanted her to have. None of it had ever meant anything to Jack.

I felt so stupid as I unfastened the buttons on her flannel, as I searched for my leggings amidst the chaos of our clothes strewn across the floor. Paul Hollywood barked and jumped on me, and I cried as I put my still-damp wool socks on my feet. I heard the sound of the shower shut off, and I panicked, not wanting her to see me with tears streaming down my face. So I tucked my boots under my arm and I fled into the snow, and I left my scarf behind.

But Jack kept my scarf.

What the hell am I supposed to do with *that*?

I can't sleep. It's one in the morning, and I toss and turn beneath expensive sheets beside a snoring Andrew, thinking about the scarf and the drawing and the copy of *Fun Home*. Thinking about Jack's feigned indifference and the way she sounded when she asked, *What did I do wrong?* So pitiful, so hurt.

I left while she was in the shower because I didn't want to humiliate myself by eating biscuits and gravy pretending like I didn't know she wanted me to leave so she could get back to her life. Back to Claire.

And now I'm questioning *everything* I thought I'd come to terms with.

It's too late to call Meredith, so I try to process it through my art. I sneak downstairs to the laundry room and draw by only the light of my iPad. I don't distill it down to a few digestible panels. I don't fictionalize it or disguise it. The images are sloppy and rough, just line work and nondescript backgrounds, recapping what happened in the Airstream last night, flashing back to the Airstream last year, moving between the past and present without an indication of the passage of time. I'm not drawing for someone else to understand; I'm drawing only for me.

When I'm done, I don't post this to Drawn2. It's not part of *The Perpetual Suck* or *The Arrangement*, even though there are thousands of followers waiting for this story. I hope that seeing it all laid out before me will provide some kind of clarity, but when I look at the pieces, it somehow makes even less sense.

• • •

Finding the perfect Christmas tree: three hours.

By Wednesday morning, Alan still hasn't arrived at the cabin, and over a French toast breakfast, Katherine, in a rare mood, snaps, "Fuck it. We're getting the tree without the bastard."

Like all Kim-Prescott Christmas traditions, this one immediately confuses me. By my estimation, there are approximately five thousand trees on the family's property, and we could easily just take an axe (*saw?*), go into the backyard, and cut down any one of the trees in spitting distance of the cabin.

Instead, after French toast, Katherine has us all load into two cars to drive somewhere noble firs grow, because apparently those are the only acceptable species of Christmas tree. Jack is back to avoiding me, so she and Dylan ride in her truck, and I end up sandwiched between the grandmas in the backseat of Katherine's Lincoln Navigator. While I know I should engage with the grandmas, my social anxiety outweighs social decorum. I slip on my headphones anyway and put "'Tis the Damn Season" on repeat so I can shut off my brain for a bit.

Using Taylor math, it takes seventeen listens to go about ten miles on the treacherous mountain roads, to an area with a little parking lot where other families pile out of minivans in their quest to murder a tree that will invariably leave pine needles and sap all over their homes. Or maybe I'm just in a weird, anti-Christmas mood today.

My mind is elsewhere as we trek through the woods in search of the perfect tree. I tune out as the grandmas sing Christmas songs and Katherine nitpicks about branch ratios for over an hour. When she finds a ten-foot noble fir that meets her specifications, Andrew cuts it down (with a saw), and he and Jack haul it out of the woods. Dylan shakes out a tarp in the bed of Jack's truck, and the siblings help strap it down with twine, the tip of the tree spilling over the cab, and the stump hanging over the tailgate.

"Why don't you ride back in the truck with me?"

I'm zoning out, so it takes me a while to realize Jack has directed this question at me. That she's making intentional eye contact with me for the first time since the Scarf Incident.

"Wait. *Me?*"

Jack nods. "Yeah. Ride back with me." This now has the essence of a command, not a request. After last night, the thought of being stuck in a truck with Jack for seventeen "'Tis the Damn Seasons" fills me with dread, and in a panic, I turn to Andrew.

"That sounds like a great idea," my traitorous fiancé says. "The two of you can bond."

"I'm not a bonder," I say. "I don't bond."

"You've bonded with me." Andrew grins. "Besides, you're going to be sisters soon. Might as well get in some quality girl time."

Jack looks vaguely ill at this statement, and I'm not sure if it's the phrase *girl time* or the idea of us becoming sisters that does it. Before I can argue with Jack or Andrew, the rest of the family is piling into the Lincoln, leaving me behind with her.

Her truck is just as huge as I remember. When Jack wrenches open the passenger-side door for me and the hinges creak like the playlist of another time, I sigh, resigned, and hoist myself into the cab.

"Paul Hollywood, down!" Jack grunts. The dog immediately leaps into my lap, licking my face and wagging his tail aggressively. I pet him as Jack jogs around to the driver's side. The truck feels too small as soon as she's inside. Shoulders and arms and thighs. A six-foot pastry chef in the body of a competitive swimmer.

She's too close.

"Listen," Jack says in the stern voice she uses sometimes, the one that does absolutely nothing to my blood pressure. "I've been thinking about this since last night. We are two queer women, and we're going to use this drive back to the cabin to do what queer women do."

Blood pressure: rising. "And, uh . . . what's that?"

"We're going to talk about our feelings."

Well. That's worse than I predicted.

"Do we have to?"

Jack nods curtly. "Yes. It seems like we've had some kind of miscommunication about what happened last year. Miscommunications are for the straights," she says with self-righteous indignation. "*We* are going to talk this out."

Jack starts the car. Before she pulls out of the parking lot, she begins fiddling with the aux to cue her playlist. Annie Lennox. "Walking on Broken Glass."

I shift awkwardly in my seat as the dog curls himself into a ball on my lap. "I thought you didn't want to talk about what happened because I'm with Andrew now?" I am not above using Andrew as a shield to protect me from this impending conversation.

Jack shoots me a look as she navigates us back to the main road. "I changed my mind. There's not exactly a guidebook for what you're supposed to do when your brother gets engaged to your ex"—I note she says *ex*, not *former one-night stand*—"but I think we need to clear the air between us so we can move on and start acting like . . ." A swallow that causes her throat to tremble. "Sisters-in-law."

Jack isn't wearing her glasses, but two fingers rise to the bridge of her nose to push them up out of habit. "Tell me what happened last Christmas."

I think about snow magic and crying with my boots under my arm.

"You were married," I say.

The truck goes silent save for Annie Lennox. When I risk a glance at Jack's profile, her jaw is clenched and her hands are strangling the steering wheel. Until she says, finally, "What?"

"Claire." It's such a pretty name. Why did her wife have to have such a pretty name? "While you were in the shower, Claire came by the Airstream. Did she never tell you?"

Jack doesn't relinquish her grasp on the wheel, but she shakes her head.

"Well, Claire came by," I continue, and I am impressed by how measured my words are, by how well I'm feigning indifference in this moment. I guess she taught me well. "She told me the two of you had some kind of agreement, and she implied that she'd wanted you to go out and have a one-night stand. So, I left because . . ." *Because I felt so silly for loving you too quickly.*

"Because I didn't want to be that awkward, clingy one-night stand who overstays her welcome. It was Christmas, and I figured you'd want to spend it with your wife."

Jack is still quiet on the other side of the cab while Annie wails through the speakers. A nervous impulse tells me to fill the space. "The family hasn't mentioned Claire at all, so I'm not sure if y'all are still together, and you spend the holidays apart, or if you're seeing other people. . . . I mean, your marriage is none of my business, but—"

The truck hits a patch of ice, and for a second, my stomach defies the laws of gravity as we fishtail. Jack quickly regains control of the car. "No," she says. "Claire and I aren't still together."

The truck goes silent, and I wait for Jack to open up the way she always has with me.

"Claire and I met after I dropped out of college, when I first moved back to Portland," Jack starts. "My family had just cut me off, and I was desperate to feel like I belonged somewhere, with someone. We got married at twenty-two. Claire and I . . ."

Jack traces her thumbs along the seam of the steering wheel, her eyes firmly fixed on the road in front of her. I notice the jut of her wristbone, so surprisingly delicate compared to the rest of her. "We didn't know ourselves well enough to meld our lives together forever. Two years into our marriage, Claire realized she is polyamorous. And at the time, it made sense to me to try polyamory," Jack continues. I stroke Paul Hollywood's ear to calm myself. It feels like we're still fishtailing.

"Monogamy felt like this patriarchal vestige I was supposed to hate, and most of our friends were poly. I didn't have any interest in seeing other people, but Claire started dating outside of our marriage, and for a while, it worked. Claire was happier, which meant I was happier."

Jack pauses, and I stare at the tendons in her throat as she works her jaw, at the leap of muscle beneath her skin. She's still not looking at me. It's almost like she's telling this story to herself, the way I told our story to myself in a series of messy comic panels.

"Unfortunately," Jack exhales ironically, "it turns out I like outdated patriarchal vestiges, and I had a hard time with Claire dating other people. And then I felt shitty for having a hard time with it, because I felt like I should be evolved enough to not be jealous. I didn't *want* to want to be monogamous. But I don't know. . . . I guess I like the idea of having that one person to be your witness through life. Maybe that's . . . regressive."

"That doesn't sound regressive," I say without thinking, my fingers stroking the soft skin of Paul Hollywood's ears. "That sounds . . . nice."

In profile, I see the smallest tug of a smile in the corner of her mouth. "Claire didn't lie to you that morning," Jack says, sighing. "She'd been pushing me to have a one-night stand, because she thought I would feel better about her dating outside the marriage if I started seeing other people, too. But that's not why I slept with you. The day we met—"

The engine releases a ghastly whine as we hit another patch of ice. Gillian fishtails, the truck bed swaying behind us. Jack holds the wheel steady with her left hand, completely calm despite the semi in the lane beside us as we pitch back and forth. She downshifts with her right hand, and the car straightens out. So confident and sure.

"That day I met you at Powell's," she repeats, "my marriage was already over. Claire had wanted to spend the holidays with her new girlfriend, and I'd stayed in Portland alone because I didn't want to explain to my family why my wife wasn't coming to the cabin with me. I didn't want them to think I'd failed at my marriage like I'd failed at everything else."

I'm shivering in the passenger seat, my teeth rattling against my jaw as I try to process what she's saying, what it all means in the context of the story I've been telling myself for the past year. "Why didn't you tell me you were married? We spent an entire day together playing the honesty game, and you never *once* mentioned Claire."

Jack releases one hand from the wheel and pushes back her hair. "Because I didn't want you to judge me for getting divorced at twenty-six. And because I *really* liked you." Jack's voice cracks again, and I crack right along with it. The scarf and the drawing and *Fun Home*. The way she smiled at me in the snow and the way she held my foot to her chest and the way she tried to reassure me. *I'm not a pumpkin.*

Why hadn't I trusted her? Why had I been so quick to assume I'd misunderstood every touch, every word of affirmation, every moment we had together in the snow?

"Look, I know this doesn't change anything between us." She grabs a handful of her hair now, and I tell myself not to look at her in profile, not to watch the way the growing dusk outside the truck paints her in pale purple. "You're with Andrew, but I just felt like we needed to clear the air. I mean, I'm really happy you and Andrew found each other, as weird as it is. You deserve . . . you deserve the best. Oh shit. You're shivering."

I can't seem to stop my body from shaking. I wrap my arms around Paul Hollywood to get warm, but it's useless, because it's not the cold that's causing me to tremble like this. It's everything else.

It's Jack *really liking me.* It's Jack keeping my scarf. Jack here, in this car, smelling like bread and telling me about her divorce. She pulls over on the side of the road and reaches for my hand. "Here, this is the only heat vent that works. Let's get you warm."

Her fingers circle my wrist as she tugs my hand closer to the middle vent, and the feeling of her skin against mine sparks my nerve endings, floods my empty insides with an overwhelming swarm of feelings. Jack touches me, and the ache in my chest fills with warmth instead. With *wholeness.*

Jack looks down at the place where her skin is touching my skin. Then she looks up, and there are the freckles. There's the white scar. In the low light of the truck, there is that stupid strand of hair I want to brush out of her face. She's close enough that I would only have to move a few inches to press my lips to hers.

And I want to. I hate that I want to kiss her again, but I do. I want to make all the same mistakes I made a year ago right here, right now, with this beautiful woman who liked me very much.

I think about our first kiss in the snow, our first *almost* kiss beneath a heater like this one.

I could kiss her. It would cost me two hundred thousand dollars, but I could kiss her.

Paul Hollywood startles in my lap, and the moment breaks. Jack quickly releases my hand, leaving me to warm myself by the only working heater vent.

"I'm sorry," Jack says, but she doesn't admit what she's apologizing for. "I just . . . I really hope that despite everything, we can find a way to be friends, Elle."

I squeeze my eyes closed. "Yes," I whisper back. "Friends."

A Webcomic
By *Oliverartssometimes*
Episode 4: *The Bathroom*
  (Christmas Eve, 4:13 p.m.)
Uploaded: January 14, 2022

"Sledding was *not* part of the plan."

I glare at Jack from across the single-stall Burgerville bathroom, but all she does is flash me that ridiculous grin. "Okay but admit it: you had fun."

We had a *plan.* We were going to walk straight across the Burnside Bridge so we could get home before the snow got any worse. But then we heard the sound of laughing children, and Jack just had to follow it, just had to trace the source of that unrestrained glee.

I think about the teenagers who happily let us borrow their lime-green toboggans; about sitting on the top of the hill in that elementary school playground with my stomach in my throat; about flying down the hill with Jack screaming her head off beside me until we both tipped sideways and fell into the snow in a tangle of semi-injured limbs. About the way she held my hand as we walked the toboggans back up the hill to go again.

I roll my eyes. "It was mildly entertaining, I suppose."

"I think what you mean to say is, *thank you, Jack*, for showing me that deviating from my rigid plans can lead to unexpected joy."

"Let's not get carried away." I bend down and try to fit my soaking wet hair under the electric hand dryer. Sledding *was* fun, with a side effect of being rather wet. Although I'm pretty sure the thing about getting sick from the cold is a lie, I forced Jack into the nearest fast-food bathroom so we could dry off anyway.

"Honesty game," Jack says as she shoves wadded paper towels inside her wet boots. "Why are you so fixated on always having a plan for everything?"

I squeeze out my thick braid and a little puddle of water forms on the bathroom floor. "If I have a plan," I explain simply, "then I can't fail."

Jack tuts. "Sounds like a logical fallacy to me. I've never planned out anything in my life, and I fail all the time."

"I don't know very many slackers who say things like *logical fallacy.*"

"I didn't say I wasn't smart. I said the education system is poorly designed. It's an important distinction." She begins to unfasten the buttons on her flannel one at a time, moving from the top to bottom. The heat from the air dryer licks the back of my neck. I drop my gaze.

"My parents have been human disasters my entire life," I tell her while staring at the puddle of water on the floor. "So I worked hard in school. I found something I'm really good at. I took all the AP classes and I got perfect grades. I took out loans for undergrad and got the fellowship I needed for grad school, and I've chosen a sensible, stable career that incorporates my love of art, because I don't want to be like them when I grow up."

I lift my gaze from the floor, and all at once there's so much of her. My eyes don't know what to do with it all. Collarbones visible beneath the slide of her white V-neck undershirt. The outline of a sports bra, the modest swell of her breasts, nipples hard from the cold through two layers of fabric. My lower stomach clenches unexpectedly but not unpleasantly.

"I—I um, you're, like, naked," I sputter awkwardly. Because of nipples.

"I'm really not," Jack says, glancing down at her T-shirt. "You know, I don't know many twenty-four-year-olds who are literally paralyzed by a fear of failure."

"I'm not paralyzed by anything," I say. *Except nipples,* apparently. Jack peels off her white T-shirt. From delicate wristbone to wide shoulder blade, she's covered in tattoos, maybe hundreds of them, grayscale ink against light brown skin. I register Mount Hood, a stingray, a line of evergreens, a compass, a desert scene with cacti in bloom.

Jack is living art. The story of an entire life stamped across her skin.

I have a sudden, irrational impulse to have *my* art on Jack's body; I want to claim a small patch of her skin for a drawing.

You've known this woman for six hours, I remind myself. *Get a fucking grip.*

"I could never do that," I mumble, dropping my head again. "Get a tattoo, I mean."

"You could," she says, taking a step closer to me, one hand holding her T-shirt out closer to the air dryer. "*We* could if you wanted. I mean, I'm sure most places have closed from the snow, but I know a few people, and—"

"Jack." She turns her head to look at me. "I'm not getting a tattoo today."

She's close enough that I can smell the damp on her, the sweat and the cold, but beneath all that, even now, is the scent of freshly baked bread. Jack smells like something I want to eat. "Not even right *here*?" She presses two cold fingertips to the exposed skin south of my collarbone. "Not even where no one would see it? Your little cardigan would hide it."

My stomach clenches again at those two fingers, at her closeness and the smell of her skin. At the thought of her picking out art that would live on my body forever.

"What's the story behind your tattoos?"

Jack takes a step back and surveys her own arms. "What, all of them?"

"Your favorite ones."

She points to her forearm, where there are three parallel waves. "This was actually the first one I ever got. I was seventeen, but a buddy of mine had a brother who did it for me. I was on the swim team in high school. It was pretty much the only reason I went to school, so I could be allowed to compete. Oh, and this. . . ." She twists around to point to the Mount Hood tattoo on her bicep. "This was my first legal tattoo. I've lived in the Pacific Northwest my whole life, and there's literally nothing better than a sunny day in Portland, when the mountain is out. And this one."

She twists again, giving me an unencumbered view of her long, lean neck, of the taut muscle between her jaw and her shoulder. "I got this one when I was twenty-one, right after I came out." She's pointing to a picture frame with two women kissing inside it.

"Wait. You didn't come out until you were twenty-one?"

Jack slouches back toward the air dryer. "Nope."

"Oh. I guess I just assumed, since you grew up here in Portland, that it must've been easier for you. . . ."

"I think it can be difficult to come out no matter where you live," she says with a shrug. "And technically, I grew up in Lake Oswego, which is like the Orange County of Portland."

I stare at the story on her skin, the story I want to read and memorize by heart. "Was it hard because of your strict parents?"

"No. My parents don't care that I'm gay. I have a grandpa who was a dick about it, but he's just generally a dick about everything, so I don't really care about his opinion. Figuring things out is just hard, you know?" She shrugs one shoulder, the tattoos dancing on her skin. "Look, I played a lot of sports, cut off all my hair, and insisted on going by Jack from a pretty young age, so I knew that people were speculating about my sexuality behind my back. Sophomore year of high school, I forced my best friend to watch *The L Word* with me, because I thought that would be the moment it all clicked."

She somehow steps even closer to me, so it's the heat of her body I feel even more than the heat of the air dryer. "But no one on that show really looked like me, and basically all the characters ever thought about and talked about was sex, so after a few episodes I was convinced I couldn't possibly be a lesbian, because I wasn't thinking about sex at all in high school. All I thought about was swimming and smoking weed and figuring out how to smoke more weed without damaging my swim times. I knew I wasn't into guys, but I wasn't actually sure if I was into girls, either. I didn't even have my first crush until I was twenty. Is that . . ." She finally lowers her voice to accommodate her proximity, the almost-whisper of the words flickering against my throat. "Is that too honest?"

"No!" I say, too loudly, too enthusiastically being altogether too much and completely incapable of restraining myself. Was it possible to have a hole inside you, cookie-cuttered into the shape of a person you hadn't met yet? Because that's how it felt when I talked to Jack. We were nothing alike and everything alike and— "No, not at all! You can never be too honest with me."

Jack's fiery eyes flash in the fluorescent lighting of the bathroom. "I guess that's the rule of the game. . . ." She lifts her right hand, like she might reach out for the tip of my braid, but lets it drop before we touch.

And I, like a bold idiot, do what I've wanted to all day. I push the wet clump of hair off her forehead. Her skin is clammy beneath my fingers, but she leans into the touch. It hits me, all at once, that none of the past six hours have felt like friendship. Jack is *right here*, close enough I can almost taste her, and Jack isn't a footstool. She's not just some person who's being nice to me because I'm having a bad Christmas Eve.

"Are you . . . I mean, have you ever considered . . . ?"

"If I'm aromantic or asexual?" she fills in for me, her smile widening. Her body arches, and our hips line up beneath the air dryer, parallel but not touching. "I have. I think I was just a late bloomer, though."

She's close, so close, I would barely have to move to kiss her. *She* would barely have to move if she wanted to kiss me. Her fingers come up to wrap around a loose strand of hair escaping from my braid. "I'm demi," I say. Then, stupidly, I clarify, "*Sexual.* Not demiromantic. Or a demigirl. Or a demigod. Like Hercules."

She doesn't move away from me, but she does release my hair. "I didn't think you were coming out to me as the mythological hero Hercules."

"Sorry, I don't always know what other people know about the asexual spectrum. I don't experience sexual attraction like most people do, but I wanted to tell you because—" Because you look like you're about to kiss me, and I want you to, so badly it aches. And I'm terrified of what that means, so soon. *It's only been six hours.*

"Because although I really want to kiss you right now," I force myself to admit, "I also don't want to kiss you. Not yet."

Jack flashes her quarter-moon smile. "I don't want to kiss you in this Burgerville bathroom, either."

I recoil from her, taking three giant steps backward until I bump against the opposite wall. "Shit. That was presumptuous. We're just spending the day together as friends, and—"

"Elle." That one syllable, one letter, rolls off her tongue like a summoning. "Stop." Her voice is a growl. "I'm not interested in just being your friend."

I swallow. "You . . . uh, you're not?"

Jack shakes her head and stalks forward like a panther, closing the distance I put between us. "And I *really* want to kiss you. I just don't find public restrooms particularly sexy."

"Oh." There's nothing but the fabric of her sports bra between me and the rest of her skin, and for some reason, that's the only thing I can think of. "But I also don't mind waiting to kiss you until you're ready," she says with another shrug. "In fact . . ."

She tugs her T-shirt back on, and for a second her expression vanishes. When she emerges again, she's smiling at me.

"I think I'm going to enjoy waiting."

Chapter Fifteen

Friends.

I'm stuck at a cabin with Jack Kim-Prescott for five more days, and she wants to be *friends*.

As soon as we get back home, I flee to the nearest bathroom to cry on a toilet seat about it.

It is, at least, a nice bathroom for crying. The kind with a gilded mirror and expensive soaps and vases full of decorative rocks. I sit on the closed toilet seat with my head in my hands, letting the tears leak down between my fingers as I try to catch my breath.

I'm not even sure *why* I'm crying. This doesn't change anything. *Does it change anything?*

Sure, Jack *really liked* me. She kept the things that reminded me of her in a drawer. Except now she thinks I'm engaged to her brother. With Andrew, I'm guaranteed two hundred thousand dollars. With Jack, there's . . . no guarantee at all.

I try to call Meredith, but she doesn't answer, so for a minute I stare at my phone screen, unsure of who I'm supposed to talk to right now. My terrible mother? My terrible therapist?

There's a knock on the bathroom door, quickly followed by, "Sugar, let me in."

I hesitate a moment before reaching over to unlock the bathroom door. Meemaw steps in, having changed into a floor-length red velvet dress that makes her look like a lounge singer doing a Christmas special. She's carrying two mugs of something that stings my sinuses. "Are you ill? Or are you avoiding dinner because you know it's my night to cook, which means frozen taquitos and Bagel Bites?"

I snort and dislodge a bit of snot. "Actually, Bagel Bites are gourmet by my standards."

"Darlin'." Meemaw stops by the sink when she sees my tears. "Whatever is the matter?"

I unspool a wad of toilet paper to dab under my eyes. "Nothing. It's nothing. I'm sorry."

"Sorry?" She sits down on the edge of the bathtub and passes me a mug. "I won't have any apologizing in this bathroom, and I especially won't tolerate any apologies for having emotions."

I snort again. I spent most of my childhood apologizing to my mother for that exact reason.

"I'm sorry that I'm in here crying when I should be out there decorating the Christmas tree with everyone else," I clarify. "It's on the schedule."

Meemaw clanks her mug against mine. "Sweetheart, we can always schedule in time for a good cry. Have a sip of mulled wine. It'll make you feel better."

I stare suspiciously at the mug of dark red liquid.

She reaches over to pat my thigh. "Tell your meemaw your woes."

I take a cautious sip of the wine. It tastes like hot nail polish remover and Christmas. "There's nothing to tell. I'm just upset over something silly."

Meemaw swirls her drink and makes a knowing click of her tongue. "Something silly like . . . the fact that you had sex with my granddaughter last Christmas?"

I choke mid-sip of mulled wine, then promptly do a cartoonish spit take. A fine mist of it spills out of my mouth and onto the front of my jeans like tear drops of blood. "What? No!" I scramble over how to approach this unexpected declaration and settle on ignorance mid-syllable—"I . . . I don't know what you're talking about."

"Sugar." Meemaw crosses her legs at the ankles and stares me down. "I might seem like some Southern floozy, but I've got sense enough to know something ain't quite right with this whole situation between you and my grandson." She taps a lacquered nail against her temple to indicate her smarts. "I mean, my bastard of an ex-husband adds a stipulation to Andrew's trust saying he's got to get married to inherit, and then Andrew shows up for Christmas with a surprise fiancée?"

I swallow the acid rising in my throat. "You . . . you know about that?"

"That's what I'm telling you. I know *everything*. Mostly, though, I know about this because Lovey told me."

"Lovey knows, too? About the will?"

My mind reels around this revelation, trying to figure out if I should apologize or beg her not to tell or burst into tears again. Two hundred thousand dollars, gone in an instant. And worse, if Meemaw tells everyone the truth, I'll have to go back to my studio apartment, back to my old life, where there are no boozy grandmas, no mothers who touch your hair, no laminated schedules of family bonding time. No Jack.

"Wait. If you know Andrew and I are faking our relationship, why have you been so kind to me? Why have you made me feel like part of the family?"

"Why wouldn't I?" Meemaw asks, like it's that simple. "Most of the people Andrew's brought home over the years have only been interested in either his money or his ass. At least he knows that's what you're about in this case." She eyes me over her mug. "You *are* getting money as part of this arrangement, yes? Or . . . ass, if that's your thing."

"Money," I answer. "Ten percent of the trust fund."

"Good." She offers me a pleased smile.

"You don't think I'm awful for marrying someone for money?"

"Hell no. I respect an entrepreneur. And I knew that a sweet girl with nowhere to go on Christmas must have her reasons for going along with this whackadoodle scheme my grandson cooked up."

"I do," I whisper. "And I swear, I have no intention of hurting your family."

"I know you don't." She taps her temple again. "I can tell. Which is why I haven't said anything to the rest of the family about the inheritance and why I won't. Oh, Lovey knows about the stipulation, but she hasn't put the rest together. Bless her heart, but she's high as a kite most of the time these days. That hip surgery really took it out of her. This is your and Andrew's secret, and you get to decide if and when you want to reveal it."

I take another sip of mulled wine and try to figure out what I did to deserve Meemaw's confidence. And also . . . "I'm sorry, but what you said earlier, about me and . . . Jack . . . ?"

"Ah." She winks at me from the rim of the bathtub. "Now that's a funny story. Last Christmas, my granddaughter calls me to tell me all about this girl named Ellie who broke her heart after they got trapped together in the snow. And this Christmas, a girl named Ellie shows at our cabin acting all kinds of weird around my Jack. It didn't take a genius to put it all together. Do you want to tell me why you ditched my granddaughter last Christmas?"

I really do not. "Does Jack know that you've put it together? That I'm the Ellie from last year?"

Meemaw shakes her head.

"Then why are you telling me now?"

"Why are you crying in the bathroom?" Meemaw snaps back.

I stare into my drink again. I could lie to Meemaw, but she's the one person at the cabin who knows everything, the one person who might understand why my body feels like it's being torn in a dozen different directions. "Because I didn't know the truth about Claire until an hour ago," I say, and I tell her about the conversation with Jack.

"Ah. I see. So, my little turtledove." Meemaw thwaps my leg

when I finish. "Sounds like you're in quite the pickle. On the one hand, you've got my grandson and the money. And on the other hand, you've got my granddaughter. What are you going to choose?"

I stare down at my fingers wrapped around a mug of mulled wine as I sit on a toilet seat, tears barely dry on my face. "I don't think there is a choice to be made, Meemaw."

Just because it turns out our relationship meant something to Jack a year ago, that doesn't change the fact that I hurt her back then and she hurt me. It doesn't change the fact that Jack thinks I'm in love with her brother, or that I've agreed to help Andrew get his inheritance and I can't back out now.

And nothing could ever change the fact that two hundred thousand dollars is a life-altering amount of money for me.

I don't have any choice at all.

• • •

Given their wealth, I expect the Kim-Prescott tree-decorating ceremony to be an exercise in both decadence and restraint. I expect color-coordinated ornaments and flawlessly arranged lights. I expect something magazine perfect and somewhat emotionally vacant.

I don't expect to find Dylan and Andrew haphazardly stringing twinkle rainbow lights around the base of the ten-foot tree. I grab a plate of Bagel Bites, and Lovey presses play on "Glittery" by Kacey Musgraves and Troye Sivan. Katherine sits on a giant ottoman in the middle of the room, and Jack moves totes of Christmas ornaments to her feet.

"Oliver," Andrew barks when he sees me, "come hold these lights for me."

The Kim-Prescotts love their Christmas traditions. This one involves Katherine pulling an ornament from the neatly organized totes—each ornament personalized and unique and definitely not color-coded—and someone in the room sharing a memory associated with the ornament. An anecdote, an inside joke, a feeling.

Katherine pulls out the first one. It's Mickey Mouse in a silver blue top hat holding a golden "50."

"Disneyland in '05," Andrew says immediately. "JayJay, remember how you barfed on Space Mountain?"

"And still rode it six more times." Jack nods solemnly.

The siblings high-five over this victory of gastrointestinal distress.

A Popsicle-stick reindeer. "One of my students made that for me during my student teaching, and it was the first time I felt like I was in the right career," Dylan says with sweet nostalgia. They're also wearing a T-shirt that says, "Merry Capitalist Consumer-Driven Corruption of a Pagan Fertility Holiday." Because there is nothing Dylan Montez loves more than ironic juxtapositions.

A sparkly rainbow orb. "Do you remember Pride that year when we drunkenly tried to smuggle Fifty Licks into that drag show, and ice cream melted all over Dylan's fanny pack?"

A giant martini glass. "Richard never let me hang that on the tree when we were married, God rest his crusty-ass soul."

"I can't believe y'all put my face on giant orb."

"Remember, Dolly Parton needs to go front and center."

"Who hid my kombucha ornament?"

I sit on the couch with Paul Hollywood snuggled against my side, sipping cups of mulled wine that magically refill themselves every time Meemaw gets up. I'm not a part of the reminiscence, but I'm not wholly separate from it, either, watching the family get lost in their shared memories of love.

I feel . . . well, a little drunk from the mulled wine, honestly. And I'm trying very hard not to think about the conversation with Jack in the truck or the conversation with Meemaw in the bathroom.

"All right," Katherine declares, staring up at the Christmas tree with a misty-eyed look. "It's done."

It is, quite frankly, the ugliest Christmas tree I've ever seen. There are mismatched ornaments hung in careless clumps and twisted rainbow lights and tinsel barfed on the branches.

It's perfect.

An Ariana Grande Christmas song starts, and Meemaw reaches for Lovey's hand and pulls her into the center of the room to dance. Andrew does the same to Jack, tugging his sister into his arms and forcing her to do some facsimile of the Charleston. She cringes, but she's also smiling, that half-moon that transforms her face into swooping angles and mischief. Jack smiles at her brother like loving him is the easiest thing she's ever done.

Andrew twirls away from his sister and finds Dylan sulking on the couch. I watch the moment of deliberation. He reaches out, hoists them up, and Dylan mock-protests for a minute before succumbing to Andrew's undeniable charms, swaying happily along. And Jack—Jack turns toward me and extends a hand.

Friends.

I take her hand. She doesn't pull me close, like she did that night on the Burnside Bridge. Instead, she keeps me at a safe distance, only her left hand touching my right, our bodies far enough apart to save room for the Holy Ghost, as well as the ghosts of Christmas past, present, and future. "Santa Tell Me" fades, and a new Ariana song comes over the speaker system.

It's "Last Christmas."

Jack stops swaying and meets my eye. I'm not sure what I expect to find there on her unguarded face, but as Ariana's breathy falsetto begins, Jack's smile widens until her eyes crinkle in the corners. And then she bursts out laughing, and I'm laughing, too, because it's all so ridiculous. Last Christmas and this Christmas and the absolute absurdity of our entire situation.

We both laugh at the private joke of this song, until Dylan snaps, "What's so funny?" which only makes Jack laugh harder, honking and quacking. It's a terrible laugh. I'm obsessed with it.

She steps closer, still laughing, so I can feel her hot breath on my throat, smell the cinnamon and cloves of her mulled wine. A wave of heat travels from the crown of my head down to my stomach. Jack's body and Jack's breath. For a moment, everything fades away. The music and the grandmas' laughter and the rest of the family dissolves, and I feel like Jack and I are back in our snow globe built for two.

But we're not. We are here, at her family's cabin. My fiancé is ten feet away.

I drop Jack's hand.

"I think that mulled wine has gone straight to my head." Without Jack's fingers to anchor me, I'm unsteady in my attempts to remain vertical. "It might be time for me to go to bed."

I'm perfectly aware of the fact that it's seven thirty, but I'm not sure I can handle one more minute around other people. I stumble in the direction of the stairs, and Jack takes a step along with me. She looks worried I'm going to fall over.

I'm worried I might fall, too. I'm going to fall right into her and never let go. I grab onto the archway leading to the stairs.

Jack comes closer. I can feel her body heat again, the warmth from the fire radiating off her skin.

"Mistletoe," Meemaw says from across the room.

"No, this is 'Only Thing I Ever Get for Christmas,'" Andrew corrects her, pointing to the playlist display, where we've switched to a collection of Justin Bieber songs.

"No. *Mistletoe*." Meemaw points somewhere north of my head, and I look up to see a bushel of green leaves wrapped in red ribbon pinned to the archway. I didn't know people actually hung mistletoe in their houses until I saw the Kim-Prescotts' cabin.

"That's cute," I say. Then I turn toward the stairs again.

"Excuse you!" Meemaw snaps, coming over to us and bringing the rest of the family with her. "You and Jack are *under the mistletoe*. You know the rules."

I glare at Meemaw, but she only smiles impishly and takes another sip of her drink. "I'm not going to kiss my brother's fiancée," Jack says before I can formulate an argument to spare us from Meemaw's cruel torture.

"I honestly don't mind." Andrew smiles and props his chin coyly on top of his closed fist. "It is mistletoe, after all."

"This seems inappropri—"

"Kiss! Kiss! Kiss!" Meemaw starts the drunken chant, and soon everyone else joins in, even Katherine. My body is attuned to the way Jack's body tenses, shifts. She is less steady on her feet now, swaying away from me, putting space between us.

"*Kiss! Kiss! Kiss!*"

"Okay, fine! You monsters!" Jack finally shouts, and she plays it off so well. I genuinely believe this kiss under the mistletoe will mean nothing to her.

I need it to mean nothing to me, too.

"One quick kiss," Jack tells her family, and then she's fully facing me. "Is this okay?" she whispers just for us.

No, it's not okay. Nothing about this situation is okay.

"Yes," I say.

Just like that, Jack closes her eyes and tilts her face toward mine. I meet her halfway, and it's nothing more than a graze. Chapped lips and a hint of oranges. Her mouth is surprisingly soft, even though the kiss itself feels sturdy and immovable.

Jack begins to pull away, to end this joke of a mistletoe kiss, but some instinct in me holds on, falling forward as she steps back, my lips still pressed to hers. And then her hand is on my waist, to keep me upright. Just one hand, through the layers of my cardigan and my shirt, but it's enough. Enough to zap feeling into my unfeeling bones, to light up my limbs like the strands of Christmas lights on the tree, to send heat pulsating between my legs, to the place where my *other* lonely ache lives.

Jack's hand is on my waist and her mouth is on my mouth, and she tilts her chin just enough that I feel the drag of her lips. I want to open my mouth for her. I want to open *everything* for her, to be that open version of myself I became with her in the snow last year.

And then I remember our audience. I let go, killing the symphony of longing inside my chest. There's a startled flash of wide eyes in my vision before Jack drops her gaze.

Behind us, the family is whooping and whistling as enthusiastically as they did during Christmas carols, somehow oblivious to the lingering tension between us.

She presses two fingers to her bottom lip, then drops her hand when she catches me watching her mouth. I want to kiss her there again. And again. *And again and again.*

It's a good thing no one is actually asking me to choose between Jack Kim-Prescott and two hundred thousand dollars. Because in this moment of mulled wine and mistletoe kisses, I think I know which one I would pick.

A Webcomic

By *Oliverartssometimes*

Episode 5: *The Dream*

(Christmas Eve, 3:54 p.m.)

Uploaded: January 21, 2022

"So you're planning to murder me?"

Jack cranes her beautiful neck to shoot me a look. "Yep. I always spend a whole day slow-burn flirting with my victims before harvesting their organs."

"Wait. *Have* you been flirting with me all day?"

With the hand not threaded through mine, Jack reaches up to pinch the bridge of her nose. "Yes, Elle. I have. And when I go home tonight, I will reflect gravely on my utter lack of romantic game. Now, come along."

She gives my hand a squeeze and pulls me forward. We'd been doing that since we left the Burgerville bathroom: holding hands. Walking through the snow with our fingers intertwined like the cross-stitch on my scarf. We've gotten off track again, wandering the opposite direction of the bridge that will take us back home.

And now we're standing on a deserted street corner in front of an abandoned building. "It's getting dark," I say. "It would make sense that you'd want to wait until nightfall to lure me back to your murder den."

"This isn't a murder den," she says, gesturing with one hand toward the boxy warehouse with boarded-up windows and graffiti on every square inch. It absolutely has the markings of a murder den. "Close your eyes."

"So you can *stab me*? I don't think so."

"Please, Elle. Come on. I told you I want to show you something."

"How will you show me if my eyes are closed?" I grumble, but I'm already closing them, already doing exactly what she said.

"Now. Picture it," Jack says. "There are real windows and the outside has been painted white. Maybe with a mural on the east side. The windows let in morning sunlight from the east—*don't open your eyes*! The floors are stripped hardwood, the walls are painted lavender, and there are long tables, communal style. The kitchen is exposed behind the counter, and there's a giant display case with cupcakes and tarts and scones and pies—the best fucking pies you've ever tasted!"

I crack open one eye and catch the look of unabashed wonder on Jack's face as she conjures this glorious image. "It's a bakery," I say.

Jack nods. "Yeah."

"It's . . ." I stare at the rundown building, then back at her. "It's *your* bakery? You want to open a bakery?"

Jack releases my hand so she can shove both fists into the pockets of her coat. "I mean, maybe. Someday. It's just an idea I've been casually playing around with off and on for, like"—she shrugs with perfect indifference—"my entire life."

My excitement gets the better of me, and I punch her in the arm. "This is amazing! You have to do it!"

Jack reels backward a bit. A quarter-moon smile slips onto her face, but she tries to Etch-a-Sketch it away. "Calm down. You're forgetting that follow-through isn't exactly my strong suit. I don't have the concentration necessary to program the radio presets on my truck, and I've been listening to the same Spotify playlist for ten years. I'm not sure how I'd figure out business loans and permits and all the meticulous, boring details associated with running a business."

"You could get help."

She scowls, like *help* is a disgusting word, but a minute ago, her face lit up like a child's on Christmas morning. "Why baking?"

Jack raises her shoulders up to her ears defensively. "What do you mean?"

"I *mean*, why baking? How did you get into it?"

She looks uncertain about answering this question on an abandoned street corner as dusk begins to settle around us. "Oh. Well, I used to help my mom cook all the time as a kid. It was something we started doing together around the third grade, when I started sucking at school. My mom thought it would help me develop concentration skills or something, to have to follow recipes and measure everything out. I didn't care very much about learning how to cook miyeok guk, but there was this place we discovered when we spent our summers in France—"

I roll my eyes, and she smiles self-deprecatingly and adds, "Yes, we *summered in France*. My parents have a place in Saint-Macaire, this little village near Bordeaux, where one of my grandmas was born. Most summers, my dad would stay inside and work the whole time, and my mom would take my brother and me to explore nearby towns. But every morning, my parents would hand my brother a fistful of euros and we'd go down the street to this patisserie."

Jack smiles faintly at the memory, her white scar twisting into a fishhook again. I take a step closer to her on the sidewalk. "The woman who ran the patisserie was this masc, Trunchbull-looking woman who would yell at us about our poor French pronunciation, but she also made the most delicate baked goods you've ever seen. Fruit tarts and chocolate croissants and macarons, and it was the first time I saw someone who looked like me creating such beautiful, delicate things. It made me feel like I could care about making things pretty and still be *me*, and I just became obsessed with baking after that. And what are you doing?"

I'd drifted even closer to her, pulled in by her vulnerable words and by that swooping scar that makes me feel like a string is tied around my insides, tied back to her. She's so beautiful, and not just because of her hair and her freckles and her eyes—not just because of her long limbs and her strong thighs and her lovely neck—but because of the messy shape of her heart, which beats wildly for macarons and pie.

And I just have to fucking kiss her.

I tilt my face up toward hers, and Jack understands. Her hand comes up to cup my chin, cold fingers against the burning blush of my skin. I need something to hold onto. I find the narrow of Jack's waist beneath her khaki jacket. Then I close my eyes.

Jack's mouth is softer than I expect. Sweet. The lingering taste of her praline mocha and maple bacon donut. But her hands are just as strong as I imagined, anchoring me until I feel elemental. My feet are deeply rooted beneath me, solid and unmoving, but when her tongue gently presses against the seal of my lips, I feel entirely capable of blowing away in the winter wind like the flakes that drift around us. The tip of her tongue presses against my lips until I open for her, like I've opened for her all day.

My skin is made of fire and my bones are made of water at the feeling of Jack's mouth and Jack's breath and Jack's body beneath my hands, beneath her clothes, arched with wanting. This loud, brash cyclone of a woman goes quiet and still in my arms, kissing me like it matters too much.

We break apart to breathe, and our glasses get stuck on each other until we carefully pry them apart. Then we burst into laughter. "You didn't make me wait long," Jack says, her voice somehow both rough and tender. I want to open Clip Studio and find the right color to capture the feeling of Jack's voice. Cerulean like my scarf, maybe. Umber like her eyes.

I shake my head, marveling at the snowflakes in her hair. "No, I didn't. What's it called?"

Jack eyes me. "Kissing . . . ?"

"Your bakery."

"Oh." Her strong hands are still on my body. "Uh. I'm thinking about calling it . . . the Butch Oven?" She squints one eye and bites her bottom lip. "Is that a stupid name?"

"Of course not."

"It's supposed to be a pun. Like on Dutch oven."

"I get it, Jack."

She presses her forehead to mine. We're touching in so many places. Touching has never felt this easy to me. "But *butch* and *Dutch* are an imperfect rhyme. They look like they should fit together, but they don't actually sound the same, so I'm worried people won't get it."

I wrap my arms around her waist until my fingers hook together in the back. Her nerves have nothing to do with the name. "You could do it, you know. You could turn this place into something truly special."

She folds herself in closer, until we're two perfectly aligned pieces, slotted together in the snow. "I'm not like you, Elle. I don't make ten-year plans. I don't have a bullet journal filled with life goals I'm checking off one by one. How would I ever open a bakery by myself?"

I reach out for her hand again, stitching our fingers back together. "Maybe you don't have to do it by yourself."

Chapter Sixteen

Thursday, December 22, 2022

"Why did I have to find out about my daughter's engagement from Instagram?"

I wake up to the lingering smell of cinnamon and cloves in my hair, the buzzing of my phone on the bedside table, and my mom's grating voice in my ear. "Hello, Linds," I grumble, half-asleep and completely annoyed.

"Don't *hello* me," Linds snaps. "You've been avoiding my calls. Were you ever going to tell me you're getting married?"

"Um . . . No?"

My mother scoffs, and I sit up in bed, leaning back against the carved wood headboard in preparation for her impending tantrum. The room is bathed in midmorning light, and Andrew isn't in bed beside me, his sheets already cool to my touch. I don't have time to wonder where he is, because *Linds*.

"Are you being serious, Elena?" she squawks. "You weren't going to tell me you have a fiancé? I know I haven't always been the best mother," Linds begins to whine, "but the idea that my only daughter would get engaged without telling me—that I would have to find out from pictures on the internet—makes me feel completely worthless, Elena Jane."

"I was kidding, Mom," I drone out the lie. "Of course I was going to tell you. Did the, uh"—I cringe at my own cowardice but barrel on anyway—"official engagement announcement arrive in the mail?"

"No, but I've been staying with a friend in Tempe," she says, her spirits sounding vastly improved already. "So, tell me everything! How did you two meet? How did he pop the question?"

I don't want to do this with her, especially not at—I pull the phone away from my face to check the time—nine in the morning after a night of mulled wine and semi-questionable choices.

I go for a subject change. "How's Ted doing?"

"Ted who?"

"Ted . . . your *husband* . . . ?" *The man you married only one month after meeting him.* Like mother, like daughter.

"Oh, that prick. Fucking gone is how he is. And good riddance. It's fine. Doesn't matter," she insists. It sounds like it matters quite a lot, but I'm not going to argue with my mother about her love life. Lindsey Oliver is an exemplary reminder that all relationships are doomed to fail. Probably within a calendar year. "I'm swearing off men for a bit. For real this time, Elena. I'm fucking done with the whole lot of them. Maybe I'll give women a try, like you did."

"I didn't 'give women a try,' Mom. I'm bisexual."

"Not anymore, apparently. Now you're getting married!"

I check the time on my phone again. What was that—three whole minutes before Linds said something biphobic? "That's not how bisexuality works. I will always be bisexual, even if I marry a man. Even if I only date men!"

Linds is not interested in a lesson on bi erasure. "Tell me about your fella! He looks expensive in these Instagram photos. You know, now that Ted and I are over, I could use a little money to get my own place, and—"

Of course. She didn't call to congratulate me on my engagement. She called me because she saw my fiancé's Gucci loafers in a photo and figured she could get more than a few hundred bucks out of me. "Look, Mom, I gotta go—"

"Don't you dare hang up on me. When is the wedding?"

And sure, Linds only calls when she wants something, but at least sometimes she calls.

"I'm working . . . a new job, sort of," I tell her. "I'll have some money coming in soon, and I'll pay for the new battery then."

The fake tears cease. "Good. Glad to hear it. Venmo me when you can. Love ya."

Linds hangs up, and I toss my iPhone onto Andrew's vacant pillow. The *love ya* is an automated response; I know it's not rooted in any true maternal affection, but still, I cling to it. I want it to mean something.

All it means, though, is that I can't do anything to jeopardize this money.

Two hundred thousand dollars. My mother's debt. My debt. My future.

There's no time for cinnamon and cloves or mistletoe.

But then I'm thinking about the kiss last night and *oh*—I still feel that kiss in every inch of my body. I can still feel the phantom press of her soft mouth, the sweet glide of her fingers. Because that's the thing about Jack—her touch is always as surprisingly delicate as her wristbone, as gentle as her words when I'm panicking, as tentative as her dreams. Jack is wild horses and rainstorms and driving with your arm out the window on a warm day. But she's also quiet moments: she's your first mug of coffee in the morning; she's watching that rainstorm through a window, wrapped up in your favorite blanket.

I forgot about her ability to make me feel both reckless and secure; the way her touch is like a lightning rod and a warm piece of bread.

I arch back against the headboard and let my fingers slide across my soft stomach in the place where my T-shirt has hitched up over my bare skin. And then I drop them lower, along the hem of my pajama bottoms. Past the hem. I'm careful, not sure where Andrew is or when he's coming back, as my fingers travel over the front of

"There isn't really a wedding. It's just going to be me and Andrew at the courthouse."

"And me, because I'm your mother."

Only biologically. "You'd have to fly into Portland, and I know you hate traveling anywhere moist."

"I will suffer frizzy hair to see my baby girl walk down the aisle."

I grit my teeth and try not to think about last Christmas, when she left me alone for the holidays. For this, though, she'll get on a plane.

"Send me the details for the wedding," my mother demands. All she ever does is demand.

"Okay," I agree, because that's all I ever do, too. "Goodbye, Linds."

"Wait! About the money you sent me . . ."

I Venmoed her two hundred dollars last week. My checking account is currently down to $13.23. "What about the money?"

"Well, see, the battery died on the Corolla, and since I don't have a running car, I haven't been able to get to work, so I'm going to need another five hundred to get it fixed."

"I don't have five hundred dollars right now."

A pause. "But that new beau of yours seems like he's got money. . . ."

"I can't ask Andrew for money."

She sniffles, inducing the fake tears that served as the insincere soundtrack to my childhood. "Are you just going to let me get fired? I have no car, Elena!"

I feel that twinge of guilt, that obligation to the only family member I have. I wish I had a mom like Katherine, so desperate to spend time with me she plans it in an Excel spreadsheet. I wish I had a sibling who called me stupid nicknames. I wish I had a grandma who called me sugar and only cared about my happiness. But I don't.

I have a dad I haven't spoken to in three years, and I have Linds.

cotton of my underwear. I think about Jack the first time I saw her: long fingers and knuckles and that impossibly fragile wristbone. It's those fingers I imagine skating over my body, and my body tightly coils at the thought.

Jack the first time she smiled, a flash of white teeth pinning that quarter-moon smile in place. I press the palm of my hand down harder over my mound, releasing the quietest moan as feeling swirls in my lower belly. Jack in the Burgerville bathroom, the first time I saw her skin, the tendons of her neck and the art on her arms, telling me she would *enjoy* waiting. I rub myself again and again, and I whisper her name into the bedroom, just to feel that hard *k* sound in the back of my throat as I bring myself closer.

Jack in the snow, Jack in the Airstream, Jack in my arms. Jack— Jack blasting "Toxic" by Britney Spears at nine in the morning?

My hand stills inside my pajamas as the opening notes of the Britney classic thump against the second-story window from somewhere outside. Only one member of the Kim-Prescott clan would blare this particular song at this particular hour of the day.

I release a sexually frustrated sigh, climb out of bed, and go to the window, pushing back the curtains to reveal the backyard of the house, the field of snow and the Airstream sparkling amidst it. The front door of the Airstream is wide open, and Jack is standing outside, throwing snowballs against the side of the trailer to the chaotic beat of "Toxic." Paul Hollywood is doing his zoomies around her feet, almost perfectly syncopated to the song.

I step out onto the bedroom balcony and shout her name, but she either doesn't hear me or chooses not to turn around. For a minute, I stand in the cold watching the frenetic energy of her body as she winds up her arm and chucks each clump of snow with intensity and force. Then I'm shoving my feet inside my boots, not bothering with the laces as I run downstairs and outside.

"Jack!" I shout again as I trudge through the snow closer to her and the portable speaker playing Britney at avalanche-inducing volumes. The cold cuts through the flimsy layers of my pajamas as I call out her name again. "Jack!"

She doesn't acknowledge me until I reach her, and even then, her face is bright red from the cold and from the exertion of pounding hunks of snow against her home.

"What's wrong?" I ask as the song skids into its techno bridge.

Jack bends down to grab another fistful of snow. "Nothing."

"You're blaring Britney and throwing snowballs at your house, so I don't believe you," I scream over the music. Then I take a few more steps toward the portable speaker resting on the front step of the Airstream, and I turn it off. Paul Hollywood barks a few times in outrage over the absence of Britney.

Silence settles over the morning. Silence, and the sound of Jack's heavy breathing and Paul Hollywood's paws crunching in the snow. "My dad arrived late last night," Jack finally says by way of explanation.

"Oh." Suddenly, the angry Britney-snowball-throwing makes perfect sense.

"And guess how long it took him to start picking apart every little thing about me?" She winds up her arm and launches another snowball. This one must have ice in it, because it hits the side of the trailer with a vicious *thwack*.

"Jack—"

"I know I shouldn't care what he thinks of me, and I tell myself I don't, but he's my fucking dad, and it would be nice if I don't know. . . ." She squats to collect more snow, and maybe to hide her face from my view as she brushes away a few rogue tears. "I know my mom puts a lot of pressure on me, but it's only because she wants me to have the best life possible. My dad can't even pretend to *like* me. But I'm not Andrew, so why would he bother?"

"Jack—" I try again.

"And I know, I know. . . ." She releases another clod against the trailer. "Andrew has his own cross to bear. I know being the anointed golden boy hasn't freed him from our dad's tyrannical expectations, but at least he hasn't been the object of my dad's mockery his entire life."

"Jack—"

"God, you're right!" She throws up one arm as another tear sneaks past her defenses. "It means a lot to my mom, and I should just be happy he's here, but—"

"*Jack!* Stop interrupting! You don't know what I'm going to say!"

Jack allows this next snowball to drop from her fingers and fall to her feet. "Okay. What are you going to say?"

For the first time since this interaction started, she's fully facing me, her body turned in my direction. "I'm sorry," I say, mesmerized by the sight of those freckles in the early-morning cold. I kissed her last night. And for a minute, under the mistletoe, I think she kissed me back. "About your dad. I'm sorry about your dad. You don't deserve to be treated that way."

A puff of white breath escapes her lips. "Are you sure? Because I've got twenty-seven years of data to support that this is *exactly* how the fuck-up child of the prodigious Prescotts deserves to be treated." She starts reaching for more snow.

"Well, the Airstream doesn't deserve to be treated this way, so at least stop abusing it! You love this trailer!"

"What?" Jack barks out a humorless laugh as she swings back toward me. "You think I love living in an Airstream?"

"Don't you?"

"No! I hate this damn thing!" She throws another snowball. "I'm six feet tall! It's like being a trout in a sardine tin!"

I'm painfully aware of the fact that we're discussing her trailer and not the fact that we kissed last night. Which is fine. I'm fine with this. We can go ahead and pretend that never happened, too.

"You have definitely led me to believe you love your Airstream."

"You know what I would love?" Jack says bitterly. "A house in the suburbs with a big yard for Paul Hollywood. A huge kitchen with *actual* counter space. Room and roots and no wheels."

"Then why do you live in an Airstream?"

Jack throws her arms wildly into the air. "Because I'm stubborn, Elle! Because this expensive hunk of metal has become a symbol of my freedom from the Prescott name"—she kicks her leg like she wants to kick the trailer, but she's a good fifteen feet away—"and because I refuse to admit that I want the normcore life my parents would choose for me. Because I'm twenty-seven years old, and I'm still basing all my life decisions around pleasing and/or pissing off my parents."

"Ah." I bend down and rub Paul Hollywood's ears, because it stops me from saying or doing something stupid after this whole passionate declaration. Like trying to kiss her again.

Her cheeks are even pinker now, her ears bright red beneath the rim of her beanie. Jack might see the Airstream as a symbol of her independence, but it's also a shiny cage. It's a sardine box that keeps her safe and separate from the rest of her family, maybe even the rest of the world. Her whole life, her dad has made her feel like a screwup; everyone has made her feel like she's not enough, or too much, but none of that can touch her inside her glossy home on wheels. Nothing can hurt her if she's always moving.

Yet what she craves most is to plant herself. And for one day last year, I felt like she let me see behind the mask of indifference, the cool aluminum exterior.

Absolutely no good can come from imagining that life of roots and routines with her.

"Look, your dad sounds like a real piece of work," I say, refocusing, "but don't let that diminish what you've accomplished, Jack. You're about to open a fucking bakery!"

"I just—" Jack winds herself up like she's going to launch into another rant, but she collapses instead, literally, her knees buckling beneath her as she topples into the snow. Her legs stick out in front of her an awkward angle, making her look much younger than twenty-seven. "I wouldn't have done it without you." She releases a resigned exhale and sends up another puff of breath.

I drop back into the snow beside her, my pajama bottoms immediately soaked through. "What?"

Jack kicks a deep groove into the snow with the toe of her boot. "The Butch Oven. I—I wouldn't have decided to do it if you hadn't believed in me that day. I thought it was spite, actually." Jack smiles a little, but my entire body is coated in permafrost, unable to move, even though all I want to do is get closer to this woman who is an arm's length away. "I was so hurt when you bailed while I was in the shower, and for some reason, I turned that into, *I'll open my bakery all by myself, and that will show her.*"

"God, you're stubborn," I say. Even as the permafrost spreads to my heart, my brain still struggles to adjust to this new version of our shared history. The version where I ghosted. The version where she kept my scarf.

Jack nods and stares at our feet. Our legs are stretched out in the snow, four parallel lines so deliberately not touching. "But really, that moment in front of the warehouse—that was the first time it felt like someone actually believed I could do it. I mean, Dylan supports me, but they also know my whole history of false starts and abandoned dreams. But you just . . . *believed.* So you being here right now, telling me to ignore my dad's criticism—it's all very full-circle for me."

Jack tilts her left foot so it bumps my right. "I guess that's me saying thanks, or whatever."

"Or whatever," I say, bumping her back. We leave our feet that way, tilted toward each other, touching. Boot to boot, leg to leg. "I'm sorry that it started out of spite, though. I'm . . . I'm sorry that I ghosted you. I should've said that last night."

"I'm sorry that my wife showed up on Christmas morning."

I stare at the place where our bodies overlap through the rubber of our shoes, and just like that, I'm ready to throw away two hundred thousand dollars, ready to tell my mom to fuck off, ready to do whatever it takes to be just a little bit closer to her.

"Do you think if—" Jack starts.

"Why the fuck were you blaring Britney at nine in the morning?"

We both whip around to see Dylan stomping through the snow. Jack folds her legs inward so she's sitting cross-legged in the snow by the time Dylan reaches us. We're not touching at all. They're wearing Andrew's herringbone peacoat over a pair of footie pajamas and scowling as they look at Jack and then me and then back again. "And why the fuck are the two of you sitting in the snow?"

I stare at Jack and imagine I can pull the rest of her sentence from her mouth. *Do you think if . . .* what?

Do I think if Claire had never shown up, things would have gone differently?

Do I think if I hadn't ghosted, if I'd given Jack the chance to explain, we might have been able to figure out a way to extend the magic beyond a single snow day?

Do I think if I wasn't engaged to her brother, then *maybe . . .* ?

But I can't make Jack finish her previous thought, and instead she smiles up at her best friend, and says, "Alan Prescott is why we're sitting in the snow."

"Of fucking course he is," Dylan says, and then they flop down into the snow beside us.

Chapter Seventeen

Alan Prescott *is* a real piece of work.

Within the first ten minutes of meeting me, he insults my jeans, my job, and my parents, and while the last might deserve it, this still seems like a dick move.

He criticizes the objectively delicious omelets Jack makes for breakfast and then launches into an offensive and ableist lecture about how Jack could have been more successful in life if she just buckled down and didn't use her ADHD as an excuse. He oscillates between berating Andrew (for the way he dresses, for the way he eats, for the way he sits in a chair) and wanting to talk business with him. The real kicker, though, comes when he insults Katherine's laminated schedule and refuses to participate in family games. This leads to the postponing of family game night so Katherine and Alan can go upstairs to scream at each other.

At which point Meemaw hands Andrew her credit card and tells us to get out of the house for a while, like an older sibling sending the kids to get ice cream while Mommy and Daddy fight.

Whatever. I love ice cream and hate fighting, so I happily accept Meemaw's suggestion.

"You know what?" Dylan says thirty minutes later from the backseat of Andrew's Tesla. "I really fucking hate your dad."

For once, Dylan's anger feels directed at the right source.

We don't go get ice cream. Andrew takes us to a bar—aptly named the Mountain Bar—a dive right along the highway, next to a gas station called "Gas" and a little market called "Market." Like the Kim-Prescott cabin, the bar is designed to look like an old-fashioned lodge, but unlike the Kim-Prescott cabin, the Mountain Bar mostly succeeds in this endeavor. It's made of interlocking logs, with wood beam ceilings that look damp with age, scuffed hardwood floors, single-paned windows, and a vast collection of original neon signs for Budweiser and Coors Light. The crowd is a mix of grizzled locals, seasonal ski instructors, and groups of tourists staying on the mountain for the holidays.

Andrew looks like a tourist but moves like a local, ordering us two pitchers of Rainier beer and leading us to a dark booth in the back. Andrew and I slide into one side of the booth; Dylan and Jack slide into the other. Underneath the table, Jack's knee brushes mine, and I need a drink if I'm going to—

No, I decide as a bearded server sets the pitchers and foggy plastic cups down on the table. Here we are, the four members of the love trapezoid, isolated together at an establishment full of alcohol. It's probably best if I try approaching Jack sober for once. A few hours ago, she touched my foot with her shoe and I was ready to give up two hundred thousand dollars for her.

Sober is my best bet.

I order myself a ginger ale and then sit in uncomfortable silence while the others quickly pound their first glass of cheap beer. I'm not sure if it's because Dylan is in love with Andrew, who's engaged to me, or if it's because I'm secretly in love with my fake fiancé's sister, or if it's because I kissed my fiancé's sister last night beneath the mistletoe, but everything feels extremely awkward in our booth as the others attempt mindless small-talk. No one seems keen to address the trapezoidal elephant in the bar.

Finally, Jack says something interesting enough to distract us from our suffering. "Dyl, why don't we work on your dating profile?"

And then everything gets exponentially *more* awkward. "Oh, uh, nah," Dylan sputters, scratching the back of their neck and deliberately *not* looking at Andrew. "I really don't want to think about online dating right now."

"Come on." Jack holds out a hand to demand Dylan's phone. "There's no time like the present."

Andrew, who has consumed his second glass of beer in the last ninety seconds, belches. "I thought you were seeing someone. Allie or Amy or—"

"Alice," Dylan grumbles. "And we broke up."

"They weren't good enough for you," Jack says fiercely, a hand on Dylan's shoulder. "And they were an idiot for ending things."

"Alice wasn't an idiot. They just weren't interested in commitment. So, you know . . ." Dylan takes a drink of their beer and shoots Andrew a look over the rim of the cup. "My type."

Jack, somehow completely oblivious to the Andrew-Dylan dynamics, continues. "Your type is serial monogamists who will carry your beets at the farmer's market, and I have it on good authority that you meet those people on Hinge."

I briefly contemplate the possibility that *Jack* is on Hinge, finding hot women to carry her beets, and frantically reach for my drink at the thought. Except it's ginger ale, and taking a swig doesn't have the same effect.

Dylan glares at Jack. "I hate dating apps."

"Unfortunately, that's how you meet people these days. You're not going to have a meet-cute in Cathedral Park."

Or in Powell's Books. I take another swig of ginger ale.

"Being bisexual on the dating apps is hard enough, but add to that being overtly not white, nonbinary, and monogamous? In *Portland*? Do you know how white and poly the Portland queer dating scene is?"

"I hated being bisexual on the apps, too." I attempt to commiserate.

Under the table, Jack presses her knee closer against mine, denim against denim. I'm not sure if this is accidental or on purpose, but

I accidentally-on-purpose rub my knee against hers. Soberness is a weak shield, apparently, when Jack's knees are involved.

"Hinge profile," Jack orders. "Now."

Dylan drops their head onto the sticky table in misery but nudges their phone toward Jack all the same.

"Fact about me that surprises people . . ." Jack says, reading the Hinge profile prompt.

"That despite the neck tattoo, I still have to sleep with a night-light," Andrew fills in. Dylan keeps their head plastered to the table but raises their middle finger in response.

"I get along best with people who . . ."

"Punch me in the face when I deserve it?" I suggest.

"Who can tell my crusty shell is just an act," Andrew answers effortlessly. At that, Dylan peels their head off the table just a smidge.

"I'm looking for . . ."

"Monogamy, marriage, mortgage, all that embarrassing crap," Dylan says with a lazy wave of their hand.

"All that normcore stuff," I say. Jack glances up from the phone, and her eyes lock onto mine. Under the table, my knee is still pressed into the indent of hers.

"I'm looking for someone to love me even when I'm being completely insufferable," Andrew grumbles into his now third cup of Rainier. Dylan sits up halfway and stares at Andrew in the poor lighting of this bar. And even though I can't see my own face, I imagine I look like *that*. I look at Jack the way Dylan looks at Andrew.

And I don't think I can do this anymore.

• • •

"We have to tell them."

"Tell them what?" Andrew asks as he leans over the bar to order another pitcher—a Breakside IPA this time, for Jack.

"Tell them *everything!*" I hiss. Over my shoulder, I see Dylan and

Jack in our corner booth looking tense and uncomfortable. "I can't do this anymore. I don't want to be a sex shield. I want to tell Dylan the truth." Never mind the fact that I want to tell Jack the truth, too. That I want to know what came at the end of her sentence.

Do you think if—

"*Why* do you want to tell Dylan?"

"Because you're in love with them!" I say at a volume not quite befitting the secrecy of this conversation. Andrew almost drops an entire pitcher of overpriced IPA. I modulate my whisper. "You're in love with them, and they're in love with you, and this whole thing is starting to feel ridiculous."

"I'm not in love with Dylan," he says calmly.

"Andrew." I put a hand on his arm. "You are, though."

"Dylan wants someone to carry their beets at a farmer's market, and while I'm great at lifting things and looking hot, I don't know the first thing about being in a long-term relationship." Andrew looks sheepish, and I realize how damn tired I am. I'm tired of lying and pretending and not-talking about things. For a year, I pretended like I wasn't hurt when I thought our day together meant nothing to Jack. For a year, I told myself it would be pathetic to hold onto any feelings for her.

But I *was* hurt, and I *do* still have feelings for her, and I can't let Andrew repeat my same idiot mistakes. "Do you want one, though? A long-term relationship?"

He opens his perpetually open mouth a little bit wider in shock, then snaps it closed. "It doesn't matter what I want. I'm not having this conversation with you in a dive bar. We're getting married. You signed a napkin contract."

A bartender with a lip ring and angel wings tattooed on her exposed décolletage raises both eyebrows at us. Andrew lowers his voice. "None of this is about love, Ellie. It's a business arrangement. This is about *the money*. I need that money."

"Why?" I demand. "Why do you need this money so badly? You

drive a Tesla! You wear Tom Ford! Please explain to me why this inheritance is worth ignoring your own desires and deceiving your entire family."

Andrew grabs me by the elbow and bodily yanks me even farther down the bar, farther out of earshot. "I'm doing this *for* my family."

"That doesn't make any sense. Your family is disgustingly rich."

He sets the pitcher down on the corner of the bar, pours himself a glass, and takes a long drink. "I'm doing this for Jack," he confesses finally, his shoulder sagging in relief.

I stare at the stress-V forming between Andrew's sleek eyebrows. "For . . . *Jack*?"

"The money. Jack, she—" He takes another drink and shakes his head. "I should have told you everything from the beginning, but I'm honestly so ashamed of my family. The money . . . my sister . . . the trust . . ."

Andrew fumbles for a second before he finds his verbal footing. "You know how my sister is opening a bakery? Well, she took out this huge business loan to do it, mostly because she believed she had this cushion to fall back on."

"The trust your grandpa left you," I say, remembering the Christmas cookie conversation.

Andrew nods slowly. "Yeah. We were both supposed to inherit one million dollars when he died. . . ."

"But your trust is two million," I correct him, even as the truth becomes so fucking clear. *Of course.* "Your grandpa wrote Jack out of the will and left all the money to you."

"The fucker," Andrew spits. "He used to go on these rants about how Jack would squander her money, used to try to manipulate her into going back to college, but that never worked on Jack. But once he realized she was content working at a bakery, he wrote her completely out of the will. I don't think he told anyone, not even Lovey. I only found out when the executor called to tell me about the new stipulation before submitting the will to probate court."

I catch Andrew staring in the direction of his sister. It's difficult to make her out from this far away in the dark, hazy bar. Just the length of her neck and the outline of her shoulders are visible. She flicks her chin, and I feel a sharp tug in my chest. Her grandfather wrote her out of his will because she didn't live up to his expectations for the family name.

"It takes about four months for the court to settle a will, so no one else in my family will know about the trust until then," Andrew explains, hushed and urgent. "And my sister will never have to know the truth if I can inherit the two million immediately and just give Jack her half."

For the first time since Andrew drunkenly put two hands flat on a table and asked if I would marry him does this whole absurd scheme make sense. "You want to protect your sister from knowing what your grandpa did."

"Yeah." He exhales, his eyes wide and glassy and so fucking full of love. Andrew is willing to marry an absolute stranger, not for himself, but for his sister. He's giving up what he may or may not have with Dylan *for his sister*.

And it dawns on me. How none of this is about me and the two hundred thousand dollars. If I tell Jack the truth—if I act on these feelings, even for a second—I'm costing *her* one million dollars.

I turn back to the lip ring bartender. "Yeah, I'm going to need a Moscow mule, actually."

Chapter Eighteen

New goal for the night: don't kiss Jack again.

I am *crushing* this goal. After my first Moscow mule, when Dylan insists on us playing a round of pool, I do not try to kiss Jack when she shows me how to hold my cue stick like we're in a Carrie Underwood song. When Dylan gets so drunk they go on a rant in Spanish about Phoebe Bridgers and bottom prejudice and skinny jeans (from what I can infer based on my AP Spanish skills), I don't stare at Jack's ass as she leans across the table to line up her shot. Not even for a second.

When Andrew switches to cheap shots of Fireball whisky (his go-to, apparently) and bats his eyes at the bartender so she puts on a Christmas playlist, I do not put my hands on Jack's hips during the conga line that forms for "Rockin' Around the Christmas Tree." I don't lean into her back or press my cheek to the rough fabric of her Carhartt jacket. When Andrew and Dylan get sloppy drunk enough to entertain the entire bar with a rendition of "All I Want for Christmas" sans karaoke machine, I don't watch Jack sway to the music, don't watch her lick beer foam off her lips after every sip, don't watch her flick her chin to get her hair out of her face.

And when Jack shimmies up to the bar for another drink, I tell myself not to follow her. And then I totally do.

"You look like you're having fun!" I shout over the Christmas music. Andrew and Dylan have now pushed aside enough tables to make a dance floor. The owner of the bar seems wholly unfazed by this development as tourists and locals alike fall under the hypnotic spell of Andrew's charm, gathering in the middle of the bar to dance out their holiday cheer.

"I am." Jack smiles at me, her hair sweaty and stuck to her forehead. She leans back against the bar on both elbows, and I don't kiss her. I'm so impressed by my own self-restraint. "I needed this. Tonight," Jack says. "I needed to get away from that house, from all the—" She cuts off mid-thought, and I watch her face, knowing her mind has gone somewhere I can't follow.

Lip ring bartender comes over. "What can I get you?"

Jack comes back into focus and orders another IPA. Against my better judgment, I order another mule. Jack watches me, something distracted in her expression. "Are we ever going to talk about it?" she asks, and I'm struggling to connect the dots amidst the leaps her drunk brain seems to be making.

"Talk about what?"

"The kiss," Jack half slurs, her eyes fuzzy. She's definitely too drunk for this conversation. And I'm too sober for it. "Are we never going to talk about the fact that you kissed me?"

"Well, I think we kissed each other," I argue. "And we only did it because of the mistletoe and your drunk family members."

Jack clicks her tongue against the roof of her mouth. I don't stare at her tongue *or* mouth. "I tried to pull away," Jack corrects me, flicking her chin to get her hair out of her face, but the hair is plastered there with her sweat, so nothing happens. "You held onto me. You kept kissing me."

My heart calcifies inside my chest in humiliation. *She pulled away. I held on.*

"I'm sorry," I say, because I'm not sure what else I can say in this situation. I can't admit that I held on because I regret letting go so easily the last time.

"Why are you marrying him?" Jack practically screams as the bartender deposits our drinks in front of us. Apparently, we've reached the point in the night where we're addressing all trapezoidal elephants.

I take a sip of my mule. "Jack . . ."

"I don't get it." She shakes her head, her expression almost angry. "I *want* to get it. I want to be supportive, but what do the two of you even have in common?"

I recoil back from the drunk woman taking up too much space in front of me. "What, because Andrew is successful and handsome and wealthy, and I'm a mess?"

Jack's hands slip on her sweaty drink. "You know that's not what I meant. Of course he would choose you, Elle. You're—shit, you're so—" She shakes her head. "You're so beautiful. You're even more beautiful than my brother. Which is, I'm realizing now, kind of a weird thing to say." Jack pauses, and once again, I don't fucking kiss her, somehow.

She once again tries to grip her drink and fails, and I can't seem to look away from the whole sloppy mess of her in this moment. "But why are you choosing him?" Jack asks me, her eyes like liquid fire, scorching me through with the intensity of their stare. And then she asks me the question. The worst possible question she could ask me here in this bar. "Do you love him?"

And I know I have to lie. I have no other choice. A million dollars and napkin contracts, and I know I have to say it. I have to tell this woman with the restless heart and the hair stuck to her face that I am in love with her brother.

I open my mouth to say it—*just say it, Ellie.*

Jack looks at me with confusion and accusation and the smallest sliver of hope, I think, right there in the corner of her mouth. It's the hope that gets me. "I . . ." I try.

And then I pivot on the heel of my boots and take off in the direction of the nearest bathroom.

• • •

My attempt to flee the scene is hindered by several factors.

One, that the sticky floors slow me down.

Two, that Jack's legs are longer than mine.

And three, that it's a multi-stall bathroom with a swinging door that I don't think to lock. Jack stomps into the bathroom behind me like she stomps everywhere and stares at me where I've propped myself against the sink. "Do you love him?" she asks me again, the door swinging closed behind her.

"Why do you care?" It's a flimsy defense, but it's the only defense I have at the moment, the only way I can protect myself from telling her the truth.

"Why do I care if you're *actually* in love with my brother, the man you're supposed to be marrying?" She folds her arms across her chest.

I fold my arms, too, mirroring her closed-off stance. "Honestly, our relationship isn't any of your business."

Jack laughs at me and flicks her chin, and I'm not sure if I'm going to kiss her face or punch it. She's so stubborn and self-righteous and *sweaty*. "Just answer the question, Elle. Do you love Andrew or not?"

And I'm tired. I'm so, so *tired*.

"Honesty game," Jack demands.

"No, okay!" I scream at her. "No, I don't love him!"

The bathroom goes silent and airless as soon as these words are out of my mouth. Jack is standing there with her arms folded, her feet planted. I'm absolutely falling apart with my back against the sink. In the distance, we can hear the thump of the bass from Andrew's impromptu dance party. I can barely make out the words to "Last Christmas." That goddamn song.

The truth dangles there between us, and I wish I could reel it back in. "I don't love him," I say again, instead, solidifying the truth until it becomes a tangible thing between us in this bathroom. Jack is motionless across from me, rigid and furious and still, all I want to do is kiss her.

I wait for her to yell at me for marrying someone I don't love. I wait for her to storm out of the bathroom. I wait for her to do *something*.

"Elle," Jack says in a voice so close to a whisper I almost don't hear her over George Michael trying to save himself from tears. And then all the tension leaves Jack's body, like someone cut her strings, like she might collapse onto this bathroom floor like she collapsed in the snow earlier. I want to go to her, hug her, hold her. I want to kiss her so badly, it's like literal thirst, a dry crack in the back of my throat.

Before I can break my vow for the night, Jack straightens. She takes three purposeful strides across the bathroom until she arrives in front of me at the sink. I think she might shake me.

I think I might kiss her.

But I don't, because Jack grabs the sides of my face, and then she's the one who's kissing me.

Chapter Nineteen

This isn't *technically* in violation of the goal for the night.

After all, Jack is the one who is kissing me, and it tastes like fire and hops and hope. Jack is kissing me, a kiss like a question mark. Her mouth is hesitant against mine, and I know I should pull away. That's the rule, that's the bargain I've struck with myself. *No kissing Jack.* For her sake.

Except I'm so tired. Except I'm so lonely. Except here's this woman who makes me feel so damn *full.* The cookie-cutter outline in my chest.

I answer the question on her lips with *yes* and *please* and *more.* I kiss her back because everything in my life is shit but this.

I boost myself up, and I wind my hands into her hair, and I kiss her like I know it's going to hurt later. I kiss her like I don't care. I feel like I'm back in the snow a year ago, tasting her for the first time, learning the press of her mouth and the sureness of her hands and the solidity of her body. It's been a year since we've done this properly, but it feels like we're remembering old choreography. It's muscle memory, the way my arms circle her waist, the way her fingers weave into her hair, the way our chins tilt, the way we arch into each other.

She drops one hand gently to my waist, two fingers on the side of my throat, and she's still kissing me carefully. I open my mouth just enough to press my tongue to that white scar, and Jack makes a soft sound in the back of her throat—because she's secretly so soft. We both are.

My hands search for her softness, for the plush fat of her hip bones beneath her flannel. Suddenly, I don't want *careful*. I want to kiss Jack while I can. Before I lose her again.

I pull her closer to me, until my back digs into the sink, until she's pinning my body in place. I coax her mouth open and run the tip of my tongue along the roof of her mouth the way she likes. She goes boneless in my arms, one hand winding around my braid until she pulls, exposing the side of my throat. She kisses me there, with teeth. With her tongue. There's nothing careful about it.

Jack kisses me into a knot that only she can untangle. She folds her body into mine, and time folds itself in half, until last Christmas feels like it was yesterday, like we're picking things up exactly where we left them. We're not kissing in a disgusting dive bar bathroom. We're outside the Butch Oven, kissing in the snow. We're in an empty bar, kissing in the dark over spiced eggnog. We're in her Airstream, kissing like we have all the time in the world.

She takes off my cardigan at some point. I take off her flannel.

Jack lifts me up and sets me down on the edge of the sink, and then she takes a step back. She *looks* at me. She steps between my open legs and stares and stares and stares. "So pretty," she says, in her Jack-whisper that's still loud enough to hear over the music. And I know this compliment comes at the intersection of too many IPAs and bad bathroom lighting, but I don't care.

I reach up, and I push that sweaty chunk of hair out of her eyes, and I stare back at her. At the beautiful slope of her jaw, at the twist of her swollen mouth, at the subtle glint of hope in her eyes. It's the hope that fucking kills me every time.

How did I manage to mess this all up last year? How do I make sure I don't mess this up again?

I take off my shirt. Arguably a great way to mess this up, but Jack's eyes go even darker. She crowds in closer to me, her hands chart their way from my soft stomach up to the front of my nude bra, and then she's kissing me again. Deep, wild kisses. Kisses that ride the wave of her body as she grinds against me, the seam of my jeans against her hip bone, her mouth on my mouth, my shoulder, my collarbone, the top of my breasts.

"You're so pretty." She breathes these words against my skin, tucks them into all my soft, fragile places. "Thank God you're not marrying him, Elle," she moans. "You can't marry him. I—I don't know what I'll do if you marry him."

I freeze on the edge of the sink.

For a moment, Jack's mouth goes still against my skin. Then she pulls away.

She stares at me again. I'm shirtless, horny, kissed within an inch of my life. Absolutely panicking. "You're . . ." Jack licks her swollen lips. "You're still going to marry him, aren't you?"

"Jack—"

That's all I manage to say before the hope flickers out of her. She blinks, and then she's taking another step back from me, reaching for her flannel on the sticky floor. "I'm sorry," Jack says, without looking at me. "Shit. I'm sorry."

"Jack, I can explain."

"This was a mistake." Jack snatches up my T-shirt and holds it out for me. I take it, drape it across the front of my body like it might protect me from this moment. "We can pretend like this never happened, okay?"

Her voice is hard as flint, her face turned away from me. Physically, she's still here in this bathroom, but emotionally, she's already hidden herself away in her Airstream again, already retreated back behind her aluminum shield.

"No, Jack, listen—"

But there's nothing I can say, and Jack doesn't stay to hear it anyway. She stomps out of the bathroom. I sit perched on the edge of the sink, listening to the sound of her footsteps receding into the distance, melding together with another Christmas song.

It feels terrible to be the one who's left behind.

A Webcomic
By *Oliverartssometimes*
Episode 6: *The L-Word*
(Christmas Eve, 6:57 p.m.)
Uploaded: January 28, 2022

"Honesty game: I feel like I've known you forever."

"Okay, that's not how the honesty game works. You're supposed to say *honesty game*, and then ask a question you want an honest answer to."

"The game has existed for, like, ten hours. And as its creator, I think I'm allowed to bend the rules to my will."

"Then why even have rules?"

"Fine. Then ask me if I feel like I've known you forever."

I sigh. "Honesty game: Do you feel like you've known me forever?"

Jack cranks out a half-moon smile that makes me feel absolutely giddy. "I do. Oh—nachos!"

The owner of the bar drops a mountainous platter of nachos onto the table and gives us a grunt. "What kind of idiots stay out all day in the middle of an unprecedented snowstorm?"

"Us kind of idiots," Jack answers pleasantly as she pulls a nacho from the middle of the stack, a jalapeño falling onto her flannel as she attempts to shove the chip into her mouth.

"Well, the nachos are on the house. I don't want your deaths on my conscience."

We are sitting in a dark corner of a dark bar, knees and calves and elbows all touching. The bar is mostly empty, save for a few regulars who live in the apartments across the street and a group of unhoused people the bartender invited out of the cold. Most places have closed, but we found a bar where the owner lives upstairs and has no reason not to stay open for anyone who needed the heat. Or any idiots who needed dinner.

And we *are* idiots.

We still haven't crossed the bridge that will take us to South-east Portland, the bridge that will take us home. We haven't discussed it, but the bridge feels like this chasm between the people we are today and the people we will be tomorrow, or in a few days when the snow melts, when this weird, magical, time-defying bubble pops.

We claimed starvation was the reason we got off track this time, but I know for me, at least, it was partially fear. Fear of what comes next. Fear of how this ends.

My fear should be about getting home, but the owner is making another batch of spiced eggnog, and Jack is kissing me between bites of nachos in our corner booth, and I can't seem to care. Knees and calves and elbows and hands. Spicy, sweet kisses.

"Honesty game: tell me about every person you've ever loved," Jack whispers into my hair.

I let myself reach out and touch the white scar on her upper lip. "I love my best friend, Meredith."

"And you act like *I'm* a queer cliché."

"No, I mean, I *platonically* love her. I've never loved anyone romantically before." Jack's fingers are still in my hair. "I thought I loved my college girlfriend, but I think I just loved what she taught me about my sexuality and myself. Is that weird? That I've never been in *love* love?"

Jack shrugs. "All types of love are *love* love."

I kiss her scar then.

"We all experience attraction differently," she continues, pressing her mouth to the soft skin behind my ear. "Some of us fall in and out of love easily. Some of us don't experience romantic love at all. Some of us have to fight to let ourselves be vulnerable enough to fall in love." She kisses my throat. "Some of us have to fight to let other people love us."

She kisses my shoulder, a small patch of my skin that had been covered by my blue scarf all day. "Some of us need emotional intimacy in order to experience sexual attraction." She nuzzles me until I laugh from the feeling of her nose against my skin. "All love and ways of loving are love, Elle."

It's just one syllable. One letter. *Elle.*

Yet I somehow feel like tectonic plates are shifting inside me, like my internal organs are experiencing subduction, pushing dormant feelings to the surface.

Because *this*. Jack in a dark bar. A jalapeño on her shirt and spiced eggnog on her tongue. Seeing and being seen. This feels like *love* love.

This feels like something huge and confusing, something too clumsy for me to puzzle through in my brain and in my chest, and it's only been nine hours.

There are rules. Plans to follow. Schedules and structures. You're not supposed to fall in love with a person in a single day, but maybe you can, when it snows.

Maybe on a snow day, you can ignore the nagging voice in the back of your head that says this won't last because nothing lasts, because the people in your life don't stick around. Maybe you can trust. At least, maybe you can trust *her*.

"Honesty game," I say, and my voice shakes a little bit. "I feel like I've known you forever, too."

Chapter Twenty

"I did not realize you were in *that* kind of romantic comedy." Meredith lets out a low whistle from my phone screen.

"Not. Helpful."

"Look, you've now kissed your fiancé's sister *twice*, so I'm not sure what you think is going to help you. There is no eleventh-hour Judy Greer pep talk coming your way."

I hunker down on the washing machine, staring at Meredith in the blue light of the 3 a.m. laundry room hiding spot. "Okay, the first kiss was not my fault. There was mistletoe and drunk grandmas involved. And the second kiss—yes, fine, I take full responsibility for that one."

"I guess you're in one of those morally ambiguous rom coms. Like *My Best Friend's Wedding* or *Four Weddings and a Funeral*."

"Which am I?" I ask, fairly certain I don't want to hear the answer. "Julia Roberts or Andie MacDowell?"

"You're Dermot Mulroney," Meredith answers. "You're the douche marrying Cameron Diaz but still overtly flirting with Julia Roberts. Because Jack thinks you're marrying her brother *for real*, and that she just *kissed her brother's fiancé*."

"But I don't want to be Dermot Mulroney," I whine.

"Tough shit." Apparently Meredith's capacity for empathy does not activate until *after* she's had her coffee. "If you don't want to be Dermot Mulroney, then you need to come clean to Jack about everything."

"I can't! Because of the money!"

Meredith already knows all of this. As soon as the love trapezoid got home from the Mountain Bar (Meemaw and Lovey had to come pick us up, and *yes,* that was the most awkward car ride of my life), I pretended to go to bed, then absconded with my electronic devices to draw until a less-cruel hour to call Meredith. The panels were sloppy, with an unfocused narrative and too much self-indulgence, but I had no intention of posting them, anyway. I hadn't posted any more episodes of *The Arrangement* to Drawn2, not since everything started feeling too personal and too private. But that hasn't stopped the number of views and likes from growing on the early episodes, my subscriptions from quadrupling, and my inbox from overflowing with unread messages. Even the numbers on the old *Snow Day* episodes have increased, new readers flocking to it in droves, and I feel slightly disquieted, knowing that story is a thinly veiled version of my story with Jack. At least, the version of our story I knew back then.

Since it was 5 a.m. Meredith's time, I decided it was an acceptable hour to call a friend in circumstances such as these, and I did. And then I told her everything.

"Look, I advised you to enter this whole marriage scam in the beginning, but that was back when I thought there was a chance for you to fall in love with Andrew, before we found out Jack is his sister. Now the whole thing is just too complicated. As your unofficial lawyer, I've got to suggest you cut your fucking losses."

"It's not that simple. I've made a promise to Andrew, and this isn't my secret to tell. And it's not about me anymore. It's about Jack."

Meredith rubs sleep crust out of her eyes, completely unperturbed. "You're lying to Jack *for* Jack?"

"You don't understand because you've never had to deal with failure"—Meredith scoffs; I politely ignore her—"but Jack is taking a huge risk in opening this bakery. And what are you even suggesting I do, exactly? Confess my love to Jack?"

"Yes," Meredith says, straight-faced. "That is literally exactly what I'm telling you to do."

"I can't! It's ridiculous! You can't be in love with someone you've known for a total of"—I count it out on my fingers, because it's three in the morning, and my brain is now nothing more than a few pulverized brain cells. "Seven days? You can't be in love with someone you've known for what amounts to a single week!"

"Says *who*?" Meredith, who's spent the last seven years studying *the law*, who loves rules and guidelines and meticulous plans almost as much as I do, has clearly lost her mind.

"Says *everyone*. You know who falls in love that fast? Teenagers. Like Romeo and Juliet. And look how that ended up."

"I don't know, they banged at some point, so it wasn't all bad."

"I don't want to end up drinking poison over Jack's not-actually-dead body, Meredith!"

"Interesting that you cast yourself as Romeo in this scenario," she calmly observes. "Are you spiraling right now? You sound like you're spiraling."

"Of course I'm spiraling! I'm in love with a woman I've only known for seven days!"

Because I am.

I shouldn't be.

It isn't logical.

I fell in love with her over the course of a single day, and I never quite fell out of love with her, and here I am, kissing her in bathrooms and screwing up her entire life. "What's wrong with me, Mere?"

Meredith takes a slow, deep breath, probably contemplating the myriad ways to answer that question. *You're a failure* and *you're a bad person* both come to mind.

You're a frozen burrito.

Or, *You have untreated generalized anxiety disorder and should probably be on meds.*

Or, *You let your mom walk all over you.*

What Meredith actually says is, "What if there's nothing wrong with you at all?"

"Seems fake but explain."

Meredith juts out her jaw. "Look. The last year has been absolute shit. You got fired from your dream job, your mom has been particularly leechlike, and you've stagnated. So when this opportunity fell into your lap, I thought, here's a chance for you to make some money, and maybe Andrew can finally help you forget about the girl who broke your heart last Christmas. But what happened instead?"

Meredith pauses meaningfully.

"Do you want me to answer, or—?"

"It turns out the girl who broke your heart last Christmas is his *fucking sister*." Meredith pounds one fist into her closed palm. "What are the *odds*? I mean, I don't know, Ellie. . . . it kind of feels like fate."

"You don't believe in fate."

"I don't believe that we should surrender our agency because we think things are *meant to be*," she clarifies. "But I do believe some people belong in our lives. Do you remember how we met?"

"Duh. Thwarting girl-on-girl crime." Meredith and I were neighbors in the dorms our freshman year. We both had roommates named Ashley who thought they were too cool for us, but we didn't hang out those first few months. We were both too busy studying and working thirty hours a week to bother making friends. Meredith had been dating this absolute tool of a mechanical engineering major named Spencer Yang from high school, and right before winter break, she'd come back to her dorm after a Business Law Society meeting to find her boyfriend and her Ashley in a rather shocking sexual position by our eighteen-year-old standards.

I caught her in the bathroom in the midst of an Aries chaos rage, about to inflict some misguided girl-on-girl crime by pouring bleach into Ashley's shampoo bottle.

Instead, inspired by *Gilmore Girls*, we decided to deviled-egg Spencer's beloved Miata, but we never actually made it past our dorm kitchen. We spent hours drinking Mike's Hard Lemonades and laughing wildly as we attempted—and failed miserably—to make deviled eggs, and Meredith forgot her anger somewhere around the fourteenth consecutive listen to "I Knew You Were Trouble." And that was it.

I saw her at her absolute lowest, her absolute *messiest*, and somehow, she became the one person I could show my messy self to in return.

"You're my platonic soul mate," Meredith says. I stare at my best friend on the phone screen. Awake at five her time to talk me through an anxiety spiral, her wild red hair held in place by a single pencil. She's the bold oil paint to my watercolor timidity, the fire to my water, the Aries to my Pisces. "You're my platonic soul mate, too," I say.

"Maybe Jack is your romantic soul mate. . . ,"

I scoff, but I'm thinking about the Jack-size cookie-cutter inside of me. About the people who've seen my messiest self and loved me anyway.

"The fact that this woman came back into your life after a year . . . I don't know. It feels like magic to me."

"You don't believe in magic, Mere."

"No." Meredith sighs. "But you do. Or, at least, some version of you used to."

I stare down at the panels sketched out in Clip Studio on my iPad. None of this feels like magic.

• • •

"Family Ski Trip: ten hours."

It's plainly written on the schedule, in a size-twelve serif font, black ink, neatly laminated. Christmas Eve *eve* is the day the Kim-Prescotts pile into two cars to drive up the dangerous, snow-covered roads to spend an entire day at the Timberline Lodge ski area. There is truly nothing I would rather do less than this family ski trip.

This core belief is verified when I walk into the kitchen at six in the morning after no sleep and find the entire family is not only awake but *energized*. Meemaw's got her snowboard over her shoulder, Lovey is doing quad stretches, and Dylan and Andrew are poring over a map of the Timberline runs as if everything between them is perfectly normal. The assholes don't even seem hungover. Jack is dressed in her ski clothes, making breakfast sandwiches that she wraps in parchment paper. She refuses to look at me when I enter the room.

Palpable shame rolls up and down my limbs. I *kissed* her. I let *her* kiss *me*. And when she asked me if I was still going to marry her brother, I said *nothing*.

I'm too tired to spend a day at Timberline trying to avoid Jack and my guilt. Plus, I haven't got the faintest idea how to ski. I'm about to tell everyone I'm too sick to go when Jack looks up from behind the stove. "Where's Dad? Am I making him a sandwich?"

Katherine, who is packing up her own gear on the kitchen island, pauses. "Your father isn't joining us today," she says with passable indifference. I wonder if that's where Jack learned it. "He'll be here when we get home. He said he's going to make us meatloaf for dinner."

The house goes silent. And *shit*. I can't bail on today, not when Alan is disappointing Katherine yet again. These traditions mean the whole world to her.

Mom-guilt, of course, is the reason I end up in a borrowed snowsuit, smooshed between the grandmas in the backseat of the Lincoln Navigator, eating my breakfast sandwich. Timberline Lodge is an *actual* ski chalet—a beautiful mountain lodge amidst snowcapped peaks, pretty enough to make you forget it was used in the exterior shots of *The Shining*. For a moment, the sight of the sweeping white landscape makes me forget all my own shit, too.

My own shit comes back to me tenfold when we get out of the car.

"Andrew and I are going to partner up, since we both snowboard," Dylan announces as we all stand in a semicircle in the parking lot. Andrew looks slightly perplexed by this declaration and by Dylan's sudden authority over family ski day. "We're going to take the Magic Mile up and start at Coffel's run. And Katherine, you and the grandmas are probably planning to stick around Molly's, right?"

I have no idea what any of these words mean, but Katherine looks at the grandmas, then nods.

"Cool. Ellie said she's never skied before," Dylan continues, "so someone will need to stay behind and help her get her equipment and learn how to use it. Jack?"

Jack is standing a few feet away, behind Gillian's tailgate. Her skis are vertical and she's leaning against them. "I'm not sure that's a good idea," Jack tries vaguely.

"Why not?" Dylan asks. "You're a skier, and you usually stick around the beginner and intermediate trails, anyway."

Jack frowns, but makes no other defense.

"Okay, everyone!" Katherine calls out, and Meemaw abandons me to rejoin the family. "We're meeting at the Blue Ox Bar at noon for lunch. The forecast says it's going to start snowing this afternoon. It shouldn't pick up until this evening, but we're leaving by four at the absolute latest to avoid bad road conditions."

Andrew and Dylan grab their snowboards and head toward one of the ski lifts. Katherine and the grandmas all walk in the opposite direction. And Jack and I are left alone with our awkward silence and avoidant glances, and—"Are you going to push me off the mountain?"

Jack finally looks at me. There are purple bags under her eyes, and her mouth is a thin, pale line in her face. "I'm considering it."

"I suppose I would deserve it. Jack, look, can we—"

"I was really drunk last night," she says quickly. She's not looking at me again. "We both were."

I wasn't, but this doesn't seem worth pointing out.

"We made a huge mistake, but it's not like it will ever happen again."

"Um, right. Of course."

Jack turns away from me, so I'm staring at her solemn face in profile. "In the future, it's probably best if we . . ." She adjusts her beanie. "If we don't spend a lot of time together. Like, any time together."

I inhale sharply through my nose and tell myself it's the cold, not tears, stinging my eyes. "Uh-huh."

"But for now, we've just got to get through today. So let's just get your skis."

Jack pivots in the snow, and I have no choice but to follow her quietly and miserably on the path up to the lodge. At the rental shop, a conventionally attractive man with an inexplicable tan for the middle of Pacific Northwest December measures my foot (huge), then the length of my leg (long), and then straps me into a pair of boots and some skinny death sticks.

"I can't do this," I tell the Tan Man in a wobbly voice.

"Sure you can," Jack answers, sounding bored.

"I *really* can't do this," I repeat when the Tan Man asks me to stand up on my skis to test the fit.

"I have total faith in you," Jack monotones, like an apathetic life coach. Neither Jack nor the Tan Man respects my protests, and soon, Jack is handing over Katherine's credit card and I'm standing outside in the snow on *skis*. Jack tells me to move so that we're not blocking the main path.

If by "move" she means wobble and flail my arms like a cartoon character slipping on a banana peel, then I succeed beautifully in meeting her demands. Before I go crashing down into the snow, Jack's free arm reaches out to steady me. I don't realize just how close she is until her arm is secured around my waist, strong and warm.

"This is dangerous," I tell her. By "this," I mean skiing. Obviously skiing.

Jack immediately releases her hold around my waist. "Skiing is perfectly safe."

"It is absolutely *not* safe," I counter, shaking the metal poles with the pokey ends. "I think you want me to impale myself."

Jack shrugs. "If you impale yourself, it will solve some of my problems, but it will also create several new ones, and ultimately, I don't think it would be worth the hassle."

"People *die* while skiing all the time," I insist. "Natasha Richardson died while skiing! Why would anyone want to partake in the activity that robbed the world of Natasha Richardson?"

I'm anxiety spiraling a bit, and it probably has nothing to do with either skiing or Natasha Richardson, and probably more to do with twenty minutes ago, when Jack said we should stop spending time together. Or twelve hours ago, when she kissed me within an inch of my life.

She impatiently shoves her fists into her coat pockets. "I promise you won't die while skiing today."

"You can't promise that."

"Well, I don't think you're going to tackle any advanced runs on your first skiing excursion, so yeah, I kind of can. Plus, you've got this super-cute helmet." She knocks on my giant black helmet three times.

"What if I fall over?"

"You will. Probably lots of times. And I will honestly probably enjoy watching it." The tiniest hint of a smile curls in the corner of Jack's mouth. I think I'm going to fall over right now.

"Everyone falls their first time," she says. "Hell, I'll fall at least once today, and I've been skiing my whole life."

"Why would anyone want to do something you're guaranteed to fail at it?"

"I said fall, not fail. It is literally impossible to fail at skiing."

"Unless you die," I say.

"Unless you don't *try*."

"Wow. Always a living, breathing motivational poster."

Her smile widens, only for a second, before she remembers she's furious with me and tamps it down. Then, she sighs, clearly distressed by the sight of me holding onto these ski poles. "I'm going to have to actually help you, aren't I?"

I do another arm-windmill, banana-peel, double-axis thing on my skis.

"I hate you right now," she says, but then she's at my side, showing me what to do, one hand on my lower back. "Like this. And then you'll push like this."

Everything is feeling dangerous again.

"I'm expected to move my legs and arms *at the same time*?"

Jack laughs her terrible, adorable, involuntary laugh. "Yes, it's a full-body experience."

I adjust my goggles over my glasses. "Okay. What now? Do we go to the chairlift?"

"No. You gotta crawl before you can walk."

I do not expect her to mean this quite so literally, but I do, in fact, spend a considerable amount of time crawling in my skis over the course of the next two hours. Jack leads us to a clearing with a small hill where children are all learning how to move in their skis for the first time. Children and *me*.

Jack is, infuriatingly, an incredible teacher, even if she does hate me right now. Even if after today, we have to stop spending time together. She takes a solid thirty minutes just to help me move my skis and the poles at the same time, then another hour teaching me how to stop, how to turn, how to fall gracefully when falling is the only option. When we're ready for actual skiing, we still don't make our way to a chairlift, but to a leisurely trail with a steady decline called the West Leg Road.

Leisurely or not, I still find myself mildly horrified as we stand on the edge of a small downward slope. Sure, there are preteens here, eagerly taking off on their snowboards. Parents are helping their toddlers. And then there's me, twenty-five and terrified, because I'm just supposed to trust gravity?

I might fly. I might fall. And I have no idea how to protect myself from failing, from having my heart splattered everywhere. Or my body splattered against the trunk of a tree. Beside the trailhead is a sign that reads, "Always Be in Control."

"I can't do this."

"There's only one way down," she says. Surely that isn't true. There must be a secret way off the mountain, an escape hatch for cowards. I can just take my skis and hightail it back to the car. "And honestly, this is more . . . *across* than down. We've got this," Jack insists.

We. For at least one more day, we're a *we.* "And I'll be beside you the whole time, whether I want to be or not."

I take a deep breath. Fly or fall.

"Should we go on the count of three? One . . . two . . ."

I push off on my poles at *two*, and let momentum pull me forward as my skis tilt onto the modest slope. And I'm flying, albeit at a rather leisurely speed. I barely have to move my legs—the mountain moves me, and wind and cold carry me as I glide along past everything. Past trees, past children, past Jack, even. The world somehow blurs and becomes more sharply focused at the same time, and this is new.

This is *everything.* I hunch lower, using my poles to move faster, to let my body exist in this new way. It protests slightly, unaccustomed to actual movement, but even as my muscles ache, my body also *sings.* I've been frozen for so long, and I feel like I'm climbing out of my icy confinements to rediscover the world isn't as terrible as I remembered.

I turn my head to the left and see Jack there, where she said she'd be, right beside me. Looking at me, too. And I wonder how much longer I have to look at her.

It's while I'm looking at her that I miss a small mound of densely packed snow. I hit it just right, and my right ski flies up and my left ski flies sideways, and if I am not mistaken, I think I do the splits midair before I fall firmly on my ass and roll several times before I come to a stop in the middle of the trail.

"Fuck, fuck, fuck!" I hear Jack shout as she comes to a controlled stop beside me. She drops to her knees and rips her goggles off. "Are you okay? Elle, say something!"

I explode with laughter.

"*Shit.*" Jack shifts her weight so she's no longer leaning over me like she's about to administer CPR. "I thought you snapped your spinal cord or something."

"I thought you said you were going to enjoy watching me fall?"

"Oh, fuck you." But she's smiling. And I'm smiling. I just skied for the first time. "Can you get up?"

I nod, but my sore ass begs to differ. Jack reaches out to grab my hand. In one effortless maneuver, she hoists me off the ground. It's not at all sexy. The laughter doesn't get caught in my throat or at this display of strength.

"Want to keep going?" she asks.

I absolutely do. If this is the last day I get to spend with Jack, I want to spend it flying down a mountain beside her.

Chapter Twenty-One

It begins to snow a little before noon, and it's almost time to break for lunch when we finally make it to where the West Leg Road intersects with the Stormin' Norman chairlift that will take us further up the mountain. Jack insists there are spectacular views and a beginners' run we can take all the way back to the lodge. Except there's no way for us to make it back to the lodge by lunchtime. Jack sends a text in the family group chat to let them know to start eating without us. Timberline, thankfully, has good service.

"That cannot possibly be safe," I say when I see the bench we're going to ride up the mountain on.

"I assure you it is."

Even though the chairlift is large enough for three, we sit pressed together, shoulders and thighs touching through our enormous layers. The world seems impossibly large from up here, a craggy ridge covered in snow in front of us, endless stretches of white all around us. Snowcapped trees and expansiveness and this undeniable feeling of *magic*. Of something so beyond the ordinary, the kind of beautiful, magical world I used to want to create with my art, back when I was a lonely kid escaping my life through the drawings in a sketchbook.

I think about Meredith, reminding me I once believed in magic. I think about the woman tucked against my side. "Jack," I say, and she turns to face me. We're inches apart, close enough that I can count the pale snowflakes as they land against her dark freckles.

We're close enough that I can taste the breakfast sandwich on her breath, close enough that I'm thinking about our bathroom kiss, the memory so fresh I lick my lips, hoping to taste her there.

"What?" she asks, just as the chairlift comes to a grinding halt, and we both jerk forward. We're not too far from the top now, but we've come to a complete standstill.

"Someone must have fallen when getting on," Jack says absently. "It happens all the time."

I turn to face her. We're stuck. On a chairlift. There are a thousand unspoken things hovering between us, and now we have a quiet, uninterrupted moment to say them before Jack starts ignoring me completely.

"Jack," I try again.

"It's Andrew," Jack interrupts.

"I know you're feeling guilty about—"

"No." She points to a man in bright yellow snow pants standing about thirty feet away, where the chairlift terminates at the top. It's obviously Andrew—those are very distinct pants, and he looks impossibly attractive even from a great distance.

He's supposed to be at lunch with the family, but of course he's here instead. Even now, during our epic stuck-on-a-chairlift moment, the specter of Andrew is haunting us.

Andrew is the reason I'm with the Kim-Prescotts in the first place. Andrew is the reason Jack is going to be able to accomplish her dream. He's the reason I will be able to salvage my wreck of a life using two hundred thousand dollars.

There is no *snow* magic. Just Andrew magic.

Jack and I both watch as, up ahead, a shorter figure in head-to-toe black (Dylan, clearly) glides up close to Andrew on a snowboard. They stand side by side for a moment, hesitating before starting their run down the trail parallel to the chairlift. Andrew leans in closer to Dylan. The snow is starting to pick up, distorting everything in a muted white film, so at first, it's difficult to see what

Andrew and Dylan are doing. It is, ironically, a bit like trying to see a shape in a Rorschach test, and Jack and I clearly realize at the exact same moment what's happening, because she sucks in a sharp breath at the same time I snort.

Dylan and Andrew are kissing in the snow. Andrew is bent down, cupping Dylan's face, and Dylan is arching up into him, curling around his body like a cat.

My first thought is: *good for them.*

But my second thought is: *shit.*

"Please tell me I just hallucinated my brother kissing my best friend?"

The extent of my contribution is an unhelpful "Mmmm."

"Elle," Jack gasps my name, then grabs onto my leg. "Are you—? Shit. That just happened. Are you okay?"

Jack stumbles and sputters, because as far as she knows, I just witnessed my fiancé kissing someone else. I turn back, but Andrew and Dylan are gone, blending into the blurs of people who are now sailing past us down below. "Elle," Jack says again. "I'm kind of freaking out right now, but you don't seem very surprised by this turn of events. Did you . . . did you know Dylan and Andrew were hooking up?"

I shake my head. "No, but I . . . I knew they used to, um . . . date."

Jack's fingers dig deeper into my leg through the layers of my snowsuit. "They *what*? My brother? And *Dylan*?"

"Um . . ."

"I know you said your relationship with Andrew is none of my business, but *what the actual fuck*?" Jack demands loudly on a stalled chairlift on top of a mountain.

Tell her the truth shouts a voice in my head. It's Meredith's voice. It's my voice. Tell *her*. Just tell her everything.

But then the chairlift jerks forward, and we both fall sideways as we finish our short ride to the top. And I would tell her the truth

at the top, but a sign has been posted at the terminus for Stormin'
Norman. The snow is coming in earlier and faster than expected,
and visibility has diminished to the point that they're shutting down
most of the chairlifts early. A seasoned skier tells us the roads are
expected to worsen quickly and warns us to get back to the parking
lot.

"I should call my mom," Jack says, all thoughts of Andrew set
aside for a moment.

"I've been trying to call you," Katherine's voice screeches loud
enough for me to hear when the call connects. Jack listens to what
she says next, nods along, a crease appearing between her eyebrows.

"Okay, yeah . . . of course. We'll get back as fast as we can. No,
we saw Andrew and Dylan . . . you talked to them? Good. If they
make it back to the parking lot before we do, feel free to leave without us. No, Mom, it's fine. Don't wait for us. We have the truck. . . .
Don't worry about us. I can drive in the snow. . . . Yeah . . . I will. . . .
Love you, too."

By the time Jack hangs up the phone, my face is as pinched as
hers. "Is Katherine freaking out?"

"Mildly, yes." Jack eyes me, and I know she's thinking about my
fiancé kissing someone else, but she asks, "Are *you* freaking out?"

"Mildly, yes."

"Then let's go."

It turns out, there is no fast way back to the parking lot, but we
get on the lodge getback trail and push forward with our poles as
ferociously as we can. I still have the same feeling of flying, but it's
tainted by the fact that I can barely see two feet in front of me in the
dense snow. I stare at the back of Jack's green jacket and follow her
movements as precisely as I can.

I'm not sure how long it takes us to get back to the lodge—I
lose track of time as I shut down my brain and go into panicked
autopilot—but when we arrive, it's obvious most people have cleared
out already. The Lincoln is gone, which hopefully means the rest of

the Kim-Prescotts made it out before the weather got too bad. Jack shoots off a quick text while we're still in range of Timberline's cell service to let the family know we're safe and heading home.

Everything feels frantic and dire as I race to return my equipment, then meet Jack back at the truck. There's a small buildup of snow behind Gillian's rear tires, but thankfully, Jack once learned this lesson the hard way, and she now carries emergency winter supplies in the back of the truck. She pulls out a shovel and clears enough of a path for us to get out of the parking lot.

Just in the time it takes her to dig us out, the snow has started coming harder and faster. The road back to the highway is slick, but Timberline was busy, and enough cars have driven the road that we're able to make it back to the highway safely.

The highway itself is a different story entirely; cars plod along at fifteen miles per hour, and Gillian's windshield wipers aren't quite up to the task of clearing snow fast enough for Jack to actually see. She cranks down the driver's-side window and sticks her head out every few seconds just to make sure we're not about to plunge off the side of the road. It's doing wonders for my anxiety.

"We'll be okay," she takes pains to reassure me every few seconds. "We are totally okay."

And she's right. We are okay, until we make it to the turn-off for the cabin, and Gillian immediately gets stuck in a bank of snow. The tires spin out until the back of the truck pitches, and Jack hits the brakes. "We'll be okay," she says quickly. "Just hang on. I can dig us out. Stay here."

She leaps out of the car, and while I wait for her to return, I attempt to warm my hands on the one heater vent that works. When she climbs back in ten minutes later, her face is flushed and distinctly unhappy. "Did it work?"

"Uh," she says, half nodding, half scowling, leaving me wholly unconvinced we're ever going to move again. She pulls off her gloves and grips the wheel. She coaxes the car from first to second, and

Gillian seesaws in the snow, gaining ground and slipping back. The road up to the cabin is steep, and despite the grueling effort Jack makes to gain ground, we end up back where we started. Jack's right hand massages the gearshift back down into first, the tendons straining against her skin. I have to give it to the Kim-Prescott siblings. They both have the unnatural talent of turning driving into something mildly obscene.

She clears her throat, flexing the muscles in her jaw. (Also obscene.) "I don't want to alarm you, but—"

"We're going to die."

"Probably not."

"*Probably?*"

"It's unlikely this is how we go. But I don't think we can drive the rest of the way home."

"I mean, we're stuck in snow and visibility is negative ten thousand, so I sort of guessed that. How far are we from the cabin?"

"Um. Maybe three miles or so?"

"Three miles! This is *absolutely* how we go!" It's already getting dark, and with the blizzard-like conditions, we'll end up lost in the woods.

But (my anxiety screams at me) we can't just stay in the truck, either—not with her feeble heat, for as long as it lasts until we run out of gas. "God, I knew this was going to happen!"

Jack shoots me a look that somehow manages to be condescending despite our impending deaths. "You knew we were going to get stuck in the snow on the way home from skiing?"

"I know you and I do not have a good track record when it comes to snow."

In profile, I see the half-moon tug at the corner of her mouth. "Fine. Here's what we're going to do. Our friends the Singhs have a cabin about a half mile up the road," she says, taking control of the situation just like she did the last time we got stuck in the snow. She leads, just assuming I'll follow. "I think we can make it there.

Hopefully they'll be home, since they usually come for the holidays. I don't think my dad can drive down the hill in these conditions, so we'll have to stay with the Singhs until things clear, and we can come back for Gillian in the morning. Does that sound like a plan?"

"Yes," I say, teeth chattering. Because I would follow her anywhere.

Chapter Twenty-Two

"Now that is what a cabin is supposed to look like."

The building becomes visible through the heavy snow and muted colors of encroaching dusk. According to Jack, the Singhs are an older couple, both anesthesiologists at OHSU, who usually spend their holidays reading mystery novels together while watching the snow come down in a cozy cabin. As their only neighbors, the Kim-Prescotts have invited them up to the cabin for Christmas Eve dinner almost every year, so they know each other in the way people with proximal vacation homes always do, apparently.

The Singhs' cabin is a small, square wood house hunkered low in the snow. There's a stone chimney, a skinny wraparound porch, and absolute darkness. Not a single window is lit. It's obvious no one is home.

The thought sends stinging tears to my eyes. Every part of my body aches from skiing and falling and walking a half mile in the snow. The wet has infiltrated my socks and the cold has lodged itself deep in my bones. All I want is to sit down, peel off these clothes, and wrap myself in a million warm blankets. But our hoped-for shelter is clearly empty, and if we can't stay here for the night, I am definitely going to have a full-on breakdown in front of Jack.

She trudges ahead and knocks on the front door. No answer. I'm shivering a few steps behind her from the freezing night and my attempts not to cry. "They're not home."

Jack walks down the porch and peers through the darkened

windows. "Jack," I croak, teeth chattering. "They're not here. What are we going to do?"

Jack looks through another window in vain. Then, without any warning, she promptly removes the screen on said window.

"What—?" I start, but it becomes clear what she's doing as soon as she begins pushing up the window from the outside.

"These old cabins usually don't have locking windows," she tells me as she slides it up enough for her long, lean body to fit through.

"We're breaking and entering?"

"Do you have a better idea?"

I do not. "I mean, *not* getting arrested seems preferable."

"No one is going to arrest us. There's no one around." She grabs the top of the window and slides one leg inside. "Besides, the Singhs are good friends. They'll understand."

I can't argue with that kind of logic, and quite frankly, I don't want to. Jack glides her body through the dark window. This is followed by a loud banging sound from inside the house, which is followed by Jack's unabashed cursing. An involuntary smile works its way across my face, but I tame it into submission before Jack opens the front door. She's turned on every light, so the cabin now shines like a beacon. She's bathed in dramatic gold, like a fucking Greek god.

"You coming inside?" she asks with an arrogant cock of her hip. "Or are you planning to sleep in the snow?"

I briefly take stock of what's happening: Jack and I are alone; Jack and I have found an empty cabin in the middle of the woods; *Jack and I are going to spend the night here together.*

So much for not spending time together anymore.

Still, relief washes over me as I step into the cabin. The relief is short-lived.

"Shit tits! It's fucking freezing in here!"

"Yeah, they clearly haven't been here in a while and didn't leave the heat on," Jack says, making her way toward a thermostat. "Also, *shit tits*?"

"I was emotionally traumatized by the fact that it's somehow colder inside than outside, and I cannot be held responsible for what came out of my mouth in that moment."

Jack smirks as she adjusts the thermostat. The cabin is filled with the hiss and whine of a heater coming to life, and we both look around the room until our eyes simultaneously land on the world's smallest and oldest radiator. We won't be warm anytime soon.

Before I say anything else to humiliate myself, I decide to take quiet stock of our current predicament. The place is so small, I can take everything in at once. It's a one-room cabin, perfectly preserved from the seventies. Wood paneling and shag carpet dominate the overall aesthetic. There's a small kitchen with outdated appliances, wooden cupboards smooth from years of handling, and a rickety little table tucked beneath a window. The living room is an anachronistic time capsule, with a record player built inside a giant hutch. I spot a patchwork rug, a bookshelf full of Dean Koontz novels, and a love seat straight out of a grandmother's sitting room. The only bright spot is a large woodburning stove.

Against the far wall is a bed. Just one. With a thin quilt thrown over the top.

Apparently, the Singhs get off on some kind of *Little House on the Prairie* kink play that's generally fucked us over.

"Maybe we can shower to get warm while we wait for the radiator to heat up," Jack suggests with the faintest hint of panic in her voice.

She marches swiftly to the kitchen sink and turns it on. There's a hollow *thunk* from deep inside the wall, but no water is produced by this act. "Except they shut off the water," Jack grumbles. "I guess they weren't planning to come to the cabin this winter."

I don't say anything in response to this horrible realization. I am busy shaking from the cold while staring at the *one bed*.

"Okay." Jack pivots, still firmly in problem-solving mode. "I'll call them and see how to turn the water back on."

She fishes her phone out from the depths of her snow pants, and her face falls as soon as she stares at the screen. "No service, but I'm sure there's Wi-Fi."

There is not Wi-Fi, but there is an old rotary phone half hidden by a stack of *National Geographic* magazines from the nineties. We call Katherine, who spends a good five minutes weeping about our imminent deaths before Jack reassures her we're fine and safe and asks for the Singhs' phone number.

The Singhs, of course, don't answer.

"Katherine is right," I say. "Death does seem like the only natural conclusion to this night."

Jack's shoulders deflate, and she drops her head into her hands. It's clear she's run out of ways to try to spin this. It's freezing, we're starving, we have very little heat and no water and (what is somehow the least of our worries) *only one fucking bed*. Even the unflappable can be flapped in circumstances like this.

Jack's falling apart, but for some reason, I feel a sudden rush of calm. I take a steadying breath. This is not the worst thing that has ever happened to me. It's not even the worst thing that has happened to me this week. We can figure this out. "There's a fireplace," I say sagely, "and that means there must be firewood."

Which is how we find ourselves, five minutes later, standing a few feet from the back porch. Me holding up the flashlight on my phone, Jack holding an axe, a wedge of wood propped in front of us. There is a pile of wood against the side of the house, covered with a tarp. They're all big, hulking pieces, none of the small stuff we're 80 percent positive you need for starting a fire, though neither of us knows for sure.

"How have you never chopped wood before?" I ask her as she grips the axe with an uncharacteristic lack of confidence.

"When would I have chopped wood before?" she practically shouts. Her panic hasn't faded yet, despite my genius plan to start a fire. "I had a very privileged upbringing!"

"But you wear so much flannel."

"Everyone wears flannel! It's Portland!"

"And the Carhartt jacket."

"What is your issue with my jacket?"

"And I've heard you talk about building a chicken coop."

"With a *table saw*." She brandishes the axe in my direction. "And why am I the one who has to chop the wood?"

"Because *you* are the butch lesbian."

She glares. "That's all I am to you, isn't it? A butch lesbian stereotype."

"No, you're very complex and multifaceted, but your arm muscles are objectively bigger than mine, so you're just going to have to do the stereotypical thing here."

"Okay. Okay," she mutters, psyching herself up. She sets down the axe for a minute and peels off her bulky ski jacket so she has better range of motion. This reveals the stereotypical flannel she has on underneath. "Oh, fuck you," she says before I can comment. Then she raises the axe above her head.

"Wait!" I call out. "Your hands! I think you should space them out, like on a baseball bat. I've seen that before."

Jack repositions her hands on the axe handle, then raises her arms again. I take a step back and watch the forceful arc of the axe as it collides with the chunk of wood.

And *oh. Oh my goodness.*

My free hand clutches at my throat. The whole lumbersexual thing suddenly makes perfect sense because *good lord.* Watching Jack chop that piece of wood in half is the single most arousing thing my demisexual brain has ever witnessed. Even though her muscles aren't visible through her flannel, I can somehow sense the way they ripple, the tendons in her neck straining, her hands flexing against the handle of the axe. Some primal instinct in me says, *This one could build you shelter.*

I press my legs tightly together and clear my throat. "That was . . . good."

She rolls her shoulders, and I stifle a whimper. This night will *definitely* end with my death.

She kicks aside the two newly cut pieces of wood and grabs another from the stack. I tell myself not to watch, but of course I do. She moves with such purpose and determination as she lines up the wood and raises the axe. I'm not sure if I want her, or if I want to *be* her, and I think it might be a little bit of both as she slices through another log.

The axe clatters to the ground as the two halves split, and Jack grabs her shoulder and winces.

"Are you okay? What's wrong?"

"Nothing." She clenches her teeth. "I have an old shoulder injury from kneading dough that flares up sometimes."

I cannot abide that sentence. "From kneading dough?"

"Fuck. You."

"I'm sorry, but you have some kind of baker's tendonitis."

"You're the absolute worst human," she seethes. "Why am I always getting snowed in places with you?"

I'm not sure how genuine this hatred is (I would guess at least 50 percent, given our present circumstances), but I smile at her anyway. "Here." I hand her the cell phone and pick up the axe. There's a meager amount of porch light reaching us, and she immediately points the phone down at where the axe is loosely gripped in my hand. Jack puts another piece of wood on the chopping block, and I choke up on the handle.

The axe is heavier than I expect, and it feels unwieldy in my hands. I'm that much more impressed by the way Jack mastered this in one try. I lift the axe over my head the way she did, or attempt to, but the weight is too much for me, and I teeter off-balance. Jack's steady hand appears on my waist, securing me in place.

"Widen your stance," she orders, but she says it gently, carefully, the way she did when she was teaching me to ski. Her hand is still resting just above my hip bone. I move one foot forward and redistribute my body weight as I lean over the chopping block. "Now raise the axe again."

Her hand is *still* on my waist, like she's forgotten the part where I kissed her in a bathroom and plan to marry her brother. She's close enough that I can smell the sharp tang of her sweat and beneath that, always, *always*, the warmth of freshly baked bread on her skin. "You should move back," I say. "I don't want to hurt you."

"You won't," Jack says, her voice confident and calm, like we're trading off who gets to be the neurotic mess and who gets to be the stabilizing force.

"I might. I've never swung an axe before. I'll probably fuck it up."

"You won't," she says again. Her hand is there, grounding me, and when I lift the axe, it almost feels like we're lifting it together. I close my eyes, terrified I'm going kill us both.

"Open your eyes, Elle," Jack whispers. Her voice is warm on my cheek. I open my eyes, and she keeps one strong hand on my waist as I let the momentum of the axe carry me through. It collides with the wood and splits it, but not in half. My aim wasn't great, and it catches the side, splintering off a small piece. Still, it's wildly satisfying to know I did that. My right shoulder does hurt, but it's the good kind of hurt. The straining of a muscle I haven't used in a while.

"This will make perfect kindling," she says, like I chopped the wood all wonky on purpose. She kicks aside the small piece and leaves the rest on the block, and she does all of this without ever letting go of me.

"Ready to try again?"

Snow Day

A Webcomic
By *Oliverartssometimes*
Episode 9: *The Airstream*
(Christmas Day, 1:12 a.m.)
Uploaded: February 18, 2022

Her hands never leave my body somehow. Not when she drives us both back into the cabinets in the Airstream kitchen, and they rattle discordantly at my back. Not when she hoists me up on to the countertop, my leggings sweeping up that small trail of flour. Not when her mouth makes a mess of me, as she smiles crookedly into sloppy kisses. Not when my hands make a mess of her.

I run my fingers through her hair, up the back of her shirt, down along the seams of her jeans, searching for skin and sweetness and maybe the source of that freshly baked bread smell.

But her hands never leave my waist, holding me in place. Holding me here with her.

I untwist my knotted scarf and let it fall onto the kitchen counter beside me, because I want nothing more than this woman's lips on my neck, her mouth on my earlobe, her tongue on every inch of my skin. Jack understands the secret code of my blue scarf removal, and she dips her head to kiss the hinge of my jaw, the curve of my ear. Hot breath and careful touches and her hands, never once leaving my body.

I've never felt this way before. Cared for. Cherished. Her kisses are some magic combination of tender and feral, making me feel both deliciously heedless and, somehow, impossibly secure.

Like she might push me off a cliff, but she's going to hold my hand the entire time. Like I can trust her, no matter what. It's safe to feel this way, my brain tells my body. So my body *feels*.

"We don't have to do this," she says as she traces the tip of her nose down the length of my throat, causing a cascade of shivers to waterfall through my body.

"I know," I say, shivering, shivering.

"We don't have to do *anything* you're not comfortable with."

"That's . . . um, nice," I manage as her kisses turn wet, as her mouth finds new places to land—my clavicle, where she wanted to put a tattoo; the top of my rib cage; the peekaboo of my breasts in my oversize T-shirt.

"Seriously," Jack insists. Hands never leaving my waist. An anchor. A life vest. "The waiting is hot."

"Uh-huh."

"And—" Her fingers squeeze into the soft flesh of my waist, and for some reason, I don't feel self-conscious about it the way I have with other people, having them hold onto a part of my body I'm still learning to love. *Trust,* my brain says. *Trust,* my body echoes. *Let go.*

"And"—Jack tries again, mouth and tongue and teeth—"I want you to want it like I want it, and if you're not there yet, or if you need more time, or if you just want to—"

"Jack." She looks up, and I press my forehead to her forehead, my nose to her nose. "I want it."

She swallows. "But . . . it's only been a day."

My fingers find the sides of her beautiful neck. "I thought we'd decided it's been forever."

She finally drops her hands from my waist. Jack turns her body, and I watch the twist of muscles in her stomach, in her neck, as she reaches across the counter and traces a finger along the trackpad of a laptop. She cues up her Spotify playlist and presses play and comically shatters the magic of this moment with—"'Call me Maybe'? Really? This song isn't sexy *at all*."

Jack swivels back to face me, smile curling in the corner of her kiss-swollen mouth. "Who says I'm trying to be sexy?"

And then her hands are back on me.

Chapter Twenty-Three

As it turns out, starting the fire is its own obstacle.

It takes more tries than I expect to get our freshly cut logs to catch fire inside the woodburning stove, especially since we're fairly certain there are different methods for arranging the logs, but we haven't the faintest idea what they are. We curse our mothers and their respective reasons for keeping us out of Girl Scouts.

My mom: lack of money, lack of interest, lack of sobriety.

Her mom: a busy schedule of piano lessons, swim practices, ballet recitals.

"*Ballet recitals?*" I gasp.

Jack gives me this bemused look, half-concealed as she bends forward to stoke the fire. "I was fucking incredible at ballet."

After thirty minutes of blowing on measly flames and praying for the bigger logs to fucking burn already, they finally do, and we both sit on the rug, close to our hard-earned fire, four hands outstretched as we try to thaw them.

And then, our mutual goal of starting a fire achieved, we seem to simultaneously remember all the rest: the bathroom kiss, and me marrying her brother, and Andrew kissing Dylan, and her hating me, maybe for real.

It's six o'clock in the evening, and we're trapped in this ramshackle little cabin together for at least the next twelve hours, and oh my God, what the hell should I say?

Thankfully, Jack starts saying things first. "We should, uh—"

Jack looks nervous. Jack *never* looks nervous. "We should get out of our wet clothes."

I want to find a way to turn that statement into a joke, but my mouth has gone as completely dry as my clothes are not.

Jack climbs off the rug and goes to the antique dresser beside the one bed. It turns out the Singhs both went to Cornell and enjoy advertising the fact on their T-shirts and sweatshirts and sweatpants. It also turns out they're both significantly smaller than we are, but we don't have any other options. Our clothes will never dry on our bodies, and my teeth have been chattering for so long, my jaw hurts.

Jack hands me a pile of clothes, and then we both stand there, staring at each other uncertainly. Without agreeing to, we slowly turn our backs like cowboys in a duel. Which is ridiculous. We've seen each other naked before.

Though perhaps seeing each other naked now might complicate things.

I can hear the shifting of wet flannel, and I imagine her removing her shirt to reveal the inky sketches of tattoos all down her arms.

But I have no right to be imagining that, so I promptly stop and get changed. It's a slow process to take off my jacket and my snowsuit and my long johns, all the way down to my bra and underwear. I slide off my bra but leave the underwear on. Mrs. Singh's sweatpants cut me halfway across the calves and the sweatshirt has a distinct crop-top vibe, but there's a pair of wool socks to keep my feet warm, and I already feel a thousand times better.

Jack waits until I say, "Ready," before turning around. She looks equally hilarious, at least, in her cropped gray sweats and her midriff-bearing sweatshirt. Jack's eyes slip down my body and get noticeably stuck around my cleavage, which is on display in these too-tight clothes.

I am not blessed with the kind of figure that enables me to go casually braless, as I learned from watching my busty mother go tits-wild in her Cleveland Browns jersey at all of my middle school sleepovers. "Sorry, but my bra was wet," I grumble.

"Yeah, of course." Jack's voice is husky, and she clears her throat. "Cool."

Cool. Nothing about this turn of events is cool. We've reverted back to standing awkwardly in front of each other. I'm trying not to stare at that patch of stomach revealed above the low-slung waist-band of her borrowed gray sweatpants.

I am doing an unbelievably bad job at trying not to stare at that patch of stomach.

"Are you hungry?" Jack asks, pulling my eyes back up to her mouth. In truth, that's not much better. I can't stop thinking about all the places that mouth has been on my body.

It's only another ten feet from the "bedroom" to the "kitchen," and the refrigerator is predictably empty. The cupboards are a different story, stocked full of dry goods, and we pull down any food we find to take inventory of our options. Without running water, we make do with a can of chicken noodle soup, a packet of saltines, and some semi-stale Fig Newtons for dessert. "I would expect more refined palates from Cornell graduates."

"I think they just have different priorities," Jack says as she pulls down a brown bottle from a high cupboard. "Do you know what this is?"

"Alcohol?" I venture.

"*Expensive* alcohol." The bottle is covered in a thin layer of dust, which she rubs against the stomach of her sweatshirt. "This is a twenty-five-year-old Macallan scotch whisky. Three hundred dollars a bottle."

I nod absentmindedly as I take out a pan from a bottom cupboard and put it on the stove top for our soup.

"We should probably drink some."

"We absolutely should not," I correct her, but she's already popping the top as I peel back the lids on the can of soup.

"Why not?"

"Well, first of all, because it's not ours. We already broke into their house and are eating their food. We do not need to also steal their expensive whisky like an Adult Swim Goldilocks."

"I'll replace it." Jack hunts for two clean glasses. "What else are we going to do for the night if we don't drink this?"

"Sit in terrible silence while contemplating the cosmic cluster-fuck that put us in this position?"

"Exactly." She nods. "Instead, we're going to drink a little bit of whisky and do the queer-women thing."

I focus on stirring the soup, and not on thinking about how I wish *the queer-women thing* meant something else. "What, uh, do we have to talk about?"

"Elle." Jack pushes a glass with three fingers of whisky into my hands. "Come on."

"Fine. I know we have a lot to talk about, but can we eat first?"

Jack props her body against the counter behind her and leans, goddamn her. "Yeah, we can eat first."

We take our gourmet meal of soup that is somehow both too salty and too bland—and crackers that contain the same inexplicable flavor palette—over to the fire, eating on the floor close to the heat. "Can I ask you something?" Jack starts, washing down the soup with a swig of whisky.

I also take a sip of whisky. It tastes like barbecued nail polish remover and goes straight to my head. Why does anyone drink hard alcohol *neat*? "I haven't finished eating yet," I argue, using the dregs of my soup as protection from a conversation I don't want to have.

Jack asks anyway, lingering soup be damned. "Do you think my mom will ever leave my dad?"

"Oh." It's not what I expected, and I take another drink of my whisky even though I despise it. "I don't know their marriage well enough to say. Relationships are complex."

Jack lounges back on her elbows, her long legs stretching in front of her, feet bobbing up and down to an unheard beat. I stare at the tattoos visible from where she's pushed her sweatshirt up to her elbows. And people are always making a fuss about male forearms, which, sure, are nice, but have these people never seen the tattooed forearms of a butch lesbian? The sleek, slender line of the humerus, the sharp jut of the wristbone, the vulnerable dip of the inside elbow, the contrast of strength and softness. Jack's lean muscles and her delicate wrists.

"I'm worried she's going to stay in a relationship that doesn't make her happy because it's safe," Jack says, looking directly at me. Because we're not talking about Katherine at all. Three fingers of whisky is never going to be enough for the coming conversation, and I reach for the bottle and give us each a splash more.

"You didn't seem surprised," Jack remarks, "to see your fiancé kissing someone else."

"Well," I say, stupidly, "I'd kissed someone else the night before, so . . ."

"So, you're not in love with Andrew, and you don't seem to care that he kissed someone else . . . ?" Jack's gaze burns the side of my face. "Why are you getting married, exactly?"

It's suddenly too hot by the fire, so I get up and take my whisky over to the record player in the corner of the room. Tucking my legs beneath me, I survey the Singhs' extensive vinyl collection, because anything is better than acknowledging Jack at the present moment.

I've honestly never seen so much Creedence Clearwater Revival in one place.

I take another, larger sip of my whisky. It's starting to taste better. Nutty and grassy and expensive. Or maybe I'm just drunker.

There's a rustling sound as Jack stands up and crosses the room to sit cross-legged on the ground next to me. She leans in to press a fingertip to the thin sleeves of the albums. She's sitting awfully close. Her forearms are *right there*. And God, she smells so good.

"God, you smell so good."

Apparently, six fingers of whisky is enough to obliterate my inhibitions.

Jack stiffens beside me. "What do I smell like?"

"Freshly baked bread."

Jack scoffs. "I definitely do not smell like bread. I haven't baked bread in days. I probably smell like body odor and the Singhs' organic laundry detergent."

I shake my head. "No. No, you always smell like bread. It's infused into your skin somehow."

Jack laughs as her fingers stop fluttering over the edges of the records. She's found what she wants. She plucks Dolly Parton off the shelf, and the record slides out of its case and onto the player with ease, her square-knuckled fingers adjusting the needle until "Here You Come Again" fills the cabin. Jack leans back on her elbows, because of course she does.

"A bit on the nose, isn't it?" I point at the record player.

Jack takes a drink of her whisky. "I have no idea what you mean."

"I'm sorry," I say, finally, "for kissing you in the bathroom last night. For putting you in an awful position with your brother, who I know you love. I . . . *shit*. I'm a fucking selfish, terrible person."

She restlessly swirls her glass a few times, watching the brown liquid create a whirlpool. "The most confusing part of this whole thing is, I know you're *not* a terrible person. Even when you ghosted me last year, I didn't think you were a terrible person. I *knew* you."

I chew miserably on my thumbnail. Jack sighs.

"So, why are you marrying a man you don't love?"

Tell her the truth. "Because . . ."

"Because *why*?"

"Because!" *Tell her the truth, tell her the truth, tell her the truth.* "Because my life was a fucking mess before I met Andrew!" I confess, because it's at least *a* truth. "Because I had hit rock bottom, and everything was utter and complete shit. I got fired from Laika, and I was stuck working for a boss who bullied me. I had no friends,

I never left my apartment, I was going *nowhere* with my ten-year-plan. I was going to get evicted! My mom only called when she needed money, and I was going to spend Christmas *alone*."

"And that's why you're marrying my brother?" Jack repeats. "Because you're *lonely*?"

"No." *Yes?*

Maybe I thought what I needed was the money, but what I really *wanted* was a family at Christmas. A mom who planned bonding time and a grandma who loved me anyway and *friends*. Maybe just for one Christmas, I wanted all the things I'd never had.

On the record player, Dolly goes quiet, spinning into static.

"Let's listen to something less melancholy," Jack declares, sitting up so she can riffle through the records again. When she repositions the needle, the cabin fills with an ominous piano and something with strings. It takes a second for me to place it. Then: "Celine Dion? *Really?*"

Jack nods solemnly. "I love this song."

"You love 'It's All Coming Back to Me Now'?"

"You sound surprised, like you don't already know about my taste in music." She stands up, and her wool socks slide along the hardwood floors. Before I have time to fully process what's happening, Jack starts dancing, swaying. It's intoxicating to watch, but I'm also just plain intoxicated, so I stand up and join the one-person dance party, bobbing and weaving beside her. Quite seriously, eyes closed and both hands balled into tight fists against her chest, Jack belts the first line in a perfect impression of Celine's breathy soprano, only awful sounding.

Laughter explodes out of me with an unexpected force, like an unburdening, and I grab my partially exposed stomach. All the tension of the moment leaves my body as I laugh wildly at her performance. Jack does not relent, doesn't stop putting her heart and soul into it, and she knows every damn line of this melodramatic song. She even sings the backing vocals.

"*I finished crying in the instant that you left*—sing with me! Don't act like you don't know the words!"

The song builds up to the chorus, and she's right. I do know the words. I haven't thought about this song in years, but it is, in fact, all coming back to me now.

And fuck—it's a good song.

I dance and dance and drunkenly dance, and the song rises and falls and rises again, until Jack and I are both screaming the lyrics. I forget about Andrew, about the money, about failed dreams. I twirl on the toes of my socks, and when I wheel around to face her, I see her eyes are on me, burning like open flames. She's watching me dance, and even when I catch her, she doesn't look away. She keeps watching, and I keep dancing.

Maybe I enjoy the feeling of her eyes on me. It's almost like she's touching me, and my skin prickles and burns in every place her eyes land. My throat, my stomach, my wrists, my ankles.

Maybe I should never drink alcohol again.

But I did drink alcohol, so as the song falls again, sweeping low into the final bridge, I do something incurably stupid. I touch her *like this*: two hands on her hip bones in an imitation of a middle school dance posture. I hold her *like this*: tugging her close, until she puts both hands on my shoulders, and we sway and sway.

It's a joke. We're joke-dancing, like in middle school. We exaggerate our movements, and we mouth the words, and I remind myself it's only a joke. But she smells tangy and sweet, and I shift my hands so they cup around her soft sides, shrinking some of the space between us. I pull her closer, as close as she'll let me. She lets me rest my cheek against her shoulder, so I do, feeling the soft fabric of a Cornell sweatshirt and the hard edge of her muscles and bones beneath. But it's obviously only a joke.

Jack whispers the final lines of the song, and I feel the way they hit my temple like a light breeze. The song slowly eases into silence, but we don't stop swaying in each other's arms, and it's not a joke, but I also don't know what happens now. A pathetic dinner and a surplus of whisky are swirling in my stomach, and Jack is letting me touch her and hold her, and I don't know what I should do next.

I know what I want to do next. I want to reach up and wind my fingers through her hair. I want to push myself up on my toes and seize her mouth with my teeth. I want another taste. I want to *devour* her. I have a huge, aching, lonely hole inside my chest and a memory of the way she once filled it, the way Jack smoothed the rough edges others had cut inside me over the years.

I don't want to be Jack-Kim Prescott's friend, and I definitely don't want to be her sister-in-law. What I want—*all I want*—is to be hers.

Except she's already pulling away. The song has ended, and now Jack shakes her head and laughs breezily as if to emphasize that it was a joke all along, that it never stopped being a joke.

I do the same, releasing my hold on her hips and giggling, so she'll never know that for one minute, dancing with her in this stolen cabin, I thought it all was real.

Jack takes her loose limbs and tucks them back into a rigid posture. She busies herself with the record collection. My body buzzes with anxiety and an almost-kiss, and I think we're both going to pretend that moment between us never happened, let it float away in a haze of whisky and Celine Dion. But then Jack settles another record on the turntable, and "Holly Jolly Christmas" fills the room.

She turns to face me. "Nothing can happen between us tonight," she says over the sound of Burl Ives. "You're still with my brother, and I can't betray him like that, even if he did cheat on you with Dylan."

"I know. I understand," I say, even though I don't. We're standing two feet apart, close enough to touch in a dozen different places, but not touching anywhere.

"Why did you kiss me in the bathroom last night?" I ask.

"Elle, let's not—"

"Honesty game."

Jack stares down at her fingers, helplessly holding onto the record sleeve like it can protect her. She exhales. "I kissed you in the bathroom because I wanted to. Because I literally always want to be kissing you. Because seeing you with my brother did *nothing* to change those feelings, no matter how much I hoped it would."

I try to take a deep breath, but I have too many ribs, too many feelings. Jack stares at me from two feet away. No, she stares at my mouth. I involuntarily swipe my bottom lip with my tongue. "Elle." Jack says my name so delicately, I can barely stand it. "Why did *you* kiss *me* in the bathroom?"

I bite down on my bottom lip.

"Honesty game," Jack says.

"Because I wanted to." I breathe the words out. "Because I'm not over you. Because I realized I was never over you the moment I saw you at the cabin, because you're all I think about, because being with Andrew could never change that, because—"

Jack is a blur of movement, her hands on my face, her body against mine, and this time, it doesn't matter if she kisses me or if I kiss her, because we're kissing.

Chapter Twenty-Four

There is something impossibly magical about knowing Jack is kissing me because she *wants to*.

Fingers in my hair, her mouth on mine. And *oh. Oh*, the taste of her whisky lips, the sweetness of her, the solidness and strength of her body holding mine.

This is even better than last night. She kisses me slowly, searchingly, like she's rebuilding something between us with each gentle shift of her lips. Her thumbs stroke my cheekbones, and I melt into her. I'll keep melting into her for as long as she lets me, savoring each kiss like she's the world's best slice of pie.

I let two fingers stroke her bare forearm until she shivers beneath my touch, moans into my mouth, and opens for me. My tongue slides along her bottom lip, and the indomitable, solid Jack Kim-Prescott mewls in my arms.

My brain feels like Pop Rocks, and I'm falling hopelessly headfirst into this kiss, holding back nothing, showing her that I want, I yearn. That I want and yearn *for her*.

When Jack jerks her head back to break off the kiss, I fall back on my heels. "Elle," she says, and her voice is raw. "We can't . . . I can't do this to Andrew. I *want* to"—she trails one hand up my arm like she can't quite help herself—"Holy shit, I want to. But what kind of monster hooks up with her brother's fiancée?"

I look up at the tortured expression on her face. I think about the two hundred thousand dollars. I think about her hands still cupping my face. I think about Jack's dream and my dreams. And fuck it—Andrew can find someone else to fake marry. "I'm not going to marry him," I tell her.

I watch as the smallest shift takes place on Jack's face, her mouth, begging to lift in the corner. "You're not?" she asks, hopeful. It's the damn *hope*.

I shake my head. "I can't marry him when I feel this way about you."

And then Jack lets loose her terrific smile. Her hands fall to my waist, and she shoves me urgently until my back is against the wall of the cabin, pinning me in place. She doesn't kiss me right away. No, for a long minute, Jack simply stares at me, and I stare at her, too. Brown eyes and freckles and the tiny white scar. She's hovering in front of me, close enough that I can see all her imperfections. The small pattern of acne scars on her chin, and the frown lines between her eyebrows, and the pores along the bridge of her nose. She's so achingly beautiful.

Jack slides a knee between my legs and kisses me again, and this is the best two hundred thousand dollars I've ever spent.

We're kissing with our whole bodies now, Jack pressing me harder against the wall, our bodies lining up like puzzle pieces that only make sense slotted together. The small swell of her breasts under my own. Her wide shoulders and narrow hips; my wide hips and narrow shoulders. Hip bones and pelvic bones, harmony and friction.

I deepen the kiss, and Jack meets me where I am, her mouth finding the pulse point at the base of my throat and sucking. I slide my hand under her sweatshirt, and her stomach is warm. I explore the inches of her, splay my hand across her back and hold her as close as I can, hold her until I get her whole body between my legs.

Our kiss turns sloppy. Tongue and teeth and her thumb on my bottom lip, the other hand gripping the front of my sweatshirt as she grinds herself against my thigh, and I move against her hip bone, and we're both wearing too many clothes.

When I fit my hands into the dimples that bracket her ass, she gasps into my mouth. "Jack," I pant. "Can I please take off your clothes?"

She takes a step back from me. I open my eyes, and *fuck*. Her mouth is pink and swollen, her eyes practically black.

"Elle," she says, hesitant.

"I'm sorry," I quickly apologize. "We don't have to. . . . I'm okay with just kissing. If you want to wait until Andrew and I have officially ended things, or . . ."

She clenches her jaw, thinking. "Oh, fuck it," she says, and when she kisses me again, she's smiling into it. I smile, too. Heat and hands, and when she shifts against me, my lower stomach tightens, pulling all the energy inside me down to my core until I feel dizzy with needing more of her touch, more of her skin. I push us across the living room until we reach the couch, and Jack falls back onto it, me halfway on top of her.

She lets me pull off her sweatshirt, and there's something so vulnerable in the action of undressing another person. She's not wearing a bra, so it's a tug of fabric, then Jack's light brown skin in the flickering firelight of the living room. Her small breasts, the ridge of her hardened nipples, which make my tongue feel thick inside my mouth. Faint stretch marks on the soft skin above her hips, the puckered skin around her belly button, the tattoos.

The *tattoos*. The images that tell her story in the way webcomic panels do, snapshots of a time and place. Of a moment in the life of this person. I need my mouth on all of it, and for the first time all week, there's nothing to hold me back.

I want to kiss, so I kiss her. I straddle her, and I kiss the hard curves of her rib cage, I kiss the Mount Hood tattoo, I kiss the deliciously soft skin of her stomach. "You're so perfect," I tell her as I slide off the couch and onto the floor so I can tug the sweatpants down her hips to reveal unisex boxer briefs with a rainbow waistband and those motherfucking thighs.

Jack's legs are a work of erotic art. Long and muscular, her shins are coated in soft brown hair, with three freckles above her left knee. Her thick thighs strain as she arches off the couch to help me along with the pants, and I think about those thighs under me, around me, squirming beneath my hands as I devoured her last Christmas.

I climb into her lap again, the hard mound of her pressed between my legs. "You're so *fucking* perfect."

I caress her breasts with my thumbs. I trace her flesh, touch and retreat, tease my fingers along the underside of her small breasts. Jack arches back, groans as I wind and unwind her, until she begs with a single word: "*Elle.*"

Here is what I know about Jack: she likes to be in charge, likes to lead; she likes to be the one who gives, the one who nurtures and nourishes, the one who makes you feel safe and protected and so goddamn precious your heart almost bursts. But one time, in her Airstream, she let me take care of *her*, and I learned she also likes to hand over that control sometimes. She likes to feel powerless, likes to be teased, likes to plead for what she wants and be denied it still, until the tension and promise and delayed satisfaction make her squirm.

And I love being the person who makes her feel that way. I fucking love to be in control.

So I move my lips closer to her nipple as if to take her in my mouth, but I only blow cool air across her skin before moving up to kiss her throat. Jack pants and makes all manner of desperate sounds as I kiss her throat, her shoulder, her collarbone. I kiss the crest of her right breast until she begs again with just the syllables of my name, and then I take her nipple between my teeth and tug, only for a second, making Jack loosen with relief before recoiling with longing.

It's so damn hot, being handed this power, being allowed to turn her all weak-kneed and wanting. I'm wet and impatient with my own game, so I push myself up on my knees to get a better angle and cup my hand between her legs. Gently, I press my palm against her, my middle finger disappearing between her legs. "May I?"

Jack growls, "You fucking better," and I think I momentarily black out. When I regain consciousness, I lift two fingers to my mouth and suck until they're slick with my spit. Jack watches me, her pink tongue darting out of her mouth to lick the white scar.

My hand dips past the waistband of her underwear, my slick fingers finding her wet and hot and waiting. It fills me with something potent to know it's for me, it's all for me, these wild feelings. It's been so long since I've been this close to another person, and she's the only person I want to be close to. I refuse to think about what this is, what this means, what we'll do tomorrow.

I sketch a finger around her, up and down the length of her, until she clenches her teeth together and doesn't unclench them. "Goddamn you," Jack growls. "*Please.* I'm not going to beg."

But she does. She begs until I burrow through her coarse hair and rub my two fingers over her swollen clit. I'm met with a *yes* and a *thank you* and an *oh my God*. I swallow a litany of curses with a graceless kiss. A *yes* and *please* and *yes, like that*. Because of course I remember how she likes to be touched.

I remember every damn thing about that night.

"Yes, Elle, holy shit." She grabs onto my hip for balance, and she arches into the pressure of my fingers, and she fucks herself against my hand. It's hot and messy and quick, but I get to watch her face the whole time. I get to watch the feigned indifference melt away. There's no shiny Airstream to hide herself away in. It's just her and me, perfect imperfections on this ratty couch.

Her bottom lip pinned beneath two white teeth; the flutter of her thick lashes as she closes her eyes and throws back her head; the way her hair falls over her forehead and the way the heat climbs up her throat and the way her mouth wrenches open with sudden, guttural moans. She's so pretty. "So fucking pretty."

And so fucking *loud*. I love every sound she makes as she grips my hip tighter and comes from my two fingers and a trail of kisses left along her hairline.

As she pants and coughs and swears some more, I stare at the freckles and the white scar, all the pieces of her I memorized last time. She presses her forehead to my shoulder and wraps her arms around my waist; I wrap my arms around the back of her neck, trailing a fingernail through the short hairs there. We sit like that for several minutes—her trying to catch her breath, me trying to remember every damn detail about this time, too.

Chapter Twenty-Five

"Well." Jack laughs into my shoulder. "That was . . . unexpected."

I sigh. "No, it wasn't."

She peeks up at me and squints one eye bashfully. "No. I guess it wasn't. I've basically wanted you to do that every minute of every day since Paul Hollywood knocked you into my mother's centerpiece."

"Honesty game," I say, wrapping my arms tighter around her, holding her in place against me. "I've wanted to do that every minute of every day since last Christmas."

I can feel Jack holding her breath. "That's . . ." She coughs. "That's not how the honesty game works."

We both laugh, her bare chest vibrating against me until she finally, fully, catches her breath. She looks up at me. We're not kissing, not talking, and somehow this feels more intimate than before. I lift a finger to trace the crescent of her scar. "How did you get this?"

Jack shivers slightly as my fingernail touches her lip. "It's not an interesting story. I fell into the corner of a coffee table when I was four and split my lip open."

"Everything about you is interesting," I say quietly. I trace my finger from that white scar to her dark freckles. They dot her cheeks like points on a map, like I could chart a new destination if I connected them just right, like there's a new ten-year-plan to be discovered in the distance between our two points. I let my finger wander through their swirling pattern, and I imagine all the things I could draw from her freckles. For a few minutes, she lets me. Jack lets me create art with the tip of my finger and the planes of her face.

It hits me ferociously. I love her. I never stopped loving her. I'm no better than that idiot Romeo. I know it's not logical, but I fell in love with a woman in twenty-four hours, because in those twenty-four hours, she did the impossible: she made me feel safe and secure; she made me feel trusted and like I could trust. With an honesty game and emotional vulnerability, she got me to open up in a way I hadn't opened up before. She let me be messy. She let me be true. How could I not love someone like that?

I love her, and I have to find a way to keep her. I want to find a way to have her beyond Christmas. I want to know Jack in every season.

In spring, when the mountain is out, when she wears a short-sleeve button-down open over a white T-shirt, the tattoos on her bare forearms flashing as she walks Paul Hollywood through Mt. Tabor Park, as she reaches for a beer at an outdoor patio on Alberta.

I want Summer Jack, in giant sunglasses and a carefree smile, holding tongs next to a barbecue, roasting marshmallows over a fire pit. Jack with melting Popsicle dripping between her fingers, Jack sprawled out on the soft grass.

I want to discover who Jack becomes in the fall, when the days get shorter and colder and gray. How does wild, restless Jack pack herself up for the winter to become the version I met in Powell's? What does she do with those last gasps of sun? I want to solve that mystery and every mystery that is Jack Kim-Prescott, through all the days of all the months.

"What are you thinking about right now?" she asks quietly into my shoulder.

I trace a finger down her spine until she shivers. "I'm thinking about what you look like in shorts in the summertime."

She looks up at me again, and she's so recklessly open. "Please,"

Jack begs, her voice soft and sweet, even as her teeth nip at my earlobe, "please let me fuck you."

I want to say yes. Even though the intimacy of receiving pleasure is always trickier than the intimacy of giving it for me, with Jack, I always, *always* want to say yes. Jack's hands travel the curve of my ass through my sweatpants, and I nod.

"Can I fuck you on the bed?" she asks plainly. As if I'm in any position to refuse such a request. Instead, I kiss her, deeply and desperately, until we both momentarily forget our mission. When we remember it, we're both hazy-eyed and swollen-mouthed, our hands joined as we rise from the couch. I'm not sure which one of us is leading and which is following, but we end up on the edge of the one bed, and it's distinctly Jack who lowers me down. It's Jack who drops to her knees in front of me.

It's Jack who undresses me, peeling off my borrowed clothes to reveal the body my mother has never been satisfied with. Just a little too tall, a little too chubby, a little too pale. "You're so fucking perfect," Jack whispers. She tries *so hard* to whisper it.

I close my eyes and try to convince myself this will last.

She traces a single finger up the inside of my thigh until I'm biting down on my bottom lip. Her mouth arrives where her finger is on the inside of my thigh, leaving a trail of kisses and the occasional press of her tongue to my flesh. I inhale sharply. She pushes herself up a bit so she can leave a kiss into the crease of my hip before she lifts my left leg over her shoulder and exhales a hot breath onto my throbbing body. "Elle," she says, her voice almost stern. *Fuck* her stern voice. "Will you tell me what you want? What will make you feel good?"

"Everything. Anything." I wiggle on the bed. "Just touch me, please."

She presses the pad of her thumb against my clit, soft at first, massaging me in gentle circles until I'm forced to do what she wants, forced to tell her what *I want*. "Faster," I demand. Jack presses harder and faster, changing patterns so quickly the room begins to spin. I respond with my own litany of curses, my own *yes* and *please* and *thank you.*

And then her tongue replaces her thumb. It's one lick, the tip of her tongue along the fissure of my body, and I'm ready to shake off my skin and soar above the bed. "Ellie," she says coyly. "Please tell me what you want."

Her raspy voice scrapes across my body, sends a tingle down my spine that curls my bare toes. "I want you to do that again."

Jack reaches up and presses one hand firmly to my lower stomach, pinning me to the bed with the force of her upper-body strength, and I squirm despite myself as I wait. Jack dips her head and plants a chaste kiss to my clit. It's demure, almost like a gentleman in a Regency romance kissing the gloved hand of a duchess, and it makes me positively *demented*. It's a game to her. Everything is a game to Jack.

"I'm going to *murder you* if you don't—"

The tough flat of her tongue presses against me, and any threats are subsumed by other, less articulate objections and protests. Like *wait, how does that feel so good?* And *oh God, are you trying to kill me?*

Jack licks me until I'm grabbing the quilt between both fists, until I'm convulsing on a stranger's bed, until I'm split open with the force of the ocean against a rocky shore, or some other, better cliché for an orgasm I can't think of at the moment, because *I am busy orgasming.*

Even as my head melts back into the bed, my bones dissolving into hot goo, another part of me tenses at Jack's continued attention. My left hand grabs the comforter while my right hand clutches her hair. Both are life preservers buoying me through the onslaught of a dozen gorgeous aftershocks.

I'm—I'm feeling too much, and these feelings—they're reckless and dangerous and so fucking wonderful.

It's been so long since I've let myself feel anything, terrified of the absence of feeling I'd be left with afterward, terrified to let the hole inside my chest grow any larger, but as Jack absolutely wrecks me with her tongue, I don't float above the scene, wondering how I'll draw it later. I just *feel*. Anchored and grounded by tongue and fingers and *her*. It's *transcendent*.

Jack responds to the sounds like we're connected by a silk thread, like the more I feel, the more *she* feels. "Elle," she whimpers as she licks me slowly, teasing out these lingering feelings, my name in her mouth a sacrament. "*Elle*."

I say her name back. It feels like dark chocolate melting on my tongue, like cutout cookies with homemade frosting, like waffles with whipped cream. *Jack. Jack Jack Jack.*

"Come up here, please," I beg, and Jack obeys, climbing up onto the bed, climbing on top of me, until our naked bodies are folded together like starched sheets. This is where I want her most. She kisses my mouth, and she tastes like me, and she tastes like her, and I kiss her back like I've forgotten how to protect myself from hurt.

Both hands in her hair, pressing her tightly against me. I wrap both of my legs around her waist and pin her to my body. Her pebbled nipples skate across my skin, and I explode in goose bumps and renewed yearning. She rubs herself against me, our bodies moving in some beautiful rhythm of pleasure while she hovers above me, watching my face.

"I'm so glad I found you again," Jack says.

She practically shouts it.

• • •

I wake up under an itchy quilt with Jack's arm around my shoulder and Jack's leg over my legs. It takes a minute for me to remember where we are and how we ended up like this, but for a moment, I revel in her body, her heat, her heartbeat against my back.

Then: skiing, snow, Gillian, the Singhs' cabin, six fingers of whisky, Celine Dion, sex. It all comes back to me, and a cold sweat breaks out across my naked skin. I feel trapped by Jack's body, unable to move my limbs. My heartbeat falls out of rhythm with hers.

This isn't a heart attack, I quickly chant to myself as I climb out from beneath her. *You are not having an unprecedented cardiac event.*

"Whatsa—?" Jack strings together some incomprehensible syllables as I slide out of the bed. She blinks up at me with sleep in her eyes, and for a second I get lost in those eyes, in their fiery intensity, even half-asleep. She tries again. "What are you doing? Are you okay?"

I'm not okay, but I'm not sure why I'm not okay. I feel fluttery and panicked, like I have an itch inside my internal organs that I'll never be able to scratch. And why, *why*? I just had the best sex of my (admittedly pretty sexless) life. I got to kiss Jack without guilt. I got to wake up in her arms. The sound of her sandpaper voice against my skin. *I am so glad I found you again.*

How could that beautiful night lead to these ugly feelings twisting inside of me?

"We . . . we should get back to the house," I say. Now I'm the one who's practically shouting.

"We should probably check the snow situation first," Jack says reasonably from the bed, where she's still stark naked, where she's not even remotely trying to hide how stark-fucking-naked she is.

Meanwhile, I'm scrambling for my clothes, searching for my bra and underwear. "I just . . . I just feel like, it's Christmas Eve, and we should probably—"

"Elle." Her voice is abrupt, stern. "It's seven in the morning. It's not even light outside yet. What's going on?"

I trip and fall my way back into my long johns. "Nothing is going on." My voice is an unholy shriek of panic, and Jack would have to be a moron to believe me. "I'm just sure the family is worried about us. We need to get back to—"

Jack is not a moron. "To Andrew?" she asks.

I glance at her on the bed. She's sitting up, the quilt around her waist and her breasts exposed to the cold morning air. Our fire went out sometime in the night.

"Elle, don't do this."

"I'm not doing anything," I sputter.

"Are you . . . ?" Jack shoves a hand through her greasy morning hair. "Do you regret what happened between us?"

"No," I say. And I don't. Do I? Why do I itch *everywhere*? "I just need a minute to, you know . . . think. Regroup."

"Elle." She keeps saying my name like it's a string tying me back to her. "Don't do this. Don't freak out."

"I'm not freaking out."

I am absolutely freaking out. A year ago, I went home with this woman and ended up with my heart broken. Ten days ago, I signed a napkin contract because I thought money was the only thing that could fix my broken life. There's a hole in my chest and a family two miles away who are never going to forgive me when they discover the truth. Andrew is a guarantee and Jack isn't and I—

On the bed, Jack clenches her jaw. "Are you going to go back to him?"

"Who?"

"What do you mean *who*?" She spits. "*Andrew*. Are you going to marry him?"

"I can't marry Andrew." Even if he *is* a guarantee, I know I can't.

Jack climbs off the bed. "Then what is this? Why are you pulling away from me?"

"This . . ." I flail a hand back and forth between her naked body and my half-covered one. "Us . . . we . . . we're going to fall apart."

"What are you talking about?"

"We've already fallen apart once, and we'll fall apart again, and I can't. I can't go through that a second time." There are tears blinding me from the sight of her, which honestly helps. If I can't see her, it's a little easier to say this to her. To be honest.

She takes my face in those large, bruised-knuckled, bread-kneading hands. "Why do you think we're going to fall apart?"

I put my hands over hers against my cheeks. "Because . . ."

"Because you think you're going to fail," she answers for me. She reaches for me, pulls me close against her chest, so her body is squeezing mine tightly, leaving no room for the panic attack. "But you've *never* failed."

"I did. I got fired from Laika because I couldn't cut it, and—"

"Elle." Jack releases me, holds me carefully at arm's length. "I'm going to say something I know you don't want to hear but is the absolute truth: you didn't fail at being an animator. You quit."

"I did not—"

Jack holds up both hands, ass naked and asking me to *hold on* with a single gesture. "What do you love about art? And the answer can't be that you're good at it."

"I'm not good at it, clearly," I say, but Jack's expression is so serious, I stiffen. There's a dull undercurrent of anxiety coursing through me, but I answer her. "Okay. Well, I fell in love with art because . . . because it used to be a way to escape. My parents would fight, and I would hide away in my room, creating these colorful worlds where everything was better than my real life. And then I used to share my art with other kids in my class, and it brought them joy, too, and it was like . . . here's this way that I can make something good, even though everything my parents touch is absolute garbage."

Jack nods, like we're getting close to the realization she's clumsily dragging me toward. "And when did you fall *out of love* with art?"

I think about undergrad at Ohio State, when I was holed away in my dorm, teaching myself Photoshop and InDesign for assignments I hated, creating fanart at four in the morning because it was the only time I had to do something for *me*; in grad school, making sure I never faltered from my ten-year-plan, never wasted time with silly doodles or stories in my head; at Laika, truly struggling for the first time and not knowing who I was if I wasn't the best, if I wasn't Artist Ellie. Nothing could ever be a rough draft.

"It just . . . it became my whole identity," I tell Jack. "I felt like I had to be perfect at it all the time, because it's who I *was*, and then I wasn't perfect at it, and my art and my identity were so tangled up in each other that I just . . ." *quit.*

I don't say it. I don't give Naked Jack that satisfaction. She is right, though. I got fired from Laika, and I just *quit* trying. But she's wrong about that not making me a total failure.

Naked Jack sits down on the edge of the bed, and the bed frame groans. "Did I ever tell you the story of why I dropped out of college?"

"I'm sort of having a panic attack–slash–existential crisis over here. . . ."

"It's related. I promise."

"Fine." I cross my arms over my chest, still halfway through the process of putting on a shirt. "Tell me the story, then."

"You know how school wasn't my thing, but it was really important to my parents that I go to college, so I enrolled at the University of Oregon anyway and declared as a business major. And the thing is, I'm pretty good at going with the flow," she explains, "at fitting in. Anyone who saw me freshman year would've thought I was having the time of my life, but I was abjectly miserable. I *hated* college. There was this restlessness inside of me all the time, this emptiness. I'd wake up in the middle of the night with so much energy, I'd have to go for a ten-mile run. Or I'd get in my car, and I'd drive to the coast or the middle of the woods, disappear in a tiny town where no one knew my name. I'd get blackout drunk at a frat party or do 'shrooms with strangers. I tried everything to fill that emptiness in me, but none of it really helped."

Jack rubs her hands up and down her thighs, like she's trying to get warm, and *shit*. She's probably freezing. I go over to the bed and drape the quilt over her naked shoulders. She looks at me with such tenderness, I feel like I'm wearing my itchy insides on the outside.

"The only time the emptiness really went away was when I was baking cookies for everyone on my floor in the awful dorm kitchen," she continues to narrate. "That was the only thing that brought me actual joy. And I eventually figured it out—the emptiness was the absence of myself. I was emptying myself to become the person my dad wanted me to be, and I kept searching for all the wrong things to fill me back up. I couldn't keep living like that, so I dropped out."

She swallows, that taut tendon spiking from the side of her neck. "I had the same feeling when I was with Claire, in the end. The emptiness came back, because I was siphoning off bit by bit who I truly am to satisfy someone else's idea of who I should be."

I swallow, too. Hearing Jack talk about the emptiness . . . it sounds an awful lot like my ache, like that pit that exists just south of my ribs, the hole I thought was loneliness. But what if the ache isn't the absence of other people? What if the thing missing inside of me is . . . *me*? It's a terrifying thought, because it means this hole inside my chest can't be filled by two hundred thousand dollars or a woman with freckles and a quarter-moon smile.

"The day we met at Powell's, the restlessness was the worst it had ever been," Jack is saying. "I knew the snow was supposed to get bad, but the thought of being trapped in the Airstream all day made me sick. So I went to Powell's on a whim and ended up finding you crying in that aisle," Jack's voice is thick with memory and affection and longing. "And you were just so—"

My heart sprouts wings and launches into my throat.

"—messy," she says, and my heart plummets back again. "You were such an anxious, lonely *mess*, and you had snot all over your face."

"This took a turn."

"No!" Jack smiles, a full, ferocious thing. "You were beautiful, Elle, even with all that snot. I thought you were wonderful because you were just *you*, and for a day, you made me feel like I could be just *me*. And that would be enough. And that feeling—that's something I'm willing to fight for."

"What does any of this have to do with me quitting art?"

"I don't know." Jack flicks her hair out of her face. "The thematic arc got kind of muddled there in the middle, but the point is"—she reaches out and takes my hand—"in my good, healthy moments, I know I'm not a fuck-up. I'm someone who spent too much time trying to be something I didn't want to be. And you're not a fuck-up, either, Elle. You're not going to fuck this up."

Our fingers are stitched together in Jack's lap, and she has no idea how badly I've already fucked this up. I slept with her, and she doesn't even know the engagement is *fake*. "And maybe, when you're panicking, you can *tell* me about it, instead of shoving it all down and pulling away."

I squint at her. "I'm not familiar with that concept."

I feel Jack's smile as she leans in close to my cheek. "For example, when your mind starts spiraling about failure, instead of putting on your long johns backward, you could take a deep breath and try saying to me something like"—she adopts a high-pitched voice for my part—"'Wow, Jack, I'm feeling really emotionally vulnerable right now, and I'm scared of taking this risk again with you.'"

"That is absolutely *not* an accurate impersonation of me."

"And then I would say, 'Thanks for opening up about that, Elle, because I'm honestly scared, too. I mean, you're still currently engaged to my brother, and we have a lot of things to work through and figure out. Maybe we take this whole thing one day at a time.'"

"Wow. Is this that queer-women communication thing you're always on about?"

"I've heard rumors it's possible for people to just . . . *talk things through*." She's sitting there completely naked in every sense of the word, a blanket over her shoulders, her face devoid of apathy. She cares so damn much, her expression raw and easy to read. Love and fear and hurt and hope.

It's the hope that gets me, every single time. She sits there without a stitch of clothing like this is all so simple. Like all I have to do is let her love me.

"Jack," I say, tightening my grip on her hand. "I'm feeling really emotionally vulnerable right now, and I'm scared of taking this risk with you."

"Me, too." Jack kisses my forehead, my chin, each of my cheekbones, in the pattern of the sign of the cross I remember from my childhood. "Maybe we take this whole thing one day at a time."

She pulls us down onto the bed, holding me tight against her chest, until I'm convinced this whole thing isn't going to crumble all around me. "What are we going to do?" I ask her.

"Do you mean right now?" she asks into my hair. "Or do you mean long-term, like telling Andrew and my parents about us?"

"Let's start with today."

"Hmm." She presses the tip of her nose to the skin behind my ear, until I tingle in all the places our skin is touching. Which is all the places. "We need breakfast."

She kisses that soft bit of skin.

"We need to figure out the snow situation."

She *bites* that skin.

"We need to figure out how to get home. But . . ."

Her mouth slides up until her lips are on my earlobe again.

"But no rush," I say.

Chapter Twenty-Six

"You made me biscuits and gravy?"

"This is a bastard shadow of my biscuits and gravy," she growls with a frown. "I make my biscuits from scratch using a recipe it took me eight years to perfect, and I would never—"

"You made me biscuits and gravy," I repeat.

She extends a plate forward with a *humph*. "I did. Granted, the biscuits are from pancake batter mix and melted snow, and the mushroom gravy is from a McCormick packet I suspect expired several years ago."

I set down the plate and pull her into my arms and kiss her deeply.

The biscuits and gravy taste like cardboard and chunky slop water, but they're still the best thing I've ever eaten. I wish we could stay here forever, in this tiny cabin, living our own *Little House on the Prairie* kink, but it's Christmas Eve. Katherine is waiting for us.

Andrew and Dylan are waiting for us.

The truth is waiting for us.

We got almost a foot of snow in the night, so digging Gillian out isn't an option. Instead, we find the Singhs' snowshoes on the back porch next to the firewood. Slowly and reluctantly, we return the cabin to the way we found it. We ditch our Cornell clothes for the ski outfits we came here in last night. Jack leaves a detailed note, along with her Venmo account name, so the Singhs can request money for everything we stole. We'll bring the snowshoes back when we come to dig Gillian out.

We call Katherine to let her know we're on our way, and then we stare at each other across the rug in the living room where we danced to Celine Dion. I try to remember the way she held me here, so I'll have it later, no matter how this next part goes.

We step outside. Neither of us speaks for the first mile as we trudge through the snow in the silent morning, my feet awkward in snowshoes for the first time. It feels like emerging from some kind of dream, and I have the same fear I did last year. What happens when the snow melts? What happens when we return to Portland?

But then Jack is at my side, reaching out for my hand, reading my mind. "It's going to be hard," she says. "Whatever comes next, with my family. It's not going to be easy. But I'm in. I'm all in."

She's right here, and her expression is completely unguarded again, and I want to tell her everything. About Andrew and the money and the trust—about the reason I went along with the scheme, and all the reasons I kept going along with the scheme. But there's still one last reason, shackled to my ankle and pinning me to my dishonesty. And that reason is *Jack*.

Jack, who is taking a huge risk in opening her own bakery. Jack, who won't have anything to fall back on if it falls apart.

No, Andrew and I will figure something else out. We'll find some way for him to get the money, and once Jack has it, once I know the Butch Oven isn't going to fail or fall apart on her, *then* I'll confess everything.

"I'm all in," I finally say back to her.

Jack leans forward and kisses me, like we're sealing a promise.

I feel my phone buzz in my coat pocket, and I drop her hand to fish it out. "I'm not sure how I have reception right now. . . . Are we back in Wi-Fi range of the house?"

I rub the snow away from the cracked screen to look at the Gmail notification. It's from a name I don't recognize—"Samantha

Clark"—but it's not the name that stops me dead in my tracks in the snow. It's the subject line. "Drawn2 Webcomics Interest."

"Is everything okay?" Jack asks.

"I think so." I fumble to open the email. *Dear Miss Oliver,* the email begins, and my brain is swimming. *How—why?* I scan the rest of the email quickly, searching for the punch line, waiting for something terrible to happen, but the bottom never falls out. I read the email a second time while Jack asks me over and over if I'm all right.

Dear Miss Oliver,

I'm sorry to email you on Christmas Eve, but I didn't want to wait and miss the chance to connect with you. I'm an editor at Timber Press, an imprint of Simon and Schuster, and I'm reaching out because like many people in the past week, I found your new webcomic series The Arrangement *on Drawn2. I was immediately drawn (pun intended) into the dynamics between your characters, Lucy, Joe, Sam, and Ricky, and it served as the perfect antidote to spending the holiday season with my family. As I eagerly awaited more episodes, I also went back and discovered your first series,* Snow Day. *Your artwork is captivating, but it's your understanding of storytelling and your voice that really kept me reading.*

It took me a while to track down your email address, and I hope you'll forgive me for being so aggressive. As an editor, I'm always looking to work with new authors and artists, and I'm especially interested in the possibility of seeing your work as a longer project. I think the market is ripe for an adult romantic comedy in graphic novel form. I'm not sure The Perpetual Suck *has quite the tone we're looking for, but* The Arrangement *and* Snow Day *could make an incredible romance (as long as we can give the characters the happy ending they deserve). I would love to set up a time to chat with you more.*

Do you already have an agent? If so, I'd be happy to connect with them moving forward. If you're not currently agented, I would love to help you find someone who would be a good fit. I'm excited to hear from you (and to see what happens between Lucy and Joe).

Sincerely,
Samantha Clark

"Holy shit!" I put a hand over my mouth and stare at my phone, reading the email a third time.

"You're freaking me out here a bit," Jack says, giving my shoulder a squeeze. "What's going on?"

"It's—it's an email from an editor! She found my webseries on Drawn2 and she loves it!"

"Your *what*?"

"I—I—" I'm not thinking clearly, not thinking at all. "I started creating webcomics after I got fired from Laika, and this editor read *The Arrangement* and she . . . she wants to publish it. She asked if I have an agent? I have no idea what an agent does! Oh my God, I should google it!"

I don't even know what I'm saying, know what I'm thinking. This mess—this absolute messy webcomic that I made just for myself . . . this thing that actually brought me joy. "She loves my work! *My* work!"

"Of course she does!" Jack pulls me into a hug, lifts me off the ground, and spins me around until I'm all warm and fuzzy again. "You're incredible, Elle! This is incredible! Oh my *God*! Like Alison Bechdel!"

"I know!" I look down at my phone again, chewing on my bottom lip as a gnawing doubt seeps in. "Well, maybe. I mean, I'm sure it's not a guarantee or whatever. She's just expressing interest."

"Still! Interest is huge!"

The thought of responding to the email turns the hope bubbling inside my chest into something bordering on panic. Jack gives my arm a playful shove. "We're going to celebrate this," she says. "Before we start panicking about what this means and what comes next, we're just going to exist in this moment and fucking *celebrate* it!"

I feel dizzy and giddy and *hopeful*. "Yes! Yes, we have to celebrate it!"

"But first . . ." Jack points up ahead, to where the cabin is visible through an outcropping of trees.

But first, we have to deal with the Kim-Prescotts.

• • •

"You're safe!" Katherine opens her arms and promptly bursts into tears the second we walk through the front door.

"Yes, Mom, we're safe." Jack allows herself to be hauled into a hug and kissed excessively on the face, then I do the same, secretly loving Katherine's kisses. Paul Hollywood flings himself at Jack next, jumping up and down and licking every inch of her exposed skin.

"Merry Christmas Eve!" Lovey gushes. "We thought you two might be dead!"

"Not dead," Jack clarifies.

"I didn't think the two of you were dead," Meemaw says, nudging me with her elbow and *actually winking*. Alan lurks in the back of the little semicircle that's forming, offering a running commentary about the deficiencies of Jack's truck, her driving abilities, and the decrepit state of the Singhs' cabin.

"Oliver!" Someone shouts across the house, and then I'm violently accosted by Andrew as he pulls me into his arms. What I assume is a performance as my doting fiancé feels surprisingly genuine as he hugs me tight. "We were so freaked out when you didn't make it back."

Dylan is there, too, wearing their penis/middle finger Christmas sweater. "Are you okay?" they ask Jack. And then Andrew is hugging

Jack, and Dylan is hugging me, and I realize both of their concern is genuine.

"We're fine." Then, quieter to Andrew: "Can I talk to you privately for a moment?"

I shoot Jack a look that attempts to convey *Don't worry—I'm all in*. Then I haul Andrew upstairs. Before I even close the door to our bedroom, he blurts, "I had sex with Dylan!" He's his face-scrunching, nose-pinching, mouth-half-open self.

"Yeah," I say. "I figured."

"You . . . figured?"

"Jack and I saw the two of you. At Timberline. We saw you kissing."

He reaches for both of my hands, like we're a bride and groom standing at the altar, about to say our vows. "Shit. I'm so, *so* sorry. I've ruined everything, haven't I?"

"Well, um, so have I, actually. . . ." I take one long, steadying breath and brace myself for the truth. "I slept with your sister."

The scrunch deepens. "Well, sure, you were snowed in at the Singhs' cabin. I assumed you slept at some point."

"No, you hot doofus! Why would I tell you we had a sleepover? *No*. I'm in love with Jack, and we *slept* together last night."

Andrew drops my hands. "You're not in love with my sister."

"I kind of am, though."

"You don't even know my sister."

"Except I do." Another steadying breath. I imagine I'm like Jack, as steady as an oak tree, confident and sure. "Do you remember on our weird not-first-date, when I told you about the woman from last Christmas? The one I met in Powell's and spent the whole day with?"

"From the napkin drawing?" He does a slow nod, and I give him a minute to get there. He gets there. "Wait, you're saying *that* was Jacqueline? That Jacqueline was your snow girl?" Andrew takes one large step back from me. "Have you been stalking my sister?"

"Andrew, *no*! I had no idea you and Jack were related!"

"You mean to tell me that this whole week, you and my sister have known each other and said nothing? My sister has been keeping a *secret* from me?"

"You've also been keeping a pretty big secret from her, buddy."

He stares up at me, mouth all the way open. "And you . . . had sex . . . with *my sister*?"

"And you had sex with your sister's best friend. It's a whole messy love trapezoid thing."

"How on earth did this happen?"

I cross the room to sit down next to him on the bed. This news all seems to be coming as a bit of a shock to his little system, and I put a comforting hand on his shoulder. "Well, I think we both entered into this fake relationship because we were trying to run away from real feelings we had for other people. And those people just so happened to be with us at this cabin. So that's how it happened."

Andrew groans. "Real feelings suck, though."

"I know."

"You . . . and *my sister*?" He side-eyes me. "Is that why you wanted to come clean about everything the other night?"

I nod. "Did you come clean? To Dylan, I mean?"

The sheepish look on his face says he did not. "I wanted to. I wanted to tell them everything. As soon as we were alone on the mountain, Dylan confronted me about why I was marrying you, and I said I was having doubts, and then they just . . . kissed me."

Good to know Dylan has no respect whatsoever for Ellie and her fake relationship.

"I really wanted to tell them everything!" Andrew dejectedly drops his head onto my shoulder. "But there's this feeling in my chest, this . . . fear, I guess. That I'm going to mess it up or let them down. That if I tell them the whole truth, then there's nothing left for me to hide behind and I'll just have to . . . to let them love me."

Andrew lets the weight of that decision settle across my skin. "I couldn't even tell Dylan I'm in love with them."

I realize that I'd used the L-word in regard to Jack with Meredith and again now with Andrew, but I hadn't even remotely dared to cross that bridge with Jack. Maybe because I'm afraid she won't say it back.

Or maybe because I'm afraid she will.

"Wait. You didn't tell Jacqueline the truth? About our engagement being fake?"

"No. I didn't think it was my secret to tell."

Andrew pulls away from me and rises from the bed. "Wait, are you telling me Jack doesn't know our relationship is fake? You *slept* with her, but she has no idea about the trust fund?"

I shake my head. "No, you told me I couldn't—"

"Okay, on the one hand, I'm pretty hurt that my sister would sleep with someone she thought was my fiancé, but on the much larger, more important *hand*." Andrew's brown eyes go shock-wide in his handsome face. "My sister . . . she's a self-righteous, stubborn motherfucker. You should have told her the truth."

The dread trickles down my insides like beads of sweat, pooling in my gut. "But the money. The Butch Oven. You said—"

"Do you love my sister?" Andrew demands.

"Y-yes, I—I think so . . . ?"

Andrew reaches out for my hand. "Then we need to come clean *right now*."

It's apparently pertinent that we run, not walk, through the hallways and down the stairs, Andrew dragging me back to the family, but even running, we're too late.

As soon as we enter the living room, still hand in hand, everyone looks up at us. There's a stillness draped over the room, a creeping sense of *wrongness*. I take in the tableau of the family and try to understand it. Jack is sitting on the couch with her laptop open, the grandmas flanking her on either side like stone statues. Meemaw looks guilty as she sips her sangria. Lovey looks furious as she stares down her grandson. Dylan is sitting on the arm of the couch, chewing on the skin around their thumbnail. Katherine is a few feet away, pacing the carpet, and Alan is behind the couch, looking at the computer screen over Jack's shoulder.

Alan sees us, sees our joined hands, and glowers.

"Everyone, Ellie and I have something we need to say," Andrew starts.

"What's going on?" I ask before Andrew can say anything else. Because it's clear *something* is.

Jack looks up at me, and her face is different than I've ever seen it. Locked up, tucked away, completely devoid of the love and affection she showed me in the last twenty-four hours. I want to understand what happened, what changed, but I think deep down, I already know even before she says it.

"I told the family the news about your graphic novel," she says, in a voice that's nothing like sandpaper, nothing like a drum. It's hollow and monotone and absolutely devastating. "You know," she spits, "the one about the girl who fakes an engagement for money and lies to an entire family at Christmas."

Chapter Twenty-Seven

I can feel my throat start to close, but I force the words out anyway. "I—I can explain," I say. Everyone in the room is staring at me, but I can only see Jack and the stubborn set of her jaw and the coldness of her blank expression. "Please let me explain."

It's not Jack who answers me, though. It's Alan. "You're going to explain how you came into my home with the intention of stealing part of my father's money?"

"I wasn't trying to steal anything. Andrew agreed to—"

"That's what your webcomic is about?" Jack asks cuttingly. "It's about how you deceived our family? How you deceived *me?*"

"No, it's . . . it's . . . fiction."

Jack snaps the laptop closed. "It seems pretty true to life from what I've seen."

"I mean, ye-yes . . . yes . . ." I stammer. "It's based on my life, but I didn't come here to deceive anyone. I didn't want to deceive anyone! I just—I needed the money, and I didn't expect to fall in love with all of you."

Katherine's arms are folded across her chest, her expression like a closed fist. "I showed you hospitality. I treated you like a daughter. And this—"

"Mom—" Andrew tries, but I'm the one who has to make Katherine understand.

"I know, Katherine. *I know!* And I'm so sorry. You don't understand what it meant to me. Every moment of family bonding time. All I've ever wanted is a mom like you."

Katherine cuts her gaze away from me, and it's clear from her silence that I'm never going to have a mom like her.

I turn to Lovey, but Lovey just shakes her head and slowly rises from the couch. "I—I think I need a joint."

I finally pivot to Meemaw, who's clutching her sangria and giving me a pitying look. "Listen, everyone, let's not overreact to a little light deception," Meemaw tries. "If anyone is to blame for this whole quagmire, it's my douche-canoe of an ex-husband. No offense, Lovey."

"None taken. Where is my lighter?"

"Richard is the one who made it so Andrew can't inherit without getting married," Meemaw continues. "He practically forced the poor boy into this situation."

Alan turns to his mother. "So it's true? What it said in her silly little cartoon? And you knew, Mother? About this stipulation?"

Meemaw takes a sip of her morning sangria.

"Is it *all* true, then? The stuff about . . . about the Sam and Ricky characters . . . ?" Alan slices his gaze between Andrew and Dylan, and there's an undercurrent to this question that makes me hold tighter to Andrew.

"Yes," Andrew says, in a shadow of a whisper. "It's all true."

Alan erupts. "You've been sleeping with Dylan? Under this roof?"

"What is it that upsets you, exactly, Mr. Prescott?" Dylan snaps up from the arm of the couch. "The fact that your almost-thirty-year-old son has sex, or the fact that he has sex *with me*?"

Alan advances on Dylan. "How dare you speak to me like that in my own house? After everything this family has done for you?"

"*Your house?*" Andrew screams back. "You're never here! You never, ever show up for this family, and we all know the *real* reason—"

"Can we not shout, please?" Katherine interrupts harshly. She presses two fingers to her left temple. "This whole thing is giving me a migraine."

Alan continues to shout. "The real reason is that I'm busy providing for this family like a man is supposed to, which you would know if you ever—"

Andrew barks a laugh. "Spare me your gender essentialism. You're never around because you cheat on Mom."

"Andrew," three people say at once, their voices blending together in the anxiety vortex that is my brain. I can't think about Andrew and Alan, can't think about what this news means for Katherine. All I can think about is Jack, still sitting on the couch, holding onto the laptop like it's another shiny shield that might protect her.

"What? We all know," Andrew spits. "He has an apartment on the waterfront for his twenty-three-year-old girlfriend, so tell me, Dad: how, exactly, is that providing for this family?"

"I'm not going to stand here and be insulted like this," Alan declares, and then he promptly storms out of the room. Katherine whimpers, only once, before she straightens like the terrifying force of a woman she is.

"Look, none of this is Dylan's fault. Or Ellie's!" Andrew says, quietly enough to appease his mother's apparent migraine. "Ellie works at one of my investment properties. I asked her to do this. I practically *begged*, and I knew she would go along with it because she desperately needed the money. All of this was so I could claim the inheritance, so if you need to be mad, be mad at me."

"Andrew," Lovey says in a low, shocked voice, clutching at her throat. "Why? Why would you put our family through this?"

"Yes, why?" Katherine demands. "Don't we provide enough for you?"

"The money wasn't for me!" Andrew finally drops my hand so he can pinch the bridge of his nose for a second. Then he releases a breath and the final truth. "I found out Grandpa wrote Jack out of the will. The trust that was supposed to go to both of us—he changed it so I'm the only beneficiary, and he added a stipulation that says I have to get married to claim the money. I did this whole thing for Jack!"

The entire family turns to look at the woman sitting on the couch in her quiet fury. I was already looking at her—already memorizing the lines of hurt and disappointment and rage on her face—so I already know better than to expect Andrew's declaration to change anything.

"For me?" Jack echoes, like she must have misunderstood the cruel irony of that claim. "You *lied* to me *for me?*"

"Yes!" Andrew says, but I can tell he knows he's losing the moral high ground already. We both are, and my arms feel numb and my chest feels heavy and I know—I *know*—that this is what it feels like to fail. "When you decided to open the Butch Oven, you thought you had the trust to fall back on, and I didn't want you to go bankrupt trying to go after your dream."

Jack rises from the couch slowly and ominously. "I didn't think I had the trust to fall back on," she says.

Andrew blinks. "What do you mean? You did. We both did."

"No," Jack says firmly, her teeth grinding together. "I didn't. You think I don't know Grandpa wrote me out of his will after I dropped out of college? That motherfucker? Andrew, I knew there was no money waiting for me. I *always* knew. I just acted like I had a safety net because it was the only way to get you all to trust me. I took out the business loan for the bakery because I believe in myself. And all I'm hearing right now is that *you* didn't believe in me."

"I do believe in you!" Andrew shouts, rushing toward his sister. "JayJay, I completely believe in you! But starting a business is always a risk! I know! I work in investments! I didn't want you to fail!"

He reaches out for her, and she bats his arms away.

"The two of you really don't get it, do you?" She jabs a finger at me, too. "I didn't need you to try to save me, Andrew. I just needed you to support me. And you assumed I would fail, just like Dad did."

"I didn't—" Andrew starts, but the rest of his defense dies in the back of his throat. Because he did, and I did. We both screwed everything up.

"Was it all a lie?" Lovey asks in a sad squeak of a voice. She's looking at me.

"No," I say, crying harder now, crying in the middle of the living room in front of the entire family. "No, only our engagement was a lie. Everything else—who I am, and how much I fell in love with all of you—that's all the truth. I loved being part of this family!"

"How much?" Jack asks the silent room. She is staring right at me, burning straight through me.

"What do you mean?" I ask, even though I know.

"I didn't get to that part of the webcomic, but I want to know what this was all worth to you. *How much?*"

I drop my head. "Two hundred thousand dollars."

Jack pivots in her boots—the same ones she's been wearing since yesterday—and barrels out of the room.

"Wait! Jack!" I shout after her, following her out of the house, out the back door, out into the snow. "Jack! *Please!*"

She stops in her tracks a few feet from the porch and looks at me with eyes like fire, eyes that want to reduce me to ash. "You were *pretending* to be his fiancée," she says, like that's it. Like that's the end of us.

"I didn't know!" I gasp. "I had no way of knowing you were his sister when I agreed to go along with Andrew's plan, and then I was here, and—"

"And what? *What?* What is your excuse for not telling me the fucking truth the second you saw me?"

"I thought I was doing the right thing."

"*How?* How could you ever think that?"

I don't know. I honestly don't know. "I'm sorry. I'm so sorry. I'll never stop being sorry."

"Do you have any idea how guilty I felt all week?" She's crying. Jack is crying in the snow because of me. "The fact that I wanted you, even though you were with my brother," Jack lashes at me. "The fact that I couldn't stop flirting with you, couldn't stop finding excuses to touch you. The fact that I was so desperate to kiss you under the mistletoe. I was so *angry* at myself for betraying my brother like that, and it turns out this entire time, your relationship with him was fake. You let me believe I was a terrible person!"

"I'm so fucking sorry!" I fall to my knees in front of her because I don't know what else to do. "I was going to tell you the truth!"

"When? When I told you the truth about Claire, you made the choice to keep lying to me. And when I asked you point-blank about your relationship with Andrew at the bar, you made the choice to keep lying to me. And when we saw Andrew and Dylan together, you made the choice to keep lying to me!" She bends forward, so she's bearing down on me like a cyclone of anger and hurt. "And when we had sex, you made the choice, then, too. And for what? For the money?"

"You have to understand! It's not *just money* for me!" I'm frenzied now, shouting at her, shaking at her, wishing I could reach up for her. "I'm broke, Jack. I'm completely broke, and I financially support my mom, and my rent was going up, and—"

"Bullshit," Jack interrupts. "That excuse is fucking *bullshit*. You didn't keep the truth from me because of the money."

"I—I did!"

"You didn't," Jack says. The tears have stopped, and I watch as she battens down the hatches on her own face, tucks away her hurt, turns to stone. "You lied to me because you always had one foot out the door, waiting for things to fall apart. Have you ever stopped to wonder why you were so fucking miserable before this week, Ellie?"

Ellie, not Elle.

"It's because you make yourself miserable! You're a self-fulfilling prophecy! *The Perpetual Suck*, as you apparently call it, is only perpetual because you expect it to be!" She jabs a finger at me again. "You only fail because you assume you already have! And you broke my heart because of that once, and now you're breaking my heart over it again. I could forgive you for everything else. . . ." She gestures around her, to the cold air and the white snow and the distance between the Airstream and the house. "I could probably forgive you for lying, but I can't forgive you for assuming we would fail."

A sob rips out of me, but I know I'm not entitled to it. Only one of us gets to be hurt right now, and it's not me.

"You know, the fucked-up irony is," Jack says in her too-loud, sandpaper voice, "that you need trust in order to have physical intimacy in a relationship, yet you violated my trust in every imaginable way."

She turns on her boots in the snow and stomps off toward the Airstream.

I know this time, Jack Kim-Prescott won't hold onto a drawer of my things.

Chapter Twenty-Eight

Sunday, December 25, 2022

I should not be surprised I find myself back here, in this apartment. Had I really believed I'd escaped this subterranean hell? That I deserved to be liberated from the smell of old garbage wafting in from the dumpster outside the one window? This place—with the crusty carpet and the water stain on the ceiling in the distinct shape of Ted Cruz's face—*this* is what I deserve. This is where I belong.

"Your capacity for self-pity is truly remarkable," Meredith responds. I am not entirely aware of the fact that I am delivering this monologue out loud until Mere pops her head out of the fridge and glares at me. "And you *absolutely* should have left. This place is the physical embodiment of depression."

She's wearing yellow rubber gloves as she cleans out my refrigerator. My brain still hasn't fully registered that she's here, with me, in Portland. That she meant it when I called her crying in the snow outside the Airstream the moment Jack walked away from me, and she told me she was buying a same-day plane ticket on her credit card. Meemaw—the only Kim-Prescott willing to acknowledge my presence after everything—drove me back to town, and I found Meredith on my front steps this morning like the best possible Christmas gift.

One look at my apartment, though, and Meredith seemed less interested in consoling my heartbreak and more interested in taking bleach to what she claims is an OSHA violation.

"I'm not sure you're aware of this," Meredith announces as she comes out of the kitchen and plops down on top of my legs, since there is nowhere else to sit as long as I'm lying dejectedly across the entire futon, "but your apartment came equipped with this magical contraption where you can step into it smelling like depression and gas station sushi and step out smelling as fresh as daisies."

"Can't shower," I manage, but even those two words feel like knives clawing at the edge of my throat. "Too sad."

Meredith pulls back the edge of the duvet to get an uninterrupted view of my face. "You could at least change out of these clothes."

For some reason, the thought of taking off my clothes from yesterday feels like finally admitting it's all over. These are the clothes I wore skiing with Jack, these are the clothes I took off in the Singhs' cabin, the clothes I put back on after we ate biscuits and gravy together. A fresh wave of tears threatens to overwhelm me at the thought of washing them. In my mind, they smell like her.

"Ellie, come on." She attempts to hoist me up. "You can cry just as easily in the shower as you can on this futon. More easily, really, since the water will wash it all away."

"Merc, I—I can't." I choke on the words, choke on the knives in my throat, choke on every second that has ticked past in the last twenty-four hours. "I fucked everything up."

"Yeah." Meredith draws out the syllable. "You kind of did."

"God, Meredith!" I sit up in my nest of used Kleenex and the blood rushes to my head. "You're not allowed to agree with me! You're the one who said it would be easy to fake a relationship for money!"

"I did," she agrees. "But I believe I also told you to *stop* fake-dating Andrew once things got complicated with Jack."

I throw the duvet back over my head. "I *never* would have gone along with Andrew's plan if not for you!"

"It's good to see you're learning from your mistakes and owning your choices like an adult."

She's right, of course. She always fucking is. But the anguish is so big inside me, so debilitating, that I crave somewhere else to put the blame. "I can't believe I failed so epically," I admit.

"Wait." Meredith flops her entire body across mine. "What does failure have to do with anything?"

I squeeze my eyes shut and try not to picture Jack shouting at me in the snow. *You're a self-fulfilling prophecy.* "I failed at being Andrew's fake fiancé," I tell the inside of my blankets. "I failed at getting the money. I failed with Jack. I've lost Katherine, and the grandmas—"

"I'm struggling to see how any of that is failure. Fuck-uppery, sure, but not failure."

"You wouldn't," I snap at her. "You've never failed at anything in your life!"

Meredith rips the blanket back again. "Where the hell did you get that idea? Everyone fails!"

"You don't! Look at you! It's Christmas, you just flew across the country on a last-minute red-eye, and your study notes are *still* all over my house." I gesture wildly to the stacks of yellow legal pads and textbooks she's already unloaded.

"Yeah, I'm studying!" she shouts at me. "Because I failed the bar exam!"

I cough derisively. "You didn't fail the bar. You haven't taken it yet. The test is in February."

"I took it in July," Meredith corrects. "I took it without telling you, and I failed."

I stare at the flushed face of my best friend. "You . . .you *what*? Wait. Why?"

Meredith takes a slow, deliberate breath, gathers her red curls into a pile on top of her head, and holds them in place using the scrunchie on her wrist. Her face looks vulnerable, exposed.

"Meredith, why would you take the bar without telling me?"

"Honestly?" She sighs. "Because you have some really toxic ideas about failure, and I was worried about how you might react if I failed the first time, which was likely, since a lot of people fail the bar. And I did."

"I . . . you . . ." I stumble over my attempt at a response. That my best friend, this person I love with my whole heart, who I talk to every single day, experienced this huge life event and felt like she couldn't tell me about it. . . .

"And it doesn't really matter if I fail the bar once or twice, as long as I keep going. Once I'm a lawyer, I won't care how I made that dream come true, but Ellie—you had this dream you worked so hard for, and you experienced one setback and just *quit*."

Why does everyone *always* make everything about Laika? "I didn't quit. I got fired," I argue, trying not to think about that conversation with Jack at the Singhs' cabin. I had a neurotically crafted ten-year-plan I refused to deviate from. And when things got hard, I couldn't cope with changing the plan. So, I just gave up instead. I got fired from Laika and walked away from art entirely. Maybe because most things had walked out of my life, and maybe because I wanted to be the one to walk away first.

It hits me, the weight of this secret Meredith kept from me. "Shit," I mutter, the tears crowding against the backs of my eyes. "I've been a terrible friend to you."

"You haven't been a terrible friend," Meredith reassures me in her non-lawyer voice, the gentle one she uses when I'm being especially pathetic. "We all have seasons of needing and seasons of giving."

"But I've been in my season of needing so long, you felt like you couldn't come to me with something really big and important. I've failed horribly at being your best friend."

"Jesus!" Meredith erupts, boomeranging back to anger and frustration. "Are you listening *at all*? You can't fail at friendship! And failure—*actual* failure—is part of life. Remember when I got that D-plus in pre-calc fall term of freshman year?" Meredith asks slowly.

"And the prof told me he only gave me the D-plus because he felt sorry for me and didn't want to give me an F?"

I honestly don't remember that at all. I can't imagine the bold, confident girl pouring bleach into a shampoo bottle over her cheating boyfriend ever getting a D-plus. And I can't imagine anyone ever feeling sorry for her.

"And it doesn't fucking matter," Meredith plows on, "because I have never once needed to use calculus."

I'm still crying. Meredith is still draped across my body like a weighted blanket.

"And I get it, Ellie," Meredith says, gentle and coaxing again. "You have parents who are shit heaps. Linds and Jed suck, and you thought being perfect and never failing was the only way you could avoid becoming them. But your trauma is something that happened to you; it's not who you are. It's time to talk-therapy your way through it so it can stop controlling your entire life."

I snort a laugh and a little bit of snot comes out with it. Meredith reaches for a tissue and wipes up my snot, and if that's not love, I'm not sure what is. "Jed and Linds don't love you," Meredith says bluntly, cutting me off at the emotional knees. "But that doesn't mean you have to be perfect to deserve love."

The thing is, I used to dream about someone who would always choose me above everything else. There was romance in that dream, sure. I wanted someone who would see all my flaws and still lean in and tell me I'm beautiful. I wanted someone who would hold my hand in public and hold the rest of me in private, a warm body in my bed, a constant presence in my life.

I wanted someone who would see the whole mess of me—all the feelings and the perfectionism and the desire for control and the shape of my heart and the ache of my dreams, the wild, imperfect *hunger* of me, and the fear that keeps me from ever feeling full—and wouldn't get freaked out or turned off. Someone who would kiss me anyway.

So yes. It was a romantic delusion. But beneath the desire to be cherished was the ever-present thrum of my desire to be *chosen*. I wanted someone who would pick me to be their family. I believed that somewhere out there was the person who would want to spend every holiday with me. The person who would pick me as their partner for every duet, the person who would always care about what I had to say, who would get me off the couch and into the world. The person patient enough to build trust and connection with me first; the person who would notice when I'm hurting and still never calculate the cost of loving me. Despite all my cynicism, I *had* to believe that person existed.

And last Christmas I thought snow magic had delivered her to me. And when I saw Claire standing there in front of the Airstream, I took it as proof that my belief was childish and naïve. My own parents hadn't loved me enough to stick around. Why did I think someone else ever would?

"Are you sure I can't just blame my parents for making me believe I'm unlovable?"

"That's the opposite of what I'm saying," Mere deadpans. "You have people in your life who already love you. People who spent a thousand dollars on a plane ticket on *Christmas Eve*, by the way," she snaps. Because Meredith—Meredith loves me enough to stick around, even when I completely fuck everything up.

"It's not failure to let people see your imperfections," Meredith says. "It's vulnerability."

I snort again. "Gross."

Meredith erupts with laughter. It's a glorious, barking laugh, like the sound of a French bulldog struggling to breathe, and it makes me start laughing, too, even though everything is complete and utter shit. I lost Jack, and I lost the money, and all I have now is this terrible apartment.

Actually, I'll be evicted from this apartment in a week.

"Ellie." Mere reaches over and touches my cheek. "You have to stop letting your fear of failure keep you from letting people in."

"That's not what—"

I'm set to argue with her, to tell her it's not my fear of failure that caused me to lose Jack twice. Except . . .

Except maybe it was. Jack said I didn't tell her the truth about the money because I was convinced we were going to fail, and maybe she was right. Exactly one year ago, I fled Jack's Airstream before she had the chance to explain Claire to me.

But I didn't need an explanation. Claire confirmed what I'd already suspected: that Jack and I were never meant to last. I convinced myself we could never have anything more than one perfect day together because I was terrified of what might happen between us when things stopped being perfect. I couldn't imagine a world where Jack might choose me after the snow melted.

Claire showed up, and she gave me a reason to leave before Jack could leave me. And my supervisor fired me from Laika after I already felt like a failure. And I didn't tell Jack the truth about the money because I assumed the Butch Oven would fail before it even opened. I didn't tell her the truth about the engagement because I assumed *we* would fail. Like a fucking self-fulfilling prophecy.

"I've been so fucking *afraid*," I say out loud.

"Yes," Meredith says with the curt nod of her head. She's crushing my ribs a bit, but it helps me feel like the world isn't completely falling apart.

"I let fear rule my entire life." I take a deep breath and try to hold it in my lungs, try to press it into the aching hole inside of me. The hole that can't be filled by another person; it can only be filled by me. "I don't want to let fear control me anymore."

"Good takeaway."

I shove Meredith. I think about Jack yelling at me in the snow. I think about Jack in the Airstream, refusing to let go of my waist. "But I—I don't know how to do that. I don't know how to move forward."

Meredith peers down at me. "You could start by showering."

Chapter Twenty-Nine

Monday, December 26, 2022

"Here's a bedroom for eight hundred a month plus utilities off something called Killingsworth, but it says water signs are not welcome to apply." Meredith squints at the Craigslist ad on her laptop screen, then promptly chucks it onto the futon between us in outrage. "That is an unethical rental practice, and these harmony-seeking assholes are lucky I'm not feeling particularly litigious at the moment."

"Mere," I say, staring at the yellow legal pad where she's created a very short list of suitable housing situations. It's a list of two places. *Two*. "I need to ask Greg to take me back at Roastlandia."

"You do not, and you will not, and we're not having this argument again."

I flick my hand toward the laptop screen. "Even if they would rent to a Pisces, I can't afford eight hundred a month plus utilities. I can't afford *dinner*. Let's face it: without Andrew's money, I need to get a job, and going back to Roastlandia is easiest."

Meredith shakes her head so viciously that the pencil flies out of her bun and red curls spill everywhere. "We are trying to move *forward*. Roastlandia is one giant step backward."

"I'm moving forward. I've showered. I've put on a real bra." I gesture to my damp hair and fully supported breasts in turn. "Progress is being made."

Meredith permitted me a single day to mope and cry and lounge around in my own filth over losing Jack. Then, this morning, she went into full problem-solving mode, kicking my shins until I agreed to wash myself and to research new living arrangements before I'm evicted from this nightmare apartment. And it does feel good—to focus on the path forward instead of dwelling on all the things I did wrong. Instead of wondering if the Kim-Prescotts are still at the cabin, if Andrew and Dylan are together, if Jack is okay, if I've caused her to retreat deeper into her aluminum shell . . .

"Look, would it be easiest to fall into your old patterns and return to Roastlandia?" Meredith asks in her lawyer-voice. "Yes, of course. But would it be *healthiest*? Especially when there is an email from a publisher just waiting to be answered . . . ?"

I begin to curl into the fetal position on my end of the futon, then catch myself. I un-fetal. "I . . . that's . . . it's not relevant. I need money *now*."

"But you *are* going to answer the email, right?"

"I—I don't know, Mere," I tell her honestly, because part of moving forward is being honest, always. Even when it's hard. "She wants to publish the comic that literally outed me and Andrew to his entire family, and I don't know how I would ever finish writing *The Arrangement*, let alone share it with the world. And . . ." *Even when it's hard.* "Drawn2 was the one place I could do art just for me. It was the one place where I didn't have to be perfect, where I could just be a messy work-in-progress. What if turning those comics into a graphic novel is more than I can handle emotionally? What if it becomes like animation, where I'm doing it for the wrong reasons? What if I become a perfectionist monster again? What if . . . what if I start *hating it*?"

Meredith clicks her tongue. "It sounds to me like you're preparing for failure before it's happened again."

I don't have time to sit with that before my phone starts buzzing on the coffee table in front of me. My heart shoots into my chest with hope, because maybe, *maybe,* it's her.

It's not.

"Hi, Mom."

"What is this about your engagement getting called off?" my mother demands without greeting or pretense, just a disapproving pterodactyl screech in my ear.

"How did you hear about that?"

"It's on his Instagram! A photo of him with *someone else*, and a caption about how the two of you ended things on 'amicable terms'?" I shoot Meredith a look across the futon, but Linds is screaming loud enough that Meredith is already opening Andrew's Instagram on her laptop. Right there, at the top of his flawlessly curated grid, is a photo of him and Dylan sitting side by side beneath the messy Christmas tree they decorated together. I feel a brief bubble of joy in my chest at the sight of them together. At least someone got their happy ending.

Linds sounds highly aggravated and mildly drunk as I shift my attention back to her. "He left you for someone else?"

"Yes," I sigh, unable and unwilling to explain beyond that.

"What did you do?" Linds demands. "How did you fuck this up?"

"I—I didn't," I say. "He was in love with someone else."

"Get him back!" my mother shouts in my ear. "You have to get him back! He was perfect! He was *rich*! You have to fix things with him!"

"There's nothing to fix."

"Tell him you're pregnant! That's worked for me before."

Nausea seizes my stomach. "I'm not going to do that, Mom." On the other side of the futon, Meredith pantomimes a strangling motion.

"Then *beg*. Beg him to take you back! Do whatever it takes. You are never going to do better than a man like Andrew."

I pinch the bridge of my nose, close my eyes, and try to pretend my own mother didn't just say those words to me. "I'm your daughter," I squeak into the phone. "Shouldn't you think I deserve better than a man who doesn't love me?"

"Don't be naïve, Elena."

"And it was Christmas yesterday." Linds emits an audible gasp of confusion. "It was Christmas," I clarify, "and you didn't call me."

"I—" She clears her throat. "I didn't want to bother you, darling. I thought you were with Andrew's family."

"It was *Christmas*. It wouldn't have bothered me to get a phone call from my mom."

"I'm sure your father didn't call, either," she snaps.

"No." I sigh again. "He didn't. But that's not really the point."

"You could have called me, too, you know. This works both ways."

"I could have," I concede. Meredith looks ready to pounce, ready to rip the phone from my hands if I dare retreat into an apology. But I'm not going to apologize to my mom. "But I'm the kid, and you're the parent, and it would have been nice if you called."

"I'm calling now, aren't I?"

"You are," I say calmly. "But if you're calling about money, I need to tell you that I'm not going to be sending you money anymore."

Meredith leaps off the futon and punches a triumphant fist into the air.

"Sweetheart—"

Forward, I think. *Not backward.* "I'm not interested in this current relationship dynamic anymore," I say, thinking about Katherine and her laminated schedule. Thinking about Meredith and the thousand-dollar plane ticket that brought her here. Thinking about Andrew, giving up everything for his sister, even if it was misguided. "If you decide you're interested in having an actual mother-daughter relationship, I would love to work on that together. But if you're just going to call me whenever you need money, then I am going to stop answering."

Meredith's victory dance in the middle of my living room takes on an interesting gyrating quality, and I feel—

The call disconnects. My phone screen goes dark. I stare blankly at it for a second, thinking it must be a mistake. The call was dropped. She's going to call back. My mother is going to call right back. She'll apologize, she'll listen, she'll *try*.

Meredith stops her pelvic thrusting. "Wait, what happened?"

"She hung up," I say, staring listlessly at my phone.

The call didn't drop. I set new boundaries and my mother isn't interested in following them.

"Fuck." Meredith deflates. "That pathetic fucking excuse for an egg donor. Are you okay? How are you feeling?"

"I feel . . ."

How *do* I feel? I've just lost my mom. In one five-minute phone conversation, I lost the only family member I have, burned that bridge, so now it's just a scorch mark on my heart. I wait for the feelings of grief to overcome me like they did in the snow when I lost Jack and the rest of the Kim-Prescotts.

"I feel . . . *relieved*," I finally say. Honest, even when it's hard. "My mom sucks, doesn't she?"

"Your mom sucks the most suck of all the people who suck that aren't, like, war criminals or Republican senators."

I spring off the futon. There's a buzzing in my limbs, but it's not panic, not anxiety. It's something else. Something *better*. "I feel . . . *good*."

"Fuck yeah." Meredith punches the air again. "You told Linds where she can shove it!"

"Yeah!" I say. Forward, not backward. "*Yeah!*"

"This calls for a celebratory dance party!" Meredith shouts as she reaches for her phone and opens her Spotify app. Somehow, of all the songs that could possibly come up on Meredith's Bar Study playlist—Bach and the Beatles and *so much* Billy Joel—it's Celine Dion's version of "It's All Coming Back to Me" that cues up next. And I promptly burst into tears.

"Shit. Fuck. Ellie, why are you crying?"

"I'm not crying," I argue as I try to brush the tears aside, but they're coming so fast, I'm more just pushing the wet around, until it looks like I'm in a face-wash commercial.

"I can see your face. You're sobbing." The doorbell to my apartment rings, temporarily distracting Meredith from my cryfest as she stumbles the ten feet to my front door. When she opens it, I expect to see my landlord reminding me of the upcoming increase in rent. Instead, Ari Ocampo is standing on my stoop in a rainbow parka and a pair of thigh-high white pleather boots, holding a pastry bag from Roastlandia.

"Ellie!" she says, swanning right inside without invitation. "I saw Andrew's Instagram post, and I came right over. I brought you some gluten-free bran muffins."

"She's heartbroken, not constipated," Meredith says.

Ari eyes her. "And who are you?"

Meredith looks rightfully affronted. "Meredith. Ellie's best friend. Who are you?"

"I'm Ellie's other best friend," Ari answers. "She may not claim me as such, but she would be wrong."

Ellie is still standing in the middle of the room with tears running down her face. "Can someone please turn off this song?" I manage through a mucus bubble in my throat. One of these days, I will stop ugly-crying in front of the only people who can tolerate me, but that day is not today.

Meredith shuts off the song, and Ari hands me the bag of muffins. "Did he cheat on you? That handsome, Gucci-wearing motherfucker."

"I'm not heartbroken over Andrew." My lip quivers. "I'm heartbroken over *Jack*."

Ari shoots Meredith a questioning look. "Andrew and Ellie's relationship was fake, they were only getting married so he could access his inheritance, and Ellie's in love with his sister," Meredith explains, in the most succinct, emotionless way possible.

To her credit, Ari doesn't even flinch at this plot twist. "Oh, Ellie, I'm so sorry. Also—" She looks around. "I got your address from Greg, and I have some questions."

"Yes, I know," I snivel. "I live in an awful hovel."

"I thought you were getting evicted from this apartment?"

"I am. I just haven't found a new place to live yet."

"That's perfect!" Ari flops onto the futon, making herself right at home among my heating pad and weighted blanket.

"How is that perfect?" Lawyer-Meredith asks with a glare.

"Ellie is going to come live with me," Ari answers.

"I am?" I wipe my snot onto my arm. "Don't you live with four other people?"

She nods. "Yes, but it's a big house."

"With an extra . . . closet?" I ask, remembering her original offer. The offer I was too full of self-pity to seriously consider the night of the napkin contract.

"It's definitely closet-adjacent in size, but it does have a little window. And we wouldn't charge you very much in rent, on account of it being, you know, not a bedroom. But don't worry— there is a ton of common-area space downstairs, and one of the housemates, Ruby, they're a psychic, and they do free tarot readings in exchange for cleaning the bathroom. And I think you'll love Winslow—he's trans like me and an artist like you, so hopefully you won't care that he has canvases up in the living room all the time. He does mostly paint naked men as part of his 'Reclaiming the Male Gays' series. . . . Are you chill about nudity in your living spaces?"

"I'm not really chill about anything," I tell her, and Ari nods astutely like she understands.

Two weeks ago, just the thought of moving in with Ari and four other people would've necessitated a three-hour hibernation under my weighted blanket. But now, I think about Lovey's calming presence and the smell of her expensive weed; Meemaw's effervescent energy; Katherine's neuroses and Andrew's friendship. Maybe it wouldn't be so terrible to be surrounded by a bunch of loud, chaotic Portland hipsters.

"Sure," I say, throwing up my arms in resignation. "I'll rent your closet."

Ari's smoky eyes go wide. "Wait, really? You will?"

Meredith cocks her hips. "Wait. You *will*?"

"Forward," I say. "Not backward."

Chapter Thirty

"Okay, so when you said closet-adjacent, you meant—"

"It's a bit cramped," Ari admits. Given that Ari, Meredith, and I can barely all fit in my new bedroom, this admission feels like an understatement. "But if Ikea can create an entire apartment in three hundred square feet, surely we can make this work for sleeping!"

Meredith sets down my one box of stuff.

"That's it. That's all the floor space, taken up by a single box. Good thing you're poor and own very little."

"Anything is better than the depression chamber you were living in before," Ari says. And no one argues with her there.

So, I move into my new closet.

Ari lives in a large foursquare house on a corner lot with a massive front porch, a pride flag over the door, and a sign that says "Welcome to Brideshead" (because one of the housemates, Bobbie, is an English professor at Lewis and Clark). There is a backyard with raised garden beds and a fire pit and all of Ari's bees, and inside the house is a *home*. A cozy, lived-in space, with walls of books and Winslow's nude paintings and the supplies for Ari's honey business and a nursery's worth of plants, all tended to by someone called Gardenia, who is at least half-plant themself.

All of the housemates are queer, most of them are artists, and they've already cleared a shelf for me in the fridge.

• • •

Meredith helps me paint my closet mint green, helps me turn my twin mattress on the floor into a chic lounging space, then sits me down on said mattress, opens my email, and forces me to write a response to the editor who reached out about my webcomics.

Every single word feels impossible to type, so Meredith decides to torture me by playing Rebecca Black on repeat, refusing to shut it off until I finish crafting the email. And miraculously, somewhere around the sixth replay of "Friday," I start remembering the way it used to feel to create art alone in my bedroom as a kid. I remember the *joy* I used to feel before I let other people's praise define the value of what I produced. I remember the way Jack looked baking Christmas cookies, like the recipes were written into her bones, like baking was an extension of her heart, like she couldn't possibly fail at doing the thing she loved most.

I think about the hole inside me, and what's going to fill it up, and the response comes a little bit easier once I know what I have to say.

On New Year's Eve, Meredith flies back to Chicago. We stand in the departures zone outside PDX for a long time, our arms wrapped tight around each other. Meredith, who is comically short, fits nicely beneath my chin.

"I'll come visit you," I promise. "After you take the bar, I'll fly out to see you and we'll party for three days straight."

"By 'party,' you mean eat Sour Punch Bites, drink hard cider, and rewatch all of *Gilmore Girls*, right?"

"Obviously."

"Have you heard back from the editor yet?"

"I promise, the second I hear *anything*, you will be the first person I tell."

Meredith narrows one eye at me. "Before you tell Ari?"

"Before I tell Ari, I swear it."

Satisfied in the knowledge that *she* is my true best friend, Meredith adjusts her carry-on bag over her left shoulder. "What are you going to do about Jack?"

I groan. *Jack.* I had gone a whole seven minutes without thinking about her (a personal record), but now I'm thinking about her again outside PDX. I'm thinking about how when I sent that email to the editor, she was the first person I wanted to tell.

We were going to celebrate together.

"I don't *know* what to do about Jack. Nothing? There's nothing I can do, right?

Meredith reaches up to give my face a not-so-gentle pat. "Let me know when you figure it out."

I'm pretty sure there is nothing to figure out. I screwed things up with Jack beyond repair. One Christmas, I ghosted her. The next Christmas, I got fake-engaged to her brother, lied to her about it, and slept with her anyway.

It's not the kind of thing you come back from.

I don't even have any means of getting in touch with Jack. We never exchanged numbers, and she's not on social media. And if I *did* reach out, what would I say?

I'm sorry?

She hadn't wanted to hear that on Christmas Eve, and I can't imagine her wanting to hear it now. No, any attempts to reach out at this point would be selfish, in service of my own needs, alleviating my own guilt.

So I don't try to reach out. I get a job working at an art-supply store, part-time for now while I finish the new webcomic series I'm working on. I eat family-style dinner with the Brideshead house-mates. I go to brunch with Ari and her amazing girlfriends on the weekends. I go to Winslow's art shows. I figure out my state health insurance so I can find a therapist who isn't awful—but only because Ari and Gardenia sit on my legs and blast deep tracks by the Pussy-cat Dolls until I finally complete the application. Apparently, this is an effective method of unfreezing me.

Then I make an intake appointment with a non-suck therapist. No Nicole Scherzinger required. Every single Brideshead housemate is in therapy, and they all refer to their therapists by their first names and talk about them in casual conversation. It's weird, but in a good way.

When I get a reply from the editor, Meredith is the first person I tell. But then I tell Ari—I tell Winslow, Bobbie, Ruby, and Gardenia—and they take me out for cocktails the size of my face at the Bye and Bye to celebrate the start of something new.

A month passes, gray days become grayer, and every night as I fall asleep, I try not to think about the woman who could make a gray world feel vibrant.

I think about her every night as I fall asleep.

• • •

"You have a visitor," Ari announces one Friday night, sticking her head through the open door into my closet. I've got my iPad on my lap, and I'm working on a fanart commission for two characters in some queer book I haven't read. I've started doing commissions again, too, as a side hustle until I get my first check for the new graphic novel. Even if it's just fifty bucks for a single character and seventy-five for two, it feels good to create this kind of joy again.

"What kind of visitor?" I ask without looking up from my line sketch.

"A knockoff copy of the person you wish it was."

"Thanks for that," a male voice grumbles, and I jerk up to see Andrew Kim-Prescott's head floating over Ari's in the doorway. "Uh, hey, Oliver."

I push the iPad out of my lap. "Hi. Andrew." I have nothing better to say, so I go with "Hi," again.

"Can I get you anything?" Ari offers. "I think Winslow has some matcha powder."

Andrew shakes his head, and Ari leaves us to talk. Andrew attempts to take a step into my room, but his loafers immediately hit the edge of my mattress. I point to the small cubby Ari helped me mount to the wall. "Shoes go there."

He toes off his shoes, slides them into the cubby, and then gets down on his knees so he can awkwardly scooch his way onto my bed.

"Wow. This is cool." Andrew gestures to the rainbow lights I've strung up around the ceiling, the curtains framing the one window, the prints of my own art on the walls of my tiny closet bedroom. "You've done a lot with, um . . . very little."

"How did you know where I live?" I ask as I make room for his large frame. He shifts until he's cross-legged across from me in an Armani suit.

"Greg," Andrew answers. "You gave him this address for forwarding your final paycheck."

"And he gave away my address? Dickweed."

"I was also . . . perhaps . . . a bit of a dickweed." Andrew pinches the bridge of his nose, and that gesture fills me with a potent cocktail of affection and heartache. "It's been a month. I should've reached out. I dragged you into a ridiculous situation—got us both into a situation that was way over our heads—and when it blew up, I just . . . I ditched you. I felt so much shame and guilt about the way my family blamed you, and I was scared that if I got back in touch, you'd be furious with me, and I'm really sorry, Ellie."

I didn't know I needed an apology from Andrew until he waltzed into my closet offering me one. It's not because I've been harboring any anger toward him. More than anything, I'm *hurt*. Andrew and I were virtual strangers when we agreed to become spouses, but over the course of our short time together, I thought we'd become something closer to friends, and I don't have many of those. Then, when it all fell apart and Andrew ghosted me, it sent a pretty clear message: our relationship was always a business transaction, and without the money, I was no longer of use to him.

"I'm not furious," I finally tell him, and I watch his shoulders unspool from up by his ears. "Just a little bit hurt. If I'm being honest—" *Honest, even when it's hard.* "I missed you."

Andrew arches a silky black brow and shoots me a seductive look. "Oh, you *missed* me, did you?"

I kick him, hard, in the shins. "What happened? With your family? After I left? Was your sister . . . Has she forgiven you?"

Andrew gives me a crooked smile, like he knows how worried I am to hear the answer. "Of course she forgave me. We're family. Jack was livid for, like, two days, and then we talked it out and everything is fine. The rest of the family is fine, too."

He says this all so easily, without the blurred edges of trauma or pain. If only that's how things were with Linds. "I haven't spoken to my own mom in a month," I tell him. "I tried to create healthier boundaries for our relationship, and my mom wasn't interested."

Andrew reaches out and grabs my socked foot, gives it a shake. "Fuck 'em," he says in a perfect imitation of Meemaw. "She doesn't deserve you or your healthy boundaries, and neither does my dad. He actually didn't take things super well. My dad, he . . . he fired me."

I study Andrew's neutral expression, waiting for the punch line of this joke. "Wait, what? Your dad *fired* you? From *Prescott* Investments?"

"Yeah, so, uh . . . my mom left him," Andrew starts, wincing. "I guess she actually didn't know about the apartment for his twenty-three-year-old girlfriend, and my dad blamed me for telling her, so I'm out."

"Wow. Fuck 'em for real. I'm so sorry."

He somehow manages to lean casually while sitting cross-legged on a bed. "Nah, it's fine. I went to Stanford. I have this face—" He gestures to the face in question with the flourish of his wrist. Unsurprisingly, it's still a magnificent face. "I got, like, ten job offers within a week, and I just accepted a new position with a hedge fund here in Portland."

"A *hedge fund*? Does this mean you and Dylan aren't together? Because there is no way they'd let you work for a *hedge fund*."

Andrew drops his head, and for the first time since I've known him, I watch a blush spread across his cheeks. "What can I say? Ours is a star-crossed love."

I kick him again. "Andrew!"

"Ouch."

"You're still together?" I realize I've raised the volume of my voice beyond the appropriate level for a closet, but it feels warranted. "You're really *together* together?"

He nods, and the blush deepens. "I don't know," he says bashfully. "I guess we're, like, trying to do this thing for real, or whatever. I—I don't have a lot of experience with, you know . . ."

"Real feelings?"

Andrew raises his hands halfway to his chest, then lets them drop again. "I don't have a lot of experience dating someone I care about, so I'm petrified about ninety percent of the time," he confesses. "But it's also good. It's really good. And after I finally told them that I *do* want a committed relationship with them . . . you know, monogamy, marriage, mortgage—"

"All that embarrassing crap."

"It was like this giant weight had been lifted." Andrew sighs. "I should've just done that from the beginning, but Dylan and I can't change the past. So here we are."

Andrew shrugs again, and there's an unexpected sweetness to it. I think about the Burberry coat, the snapback, all the versions of Andrew Kim-Prescott I tried to pin down. But Andrew is just this— just a messy person with feelings he doesn't always understand, just a person who is mostly trying to do his best.

I can feel him studying me from across the bed as I pick pilly bits off my sweatpants. "They miss you, you know?"

"Dylan does not miss me, unless it's because they need a human target for their glowering."

"Glowering is Dylan's love language," Andrew clarifies. "They do miss you, but I meant *everyone*. The grandmas ask me about you all the time. Lovey wants to know when you're going to finish *The Arrangement*, even though I keep telling her she already knows how it ends. And Meemaw told me the truth—that she knew our relationship was fake all along, that she knew about you and Jack. I think she blames herself a bit for not stepping in. Also, she wants her snowsuit back."

She can't have it, I don't say aloud. It does, a little bit, still smell like Jack.

"And my mom mentions you a lot. At first, it was in a not-so-positive context. Like *How could we have let ourselves be taken in by that charlatan?* And *Who raises their daughter to infiltrate a family at Christmas?* But once her initial anger wore off, I think Mom started to realize you weren't a charlatan so much as a desperate poor person, and that the whole point was that your parents didn't really raise you. Now she mostly worries you're not eating well and wonders if it would be acceptable to drop off Tupperware containers full of food."

I want to smile, imagining Katherine stealthily depositing reusable grocery bags outside of Brideshead, but instead I'm holding my breath, waiting to hear if "everyone" includes her.

If Jack ever talks about missing me.

But Andrew doesn't say her name, and I'm forced to exhale my disappointment. Jack doesn't miss me. Why would she miss someone who did nothing but hurt her and violate her trust?

Andrew seems oblivious to my own hurt as he reaches into the inside pocket of his blazer and pulls out an envelope. "I've missed you, too. I know you were supposed to be my wife, but I started thinking of you as a sister, and—" Andrew cringes. "Wait, did that sound creepy?"

"It's the situation that got creepy, honestly. That's not on you."

He pushes the envelope awkwardly toward me. "Anyway, since

you're my almost-wife, sort-of-sister, I've been feeling really guilty that you went through all of this and still didn't get the money, so I—"

"I don't care about the money," I interrupt. "I mean, of course I *care*, because that kind of money is the difference between Grocery Outlet frozen burritos and Whole Foods fresh vegetables, but the money was just a Band-Aid. A golden parachute I thought would fix my life without me actually having to, you know . . . fix my life."

"Well, it seems like you've been fixing your life, so . . . take this."

I do. The envelope is heavier than I expect. "What's this?"

"It's not two hundred thousand dollars, so adjust your expectations." He flaps his hands. "Just open it."

Inside the envelope are several sheets of expensive paper folded neatly into thirds. They fan apart, and there, across the top, in official block letters are the typed words "Andrew and Ellie's Non-Marriage Contract." Below is a paragraph of legalese, followed by enumerated stipulations, the words blurring and blending together.

"Seriously, Andrew, what is this?"

He tilts forward so he can point to the words on the page. "It's a contract that says that whenever I do get married—if that's in two years or five or fifty—you are entitled to ten percent of my inheritance."

The pages slip between my fingers. "Andrew! No, you don't have to do that!"

"Well, don't get too effusive with your gratitude. I do *actually* have to get married at some point, which is statistically unlikely."

I look up at Andrew, at the blush on his throat and the smile on his face. I think the statistical probability is changing. "You're prepared to give me ten percent of your inheritance regardless of when you get married . . . ?"

"And bonus, *you* don't even have to be the person who is marrying me. You're welcome."

I stare down at the creamy pages, at this huge symbolic gesture he's handed me. "How will your future spouse feel about you giving away two hundred thousand dollars to some random woman?"

Andrew shrugs. "Dylan firmly believes you're entitled to that money for what you had to endure."

I lift a suggestive eyebrow, and Andrew's blush deepens as he realizes what he's said. "Not that I think Dylan is going to be that spouse. Just, you know. An example. A sampling of potential partners and their attitudes toward me giving away our money."

"A sample size of *one*?"

"Please shut up." Andrew snatches the papers out of my hand and awkwardly shoves them back into the envelope. "The point is, I want you to have this money, and I understand you might be hesitant to take it, and I want to reassure you that—"

"Oh no, I'll take it."

Andrew frowns.

"Yeah, I'm not going to fight you on this. I live in a closet." He looks around, remembering where we are. "If someone with generational wealth wants to offer me a boatload of money, I'm not going to turn it down. I'm just also not going to wait for that money to start building the life that I want."

"Well, good." Andrew gives me a curt nod. "So does that mean you're getting back to your art? The family mentioned there was an editor who maybe wanted to publish you?"

"Yeah. Yeah, that's sort of . . . happening? Maybe? I had to sign with an agent first, which I did. And the editor wanted me to adapt the original webcomics, but it didn't feel quite right, writing about . . . *her*. So I'm taking the parts that worked, and I'm writing something new. Something a little more . . . magical. It's possible the editor won't want it when it's done, but . . ." I shrug, and I mean that shrug. Maybe this won't work out. I don't really have a plan for what happens next.

Andrew flashes me his most charming, most sincere smile. "I

hope you'll let me read it when you're finished. I could use a little magic. Speaking of . . ." He reaches for his pocket again. "I have one more thing for you."

"Is it a car? Because I could really use a car."

He pulls out a sheet of paper, this one folded haphazardly into quarters. When I unfold it, I see that it's a flyer.

THE BUTCH OVEN SOFT OPENING.

"Andrew . . ."

The paper is glossy, with a purple background, the words in white, loopy script. In the middle of the page is a cartoon, rainbow-colored Dutch oven.

"Andrew . . ." I start again.

"Yeah," he says, like he understands this one glossy sheet of paper is worth more than the pages folded inside that envelope. "She's really doing it."

Ridiculous, sentimental tears prickle in the back of my eyes. "I always knew she could."

"I didn't," Andrew admits, his voice low. "I should have, but I didn't. You know, one night a few weeks ago, we got drunk and she told me everything about what happened between the two of you. She told me she never would've believed she could do it if you hadn't believed in her first. I never thought my sister could stay focused on a goal like this long enough to achieve it, and I know that makes me an asshole."

I set the flyer down on the bedspread in front of me, too over-whelmed to look at the cute font and the even cuter Dutch oven. "Jack was always capable of this. She just spent her whole life being told she was a slacker and a fuck-up, and she just needed—"

"Someone who could really see her?" Andrew fills in, looking at me pointedly. "Ellie, what happened between the two of you?"

I shift back against the pillows. "You just said Jack told you everything."

"I want to hear it from you," he says. "Because based on what I do know, I'm having a difficult time understanding why you're not together right now."

"Probably because I was fake-engaged to her brother and lied to her about it," I joke.

Andrew isn't joking. His tone is completely serious when he asks me, "Why did you and Jack fall apart?"

I shift again. "Because—because I assumed we were always destined to fall apart. Jack and I were never supposed to meet. We were two lonely girls searching for the same book who found each other on Christmas Eve."

And it's hard not to believe some part of that was fated, that it wasn't random chaos that brought us together and trapped us in the city for the entire day. It's hard not to feel like Jack was created especially for me, and me for her. Some divine being who built her out of hard angles and tough sinew built me out of softer materials, curves and dimpled flesh. Jack is the steadiness to my sway, and I'm the control to her chaos, yet I'm the one who screwed us up.

"I convinced myself that someone like her could never love someone like me, so I self-sabotaged in the most epic way possible by assuming we weren't meant to last. And I did that *twice*."

Andrew looks serious for a moment. "Third time's the charm?" he tries.

I shake my head. "People don't give third chances. And it's okay—Jack clearly doesn't want to talk to me and that's *okay*. I'm trying to change my patterns. I'm trying to be better at accepting failure is a part of life, and that means accepting that I messed things up with your sister and moving on."

"Are you actually trying, though? I mean, sure, with your art and your life, A-plus for effort, but"—he places both hands flat on his knees, the way he placed those hands flat on a table before he asked me to marry him—"did you really try with Jack? Look, as we've established, I'm not your fiancé, and I'm not your brother, and if you want to tell me to fuck off, you can—"

"Fuck off," I say. I halfway mean it.

"But," Andrew continues, "it seems to me like you're still assuming you're going to fail before you've even tried. You said Jack doesn't want to talk to you, but have you even reached out to her? Did you even *try?*"

I stare down at the purple flyer crumpled on top of my duvet.

"People do sometimes get third chances," Andrew says. "Dylan and I did."

On the bottom of the flyer, beneath the details about when and where, is a little postscript. *Come exactly as you are. All are welcome.*

"You should go," he says.

"Go where?"

"To the soft opening. It's on Valentine's Day."

"I can't show up to her soft opening. She doesn't want me there."

"You don't know that."

"Do you know she *does* want me there?"

"No. That's kind of the point. You have to take a risk and find out."

My finger traces the glossy paper over the words *Butch Oven.* An imperfect rhyme.

"I don't want to show up to her big event and ruin it," I tell Andrew. "That sounds like a ridiculously idiotic plan."

He reaches across the bed to grab my foot again. "Sometimes," he says, "ridiculously idiotic plans work out mostly for the best."

Chapter Thirty-One

Tuesday, February 14, 2023

The air smells like the possibility of snow.

I step out of the car and into the cold evening, wrapping my blue scarf closer to my face. It hasn't snowed in Portland all winter, but now the promise lingers in the sharpness of every deep breath I take. And I'm taking a lot of deep breaths.

"Is this a ridiculously idiotic idea?"

Ari finishes paying through Parking Kitty on her phone, then loops her right arm through my free one. "Oh, it's definitely a ridiculously idiotic idea. That's why I love it."

She gives me a tug, as if she knows my internal resistance is about two seconds away from becoming external, that I'm about ready to plant my feet into this sidewalk and never move. That I'm ready to freeze.

Ari doesn't let me freeze.

"How are you feeling?"

"Like my stomach is going to fall out of my ass."

"God, it's so sexy when you talk about your anxiety-based GI issues," Ari says, and I laugh as she nestles closer to me while we walk, pressing her crown of hair to my shoulder. She smells like coffee and essential oils and unconditional love.

"But is this fucked up? That I'm crashing her soft opening?"

"You're not crashing," Ari argues, "because her entire family invited you."

"Yeah, but what if it was a pity invite?"

"Now. What have we talked about?" Ari says in her most patronizing voice.

I roll my eyes and repeat back Ari's words. "I should not assume people invite me to social events out of pity, since that's not a thing that actually happens very often."

"*Exactly*. You're not showing up to shit all over her special day. All you're doing is walking in, congratulating her, and giving her your gift."

The gift in question is tucked under my other arm.

"This is a totally normal gesture between friends."

Friends. The word leaves a sharp, metallic tang in my mouth, sits like a knot in my chest. *Friends.*

Three months ago, I had *one* friend, singular. Meredith.

And, of course, I still have Meredith, sending me TikToks I never watch and screenshots of dating profiles for people I have no interest in dating. We have our constant video chats and my upcoming trip to Chicago. I don't know what I would do without Meredith, but I also have so much *more* than Meredith now.

I have Ari and her occasional condescension and her unwavering loyalty and her admirable confidence that she is, somehow, my best friend and always has been. I have the Brideshead housemates. I have Andrew, who walked back into my life and then kindly refused to walk back out again. And he brought others with him.

Like Dylan, who showed up at Brideshead to drag me to brunch two days after Andrew's surprise visit. ("A *hedge fund*?" I asked. To which Dylan scoffed, "I know, I truly can't take him anywhere in this city anymore.")

Like Meemaw and Lovey, who called me out of the blue one evening and invited me to a sip-and-paint. Apparently, it happens twice a month at their favorite wine bar in Lake Oswego, and after we did amazing drunk-replications of *Starry Night*, we made plans to come back.

Like Katherine, who dropped off a bag of food one Sunday afternoon and then invited herself inside for a bottle of wine that soon turned into three. It turns out she's a little lonely post-separation from Alan. I've agreed to come over next weekend to help her paint the walls of her new condo.

I used to think letting more people in would mean having more people who could ultimately disappoint me. Hurt me. Walk out of my life. But having more people means there are more arms at the ready to catch me when I fall. And I fall *a lot*.

And it feels good to be the arms for someone else, too. It feels good to both need and be needed—to have seasons of needing and seasons of giving—but when I think about *Jack*. About being Jack's *friend*. The thought calcifies inside my lungs.

I haven't seen her, even since I've started seeing her family. Dylan and Katherine and Meemaw all assure me that she's doing well, that she's moving on, that *friendship* between us is possible. And if I want to keep the rest of the Kim-Prescotts in my life, friendship seems like the right path forward.

"You ready?" Ari asks as we cross the street toward the building. There's a small banner out front announcing the soft opening with those same words printed in purple: "All Are Welcome."

I hope that includes me.

The building is almost unrecognizable from the place she showed me a year ago. New windows, new paint, and a new sign out front. There's an awning and a pride flag, and I feel slightly untethered when I think about all that has happened between last Christmas and this moment so that Jack could achieve her dream.

But I remind myself I am tethered. To Ari's arm.

"Ready."

We step inside the converted warehouse, and I'm overwhelmed by the size of the crowd, by the volume of the room, by the sugary smells and rising heat. There's a small stage where a trio is playing acoustic music, and laid over that is the sound of dozens of different voices, grating and out-of-tune.

Ari pulls me in tighter, and I take a deep breath and try to calm my anxiety by focusing on how I would draw this place—this beautiful place that belongs to Jack. The first thing I notice are the lavender walls, bright and cheerful and so damn *gay*. Industrial lights wash the room in a warm glow and a giant window facing the east must fill the space with natural light every morning. On the opposite side of the room from the stage there's the giant counter, the exposed kitchen, the glass display case filled with a million different colors of pastries and pies and cookies and cupcakes. In between is a hodgepodge of tables. Some customers are sitting down, using forks to dive into delicious desserts, but most people are standing, milling around, sampling the food as it's carried around the room on platters.

I spot the grandmas, passing out macarons on serving trays. Katherine is wearing an apron and refilling coffee cups. Dylan and Andrew are surrounded by hip-looking twentysomethings, and I can see Andrew animatedly talking up the place: he's in full investment-bro mode, but he's out here putting that broiness to good use. And he's holding Dylan's hand as he does it.

And then there's Jack. I spot her immediately, as soon as we step inside. She's wearing her usual uniform of loose-fitting jeans and black boots, but on top, she's gone with a linen button-down cuffed at the elbow, a purple apron with the Butch Oven logo splashed across the front. She looks like herself—like *more* of herself, in this place she made into a reality by sheer force of will—taking up space, demanding all the attention. Forearms and thighs. Her dark brown eyes and her half-moon smile and her extremely heavy gait. She's not restless, not fidgeting. She seems at peace. She's too loud, and she's absolutely everything, chatting with the people who came here to celebrate this, to celebrate her. She accomplished her dream.

The force of feelings hit me like a train. I don't want *friends*. I want to kiss that white scar. I want to be the person standing at Jack's side. I want to be the person who celebrates with her after everyone else goes home, a bottle of wine for just the two of us, toasting her, whispering, *You did it, I knew you could*. I want to be Jack's arms and her everything else, to be there for all the seasons, and the past seven weeks have done nothing to dull the intense certainty of these feelings. I want her so badly, it pins me in place by the door. It's the ache, in my heart, in my stomach, between my legs, but it's not an ache of loneliness. It's the ache of wanting something so badly, you will throw yourself down a flight of stairs if you can't have it. It's the ache of wanting to risk everything for the smallest chance at something.

It's a good kind of ache.

"Girl, wipe that horny look off your face," Ari hisses. "We're in public."

My eyes are on Jack, watching as she whips her head around. She's wearing her glasses, and her hair is freshly cut, shaved on the side and neat, like that day I first met her. She turns again, and she finally sees me and Ari by the door.

Her expression shifts, but I'm not sure what it's shifting *to*; I'm too anxious to read the nuances of her mouth and eyes. "Shit. She's seen me. What do I do?"

"Um, go talk to her?"

"What? No. Gross."

"Continue standing in the doorway like a weirdo, then. You're right, that's a better plan."

"Ugh. Fine. I'll go talk to her."

But before I can even motivate my legs to move again, Jack comes across the room to talk to me first. "What are you doing here?" she asks in her too-loud, easy-to-overhear voice. She doesn't sound angry to see me, but she doesn't sound quite happy, either. Approximately half the room turns to face us.

Ari slips her arm out of mine and vanishes into the crowd without a word.

I need to say a word, so I go with, "Congratulations!" and I sort of shout it at Jack while throwing one arm needlessly into the air. "You did it. I knew you could."

It's not the way I want to say those words to her, but Jack gives a little waning crescent of a smile, and it's enough to turn my ache into a gentle, pulsating heat throughout my body.

"It's not bad, is it?" Jack looks around the room—at the beautiful space she's built with her own two hands and her willingness to fail.

"It's incredible," I say.

Jack's eyes flicker up and down my body. "What are you doing here?" she asks again, and there's a tiny quarter-moon tugging on her lips. That quarter-moon smile almost looks like hope to me, but it's too soon to get carried away on Jack's hope.

"Your family invited me. Insisted I come, actually."

"You didn't . . . *want* to come?"

Honest, even when it's hard. "Of course I wanted to come," I admit. "I wanted to see your dream come to life. I wanted to support you. I wanted to . . . to see you. I just didn't want to ruin your event."

She tilts her head and half-moons at me. "Are you planning on ruining it?"

"No! But I have a pattern of unintentionally ruining things with you, so . . ."

"You have a pattern of *thinking* you're going to ruin things," Jack corrects, "and then when they're ruined, you take that as proof that you were the ruiner."

"Yeah, I know. You already told me I'm a self-fulling prophecy, and I'm working on it. Trying to become less . . . prophetic."

"I said that to you?" Jack leans back against the table behind her, and *shit.* This woman should not be allowed to lean in my presence. Everything has gone sweaty.

I peel my blue scarf away from my throat. "Well, you sort of shouted it at me? In the snow? You know, after you found out I horribly betrayed you."

"Ah." Jack winces. "I maybe blocked some of that out, on account of how awful it was."

"Very fair. Unfortunately, when the woman you love tells you you're the reason your life is miserable, you tend to remember it forever in a very self-punishing sort of way."

Jack's smile disintegrates on her face. "What did you just say?"

"Not that I didn't deserve it!" I backpedal. "I did! I am so sorry for the way I hurt you. You were totally right to say all of that to me! You were right about a lot of things, actually, and I've really been trying to make some changes based on your very honest feedback. It was sort of like a comment card, but for a romantic relationship, and I've . . . um . . . taken those comments under advisement."

Oh, *fuck*. Thank goodness I finally stop talking, but I'm pretty sure now the *entire* bakery is staring at me.

"No." Jack shakes her head. "You said *when the woman you love* . . . Do you? *Love* me?"

"Did I say that?" God, why did I wear a scarf indoors? So, so much *sweating*. "I don't think I said that."

"You did," Jack counters. "Basically everyone heard it." She turns to some random person over her right shoulder. "Sorry, but did you just hear this woman with the braid and glasses say she loves me?"

The stranger nods, and Jack turns back to me.

"See?"

"Well—" *Fuck*. My brain is 90 percent white noise and 10 percent whatever the trio on the stage is playing at the moment. And that 10 percent finally recognizes the song: it's an instrumental version of Carly Rae Jepsen's "Call Me Maybe."

And if that's not a sign, then I don't know what is. "Yes, actually, that's right," I say to Jack. And the entire bakery. "I love you. I'm, like, hopelessly in love with you. And I was supposed to come here tonight and offer you this gift in friendship, but I don't want to be your friend."

Jack can't stop the smile from curling in the corner of her mouth. "You don't?"

"This was never about friendship." I don't want to be Jack's friend. I have friends. What I want is a witness. I want someone who sees me, someone who experiences every failure alongside me, someone who chooses me. And I want that person to be Jack.

So I'm going to go ahead and embarrass myself in a room filled with fifty strangers. "I fell in love with you after spending one day with you, which is a lot, I know. Definitely not something you're supposed to admit, because it's love-bomby and Romeo-ish, but it's true. I fell in love with you that day, and I was so scared of getting rejected, that I convinced myself it didn't mean anything. But it did. It meant so much to me."

Jack bites down on the edge of her smile, and she's about to reject me. The trio is playing the chorus of "Call Me Maybe," and Jack is about to tell me it doesn't mean anything to her anymore. I'm scared, but I'm trying so hard to be honest. So I tell her: "I am feeling very emotionally vulnerable right now, and I'm afraid of taking this risk with you, Jack. But I also know that you're a risk worth taking, and if there is any part of you that thinks you might be able to forgive me—"

I stop. Around me, the room has gone quiet. The clang of forks and the din of happy conversations has muted. The band has stopped playing Carly. Even the lavender walls are holding their breath as Jack looks at me without an ounce of hope in her eyes. "Ellie," she says, as quietly as she can, "I'm sorry, but I don't think I can take that risk with you again."

A few people in the room make sounds of sympathy. One person *laughs*.

"I understand, and I appreciate your consideration," I say with all the dignity I can muster as I attempt to swallow down the impending tears. "I'm extremely proud of everything you've accomplished here, and I hope you enjoy the rest of your night."

I turn to leave before Ari and Dylan and all the Kim-Prescotts and a roomful of strangers see me cry, but then I remember the gift still tucked under my arm. I turn back. "Sorry, this is for you. It's a . . . a friendship gift. You don't have to take it if it makes you uncomfortable."

Jack takes the gift from my hands without looking at me, and I turn back toward the door.

Except, shit—for some reason I'm turning around again. "I know you're afraid of letting other people see you and help you— that you're afraid you'll disappoint people if you let them in. But you never once disappointed me, Jack."

I clear my throat, and damn—my voice is cracking. Because I am crying *quite* hard. I steel myself. "I love that you're restless and unsatisfied, that you're both allergic to boredom and somehow crave a boring life in the suburbs, and I think other people will love that about you, too. If you let them see it. You have so much love to give, and I know you want your witness."

Jack frowns, and I cut in with—"And that's not me! I'm not your person, and that's fine!" This snot situation is getting a little out of control at the moment. I'm about two seconds from needing to wipe my nose on my sleeve, so I better end this thing. "But I hope someday you'll drop your shiny shield so someone can see the messy, honest you."

And before the snot becomes visible on my face, I turn away one last time and flee the Butch Oven.

Chapter Thirty-Two

There is almost an inch of snow on the ground when I trip out of the bakery.

Even though I'm crying and snotting, I also have to laugh at the fine layer of fresh snow on the sidewalk. I've overcome so much—grown and changed *so much*—yet here I am, heartbroken in the snow over Jack Kim-Prescott yet again. I'm alone now, so I might as well rub all my snot all over my sleeve.

I *failed*. In a passionate, public display of love, I failed in epic fashion. I grand-gestured the woman I love in full view of all her family and friends, and I crashed and burned. And—

I take a deep breath. *And it's okay.*

It's not okay right now, obviously. Right now, I need to take off my pants and crawl into my bed. I need to eat all the things and draw through this pain. I need my heating pad and my weighted blanket and a very long *cry*.

But I think it *will* be okay, someday. Probably.

Hopefully.

I pull out my phone to send Ari a quick text letting her know that I need a little space and I'm walking home. Soon I'll want to call Meredith so she can jump into problem-solving mode. Soon I'll want Ari to wrap me in her soft arms and tell me I'm pretty. For now, though, I just want to be alone.

It's not a long walk between here and the Burnside Bridge, and I make my way down quiet, dark streets as snow swirls around me, tiny flakes, illuminated in the streetlamps. And damn if it isn't a little bit magic, the way it floats in all directions, the way it paints the ground a pristine white, the way it immediately transforms the world into something new, right before your eyes.

Snow days mean freedom, and some part of me does feel impossibly *free*. I finally told Jack how I feel—full honesty game. And she doesn't feel the same way, but at least . . .

At least I tried.

I slide my hands into the pockets of my coat. Maybe this snow will bring its own magic. Maybe it will bring me something new.

Two Christmases ago, the snow brought me Jack, and even if we didn't work out, we had one perfect day together.

This last Christmas, the snow brought me Andrew and the Kim-Prescotts.

Maybe this snow will bring me a new person—a messy, honest, too-loud person, one who can love me back. Someone else who shoves their fists into the pockets of her Carhartt jacket, someone else who flicks her chin to get her hair out of her face, someone else whose smiles come in increments like the phases of the moon.

I know there's only one Jack. But maybe someone else will make me feel the way she does. In time. If I can be that open version of myself I was with her.

I step onto the sidewalk on the edge of the Burnside Bridge.

Last year, with Jack, we walked down the middle of the bridge. There were no cars, no boundaries, no restrictions at all. Everything was blurred and indistinct. Now, I stick to the path as cars chug by, slowly, windshield wipers pushing aside the mounting snow. Yet, even now, there's something magical about this bridge, too.

Maybe the someone new this snow will bring me is myself.

Behind me, a car honks, and fuck it—*nope*, I'm still the Ellie Oliver who despises being honked at by strangers. I fold my arms across my chest and hope they pass quickly.

They don't pass. They honk several more times. The car pulls up beside me and slows down to match my pace, and it's only then that I realize there is a vast difference between walking across the Burnside Bridge in the middle of the night during a snowstorm with Jack and walking across the Burnside Bridge on a random *Tuesday* at eight o'clock *by myself.* I avoid looking directly at the vehicle—a truck, I think—that has decided to crawl along beside me, honking.

I pull out my phone, ready to utilize the emergency call feature just as the driver of the truck rolls down the passenger-side window and yells, "Hey!" And I swear I recognize that voice.

"Elle! Hey, Elle, *stop!*"

The truck pulls up beside me with its emergency flashers on. "Holy shit! You walk fast!" the driver shouts, and then they're leaping out of the car, and the driver is Jack.

Jack, on the Burnside Bridge. Jack, in the snow. She's silhouetted in the harsh glare of Gillian's headlights, so all I can make out is the breadth of her shoulders and the length of her legs, her entire body dotted with snowflakes.

"What the hell are you doing?"

"What am *I* doing?" she shouts. Jack always thinks she has to shout when she's outside, as if somehow the fresh air makes it impossible to hear her naturally loud volume. "You're the one who's walking alone in the snow!"

"I—I needed some space," I say. "To think."

She takes a step forward and shifts from silhouette to full, in-color person, and even though I just saw her twenty minutes ago, and even though she literally just *broke my heart*, the sight of her makes me feel invincible and devastated all at once.

"That was pretty humiliating back there," Jack screams at me, even though we're ten feet apart.

Fuck. "I'm so sorry, Jack. The last thing I wanted to do was embarrass you at your event."

"Oh no, I wasn't." A chin flick to get her hair out of her eyes.

"This is a soft opening. Everyone in there was a friend. I meant, that was humiliating for *you*."

Even bigger *fuck*. "Well." I give an awkward shrug. "You're worth the humiliation, I guess."

Jack sucks in a breath and pulls herself up taller.

"Is this . . . is that why you followed me all the way to the Burnside Bridge, Jack? To tell me I should be embarrassed?"

"No, I . . ." She shoves her fists into the pockets of her Carhartt jacket, goddamn her. "I opened your present after you gave your humiliating little speech. It is—"

"I know it's kind of weird," I insert, feeling more humiliated by the second, "to draw you a picture of what the Butch Oven looked like before, but I thought it was a good reminder of what you did. You know, how hard you worked to turn it into what it is. Where you started, and where you are now. I framed it so you can hang it on the walls of the Butch Oven. Or not. Whatever."

"I will absolutely hang it on the wall. Did you . . . did you draw the building from the memory of when I showed it to you last Christmas?"

I nod. "I have a very good memory for artistic details." *Honest, even when it's hard.* "And I remember basically everything about that day."

There's a small sliver of hope in the corner of Jack's mouth. It's always the fucking hope that gets me. It makes me feel like a weird pile of goo, held together by a purple puffy jacket.

"Andrew says you're working on something new?"

I nod uneasily, aware that we're still standing on the side of a bridge, in the accumulating snow, as cars crawl past.

"Am I in it?"

I open my mouth to tell her that—

"Honesty game," Jack demands before I even have the chance to respond.

I roll my eyes. "I was about to say—*yes, Jack*. You're in it." It's the hope that makes me feel as reckless and wild as she was our first day together. "I don't think I could stop drawing you if I tried. You . . . you're the best parts of every character I create."

She exhales. Her breath is white like the snow.

"I sold the Airstream," she blurts. Then she looks down at her feet. Or my feet. Or maybe she's looking at both of our feet, toes pointed toward each other in the snow. "And I made a ton of money from the sale, because it turns out Airstreams are ridiculously expensive, which I didn't know, because it *also* turns out that Patty's brother sold it to me at a huge discount out of pity."

"Not quite the embodiment of financial independence you thought?"

She shakes her head. "No, but I was able to use the money I made selling it to give myself a nice safety net until the Butch Oven starts making money. And now I'm living in the spare bedroom at my mom's new condo. She's . . ." Jack inhales a rattled breath. "She's helping me get on my feet, at least for a little bit."

"Jack, that's. Wow." Selling the shiny symbol of her freedom, letting her mom *help* her . . . "That's just *wow*."

"Yeah." She looks up from our feet, and her face is half attempted apathy, half unadulterated hope. "You wore the blue scarf tonight."

My fingers graze the well-loved yarn around my throat. "I did."

"And we're"—she glances around us, at the snow and the dark water below—"on the Burnside Bridge again."

"We are."

She grinds the toe of her boot into the snow. "And you humiliated yourself for me tonight."

No point in pretending now, not when she can probably see the snot crusted onto my face. "I would humiliate myself a thousand times for you, Jack."

There it is—her half-moon smile, right there, on this bridge, just the two of us. "Maybe one more time. Since you did get fake-engaged to my brother . . ."

"One more time," I say, and I hope, hope, *hope*. "Jack. I'm in love with you. It took less than fifteen hours for me to fall in love with every damn thing about you. In particular, your hair, and the stupid way you flick your chin to get it out of your face."

"The stupid way I *what*—?"

"And your thighs, which are thick and magnificent, and the way you either stand solid like an oak tree *or* have to lean against every available surface, there's no in-between."

"An *oak tree*? Are these supposed to be compliments?"

"Yes. You are a sexy oak tree. And you're brave and you're outspoken, and I love your heavy gait and the fact that you always shout, even though you're really far too loud to take to any museum or formal restaurant, and you're the smartest slacker I've ever met—probably because you're not a slacker at all, you're just a kinesthetic learner who's been bombarded with really negative messages about the way your brain works."

"You're in love with my learning style now?"

"You're not getting it," I say impatiently, plainly. "I'm in love with every single thing about you, Jack Kim-Prescott."

She takes one hand out of her pocket and reaches for mine. As she knits our fingers together, I fall apart. Jack doesn't move. She just stands there with a mocking half-moon smile. I want to grab her by her indifferent shoulders. I want to dig my nails into her skin and kiss her collarbone, memorizing the musculature that allows her to be so relaxed while my entire body riots. "Go on. Surely there is more to the humiliating speech."

"I love you." I shrug. "And I don't have a plan for what happens next. I live in a closet, and I work in an art-supply store, and hopefully maybe someday, I'll also get to tell stories with my art. But maybe not. Maybe I'll have to figure out a different dream instead.

I . . . I know I hurt you. I know I betrayed your trust. But if you give me a third chance, I will *never* do that again."

"You'll never get engaged to my brother in exchange for money and lie to me about it again?"

I shake my head. "That's a mistake you only make once, I promise."

Jack shakes her head, too, dislodging a few snowflakes. There's almost three inches on the ground now. The sidewalk and our jeans are both covered in white. I want to draw Jack like this. I want to spend the rest of my life drawing Jack, in the snow and everywhere.

I think, *Maybe I'm not getting my heart broken on a bridge right now.* I'm really not sure.

"So I think the Claire thing kind of messed me up more than I realized," she says, puffing out her cheeks. "Just, like, in terms of making me feel like a fuck-up at relationships, too. And I definitely haven't reconciled all the issues I have with my family not believing in me. And my parents' divorce is sort of messing me up more than I expected, considering I've been actively rooting for it since I was ten. And then there's all this stuff with my grandpa writing me out of his will. It's just—"

"You've got a lot on your plate, sure." Never mind, I *am* getting my heart broken. In the gentle way, where she's going to tell me she's too "busy" to date me. Which everyone knows is just something you say when you're not very into a person but you don't have a good reason *why*.

"I'm telling you all of this so you *know*." Jack licks her lips, and I think miserably about how I'll never lick those lips again. "I'm not perfect."

I snort. "Jack, I was not operating under the assumption that you're perfect."

She moves closer to me. Her body sways, then replants itself. "It's just . . . I'm really fucking scared of letting you love me back.

I'm afraid I'll get hurt again. And worse, I'm afraid I'll get lost in a relationship again."

"*Back* . . ." I repeat. I have eight hearts, thirty ribs, and no idea what's happening.

"Duh." Jack rolls her shoulders uncomfortably inside her khaki jacket. "Of course I love you, too."

"*Duh?* Jack!" I relish in the sound of her name on my tongue, the sight of her crooked smile. "That's a terrible declaration of love."

"Should I compare you to a tree and insult the volume of your voice?"

"Fair point." I take our joined hands and lift them to my mouth, kissing her cold knuckles in the snow. "And Jack—I don't want you to lose yourself in this relationship. I don't want you to siphon off any part of who you are."

It happens quickly. One second, there's a flurry of snow between us, then there's nothing. Jack's thumb on my jaw, Jack's hand on my waist, Jack's cold mouth on mine. She tastes like macarons and *home*. Like warm bread, like a home-cooked meal. Snowball fights and Christmas carols and making cookies. Kissing Jack makes me feel like home is the place we'll build together, and I kiss her back frantically.

I open myself up entirely for Jack, with tongue and teeth, with fingers scraping the short hairs on her neck, my body arched. I want Jack, now and always, and there's no point in hiding it. The way Jack kisses me back is everything I've ever wanted with the only person I've ever wanted it with.

This isn't a last kiss or a goodbye kiss. This is a first kiss. Our first kiss as the best versions of ourselves. When we pull apart, our glasses are fogged up, and we're both covered in snow. "I want to help you shine, too, Elle," she says, gruffly and loudly. Like Jack.

"Is that a yes, then?" I pant. I'm out of breath but too in love to be embarrassed. "You'll let me love you back?"

Jack's hands are still on my waist. I believe she'll never let go. "We have no idea how to be in a relationship together."

"I don't know how to be in a relationship with *anyone*," I clarify. "We can figure it out together."

I wrap my arms around her. I know there's no guarantee this will last. We could fall apart in a year or five years. We could fall apart tomorrow. I could give Jack everything and lose her again anyway. I take Jack's face in my hands and kiss her one more time, on the little white scar across her upper lip.

If it's twelve hours, or twelve years, or the rest of our beautiful lives, I'm going to savor every damn second of it. Starting with this second outside in the snow, in the glow of Gillian's headlights.

I pull Jack into my arms on the Burnside Bridge, swaying back and forth, slow dancing with her in a snow globe somehow big enough for all of us.

Acknowledgements

Thursday, April 28, 2022

For some reason, I decided to write a book about failure at a time in my life when I was paralyzed by a fear of failing.

I didn't *set out* to write a book about failure. This was supposed to be a fluffy holiday rom com about a lesbian Bill Pullman, but fairly early in the drafting process, it became clear to me that fear was at the core of Ellie's story. And it makes sense. I started writing this book in June 2020, right after I'd sold my debut novel, and I was coming to terms with the fact that people were actually going to read something I wrote. That I was going to be PERCEIVED. It was a dream come true, yes, but for a closeted perfectionist, I couldn't imagine anything more terrifying than showing strangers all of me. In many ways, this book is my way of processing that fear, of trying to convince myself that some things are too spectacular for fear.

So, thank you first and foremost to my therapist, Karen, always, for helping me redefine what it means to fail and what it means to succeed and what it means to be proud of yourself just for showing up. You know this one was entirely a joint effort.

Thank you to my brilliant and tireless editor, Kaitlin Olson, for always taking a leap with me. Thank you for your insights and your patience in guiding me through this process, and thank you for believing I could do it, even when I wasn't so sure.

Thank you to my agent, Bibi Lewis, who supported this book back when it was nothing more than a poorly fleshed-out, gay *While You Were Sleeping* fanfic, and who helped me find the story

I truly wanted to tell. Thank you for talking me out of so many bad ideas (including the coma). I'm so fortunate to have an agent who is compassionate about mental health and who treats clients with such care. I wouldn't want to go through this with anyone but you.

Thank you to all the passionate people behind the scenes at Atria and Simon & Schuster who helped bring this book into the world. Thank you to the greatest publicist of all time, Megan Rudloff, who works so hard for her authors—I can't believe how lucky I am to work with you. Thank you Raaga Rajagopala and Katelyn Phillips, for your marketing acumen, and Polly Watson, for always making copyedits so darn fun. Thank you Sarah Horgan, for the gorgeous cover, and Lexy Alemao, for your equally gorgeous interior designs. Thank you to editorial assistants Jade Hui and Elizabeth Hitti; my production editor, Liz Byer; my managing editor, Paige Lytle; and my managing editorial assistant, Iris Chen. Thank you to Nicole Bond, for getting this book and *The Charm Offensive* into foreign markets. Thank you to all the people in sales and production I neglected to mention but whose tireless work is the backbone of this industry. It takes so many people to make this dream a reality, and you're all appreciated beyond measure.

Thank you to the sensitivity readers who put in emotional work to help me tell this story in the most thoughtful way possible. Esther Kim and Ellie Mae McGregor, your insightful perspectives meant the world to me. Any oversights are my errors alone.

Thank you to my sister, Heather, for reading this book so many times and always offering to read it more. Thank you to Meredith Ryan, for allowing me to borrow your name, and your career, and your amazing hair for the best friend character in this book, and thank you for always being the Aries to my Pisces. Thank you to Michelle Agne, whose name I didn't use, but who can be found in the best parts of every character I write. Not to be weird, but you're the person I want to be when I grow up. The three of you make up my heart, and I couldn't write about love and joy without you. Thank you for sticking beside me through all my seasons of needing.

Thank you to Andie Sheridan, for giving me the title of this book, and for giving me so much of your time and energy. Thank you for all the emails and Google Docs and brainstorms it took to unlock Jack's character.

Thank you to Jordan, who took on so much during the line edits of this book (aka the hardest four weeks of my life). Thank you for feeding me and cleaning the house and taking care of the dogs while I cried in front of my computer screen. It seems only fitting that I met you while revising this book; you're worth every risk.

Thank you to the rest of my family—Erin, Mark, Bill, Kim, Brooklyn, and John—who celebrate every victory, no matter how small. Thank you to my grandma, Laverne O'Reilly, who passed away in January 2022, and who influenced so much of who I am today.

Thank you to my Portland friends—Leanna, Sarah, Hayley, Bryan C., Jill, Bryan B., and Julianne—who are so supportive and so very generous with their preorders. Thank you to Nicky, Tiana, Tiffany, Jill, and literally anyone who has ever sent me a photo of *The Charm Offensive* in an airport bookstore.

Thank you to Portland itself, for being a weird little city where so many queer people feel at home. If you're not from here—it's not as awful as they make it out to be on the news, I promise. But Portland, like so many cities in the US, is struggling with a major housing crisis that has only been exacerbated by the pandemic, leaving many of our neighbors housing-insecure. If you're interested in learning more about how to support the unhoused population in Portland, you can check out resources on my website www.alison cochrun.com.

Thank you to Venessa Kelley and Leanna Fabian, for the incredible art that helped bring Ellie and Jack to life in my mind. Thank you to all the other artists who answered my questions about animation. And thank you to all the fan artists who are so integral to the romance community and the book community at large.

Thank you to everyone who answered my questions while I researched this book. In particular, thank you to the dozens of Ohio State alums who flooded my DMs so I could include one tiny throwaway detail in this book. Go Buckeyes!

I'm so grateful to other writers who make the process of publishing books a little less lonely. In particular, I want to thank Rachel Lynn Solomon, who is one of the most generous people I've ever met, in and out of publishing, and who continually reminds me what it means to show up for other people and be vulnerable with your art. I want to thank Anita Kelly, for being my IRL writer friend. Thank you to Chloe Liese and Mazey Eddings, who write about mental health and neurodivergence so beautifully.

The most specialest of thanks to Timothy Janovsky, because I *literally* could not have written this book without you. Thank you for reading the prologue over and over again (even though you hate prologues), thank you for letting me word-vomit all my plot problems, and thank you for constantly reminding me you can get away with a lot in a Christmas book.

Thank you to the other #holigays22: Courtney Kae, Helena Greer, and Jake Maia Arlow. It was an honor to release a queer Christmas book alongside you, and I can't wait to see our books on shelves together.

Thank you to Taylor Swift, for writing *evermore*, the perfect Christmas album, and for releasing *RED TV* in the middle of my developmental edits, so I could listen to "Forever Winter" on repeat while rewriting the flashbacks in this book for the millionth time.

"Thank you" is a feeble term to express my gratitude toward all the booksellers and librarians who've placed my books into the hands of readers. The same is true of the Bookstagram community. Thank you for reading my books, talking about my books, sharing my books.

Thank *you* for picking up this book and supporting queer romance authors. Thank you to all the queer romance authors who came before me and paved the way so I could tell a story about two women falling in love.

And finally, thank you to everyone who reached out to me after reading *The Charm Offensive* to tell me they felt seen or validated by the characters and their experiences with mental health and sexuality. By sharing your stories with me, you made *me* feel so seen and validated. You made me feel less alone. Putting your art out into the world is always a risk, but you all make it so worth it. I feel so fortunate to be on this writing journey with you.

If, like Ellie, you find yourself frozen by fear, afraid to share your story and yourself, please know I've been there, too. And there is joy and connection on the other side.

About the Author

Alison Cochrun is a former high school English teacher and a current writer of queer love stories, including her debut novel, *The Charm Offensive*. She lives outside of Portland, Oregon, with her giant dog and a vast collection of brightly colored books. She controversially believes *evermore* is the greatest Christmas album of all time, and she's probably sitting by a window right now hoping for snow.